By KATHY LYONS

WERE-GEEKS SAVE THE WORLD
Were-Geeks Save Wisconsin

Published by DREAMSPINNER PRESS
www.dreampsinnerpress.com

WERE-GEEKS SAVE WISCONSIN

KATHY LYONS

DREAMSPINNER
PRESS

Published by
DREAMSPINNER PRESS
5032 Capital Circle SW, Suite 2, PMB# 279,
Tallahassee, FL 32305-7886 USA
www.dreamspinnerpress.com

This is a work of fiction. Names, characters, places, and incidents either are the product of author imagination or are used fictitiously, and any resemblance to actual persons, living or dead, business establishments, events, or locales is entirely coincidental.

Were-Geeks Save Wisconsin
© 2020 Kathy Lyons

Cover Art
© 2020 Paul Richmond
http://www.paulrichmondstudio.com
Cover content is for illustrative purposes only and any person depicted on the cover is a model.

All rights reserved. This book is licensed to the original purchaser only. Duplication or distribution via any means is illegal and a violation of international copyright law, subject to criminal prosecution and upon conviction, fines, and/or imprisonment. Any eBook format cannot be legally loaned or given to others. No part of this book may be reproduced or transmitted in any form or by any means, electronic or mechanical, including photocopying, recording, or by any information storage and retrieval system, without the written permission of the Publisher, except where permitted by law. To request permission and all other inquiries, contact Dreamspinner Press, 5032 Capital Circle SW, Suite 2, PMB# 279, Tallahassee, FL 32305-7886, USA, or www.dreamspinnerpress.com.

Mass Market Paperback ISBN: 978-1-64108-176-4
Trade Paperback ISBN: 978-1-64405-310-2
Digital ISBN: 978-1-64405-309-6
Library of Congress Control Number: 2019953336
Mass Market Paperback published July 2020
v. 1.0

Printed in the United States of America
∞
This paper meets the requirements of
ANSI/NISO Z39.48-1992 (Permanence of Paper).

There are so many people to thank for this book. I'd love to say it was all my inspiration and talent, but it turns out a project like this comes together because of many people. Damon Suede pushed me to go for it, and Lynn West was right there making me feel comfortable, which ultimately swung the balance. In fact, all the folks at Dreamspinner have been a dream to work with (pun intended). Elizabeth North (brilliant publisher) gave me amazing support, Nicole Resciniti (brilliant agent) held my hand, Brenda Chin (brilliant editor) kept me on track, and even my husband kept the chocolate well stocked. (Nothing happens in my life without chocolate.) But this book owes its existence to Cindy Dees, who said, "You love geeks. Write geeks!"

I do, so I did.

Thank you, Cindy, for being with me every step of the way.

Chapter 1

"I AM not going to wear that to a demon slaying." Nero Bramson stood naked to the waist in the Wisconsin snow. He was surrounded by his werewolf team, and they were headed into serious business. But apparently Pauly's brain was still on last night's Trivial Pursuit game.

"You lost, so you have to wear this," he said as he held up a pink tee. It read *Crazy Cat Lady* and was covered in stupidly cute kittens.

"We're here to do a job—"

"Yeah, yeah." His friend rolled his eyes as he waved toward the lake. "We're here to kill a basic demon who's been eating ice fishermen for who knows

how long. Human body, big teeth. We can take care
of one of those in our sleep." He shifted the tee in the
predawn light enough to show off the glitter on the
kitten collars. "You lost, you have to wear this today."

Nero bared his teeth, not surprised when it had no
effect on his team. Pauly's partner, Mother, actually
snorted as she started to strip out of her clothing. "You
shouldn't bet on trivia when you suck at it."

"I grew up in Florida. What do I care about Big
Ten football?" He'd lost the game—and the bet—on
some obscure Michigan versus Ohio State statistic.
"But I'm not going to wear something stupid and
endanger this mission." He looked to the other two
members of his team for help, but Cream and Coffee had already shifted into their animal forms. They
were timber wolves and were prancing about in the
snow, oblivious to Pauly's attempt to humiliate their
leader.

"The fabric's so thin it'll rip in a stiff breeze,"
Pauly said. "It's not going to endanger anything."

Just his pride. Bad enough to wear pink, but the
cat lady moniker was going to stick. And for a werewolf, that was adding insult to injury.

But Pauly was grinning as he tried to hide his cell
phone, no doubt ready to snap pictures the moment
Nero put on the garment. Mother was chuckling as she
shucked the last of her clothing. And even Cream and
Coffee had laid off rolling around in the snow to watch
him with expectant expressions.

It was what he'd wanted for his team. They'd been
going full-out for the past few months, and everyone
was starting to feel the strain. They'd taken out a ban-
shee, two sewer demons, and his personal favorite: a

zombie wizard on a bad acid trip. When Pauly had suggested a night of trivia and shots, Nero had thought it was the perfect stress relief. Who knew the guy had an encyclopedia of sports facts in his brain? Or that they'd finally get a location on the demon chomping on unwary Wisconsinites next to Lake Wacka Wacka? That wasn't its real name, but it was all he could remember.

He fingered the garment. It really was paper thin, and though the pink would stand out against the snow, his team was the best. They'd have no trouble taking out the demon, even if it spotted them a few seconds early. Maybe he could manage to rip the shirt on one of the evergreens.

"Come on," Pauly wheedled. "A gentleman always honors his debts."

"Now you're just being rude." He was not a gentleman by any stretch of the imagination, but damn it, he'd fake it if it meant keeping those smiles on his team's faces. "Fine," he said as he pulled the shirt over his head. "But you're paying for breakfast." It was his favorite part of every mission—the celebratory meal afterward. He had the perfect pancake house in mind, and it would cost Pauly a pretty penny since they'd all be starving after a demon killing followed by a glorious romp through the snow.

"Totally worth it," Pauly said as he snapped pictures rapid-fire.

"Get into position," Nero grumbled, and then he stripped out of his pants.

Damn, it was cold. He waited until everyone had gone full furry to slam and lock the van door. He put the keys in a box hidden inside the driver's side wheel well, then gratefully sprouted fur as he turned into the big, bad wolf of all those childhood fairy tales. Only this wolf was going to kill a demon before breakfast.

All in all, today would be a great day… even if he was going to be staring at pictures of himself in a pink tee for a long time. It stretched tight across his wolf chest, and though he tried to rip it as he breathed deeply, the fabric strained but didn't tear.

Pauly's gray muzzle pulled wide in a wolfish grin, and even Mother yipped quietly in laughter. He growled to silence them, but that only made Cream and Coffee snort. Nero then let out a stern bark and everyone settled. It was time to get down to business.

After five years of working together—three with him as alpha—they knew his moves as well as he did. They peeled out in formation, ranging wide as they searched for the demon. Cream scented it first, but the stench soon enveloped them all—brine badly covered by Axe Body Spray. Gah. Even a human nose would notice that. They picked up speed, and Nero quickly forgot the embarrassment of his attire. They were all caught up in the chase.

They found the demon squatting behind some young evergreens near an iced-over lake. It looked to Nero like a maraschino cherry: all its colors were off. Sure, it was shaped like a normal human male, but the skin looked pinker than flesh, the hair had green undertones, and the eyes seemed flat and creepy. Like glass eyes because—according to the fairy who had put them onto this thing—the demon didn't use its eyes to see. Those empty baby blues were for appearance only, since its whole body pulsed with paranormal radar and its receptors were on its skin. The only part of it that seemed normal was the mouth, though it was too wide and the teeth were sharp.

He went in first. It was his right as alpha. Plus, it was just plain fun to get in the first swipe.

The creature was focused on the lake, probably waiting for careless ice fishers, since there were some winter cabins nearby. It had been chomping on them, as well as cross-country skiers, for at least a decade before it had caught the Paranormal Alliance's attention. Thanks to the internet and cell phone cameras, it was getting easier to find the silent munchers. And now that it had been located, Nero's strike team would end it forever.

Seeing that the others were in place, he bolted forward through the snow. God, he loved this part— the sheer joy of his body moving like black lightning through the white landscape. Something about his wolf body erased his human aches. Bum knee, stubbed toe, achy shoulder—it all disappeared when he was a wolf.

He took a wide arc around the creature's hiding place, then dashed in to hamstring it.

The thing was prepared. Whatever radar it had had alerted it to the danger, but it was hemmed in by evergreens and too slow to leap away. It was faster than a human but not than a werewolf, and Nero dodged the swipe with ease. Better yet, he timed it just right, swerving around, then ducking under the swing, taking a bite of demon calf.

Score! He ripped out a solid chunk of the demon's leg. He was grinning around demon flesh.

Then the taste hit. *Gah.* Brine. It tasted like shit, but he'd done his job. Blood spurted from the creature's leg. Like everything else about this thing, the color was off. Orangey-pink like shrimp. He darted away before he could get covered in the crap.

He spit the mouthful out as soon as he could, his momentum taking him well out of the reach of the demon's hands. Mother and Pauly went in second. She'd go for the throat or crotch—she was vicious that way. Pauly would take out the other leg. Then it would all be over and they could go for a real run in the woods.

He kept his tail high as a message that said, *All's good.* He was spinning around when the first gunshot rang out.

It was the demon. Clearly it had been in this world long enough to learn about firearms, and it was getting off rounds with a surprisingly steady hand, given that Mother and Pauly had done their jobs. Both its legs were torn to hell and back. Some of its crotch too.

That was the thing with demons. They could section off parts of their bodies like a starfish. Its entire lower half could be torn away, and the upper body would still work. Good thing they'd trained for this possibility.

Cream and Coffee were already on it. Cream would take out the gun arm; Coffee would go for the throat. Some demons had to be dismembered. Mother and Pauly were rounding the trees, cutting closer and obviously anxious to take the bastard down. Nero tensed, ready for his pass as soon as Cream and Coffee delivered their strikes.

Bingo! Coffee got it across the neck, and weird blood sprayed. Cream had the gun arm clamped between his teeth and was ripping it off the bastard's body, but the thing was way more dexterous than they expected. The demon managed to toss the gun from one hand to the other—while being dismembered—and got off a shot.

Cream yelped in pain and dropped the arm. He still tried to run, but his back leg was fucked-up, and he tumbled nose over tail. Coffee's momentum had already taken him past Cream, but that was okay because Nero had already started his pass. He'd forgo the demon in favor of pulling Cream's ass out of the way while Mother and Pauly followed up with the killing blows. But he couldn't carry Cream as a wolf. It was way easier to scoop up a lupine with human arms, though the wolf weighed a freaking ton. He needed to get the guy out of the line of fire long enough to dig out the bullet. It was much too dangerous to attempt a shift back to human with a bullet in the body. There were too many bad places for the metal to lodge.

Not many shifters could make the change while moving, but fighters didn't often have the luxury of a quiet place to shift. He had been a year into training with Wulf, Inc. when he'd perfected the moving shift. It was one of the reasons he'd become a team alpha so young. He did it now, slipping into an energy place before resolving into a human still on the run. He even knew how to time his balance so that he could keep running while scooping up Cream's back end. The wolf would then run on his front legs while Nero managed the back.

That was the plan, and it started with flawless precision. He went from running on all fours to a dissolving flow of energy. His awareness took in the stupid T-shirt he wore, the ground and the air, the pulse of the demon's radar, and something more. There was a buildup of power from the demon's head. Coffee hadn't fully decapitated the thing, and there was growing magic centered at the spine, right behind the jaw.

That couldn't be good, but in this state, he didn't have the ability to broadcast a warning. It happened so fast. He'd barely sensed the power when it detonated.

The bastard demon exploded in a fireball that could be seen from a satellite. Fortunately Nero didn't have a body to burn. He didn't even feel pain—just a surge that tried to disrupt his energetic state. It was a mental scramble for him to ride the wave without disintegrating, but he managed, and then he resolved himself into his human body. He needed to scream a warning to his team. He needed....

The smell hit first. Even in a human body, he relied on his sense of smell.

Burnt flesh and smoke.

His bare feet registered blistering heat next. It burned his soles, even as he kept running.

Vision came next, and he saw a landscape that was no longer a winter wonderland. He was running through the center of a blast zone, and when he bent to scoop up Cream, all he got was charcoal.

He couldn't breathe. Everything felt choked off, even as it burned through to the bottom of his lungs. And all he heard was absolute silence.

He stumbled, falling to his knees but unable to release the charred bones of his friend. He looked down, his hands tightened, and the fragments slid between his fingers. He turned, frantically searching for his teammates, someone to share the shock with, but all he could see was burnt bodies and the melted ice of the water.

He saw the demon then, and shit, how could that thing be still alive? Sure, there were demons that could shoot fireballs, but he'd never heard of one that could create an explosion on such a massive scale. But the evidence was clear, as was the pink blob of partially dismembered demon body. It was beside the lake, rolling to the edge before it fell in. It wasn't going to drown. It would sink to the depths of the lake, where it would reform into a smaller, simpler body. Nero wanted to chase it. He could dive into the water and tear it apart with his bare hands.

But he couldn't leave Cream.

Or Pauly. Or....

He scanned the area, identifying the bodies, not from anything recognizable but from their locations on the blackened ground. Cream at his feet, Pauly just a few feet away. Mother beside her partner. And Coffee farthest away but facing toward him, because he'd been running back to help.

Four bodies. And a half-mile radius of scorched earth.

He started to shake, and his knees blistered. The heat from the ground was intense, and he was naked except for the tee. He stripped out of it and put it under his feet as he stood. He'd have to walk back to the van, thankfully out of the kill zone. His phone was there too. For some reason he thought he could call for help. Maybe someone could do… something.

It took another moment of staring before he realized he didn't need his phone. He had someone to call on for help: a fairy prince who owed him a favor. He'd saved the guy's life in a bar fight, of all things. He'd been at the right place at the right time, and by fairy rules, that meant Bitterroot owed him. The bastard also owed Nero an explanation as to why he'd sent them after this demon without telling them the thing could blast fire.

Clutching his hands into fists, he called out Bitterroot's full name three times. The condescending prick appeared instantly, almost as if he'd been waiting. He was a short guy or a tall elf, standing about two foot four, with bright eyes and a collection of butterflies attached to his body. The fairy was a collector of sorts.

Bitterroot appeared wearing his usual smug expression, but his eyes widened in shock as he took in the surroundings, including the charred remains at their feet.

Nero didn't let him get his bearings. "Why didn't you tell me?" he demanded. "You didn't say it could blast fire."

"You didn't ask," Bitterroot rasped, his expression still shocked. "There are rules."

Fucking asshole fairies, always with an excuse. But it didn't matter. They needed to handle the problem now. "Can you fix this? Can you help me?"

Bitterroot shook his head slowly, his gaze landing with horror on the ash outline of Mother's body. "I can't—"

"You can." Nero swallowed, the solution sitting heavy in his mind. The brass at Wulf, Inc. didn't have a lot of rules. The main precept was "complete the mission and don't die." But there was another: Never negotiate with the fae. Wolves always lose. But Nero didn't care—he did it anyway. "Give me a mulligan."

The fairy's gaze snapped back to Nero's. "That's not an easy thing." He took a deep breath. "It's an *expensive* thing."

"You owe me. I saved your life."

"Which gives you one wish." The fae rubbed his hand over his face in a weirdly human gesture. "A mulligan is complicated." Then he waved at the center of the blast zone. "What would you do different? How could they survive that?"

Nero didn't have an answer. He'd been lucky to have been in an energy state when the boom hit, and he'd barely survived it. The others might not be able to ride the wave like he had, and Coffee was a traditional werewolf. He never fully dissolved into energy but sprouted his snout and tail in an excruciating agony that took time. Coffee definitely wouldn't survive, but Nero had faith in his team to figure it out.

"We wouldn't attack at all," he said. "We'd take time to plan—"

"Not possible. You still have to attack today." Then, before Nero could argue, Bitterroot held up his hand. "I don't make the rules."

Nero choked back his frustration. Much of his brain was still screaming in horror, but what focus he had found a solution. "Can you hold on to the mulligan? Let me use it when I'm ready."

Bitterroot frowned, and a single brilliant red butterfly set off from his arm to flutter in front of their faces. He caught it gently, speaking quietly to it in a language Nero didn't understand. The fairy waited a beat, then another, as if listening to an answer. In the end, he looked up at Nero. "I can hold it for seven-times-seven days, that's all. And you'll have to pay."

Forty-nine days to find an answer to an explosion that had taken out a mile of Wisconsin. "Deal." His team was worth whatever the cost. No question.

Bitterroot's expression hardened. "You'll serve me, Nero. A year of your life for every day that I hold the mulligan open."

Nero's breath caught. Fairyland was a place of nightmares. No mortal belonged there, and no one came back sane. "Deal," he repeated, his voice strong, though inside he shuddered at the magnitude of what he'd promised.

"Standard rules apply. You can't tell anyone about this, and you can't go bargaining with another fairy to change this one."

Nero nodded. That part he'd already known. "Agreed."

"Agreed." Then Bitterroot stuffed that bright red butterfly in his mouth and swallowed it whole. He grimaced at the taste as he glared daggers at Nero. "Don't ever make me do that again."

Then he disappeared.

It was done. When he was ready, he'd call on Bitterroot and be zipped back in time to fifteen minutes ago—before the blast, before they even attacked. He'd be able to redo everything, making sure everyone survived.

But how?

He didn't have time to figure it out now. Police sirens were wailing in the distance, and he needed to come up with a cover story before they got here. The good news was that whatever he said wouldn't ultimately matter. Eventually he'd go back in time and fix the problem before it started.

In fact, he realized, everything he did for the next forty-nine days didn't matter. So long as he figured out how to defeat that fire blast, everything would reset once he used the mulligan. His team would survive, and life would go on as if this never happened. For them, at least. For him, he'd have to pay Bitterroot back. Which meant he'd be in Fairyland trying to hold on to his sanity, but that was a small price to pay for their lives.

Chapter 2

"THERE WAS nothing anyone could do. It's not your fault."

Captain M spoke with compassion, and everyone at the conference table nodded sagely at Nero. He gave them a weak smile, trying to make nice with all the Wulf, Inc. brass. There were three of them there—all badass werewolves looking dour—plus a thick-lipped ghoul representative from the Paranormal Alliance who never spoke to anyone and a gelatinous alien in the shape of a man. At least Gelpack was familiar to him. The see-through alien had shown up a month ago, talked with this same brass, then moved in as if he was one of the team.

"This was not your fault," emphasized the wolf version of a wizard. He was the only werewolf who could throw magic, and that had earned him a spot as VP and the handle Wiz. A little bit on the nose, but it was appropriate.

"I know," Nero said, trying to invest his words with conviction. "It was a failure of intelligence. We should have known that the demon had fireball capability."

"On a galactic scale." Captain M shuddered as she looked at satellite imagery of the now-renamed Burnt Lake. "And you needed better gear. Stuff that resists plasma fire."

"Fire is not a plasma," corrected Wizard. Arrogant bastard. "This appears to be magical plasma that burns."

Captain M's head snapped up. "Do you have anything that's *magic plasma*–resistant?"

Wizard closed his mouth. Up until a day ago, magic plasma was a myth. But then, a year ago, no one believed in gelatinous aliens, spell-casting wolves, or that a ghoul could make it into the upper echelons of the Paranormal Alliance. But there you go. The conference table was filled with myths turned into reality. And apparently his entire team had been decimated by just another myth.

"What we need," said his captain, her words laden with the anger of a woman who'd been banging this drum for a while, "is some science skill."

Gelpack spoke up, his voice sounding like it was coming from under water. Which, given the "man's" consistency, it probably was. "I thought magic and science were different."

"They are—" said the captain, but Wizard interrupted.

"Magic is science we don't understand yet."

Gelpack didn't answer. Nero guessed that the complexities of human language were difficult for the alien to process. Meanwhile, Captain M was folding her arms.

"Either way, we need researchers, and not the librarian kind. Call it tech support, a geek squad, or Fitz-Simmons. I don't care. We can't go out with just fangs and claws anymore. Not since half our calls are more than the occasional vamp or an idiot demon. Hell, I can't remember the last demon that could dress itself, and this one came with magical fire."

"And could use a handgun," Nero reminded her. That bit tended to get forgotten in the whole atomic explosion part at the end.

She nodded. "How the hell did a demon figure out firearms? Before you know it, they'll be on the internet and taking over Amazon."

It was a joke. Sort of. But Captain M had a point. Magical baddies were getting more capable and more weird by the second. No one could keep up, least of all the lowest grunts on the take-'em-out scale.

All the species in the Paranormal Alliance took turns handling paranormal threats. It was shifters who bore the brunt of them, though. Wolves, bears, and cats all had their own organizations, and they usually dealt with the grunt work. The Non-Corporeals were less capable, limited to hauntings and driving people crazy, but they had their place, especially since they included some unspecified number of fairies who focused on stopping mystical mischief. That included, of course, the Fairy Prince Bitterroot, who had started this particular problem. Then there was the catchall of witches, warlocks, and whatnot in the Religious Crew. That was the unofficial name for demons turned good-guy and angels turned not-so-good. Throw in a few surviving demigods for their board of directors and you had Halloween, Inc., the third leg of the weird world tripod.

Nero had no idea where Gelpack came in except that he arrived like the Silver Surfer. He just showed up and asked to hang out with the wolves. As far as the World of Weird went, Gelpack was almost blasé. Completely see-through, he was like a living Jell-O mold in the shape of a human body. He had a mouth, but sound seemed to come as a vibration of his whole form. His eye indents were there, but no one thought he could see through them. He was like a talking ge-latinous mannequin. Why the creature was in this meeting was anyone's guess.

"We have to figure out how to defeat that fire-ball," Nero insisted. "Can we tap Halloween, Inc.? They've got to know a way."

"Already done," Wiz said mournfully. "If they know the answer, they're not telling." Wiz rolled his eyes. "They're *religious*, and they think we're another form of demon. So if a demon takes us out, all the better for them."

Well, shit.

"But what if—?"

Captain M cut him off. "We don't make fairy deals. Ever. That comes down from the founder him-self, and if you don't like it, then take it up with him." Wulfric was still alive, even though he and his magical mother were more than two hundred years old. They were the creators of the original Paranormal Alliance back in the 1800s, and whatever bullshit had gone on then, the fairies were responsible for it. Hence the rule: no negotiating with fairies. Nero kept his mouth shut.

"We need geeks," Captain M repeated. "We need to *recruit* geeks."

No one argued, though everyone wanted to. The problem was that paranormals weren't exactly in the open. Lots of people had experience with the woo-woo, but those who were touched by it—by the real shit—tended to die. Survival rate was highest among those born as werewolves. The infants were stronger and as they aged, they knew how to handle themselves against scary stuff. Nero was a lycanthropy were-wolf—bitten when he was a teenager—and the odds on him making it were one in ten. Others manifested from curses or mystical bullshit, but again, the surviv-al rate was low. Weak minds and bodies crumpled un-der the strain. Heart valves broke, asthmatics stopped breathing, and those with bad allergies? Their bodies attacked themselves and they died ugly. And that was nothing compared to the ones who went nuts. Geeks and nerds weren't known for their physical stami-na. And who knew what mental hang-ups wandered around in their massive brains? At least that was the perception, and no one wanted to test it. So geeks had been noticeably absent from the werewolf rolls. Un-fortunately, the need for scientific mojo was becoming more obvious by the second.

Captain M looked around the room, her gaze heavy on each of the wolf higher-ups. "We're agreed?"

One by one, they nodded, their expressions blank except for their tight mouths. Seeing werewolves that quiet was downright creepy. Meanwhile, Captain M grunted her acknowledgment and gestured to the stacks of file folders on a side table behind her.

"Pick whoever you want," she said to Nero. "I've listed my recommendations. Then get with Wizard to figure out how to make it happen."

Nero's head snapped up. He'd been staring blankly at the dozen or so folders when his gaze shot back to her. "What?"

Her expression softened. "We're not putting you back out in the field right now, but you've got more than enough experience to identify what kind of scientific support we need."

"I haven't a clue, beyond the obvious."

She smiled. "That's more than most people have. Go through the folders, talk it over with Wizard, and figure out who we can activate."

"That's a pretty word for destroying someone's life. And that's assuming they survive."

"Your life wasn't destroyed."

"I was infected by an asshole, and I got lucky." He folded his arms across his chest. "I'm not going to bite some random geek on the prayer that they—"

"They're not random," said the Director. His voice was whisper-soft. Rumor had it that he'd had his trachea decimated by an angry vamp but had gotten some kind of magical replacement. Either way, he never spoke above a whisper, but everyone listened. "We've had our eyes on them for a while. Most of them are genetic werewolves, a few from the founder's line. Someone in their near past carries the werewolf gene, and so the odds are they'll manifest someday."

"*Someday* is a far cry from *today*."

"Do you have a better idea?"

Captain M spoke up "There wasn't a lot to choose from, but those are all the scientists, programmers, and researchers we know who can become werewolves. People who can research the demons ahead of time, who can figure out our biology when we're hurt, and—"

"Who can figure out how to defeat magical fire."

"Yes."

Nero didn't like the idea of forcing the paranormal onto someone who hadn't chosen it, but he understood the need for researchers and scientists. Neither the religious nor the magical folk were keen on helping them, and he was the first to admit they needed more than brute force.

"It's a big risk," Captain M continued, "but we're not the only ones dying from the threats. Normals die every time there's a problem we can't anticipate or defuse. Better we get the support we need now, before the situation gets more out of hand and wholesale disaster happens."

An ominous silence fell at the words *wholesale disaster*. That was the werewolf term for it. The Religious Crew called it the apocalypse, and the ghosts referred to it as the post afterlife. Bears growled instead of using words, and no one knew what the cats called anything, but the meaning was all the same. At some point there would be so much weird shit happening that they would reach a tipping point. Normals would finally open their eyes and see what was around them.

Then there would be mass hysteria, targeted genocide, and/or a big party, if a person was part of the winning belief structure. It was the Big Bad of the paranormal world, and everyone worked very hard to prevent its onset.

In this case, that meant forcibly converting brainiacs in the hopes that they could keep up with what was going on. Because right now everyone was in the dark. And in the paranormal game, ignorance was deadly.

"Can't we just talk to them?" Nero asked. "See if they'll come on board like normal hires without making them furry?" He knew it was a stupid thing to ask. He even knew the answer before the DIRECTOR said it, but he still had to voice the question.

"We will not violate the Paranormal Accords. That's like fixing a house fire with a nuclear bomb. We will not do it."

The Paranormal Accords stated that vanilla humans did not get purposely drawn into their world. Period. Only someone already paranormal could be asked to work on the weird and violating the accord was punishable by more than death. Unfortunately, they were already stretching the law to activate latent werewolf genes. A frank discussion—like a job offer—with a vanilla human would plunge Wulf, Inc. into legal disaster, and no one was willing to risk that. When a demigod judge said, "More than death," everyone grew very, very afraid. "Okay," he said, though the word felt like ashes in his mouth. "I'll look at the files."

"I will help," said Gelpack.

Everyone turned to stare at the gelatinous alien, but it was Captain M who found her voice first. "Great. Um… how?"

"I will read the files."

Silence. Apparently no one was willing to point out that reading the files in and of itself was not helpful.

"Okay, sure," Captain M finally said. "Nero, let him… um… help."

"No." The word was out before he could think better of it. It wasn't exactly politic to refuse a direct order in front of the Director, but he couldn't keep quiet. "Personnel files are private. This task is dicey enough. I'm not going to let just anyone read through the dossiers without good reason."

"Gelpack isn't just anyone," Captain M said, but he could tell she was nervous. "He's…. He's…." Her stammer ground to a halt as she obviously had no idea what Gelpack was here to do.

"He's here to explain magic to us," the Director whispered. "And for us to explain emotions to him."

Everyone gaped at their director. Finally, Nero said what everyone was thinking. "Come again?"

"Gelpack is from a different… um… dimension. He's studying us—our emotions—and in return, he'll help us use magic."

Everyone in the room suddenly sat up straighter, and their eyes focused tightly on the gelatinous being. It wasn't surprising that Wizard was the first to ask questions.

"Explain which kind of magic? Who is he explaining it to? Why wasn't I informed—?"

The Director held up his hand, and Wizard immediately snapped his jaw shut. "It's a one-on-one exchange. You tell him about how you feel—*honestly*—and he'll help you...." The director frowned at Gelpack. "Can you help turn on a latent werewolf?"

"Perhaps."

Captain M grabbed a file folder off the top and pushed it toward Gelpack. "What about him? Can you activate him?"

Nero winced as he watched Gelpack open the folder. Nothing about him was fully solid, so he seemed to sink into the paper as if he was going to slice off his thumb, then gently pulled it open. When he removed his hand, Nero couldn't see any residue, but it still gave him the willies.

"No," Gelpack said.

"Then—"

"But Wizard can."

"What?" said Wizard.

"Excellent," responded Captain M as she pulled the folder away from Gelpack and slid it to Nero. "Look at him first."

Nero frowned at the name. *Joshua Collier.* The name was as unimpressive as the picture, but then again, the image showed a too-pale guy in shorts and flip-flops as he bought no-name corn chips at a corner market. No one looked cool buying generic chips.

"Then it's decided," the director said as he stood up from his seat. "Nero, I want four new geeks in training by Monday next week."

"That may be too fast—" Nero argued, but he wasn't given a chance to finish.

"Our people are dying. You fix this by Monday or I'll find someone else who will."

A chill went down Nero's spine. It was a standard threat, used often in Wulf, Inc., but it scared the bejesus out of him. Sure, a lot of the people who worked here had families and friends, a life outside of searching for paranormal baddies. Captain M had a husband and four kids, all werewolves living normal suburban lives except during the full moon. She was of a breed that went loony during the moon.

But Nero didn't have anybody. Since his infection with lycanthropy ten years before, he'd cut ties with anything that wasn't part of this life. Captain M and so many others might find a civilian job, but running a team that fought bad guys was all he knew how to do. And there were no private sector companies who hired guys without a civilian résumé that made sense. He didn't have one because Wulf, Inc. didn't talk to civilians about what it did. Which meant if he didn't do what he was told, he'd be out on his ass without references.

"Monday," he said glumly. That meant he had seven whole days to screw over five new werewolves and pray that they lived to hate his guts.

Just as well. He was working on a time clock too. Bitterroot had set a forty-nine-day time limit on his do-over, and the faster the geeks solved that problem, the sooner he could be done with this whole timeline and go back to the way things used to be.

Chapter 3

"GODDAMNED TECH support! Fucking idiots."

Josh Collier's brows went up as he joined Wednesday Addams, aka his best friend since high school, Savannah Nielson, where she sat at the hotel coffee bar. She was glaring at her phone, and he gave it even odds she would throw it across the room any moment now.

He sipped his triple-sweet black coffee and waited.

"What kind of losers take a job answering moron questions all day? I'll tell you who. Losers who can't read emails, who won't give a straight answer, and can't think for themselves, that's who."

"Wow. Quite a statement about an entire career path." He glanced around the room at a couple of Klingons, two wizards, and three scantily clad elven princesses. Given the usual gaming convention crowd, a good half the room had probably worked tech support at one time or another. Savannah obviously didn't care.

"You know what I mean," she huffed. "My *Destined Mayhem* game keeps throwing me out at the final battle. I can't figure out why, and tech support is all, 'Did you update your software? Do you have the latest version? Perhaps if you turned off your machine and restarted it?'" She rolled her eyes. "Like I didn't think to do that before I contacted them."

He winced, knowing her problem immediately but reluctant to give her the bad news. Hell, he'd lost a few months of his life in the exact same way only to discover the horrible, betraying truth.

She sighed as she pulled at her dark black Wednesday Addams hair. Given that she was normally all curls, it had probably taken her an hour to straighten it… as opposed to the hundreds of hours it had taken him to make his seemingly benign wizard cape costume.

"Okay," she groaned. "Tell me what the problem is. And laugh that I didn't ask you first before I tried so-called customer service."

"You need a faster rig to play the final level."

She shook her head. "No, I checked that. The game specs—"

"Are a lie. The latest expansion requires more, and they're behind on updating the website." He gave her a sarcastic grin. "But they will sell you a cheat for a mere fifty dollars."

"That's obnoxious!" she cried, and he agreed.

Games were one of the few places in the world that followed rules. Even in-game surprises could be discovered ahead of time if one scoured the internet hard enough. That a gaming company would do a bait-and-switch like this was heinous, which is why he'd initiated a revenge campaign out of sheer moral outrage. He didn't have the technical skills himself, but he did know who to contact to point out the company's perfidy. He expected that sales of *Destined Mayhem* were about to tank due to an insidious malware infection, but that didn't help Savannah.

She eyed him over her mocha. "Tell me you have the cheat."

"I don't play that game." Anymore. He figured out the truth two weeks ago and sold all the games he owned that were made by that company. It cut his game collection, but it was the principle of the thing. Plus, he needed the cash to pay for MoreCon.

"But you know it, right?"

He flashed her a grin. "I might know a guy who knows a guy." He pulled out his phone and texted her the steps.

"Why is it always a guy? Why don't you know a girl who knows a girl?"

He arched a brow at her. "Me? Girls?"

She snorted. "You have to get out of the lab sometime."

"No," he laughed. "I really don't."

She was the only person in the world who knew all his secrets—except for this one. She knew his father was an asshole, that Josh had cheated all through AP English, and that their romantic relationship in high school had never worked. They were too good at being friends, and all that sex stuff had ruined things—or nearly ruined them. What she didn't know was that he'd given up on girls completely and had started dating guys.

It was a new thing. He wasn't about to come out of the closet just yet because he hated labels as much as she hated tech support. But he'd thought he'd broach the subject during their annual weekend at MoreCon. He imagined telling her that he'd met a guy at a bar and that something had stirred. Part of him had heated and thickened, and all those things that were supposed to happen with a girl, but rarely did with him, happened with this guy.

Did that mean he was gay? He was exploring the possibility. He'd gone to a movie with the guy and found out he was a jerk. But that had opened a door, and so he'd gone on a few more dates with a few different men. He'd even kissed a couple.

All new. All exciting. And he wanted to share it with his best friend, but he wasn't sure how to broach the topic.

Then she changed the subject.

"So you're part of the opening ceremony extravaganza, huh?"

His eyes widened in mock surprise. "I don't know what you mean."

She laughed as he knew she would. "Usually you hate the opening event, but this year you're all about how I have to take Friday off and be here in time for the 7:00 p.m. kickoff. That can only mean you finally wore down the management team enough that they let you be part of it." She eyed his cape, no doubt seeing some of the badly hidden pockets on the inside. A seamster he was not. "Is that some of your dad's special fire-resistant fabric there?"

He looked down and saw the exposed shimmery green fabric called Volcax that he'd stolen from his father's factory. Years ago his father had teamed up with a brilliant chemist named Craig, and together they developed a fiber that was impervious to heat up to five thousand degrees. He'd been a kid at the time, sitting on the lab bench, listening to what they said, watching all the mixing and blowing up of stuff, and he'd gotten hooked. Chemistry was his jam, thanks to all those wonderful afternoons watching his father and Craig make things go boom. Eventually they'd figured out the formula and Volcax was born. Soon afterward they sold it to the government, and the fabric was now so hush-hush, Josh could end up in prison for what he was wearing.

Josh adjusted his cape. "I have no idea what you mean."

She arched a brow. "You're not going to set the hotel on fire again, are you?"

"That was one time!"

"Twice."

"A stink bomb does not count as fire," he said stiffly.

"The hotel manager didn't see it that way."

True. And he'd had to do some major pleading not to be banned from the entire hotel chain for the rest of his life. "No stink bombs this year." Just pyrotechnics, some cool electrical effects, and a sleight of hand that he'd spent months perfecting. He grinned. "And the con comped my hotel stay."

"That's cool."

It didn't come close to covering what he'd spent creating his costume, but every bit helped. Especially since he was a lowly PhD student on a University of Michigan stipend. That covered rent, cheap food, and a heavy winter coat, but not much else. She, on the other hand, had gotten the holy doctorate at Michigan State and was now working in Big Pharma for more money than he'd make in years as a student.

"How goes the dissertation?" she asked.

"Need a couple more experiments."

"That's what you said last year."

He shrugged. That was the problem with research. There was always more to learn, more to do, and more ways to delay writing the dissertation that would end his comfortable life in Ann Arbor and send him off into the big bad world looking for a job.

"You can't spend your life doing rando experiments in a basement," she said.

"I do them in a university lab now." In their basement.

"I do them in a multimillion-dollar lab, and they pay me lots of money to do it."

He nodded. "But they tell you what to do, when, and how to do it. I'd rather go where my curiosity leads me." And right there was his problem. He liked exploring chemistry and was damn good at it. And he hated having anyone else tell him where his mind should go. There was no compelling reason—other than money—to pick their research over his own. He could live with a tiny bank account. He couldn't live bored.

She sighed. "No one will pay you for that."

"Yet. Eventually someone will recognize my genius."

"You have to do something cool to be considered a genius," she drawled.

"I won the Chem Hack Contest again this year. Five years straight. That's pretty impressive."

"And no one outside of the university even knows what that means."

Yeah, that was the problem. He'd had rotten luck in his research as he tried to invent something better than Volcax. It didn't exist, and he'd spent years figuring that out, though he did learn all sorts of cool stuff about how things burned, blew up, or melted. But rather than talk about that, he dove into their usual round of what-have-you-been-doing questions.

About halfway through her latest tale of coworker stupidity, his phone alarm went off. He thumbed it off, then drained his coffee.

"Gotta go."

"This early?"

He nodded. It was going to take him hours to get the stage set just right for his show. "I'll save you a front-row seat. Promise you'll be there."

"Of course I'll be there! This is our weekend. I look forward to it every year."

"Good, because afterwards...." He swallowed. It was time to take the plunge. "I've got something I'd like to tell you. About me. And maybe dating... or something."

Her brows went up. "Dating... *or something?*"

"Yeah." Then, before she could ask any one of the thousands of questions he saw in her expression, he got up from his chair. "Afterwards. Don't miss it."

"Like I could miss this now?"

He laughed as he headed off to the main stage. He'd been planning this show for a year now. By tonight, he was going to be the talk of the con.

Chapter 4

IT TOOK Josh two hours to get all his pyrotechnics set right. He went through them twice for his own peace of mind, then again for the hotel manager. Everything was perfect, and his belly was tight with excitement. After a year of planning, this was going to be amazing. He was going to step on stage as a drunk wizard throwing mismatched spells everywhere. But then, when the master of ceremonies tried to throw him out, he would disappear in a burst of multicolored flames.

Thanks to the low balance in his bank account, planning this had been his entertainment for the past year. He'd spent nights dreaming about this glorious moment and days searching for the cheapest, best way to do it. Some might think it lame, but he'd rather spend his time figuring out how to safely blow up a stage than binge-watch the latest Netflix offering.

He was setting his wizard's staff behind the curtain, stage right, when a deep voice interrupted him going through his mental checklist for the billionth time.

"Josh?"

A shiver went down his spine at the resonant sound of his name. It was the kind of voice used by grand wizards in video games or old trees dispensing wisdom. It silenced every random thought in his head so he could listen, and he quickly turned around to find the source. In so doing he nearly collided with a stripper warrior and Doctor Strange.

They were in costume, obviously, and he really hoped the mesmerizing voice was from the Benedict Cumberbatch wannabe. It would fit with the wizard costume. But even so, his gaze was caught and held by the warrior guy.

The man was huge, as in mountainous. He wore a simple leather vest, no doubt to show off those ripped abs, and surprisingly good quality tearaway pants, hence the "stripper" tag. His face wasn't model-beautiful, but there was a craggy beauty to it. Hard jaw, slight scruff of a beard, and a sharp cut of a Roman nose. Truthfully, he would have fit better in a Trojan skirt with a sword, but Josh wasn't quibbling. Honestly, he wanted to get a look at the guy's legs.

Then there were those eyes. Technically they were brown, but the coolest brown he'd ever seen. There was red and yellow there, and rich, dark mink. Like a hawk's eyes or a lion's. Maybe a werewolf from some movie. He got momentarily lost in them, trying to see if they were real or contact lenses.

"Josh Collier?"

Okay, so Warrior Guy was the one with the voice. Sweet. "Next time go for the Roman centurion look. You've got the shoulders for a cape, and stripper pants cheapen the look." Josh grinned. "Besides, skirts are better advertisements anyway."

He might be new to his own sexual orientation, but he'd learned the lingo at his first con. No one judged preferences here, and the dirty jokes usually worked for any orientation.

But clearly the warrior wasn't used to conventions, because he blinked in confusion. Eventually he stammered out a "Wh-what? No!" He looked down at his pants. "Not stripping."

Josh shrugged. "I'm not judging. Well, I guess I am, but just of your costume choice. Hey, if you've got the build, I say flaunt it. You probably worked hard to get all that muscle definition." Then he tried a flirtatious smile.

He was new to flirting with guys and his gaydar wasn't even close to 100 percent, but anyone who wore stripper pants to a con had to be hoping for something. And Josh wasn't opposed to testing out the guy-on-guy waters with a con neophyte. Especially one who looked like he could bench-press a bus. And who blushed like he was a vestal virgin.

Wasn't that adorable?

Then Doctor Strange had to interrupt. His voice was dry, classy, and had the perfect ring of arrogance. "We are here to offer you a job."

Josh nodded, surreptitiously looking around for whoever was filming this. He saw the regular con staff, but none of them were paying any attention.

"Okay, I'll bite. What kind of job at which con? And most important, who told you I was looking? You haven't even seen my show yet."

"It's fulfilling work," said Warrior Guy in that beautiful voice. "Life-changing stuff. Your science background is impressive, and we'd like you to start immediately."

"My science background?" He'd published two papers, both in midlevel journals. Not exactly a NA-SA-level résumé. But he supposed to most people, even being in a PhD program was an accomplishment.

"We looked at your papers. The ones on carbon chains and um…. Look, I didn't understand a word of it, but—"

"I did," interrupted Doctor Strange. "And we need your help. We offer excellent benefits and—"

Josh laughed and held up his hand to stop them from talking. Whatever this was, it had already eased his nerves before the show, and he was grateful for that. But they were about to open the doors, and that meant he was in the last few minutes of preparation. He was beyond excited for his big con moment, and these guys were distracting him from living his glory to the fullest.

"Mr. Collier—" Doctor Strange said.

"Guys, I have no idea what you're trying to do, but I don't have the time to discuss it now. You can buy me a drink afterwards and—"

"It would be really better if we talked now," Warrior Guy said. "This is going to happen, Josh. You're

going to love this job, but it has to happen now."
There was a clear note of desperation in his voice as
he added, "Please, just come with us. Take the pill,
step through the magic mirror, grab on to adventure
with both hands."

Josh smiled. He had to hand it to Warrior Guy.
He certainly delivered corny lines with true passion.
"Okay, sure," he said. And at the sudden brightening in
the warrior's eyes, he laughed. "Right after the show. I
promise, you guys get to buy me the first drinks."

"Wait—" the warrior began, but Doctor Strange
shook his head.

"Save it," he said. "We can't give him enough details to convince him of anything. It has to happen the
hard way."

That sounded threatening, as did the way the
warrior's face shut down before he gave a clipped
nod. Josh frowned and then gestured to the stage
manager. Her name was Megan, and she couldn't do
anything to either guy, but she had a walkie-talkie and
a direct line to hotel security. "Megan, you need to
call hotel security. I don't think these guys are registered attendees."

Megan nodded from as far back as possible. She
knew she was no match for these guys if they ended up
belligerent, but she was quick with her walkie-talkie.
Fortunately, there was no need. The warrior held up
his hands in surrender.

"No security necessary," he said in that still-beau-
tiful voice. "We'll find our seats." His expression was
so locked down that his glorious eyes seemed even
brighter.

Not one to be a full pushover, Megan nodded. "That's great, but I'll need to see your con badges first."

The warrior shot a dark gaze at his wizard companion. "I told you we needed to buy badges."

"For thirty minutes?" the other one countered. "We have a flight to Seattle in three hours."

The warrior grimaced. "Josh, please help us out. Look, my name is Nero, and this is Wiz. We came here just to meet you."

"Me." The word was heavily laced with skepticism. "Why?"

"To offer you a job. On the level."

Josh didn't believe a word of it. This was not how his life worked, but his game-loving soul wanted to believe it could happen. Wasn't that how all good stories started? With a call to adventure? He still thought it was a joke, but he wasn't immune to the flattery of it all. These guys had gone to a lot of trouble to do whatever-it-was to him. He could give them a break.

"Megan, let them watch the show."

"They don't have badges—"

"I'm allowed a couple guests." And since his family wouldn't be caught dead at a fantasy convention, he was here solo. "Put them in the front row, keep an eye on them, and I'll make sure they leave right afterwards."

She frowned at him. "Are you sure?"

No. He hadn't a clue how he would get these guys out if they resisted. But that was a worry for after his show. "Yeah. I'll take care of it."

"Okay," she said. "This way, gentlemen." She started escorting them away but then paused long enough to wink at him. "Break a leg, Josh."

He grinned at her. "Thanks." He watched as she led them to seats in the front row, far left. They got there just in time, because a moment later the doors opened and people filed in. People, fairies and elves, heroes and heroines from a wide variety of literature, and a whole bunch of Star Wars and Star Trek characters. Not everyone was in costume, though. Some people didn't bother until tomorrow, but the cool ones did. And Savannah was front and center in her Wednesday Addams outfit. Thank God he'd reserved her seat, because otherwise she'd have been stuck in the far back.

He wanted to wave to her but couldn't step out from behind the curtain, so he distracted himself from his nerves by checking out costumes and hot guys. No one compared to the warrior who ought to have gone with the centurion costume, assuming his name really was Nero. It just made sense. What didn't track was the way the guy was sitting mountain-still in his seat, his expression so tight it could have been carved.

What was up with that? It was just an opening ceremony show.

And even more bizarre was the Wiz next to him. The guy had his nose in a cheap three-ring binder, moving his lips as he read. No kidding. Josh could see it from the stage. The guy's mouth was moving as he read whatever was in his hands.

Then the show started. David Jenkins, the president of MoreCon, stepped onto the stage and spoke into the microphone. The guy was in his late forties, gay, and had the most amazing anime collection Josh had ever seen. Josh had been to his house a few times for viewing parties that came complete with great nachos. David and his partner, Glen, were the living example of a healthy gay couple. They weren't weird or cartoonish. Glen was an accountant, David owned a couple of Taco Bell franchises, and they loved each other, which was more than Josh could say about his own parents. It was what Josh aspired to have some day: quiet, suburban anime parties with his sweet husband. Though he wouldn't be opposed to some hot flings with a mountainous guy in stripper pants along the way.

David finished the greeting, listed important changes to the programs, and introduced the fandom guest of honor. He was a minor character in a long-running TV show, but it was the most the con could afford, and two minutes into the guy's self-important chatter, Josh got his cue.

He stumbled onto the stage as if he was drunk. He had his staff in one hand and an empty goblet, which he turned upside down so everyone could see it was empty.

"Get to the important stuff!" he cried. "Where can a humble wizard get a drink?"

Grinning, David went back to the mic. "Well, the bar is right through those doors—"

"Never mind. I'm a wizard, right? I can conjure my own drink!"

"Um… I don't think you should be doing magic, sir. You're clearly not fit—"

"Fit, Schmidt!" Josh pointed and winked at one of the con regulars, Tom Schmidt, who waved from the fourth row. "I'm as fit to cast magic as a Schmidt!" He really put some gusto into Tom's last name, making sure to spit a bit as he slurred the name.

Everyone thought it was funny, Tom included, and so Josh got ready to detonate the least of his pyrotechnics: a small explosion from a lined pocket on the outside of his cape.

"Spirit of the grape," he intoned as he held his goblet high, "the grain, and the hop." He did a little hop at that. "Refill and renew my goblet, and not with pop!"

He pressed the detonation button, and sure enough, his pocket exploded with a shower of sparkles.

"Oops!" he said to everyone's amusement. "That's not what I meant at all." He peered owlishly into his empty goblet, but as he did so, a strange heat began deep in his belly. It was a weird sensation, like inferno-sized acid reflux, only lower and with accompanying cramps. Was he getting sick? Had some of his more dangerous chemicals spilled out of an inside pocket?

It was alarming to be sure, but he was in the middle of his big moment. Although he felt like he was about to vomit, he locked it down and tried to go on with the show.

Just like they'd planned, David scrunched up his face in mock alarm. "I really don't think you should be doing that—"

"Riddikiiiieeeee!"

He'd meant to say, "Riddikulus!" but the word burned like fire in his throat and became a scream of agony. That killer heartburn exploded through his body, setting his nerves on fire. His eyes felt like they were bulging out of his head, and his gaze shot to Savannah's. Her mouth was open and she looked worried, but everyone else around her was grinning. He

was about to vomit his lunch all over the stage, and
they thought it was part of the show.

At least David knew this wasn't planned. He
stepped forward, a look of concern on his face. "Josh—"

Lightning struck him. It wasn't real lightning,
but that's what it felt like. Electricity shot through
his body, making every muscle tighten unbearably.
His head flew back, and he screamed as his bones
snapped from the strain. Spine, hips, legs. Crackle,
crackle, pop.

He collapsed to the floor, the pain making his vision burst with stars. His cape fluttered down across
his back, but it didn't fit right and slid to the side of his
body. His mind was white with agony, and he tried to
cry out, but no sound emerged.

He felt his jaw unhinge, his mouth and face burst
apart. He could hear the audience gasping, but he
couldn't see. Damn it, he couldn't see! And then he
completely dissolved. As if he melted into air while
his body shifted horribly, and everything felt wrong,
wrong, wrong. It wasn't pain so much, but his hands,
legs, face all stretched or compressed or just plain
broke. At least that's what his mind was telling him,
while everything also felt completely incorporeal.
Like he was energy soup and not form at all, except
suddenly, he coalesced. He had a body and it was
hunched on all fours. Well, that was good, right? He
tried to straighten up, but he couldn't stand.

Then the audience burst into thunderous applause.

What. The. Fuck? He was dying, and they
applauded?

He turned his head, and now that his vision was
clearing, he could see everything. People clapping,

elves laughing, movement everywhere, but where the hell was Savannah? He found her eventually, though all the standing and clapping was blinding him. She was there, right where she'd been, with her mouth ajar and her eyes huge.

Savannah!

He screamed out her name. She needed to call 911. He needed a doctor. But what happened shocked him to his bones.

He heard a howl instead of her name. And he felt the noise come from his own throat.

He skittered backward, startled and confused. And as he moved, he saw paws. Big, thick dog paws where his hands should be. And his footing was fouled in clothing and shoes that fell off him. The audience was starting to whistle their approval. Fucking idiots!

He glared at them, trying to speak. He had to make them understand!

He heard a growl and felt his lips pull back. The clapping faltered, and no wonder. The sound was rabid.

He felt his body tense and his ears flatten. He stepped free of the fabric around his feet and howled again. He was already salivating from the hunger that churned through his stomach.

Then something tightened around his neck and jerked him back. The feeling was abrupt, it choked him, and he wheeled around at the thing that held his neck.

It was a leash… held by Doctor Strange. And in front of him, smiling at the crowd, was the warrior.

"That was impressive, wasn't it?" Nero said to the crowd. "But now we have to get the wolf back to the zoo. Can't believe he escaped like that. Ha. Ha." He waved and started backing away.

Doctor Strange hauled on the collar and dragged him backward as if he was a dog. A fucking dog!

Josh leaped, teeth bared. He was going to bite off the damned hand holding—

Electrical shock jolted through him. Real electricity exploding out from his neck and frying his neurons. And while he was twitching from the torture device, Nero squatted down. Josh saw the hypodermic a split second before Nero shoved it into his side.

He growled when it went in, but what he heard was more of a whine.

Fogginess came quickly after that, a numbing weakness that softened his mind and made his whole body go limp. But he was still awake enough to feel Nero lift him up and carry him off stage.

Help me! Savannah!

He listened from a distant place as Nero's heavy tread made it through the hotel lobby. He smelled the man's scent and felt the muscles strain under Josh's weight. But most of all he heard the bastard's words as he walked.

"You're going to be okay, Josh. There's no easy way to say this, but you're a werewolf. It's a grand thing, really, and now you work for Wulf, Inc. See? I told you we were here to give you a job offer. Congratulations. You're going to love it."

With the last of his fading strength, Josh opened his mouth and bit straight through the bastard's throat. Then the world went dark.

NERO REARED backward as far as he could go without dropping the unconscious wolf, who weighed a metric ton.

"Did he try to rip out my throat?" he gasped.

Wiz chuckled. "Serves you right for cradling him like a baby. I'd bite you too."

"And get a mouthful of lycanthropy." Not that it would matter, but still…. "Am I bleeding?"

"Nothing to worry about. Burn your shirt when you get back."

He was going to do that anyway. God, he'd never live down wearing a kitschy fake leather vest, but it was the cheapest costume they could find on short notice. He knew Wiz had taken pictures. Fortunately the guy tended to short out modern electronics, and so it was even odds that the digital image would survive his wizardly aura.

"I can't believe that spell worked," he said as he looked at Wiz. "Can you activate anyone with the werewolf gene?"

Wiz shrugged as he opened the back of their van. Gelpack was in the driver's seat looking like he was staring straight ahead, but Nero knew the alien saw and heard everything they did, no matter where his head was facing.

"According to Mr. See-Thru"—Wiz gestured at Gelpack—"I can turn anyone with the right energy signature." That was vague, but pretty much what Nero had expected. He waited while Wiz opened the reinforced cage inside the van. As gingerly as he could, he set Josh down, mentally apologizing to the guy the whole time. It was bad enough to be surprise-converted into a wolf in front of all your friends, but to be caged afterward was rubbing salt into the wound. Sadly, it was the only way, and he had more wolves to collect this weekend.

From the front seat, Gelpack twisted his head—just his head—around to face them. Nero didn't like having a gelatinous being as their driver, but he had too much to do to take the wheel as well. Especially since he was going to O'Hare airport and Gelpack was taking Josh to their facility in Michigan. "How long will he be unconscious?"

"About twenty hours," said Wiz as he locked the cage and slammed the back door shut. "He's going to wake up spitting mad and hungry. We'll try to be back by then, but no promises."

"I will talk to him when he wakes," said Gelpack.

And wouldn't that put the cap on poor Josh's weekend? To wake in a cage and be "talked to" by a see-through guy. The brass claimed that this would be less traumatic than the usual wolf manifestation. They said it was better to change around people who knew how to keep you safe—and caged—than to unexpectedly transform and kill your nearest and dearest. They had a point, but it still sucked.

"Why are you looking so down in the mouth?" Wiz poked him as they settled into the back seat. "This went off without a hitch."

"I doubt Josh will see it that way."

"Josh will adjust. We all did."

Yeah, but everyone else wasn't cut from the same cloth as Josh. Nero had gone to the conference, expecting to meet a stammering guy with thick glasses and bad acne. Instead he'd met a funny guy with a flirtatious smile who wasn't in the least bit fazed by two big costumed baddies trying to make him an offer he couldn't refuse.

Josh had laughed and let them sit in the front row. Nero had half hoped the guy would make good on his threat to kick them out. That would have delayed them, and Josh could have at least finished his act, but they had a timetable to keep and couldn't wait.

"Cheer up," Wiz said as he peered behind him. "He's not dead yet. No signs of rejection or fever. With any luck he'll wake up healthy and hale just in time for Gelpack to scare the shit out of him." He turned to the alien with a grin. "Can you eat something especially bloody and forget to wear a shirt? That always makes an impression."

Gelpack answered in an honest deadpan. "My digestive system is not up to meats yet. But I will try some red Jell-O."

"Perfect," Wiz said with a grin.

Great. If the werewolf curse didn't kill Josh, his new teammates surely would.

Chapter 5

NERO FELT a weird kind of euphoria. It might have had something to do with being up for three days straight, but it was more likely because every single one of the new recruits had survived the transformation to wolf.

Every single one, including a surprise recruit, thanks to Gelpack. Nero didn't understand what the alien had done, but it had worked. Wiz said he made adjustments to the activation spell. Words, tones, something that seemed completely insignificant to Nero but apparently made a world of difference. He'd also insisted that the recruits be brought here to the cage room in the basement as soon as possible instead of closer interim facilities. Good thing too, because two of the recruits had spiked fevers and gone into seizures within an hour of getting to Michigan. Everyone had written off the wolves then, because once the seizures hit, there was nothing anyone could do. But Gelpack had stared at them for an hour and the wolves had eventually settled.

It was a flat-out miracle, and Nero would never again speak of the gelatinous alien as anything but a blessing, even if he was now sitting in board shorts and nothing else in front of Josh Collier's cage. Worse, he had taken Wiz's suggestion seriously and there was a bright red Jell-O smear where his stomach should be in his otherwise tannish-clear body.

Gross.

"I came as soon as I could," Nero said as he walked into the huge concrete room of steel-reinforced cages. He noted with pleasure that four of the five wolves were sleeping deeply. That was the most healing thing for them. It was the fifth who had him concerned.

Josh Collier. The charming blond-haired geek boy was now a black timber wolf with white along his lips. That made his snarling, growling fury all the more frightening because the white made his teeth look bigger, sharper, and scarier. Nero had seen his fair share of furious wolves, so Josh shouldn't scare him. He shouldn't, but damn it, this wolf radiated rabid fury like he'd never seen. Hatred burned through his burnt orange eyes, and even the drool looked malevolent. Then he noticed that the steel bars of the cage were bent.

"Did he break his cage?" No wolf should have the strength to do that.

"No," Gelpack answered. "He bent the bars. They should not break. He is too near exhaustion to finish the task."

Really? Josh didn't look exhausted. He looked tense, blindly furious, and—

Wham.

Nero flinched as Josh rammed the cage bars. He'd leaped straight into them with claws extended at Nero and jaws that latched on to the bars like they were a filet mignon. And when he couldn't crush them, he shook his head, growling and pulling on the metal as if to tear them apart.

The sight was bad enough, but the sounds.... Guttural animal hatred formed into an endless roll of snarls and growls. Not a single bark or howl. That would be too polite. And Nero had no doubt that if the bars broke, Josh would make those same sounds while ripping out their throats.

"How long has he been like this?"

"Since he woke several hours ago."

Hours? Oh hell. He searched the creature's eyes, hoping for a sign of sanity, some spark of human rationality beneath the animal hatred. He found nothing, which meant Josh's mind was gone. The brilliant chemist was lost to the beast.

"What does Captain M say?"

"To euthanize him. No one has come back from this level of fury before."

Even though he'd already guessed that, the words sank like a stone into his gut. He'd done this to Josh. He'd been the one to select him for the team, to stand by while Wiz activated his DNA, to plan every second of the operation that brought Josh to this rabid animal state.

His stomach cramped like a vise and he dry-swallowed to fight the pain. It didn't help. Nothing would help, especially when he added the mental image of putting a couple of bullets into the wolf's brain. God, he didn't want to add one more death to his already black soul. Meanwhile Gelpack kept speaking, his voice the same monotonous underwater burble that he always had.

"Her orders are there." Gelpack pointed to the clipboard attached to the misshapen cage. Nero didn't have to read them to know they told him to end Josh's life as quickly as possible. It did no good wasting resources on someone who would never come back, not to mention the danger to everyone in keeping Josh alive.

"Isn't there something you can do?" he asked. It was a vain hope. Gelpack would already have done it if he could, but Nero was looking for any possibility, no matter how small. "You stabilized the other two."

"Your minds are a mystery to me. That is why I am here."

Nero pounced on the distraction. "You're here to study our minds?"

"Thoughts and emotions are unknown to me. I studied for a hundred of your years to learn your language."

"A hundred?" he said weakly. "How old are you?"

"Without bodies, we do not age. I am the only one of my kind to attempt a body, so perhaps I will age now too."

Nero didn't have a response to that and had nowhere to go except back to Josh. "Have you tried talking to him?"

"I have tried many forms of discourse. Most recently I have been reading his paper to him. Captain M said to expose him to familiar human things that will engage his mind."

It was standard protocol, and Nero scanned the list Gelpack had made of all the things he'd tried. Every line item was followed by the words *no noticeable effect*. He also glanced at the array of Josh's personal items scattered on a table beside Gelpack.

Walking over to it, he tried to see if there was anything that would help Josh. They had his suitcase and backpack, all of which had exactly what he'd expect. Tees with emblems or sayings that Nero didn't recognize. Something was "shiny," someone was from the Colonial Squadron. The jeans were worn soft, the socks worn old, and the toiletries cheap. His backpack wasn't any different. There was a spiral notebook with diagrams of his big show and a laptop that they hadn't opened because it was his and they were trying to respect his privacy as much as possible.

Nothing. Not even the crumpled receipts were interesting. A grocery store receipt for generic cereal and Campbell's soup. Another one from Target for needles and thread, presumably to sew those shiny pockets into his wizard's cape.

"What happens when you read his paper?"

Gelpack lifted the printed paper in his hand and began to read. The words were strange enough, but in his weird voice, they were downright creepy.

"To confirm that the defects of NOB mutants result solely from telomerase binding deficiencies, we performed primer extension assays with a series of chimeric proteins—"

"Okay. Never mind."

Josh hadn't reacted at all to the string of words. If anything, the creature's eyes had glazed over as much as Nero's had. Frowning, Nero ran through everything that had been in Josh's file. The guy's social media had been minimal, his family tree, all the way back to the ancestor with the werewolf gene, was useless, and even his grades, which had been excellent in the sciences and lackluster in liberal arts, couldn't help.

"Wait a minute…," he murmured as he looked back at Josh's threadbare socks and the generic chips on his IGA receipt. Everything indicated he lived a stripped-down, impoverished lifestyle. Nero hadn't thought it odd because that had been his own life before lycanthropy bit. But Josh's father owned his own business making Volcax for the government. Though it sounded blue-collar, it was actually a multimillion-dollar company that was run like a fine-tuned watch. He knew that the Collier family's income was in the top 1 percent. Josh had attended Harvard at full-price tuition. From his sister's Facebook pictures, Josh ought to be wearing designer jeans and shopping at Whole Foods. Instead, his sneakers were ripping in two places, which sure as hell would be cold in the winter. Obviously the guy was living on his graduate stipend from the University of Michigan. He'd bet that not a cent was taken from dear old Dad.

Josh wouldn't be the first guy to have an overbearing father. Maybe Nero could reach him that way.

So he turned to the glaring, growling wolf and spoke in his sternest tone.

"Joshua Dyer Collier, look at you drooling on yourself and destroying your cage. I spent all that money sending you to a fancy school, and what do you do—?"

Josh went insane. Where before he'd been simply growling and chewing on the cage, now he slammed against the bars over and over again. And when those didn't break, he howled with rage loud enough to make the other wolves stir in their unconscious state.

Nero's insides stiffened, his body tightening unbearably every time Josh hit the cage bars. Which would break first? Josh or the bars?

Gelpack spoke above the din. "I do not believe this violence is a good sign."

Maybe not, but then again, it was certainly more of a reaction than anything else they'd seen. He decided to keep going.

"Four years at Harvard and now how many at Michigan? You don't have a trade, you certainly don't work for a living." He winced at that. He didn't know anything about higher education, but he did know about being the lowest grunt on the pay scale. He would bet anything that PhD students were the slaves of the academic world. "You're just lazy, freeloading off of my money. You will quit playing around at school and learn a real trade. Now change back to human and talk like the man you claim to be."

The frenzy in the cage doubled, then redoubled. Josh was a whirling blur as only a werewolf could be. He thrashed at the cage on all sides, including the top and bottom. He snapped at the bars and exploded upward to try to break the lid. The sounds he made were no longer identifiable. Snarls or growls were indistinguishable from yips of pain or howls of fury. It was all one explosive disaster, and Nero saw blood and spittle fly from the bars. And still he couldn't stop.

"Good God, what a *disappointment* you are!"

The cage broke.

One of the hinges snapped and Josh bashed at the weakened side until the seam split. One slam to break the hinge and a second to burst through.

Shit, shit, shit. Nero was about to die.

There wasn't time to react. And after being up for three days, Nero didn't have the reserves to go wolf. All he could do was step in front of Gelpack and hope the alien would become goo instead of die like Nero was about to.

Josh hit him square in the chest and they tumbled backward into the table of belongings. Nero got an arm up and felt a flash of pain as it got shredded. He kicked Josh in the ribs, knocking the wolf sideways, because this wasn't his first wolf-on-human fight. Josh was back before Nero could draw breath, and it was all he could do to dodge in time to save his face.

Bzzzzz!

The cattle prod. Gelpack had it in hand and was shoving it in Josh's near side. The wolf yelped in pain and slammed sideways. Nero's legs fouled the wolf's footing and the two ended up tangled together on the floor.

Bzzzz!

The next electric shock carried into Nero's body, but it was nothing compared to what Josh must have felt. The wolf scrambled to get his feet under him, but he didn't have the coordination. Nero did, and he pulled himself aside barely fast enough to avoid losing a kneecap to Josh's bite.

Bzzzz!

Gelpack got him again, and this time Josh's wolf body rippled in agony from the impact, but he wasn't jerking away. Instead, his head was coming around and his lips were peeled back from his very sharp teeth.

Bzzzz! Bzzzz!

Nero got his feet under him. His breath was quick and tight, but his hands were steady as he grabbed a pistol from the locked cabinet on the far wall. He didn't want to do this. God damn it, he didn't want to kill someone who'd just had the misfortune of being born to the wrong family tree. But he didn't have a choice.

Josh was rabid. There wasn't a choice.

Bzzz! Bzzzz!

Nero raised the pistol. He took a breath and sighted Josh, only to see the wolf body begin to shimmer. Nero's heart pounded and his brain screamed to pull the trigger, but he didn't do it. Not yet. He couldn't—

Josh resolved into a human form with pink skin and dark red welts on the side.

"It's telomere-*ace*, fuckface," Josh bellowed. Then he launched himself at the cattle prod. He got ahold of it and ripped it through Gelpack's gelatinous hand. Nero's finger twitched on the trigger, but there was no time to save Gelpack.

"Josh, no!" he bellowed, but it was too late.

Chapter 6

JOSH RAMMED the cattle prod hard into the gut of the bastard who had been torturing him with it. He shoved it straight into the weird-colored creature and pulled the trigger with a vengeance. He saw the voltage go through the thing. Ripples of burnt color expanded outward from the point of the prod, and the smell was… unsettling. Like burned marine life. But he didn't care and he sure as hell wasn't going to stop. Fury rode him in rolling waves of hatred as he jammed that fucker with—

A Mack Truck tackled him. The cattle prod went flying, his bare feet left the concrete, and he landed on his hip, then shoulder, then head hard enough to make

his brain rattle. It didn't matter. He was fighting even
before his consciousness caught up to what had happened. Every cell was punching or kicking or biting.
If it could move, it was attacking.

Except the truck was fucking huge and the weight
was suffocating.

His arms were pinned first, and his hips immo-
bilized. Legs were trapped next, and when his vision
cleared enough for him to focus, he saw the weird asshole holding the cattle prod. And all the while, someone was screaming, dogs were barking, and the Mack
Truck was saying his name. Over and over.

"Josh, calm down. Josh! Ow! Joshua!"

He didn't stop fighting. He couldn't. The fury inside him was too hot for him to rest. But he didn't
have the strength. And though in his mind he might be
Wolverine, slashing and bashing his captors, in reality,
his body strained to no effect. He gasped for air, his
muscles twitched as he still commanded them to fight,
and in the background a woman was screaming while
dogs were barking.

"Josh, calm down," the truck was saying. The
words came out breathless, and he had some satisfac-
tion that he'd tired out the guy. "You fight like you're
possessed."

Yes, he did. Always.

"Gelpack, you okay?"

"That was an unusual experience. Should I have
experienced pain? I do not have nerves yet to transmit
sensations."

The guy huffed out a breath, dropping his weight
more fully on top of Josh. "Be thankful you don't.
Hell—" He turned and looked at something to Josh's

right, then did a double take. "The girl changed back to human. Call Wiz to help her and sedate the other wolves. We can't handle them right now."

Josh turned his head enough to see what his captor was looking at. What he saw shocked him into momentary stillness. Cages. Rows of cages, three with barking wolves and one with a naked redheaded woman clutching her head and screaming. She must be the girl they were talking about. He'd been so busy fighting that he hadn't registered the noise.

God, she had a set of lungs on her. Good. He hoped she was loud enough to bring in the cops, but somehow he doubted it. This had all the freezing-cold feels of an underground laboratory. And didn't that just make all his body parts clench tight.

"Send us back to Earth," he said loudly. "It's not right to experiment on us."

He felt the truck pull back, and Josh focused enough to see that it was the big warrior guy from the convention, the one with the Roman name. And he was frowning at Josh.

"What are you talking about? This is Earth."

"He's not." He jerked his chin at the see-through guy in board shorts. And what the hell was that red smear in the middle of his chest? It looked too bright to be blood, but then how would he know what blood looked like inside a guy who was made of Jell-O?

"Um, yeah. His name is Gelpack. He's not from around here."

No shit, Sherlock.

Then he watched as the weird guy picked up a tranquilizer gun and steadily shot each of the wolves.

Pfft. Pfft. Pfft. Three wolves yipped in surprise and then dropped down onto the ground with a thud.

It was chilling, especially when he aimed at the redhead, who had quieted into soft sobs.

"No!" Josh cried out, suddenly pushing himself up so he could stop the creature. But the big guy didn't budge off him. All he got was a grunt and a renewed grip on his wrists. "Damn it—"

"He's not going to shoot her." He cast a glance at the alien. "Right, Gelpack? You're not going to shoot her."

The redhead lifted her head to stare at them with huge green eyes.

"There is no dart loaded in the gun. I wondered if the air pressure would be comforting to her. Captain M said this morning that she found the breeze soothing."

"It's not—" Nero said, but it was too late. Gelpack had already pulled the trigger… to no effect.

"It appears I have miscalculated," the creature said as he put the gun away in a locked cabinet. "I will go wake Wiz now." He paused. "Will you be okay alone with Mr. Collier?"

"Yeah," he said as he started to peel back off of Josh. "His big ole brain is engaged now, right, Josh? You're not a mindless lunatic."

No, he wasn't, though hatred still boiled just beneath his surface. And to think he had actually flirted with this bastard. "Of course I'm fine," he said, sarcasm heavy in his voice. "I've only been attacked, abducted, and…." Shit. Certain parts of their bodies were intimately close. And damn it, his dick didn't seem to care about who was pressing against it. It was hot and throbbing, and given that he was stark naked, it wasn't something he could hide.

It also told him that he probably wasn't in as much danger as he feared. If the Mack Truck was trying to harm him, Josh wouldn't be getting aroused, right? Subliminal cues and all that would keep his dick shriveled. Maybe.

And while he was still processing that, the alien left the room, shutting the door with a heavy thud.

"Before you get any bright ideas, the door is locked and sealed. You can't get out without a handprint."

Yeah, he'd already figured that from the way Gel-pack had pressed his palm on a hand reader. Though that did bring up an obvious question. "Does he have a handprint?"

"I don't ask questions that make my brain hurt," Nero answered. Then he gently disentangled himself from Josh's legs. "So we're good here? I can get off you?"

"Yeah, sure," Josh lied. "We're peachy keen." He shoved his hips sideways, trying to toss the guy off. It would have been wasted effort, except Nero rolled with the movement and suddenly Josh could breathe again.

He looked around, trying to be covert about it. He needed a weapon. The dart gun would be great if it was loaded and not locked in a cabinet. Meanwhile Nero was talking in a calm, reasonable voice.

"You're right. You've been assaulted, sort of. And kidnapped. And traumatized, I'm sure." He glanced guiltily at the girl, whom had quieted enough to listen. Then Nero stood up and opened a drawer across from the girl's cage. He pulled out gray sweatpants and a sweatshirt, which he fed her through the bars. Then he glanced at Josh. "Your clothes are over there. Or you can grab some sweats."

Josh wanted to argue out of spite, but he felt defenseless crouched naked on the floor. So he went to his luggage and quickly pulled on jeans and a tee. He didn't see his shoes anywhere, so it was bare feet on the cold concrete. Nero, he saw, was casually attired. Khaki pants, a butter-yellow polo that stretched across his broad chest, and Dockers for shoes. Preppy much?

The girl, however, didn't move from the back corner of her cage. She stayed where she was, arms wrapped around her knees as she glared through her short red hair. At least she'd stopped screaming. Meanwhile Josh had to think of a way out of this place. For himself and the girl.

But first things first. He needed more data.

"Why have you kidnapped us?" he demanded.

"We didn't…." Nero grimaced. "Well, okay, we did, but let me start at the beginning." He took a deep breath. "You are werewolves." He gestured at the rows of cages. "You all are. I am too, if that makes you feel any better."

"It doesn't." That was a lie. It kind of did. The guy seemed… normal in an evil Hulk kind of way. Josh chose to focus on that rather than the idea that he had turned into a wolf and been trapped in a cage. It wasn't possible, and he didn't want to even look at the memory. But it was hard to deny when the cage was two feet away. "How can I… how can we be…?" God, he couldn't even say the word.

Nero pointed at him. "Romani magic." He pointed at the girl. "Family curse." Then he went down the line of wolves. "Native American thing. Family heirloom, we think. And we haven't got a clue about him. He was an accident." Then he turned his thumb toward himself. "Lycanthropic bite from an asshole."

"And Gelpack?"

"He's his own special kind of we don't know what." Nero looked at the bloody gashes on his forearm, then crossed to a nearby cabinet. While he spoke, he pulled out bandages and tape, wrapping up his arm with casual ease. "That's why we need you guys." His voice had dropped to a lower pitch, the one that drew Josh's attention like a bee to a flower. But his next words pulled out of that resonance, enough to make Josh listen even closer. "Whether or not you realize it, you guys were always going to manifest into werewolves. We did it in a controlled environment where we could keep everyone safe. Including you."

Josh shook his head. "I was perfectly safe. I was doing a show on…." His eyes widened as he remembered what had happened. "You turned me into a wolf in front of the whole con! I worked for a year on that show!"

"And everyone loved it. It just wasn't the show you planned."

"No…," he murmured, memories flooding back. The terror of a body gone insane. The hatred boiling in his mind and body. And then… they'd choked him! And shot him! His hands went to his throat in memory, and fury burst through him. "You fucking asshole!"

He shot forward, going for a grappling hold. He'd had a little martial arts training in college, and he used that in his attack. But whatever little training he'd had, Nero had more. The guy took his attack and rolled through it, sending Josh flying across the floor until he slid against the tranq gun cabinet.

That didn't stop him, though. He jumped up and ran straight at Nero. He had no plan except to beat the guy senseless. Then he'd figure out how to open the girl's cage and get them both out of there. Time after time, though, all he did was get tossed onto his ass. And once—as if the whole thing wasn't insulting enough—Nero flipped him to the floor and protected the back of Josh's head while doing it. The fucker was looking after him at the same time he was kicking his ass.

Which made Josh all the more pissed off. So he threw all his energy into what he was doing. If he couldn't beat the bastard with skill, he'd do it with frenzy.

Didn't make any difference.

Five minutes later he was on his back, sucking air. He tried to get up again but was too dizzy, and damn it, every single joint felt like it was on fire, and his muscles seemed to be weighed down with lead. He tried to roll over to at least crawl, but another wave of vertigo put him flat on his back again.

"Are you done yet?"

The fucker wasn't even winded. Though he did have to retie the bandage.

"How could you do this to us?"

"You were going to change eventually. We just did it safely."

It wasn't possible. It wasn't fucking possible.

Except he had the memories. He knew it was true. And if he doubted it, all he had to do was look at the cages. And damn it, the redhead was still curled into a tight little ball, her green eyes huge in a very pale face.

"At least let her out. She doesn't deserve to be caged like that." And maybe together they could take down the Mack Truck.

"Wiz will take care of her. You're my problem." That commanding tone was back, the one that made it clear that he meant what he said. Whatever else was going on, apparently Josh was stuck with Nero on his ass.

Great… not.

"Look, I'm hungry, and you've got to be starving. I think I ate a cow after my first shift." Then, at Josh's horrified look, he hastily amended his words. "Not literally. We went to McDonald's and I ate like ten Big Macs." He rubbed a hand over his face. "We're not monsters. We're the good guys."

"Except when you turn them into werewolves and throw them in cages." Josh couldn't keep the bitter tone out of his voice, and he was childishly satisfied to see Nero wince.

"Do you want some food or not?" he finally said.

He hadn't thought he was hungry before, but at Nero's offer, his stomach cramped with need. Not hunger exactly. More like fury translated to his stomach. But even as he was struggling to his feet, his gaze caught on the girl. He couldn't leave her behind. But what the hell could he do here?

"She's hungry too. We go together or not at all."

Nero's brows rose in surprise. Apparently he'd thought Josh was an asshole. Sorry, dude. He didn't abandon caged girls. Except Nero was shaking his head.

"Wiz has food for her. She's gluten-intolerant."

Then, before Josh could respond, the door unsealed and the guy called Wiz strode in. He'd been Doctor Strange when they'd met at the con, and the guy looked tired to the point of being haggard. But his eyes were bright, and they landed heavily on the girl, who Josh had started calling Red in his thoughts. And even better, Wiz had brought a full tray of food that included a rib eye, a few protein bars, a water bottle, soda, flourless chocolate cake, and buttered broccoli. Josh took a step toward it, but Nero grabbed his arm.

"That's hers. We go upstairs." Then he turned to Wiz. "You got this?"

"Yeah. How you doing with yours?"

Nero shrugged. "At least I didn't have to put a bullet in his brain." It didn't sound like a joke, and the horror of that slid chills right down Josh's spine.

Wiz nodded. "Yeah. Looks like I'm good too," he said with a grin as he turned to the girl, though his smile faded pretty quick when he looked in the cage. "Shit," he murmured under his breath so quietly that Josh shouldn't have been able to hear it.

"Come on," Nero said as he manhandled Josh to the door. "I've got a feast for you upstairs."

Wiz snorted in response, but there was no way for Josh to ask. He could do something for the girl, at least. He dug in his feet and twisted to look at her.

"I'm not abandoning you. Get what info you can. I'll come back."

Wiz rolled his eyes and glared at Nero. "Get him out of here. He can come back when you've explained the facts of life to him."

"Yeah," Nero said as he tightened his grip on Josh. "Come on, hero. Let me explain how you are *not* prisoners here and that this is a *job offer*." Then he hauled Josh out of the room.

Chapter 7

NERO HATED lying. He'd been glib with his lies as a kid. Damned good at them, in fact. But ever since he became an alpha, every dishonest word bothered him. Most of the time he and his team were working with less than the full facts. The idea of purposely giving false intel set his teeth on edge. That he was lying to Josh made him sick to his stomach, but it was the only way to bring him into the fold. They needed him, and the world needed Wulf, Inc. So it was all for the greater good. And most important, Nero needed him to figure out magical fire.

Too bad his head didn't care. It felt like it was held in a vise. He'd feel better after he slept, but for now he had a job to do, and that meant initiating Josh to the werewolf facts of life.

"The center of werewolf life is the kitchen. Sounds obvious, but we werewolves like to eat. You'll take turns with kitchen cleanup, but unless you're a gourmet chef, I'll do most of the cooking. I try to make it healthy. You know, with vegetables and stuff. But we like our meats. Don't know what we'll do for Aine. I've never thought about gluten, but I guess I'll have to research that soon."

"Is that the redhead?" Josh asked.

"Yeah. But let her tell you that. She's got a gaming name that she usually goes by. Straw—Strat—"

"Stratos?" There was shock in the word.

Nero looked hard at his newest charge. "Yeah. How'd you know that?"

"Because she's infamous. In the gaming community, at least." His tone was layered with "how could you not know this?" attitude. "She's a kickass player with gorgeous looks. The whole package." He looked back at the door to the basement. "That was her?"

"Yeah," Nero said slowly. "So why is she *in*famous?"

"Because she'll do whatever it takes to win. She'll wear a push-up bra with drawn-on nipples, she'll flirt outrageously with the opponents and promise the judges dates, and then when she feels like it, she'll go all goth and tell everyone to keep the fuck away. She's the definition of female attitude. Gamers *hate* her because they can't stop watching, even when she gives them the finger. Especially when she gives it to them."

Nero snorted. "Sounds like a female werewolf to me."

"Seriously?"

Nero shrugged. "I was infected by a female wolf. I'm a traditional lycanthrope, like in the old movies. She bit me, and I got infected. She told me later it was because she wanted someone to be a bitch to." He held up his hands. "Her words, not mine. And then she pranced around naked to see if I would get it up."

"Did you?"

He looked away as he palmed the security reader on the way into the main floor of the west wing. "When I first changed, yes. At least I think so, it's kind of fuzzy now." Thank God. "But by the time she got around to explaining what had happened, I was traumatized and starving. I wouldn't have gotten it up for a Playboy Bunny. Unless she was a real bunny—then I probably would have eaten her." It was too soon to mention that he'd already figured out he was gay by then. Josh, on the other hand, had completely surprised him in that department. Something about the way the guy had gone thermonuclear meltdown in his attack turned him on like nothing else. No holds barred, full-on destroy, take out everyone and everything in his path. That was apparently the way to Nero's heart. It didn't make sense, but then he'd learned that nothing about sexuality made sense, so he should go with his gut. Or his dick. After all, a lycanthrope like him didn't have many options. And he hadn't missed the woody that Josh had sported when he'd been pinned. The guy hated Nero right now. He sure as hell didn't trust him. But that hadn't stopped the old dick from rearing its head.

Fortunately Nero was in better control. He knew not to play with the trainee. So he stepped back far enough to give Josh room to set his hand on the reader.

"Palm it. You're already in the system, so the door will open for you."

Josh frowned. "It already opened for you."

"Yeah. Palm it anyway, okay? There are holes in our security system, so it's best to be sure. Maybe you guys can help us out with that."

Josh nodded and did what he was told. The reader scanned his handprint and beeped the okay, unlocking the already unlocked door.

"So I'm free to go?" Josh asked as he stepped through the door.

No. "Sure. But we're hoping you'll stay around long enough to hear what's going on. You're a were-wolf now. There are precautions you have to take for your own safety and everyone else's."

"Like chaining myself up every full moon?"

Nero shook his head. That was the curse of humans who caught a specific strain of the lycanthropy virus. Not him, thank God, though he had his full moon moments, but some of his wolf-kin were really screwed when it came to the lunar cycle. "As far as we know, you should be fine on full moons. None of your ancestors were ruled by it. But we can never be sure until you live through one, so don't go running off. If you do, I'll probably be assigned to watch you until after the full moon, just to be sure. Don't make me do that. I haven't slept in…." *A week.* "…my own bed in forever."

Josh looked at him, his eyes narrowing. "I can tell when you're lying. You know that, right?"

"What? I'm not—"

"Your voice changes. It's not as compelling as when you're being honest."

Nero felt his jaw drop and made an effort to snap it closed. He didn't know where to examine that statement first. That he had compulsion in his voice or that it went out when he was lying. Or that Josh could tell one from the other. It wasn't possible, but then again, this was a new day and age. All the normal rules— what few there were—seemed to be on their head right now.

"Josh—"

"Save it. I'm going to assume I'm a prisoner, what with the cages and all. So, are you going to feed me, or do I make a break for the nearest McDonald's?"

"It'd be a long, cold walk. Nearest one is thirty miles away."

"So where's the kitchen?"

"This way." Nero walked ahead of him, knowing he was on borrowed time. Eventually Josh was going to make a break for it. It was his job to start laying out the breadcrumbs and making sure that Josh gobbled them up. But first things first. They made it to the large kitchen with a center island and long dining room table. Waiting in the oven was a massive dish of shepherd's pie. It had everything the new werewolf could want: meat, meat, and more meat layered over with cheesy mashed potatoes. He pulled it out and dished up a huge plate, which he kept for himself. He pushed the remainder of the casserole straight at Josh. Given the rumbling in the guy's stomach, it was a miracle he'd waited long enough to grab silverware.

Josh ate with speed. That was part of the glory of shepherd's pie. You didn't really even need to chew.

Water from the filtered tap was next, as well as a dish of green beans. All of it went down Josh's gullet, which wasn't a surprise.

What did surprise Nero was the way he seemed to be taking in all his surroundings even while he was shoveling food in his mouth. The guy's eyes were never still, and he even picked up his dish to eat while walking around. Nero followed, fighting the urge to sit and let the guy run for it. Nero was drooping with fatigue, and frankly he doubted Josh could make it out of the estate, past the gate, and out into the world. But it wasn't worth the risk, so he dug deep and tried to be persuasive.

"So while you're checking out the mansion, how about I go through who we are and what we want you to do for us?" It was a rhetorical question, but Josh nodded anyway. "The company's called Wulf, Inc. We're all werewolves, except for Gelpack. We fight paranormal baddies. That's mostly demons, but there are rogue vampires, evil fairies, and shifters who can't control who and what they are."

Josh gave him a wide-eyed look, but he didn't stop eating. And when Nero paused to finish his own meal, Josh tried to slide open a glass door to the back lawn. It didn't work, of course. It was locked and the glass was bulletproof.

"You might take note of what I said," Nero said. "If you don't stay here long enough to learn how to control your new abilities, it'll be my job to hunt you down and force you through our training course."

"And if I refuse?"

"We have permanent cages at a different facility. Sorry, but it's for your own safety and everyone else's." He set down his plate. "But we're hoping you'll pick up the basics pretty fast and then help us out with a problem we have."

Josh tilted his head as if he were listening closer, but Nero suspected he was looking out of the corner of his eye to their entertainment setup. The lounge was right beyond the kitchen, and it included a widescreen TV, couches, and several gaming systems. It was pretty sweet, and he wondered if Josh was tempted to forget everything and lose himself in video games. Nero certainly had been, especially lately.

Nero let himself wallow in yearning for a moment. Grief was still his constant companion, but work helped. As would video games, if he had the time. But his whole focus was on finding a way to defeat the plasma fire so he could go back in time and kill the demon bastard. That meant bringing Josh and the others up to speed. Surely one of them could figure it out, but they'd have to work fast. The fairy mulligan was available for seven weeks, and the clock was ticking.

A sound interrupted his thoughts, and he came back to the present with a lurch.

Holy shit, Josh was gagging. It began as a small cough but quickly progressed. Nero got to his side in a second, but it was too late. Josh's body was rejecting the food. The guy was about to projectile hurl.

He half dragged, half carried Josh to the kitchen sink. They barely made it in time before Josh started heaving. His body convulsed and his hands gripped the counter until his fingers were white. Nero turned on the water and the garbage disposal, but beyond that, there was nothing he could do. He held the man,

supporting his slender shoulders while his body reject-
ed every bit of food he'd consumed. And he'd consumed a lot.

"You're okay," Nero murmured. "This happens
sometimes. Let it go. You just need to get grounded a
different way. Coming back to human is always hard,
especially the first time." He kept speaking like that.
Soothing bullshit. The truth was that some wolves had
trouble *every* time, but it did no good to tell Josh that
now. He held the man while Josh's body wrung itself
out. And when it was done, Nero handed the man a
glass of water and a paper towel, supporting Josh's
weight as the man rinsed, spit, and shuddered with
revulsion.

"What. The. Hell," Josh finally said. He was leaning heavily against the side of the sink, and his skin
looked wan and dotted with sweat. Nero had a pretty
good idea what was going on, but before he answered,
he tried an experiment.

He rubbed his hand up and down Josh's back in
a soothing caress. The man shuddered and closed his
eyes, clearly appreciating the touch.

Yeah, Josh was one of *those*, and it was going to
be fucking hell on his own psyche to do what came
next, but Josh was the important one here.

"Come on, let's get you onto the couch." He'd
rather get the guy to bed, but that was too far away,
and Josh needed care ASAP. "So look," he said as he
guided Josh in tiny steps to the nearest game room
couch. Thank God it was the middle of the night and
no one else was around. This could be really embarrassing for them both otherwise. "When you shift
from human to wolf or back, you go through an energy

state. Not everyone does, but most of us do, including you. Everyone has to learn how to settle into the body again afterwards. I think the Earth helps in the wolf state. There's something about being an animal that connects you closer to Mother Earth. Don't roll your eyes at me like that. I don't fucking understand the details. I just know that no one has trouble grounding in their wolf state. In fact, many prefer being lupine instead of human."

They'd made it to the couch, and Josh half sat, half collapsed onto it. Nero joined him there, keeping a hand on his arm as he settled in as close to the man as possible without full-on embracing. That would have to come next.

"Grounding back in your human form is harder. Wiz thinks it's because we're so much in our heads that we don't really know our bodies that well. At least not the way we should. So coming back to human form requires some form of grounding."

He pulled his hand away from Josh, watching closely for the effect. The guy visibly paled, wavering in his seat. Nero quickly returned to him, not only stroking his arm, but twisting him slightly on the couch so that he could fall more fully against Nero's chest.

"For me," Nero continued, "I eat a lot of food. The more meat, the better. I love food in every way, shape, or form, so for me, going human means eating. Obviously that doesn't work for you."

Josh released a low moan. "Obviously."

"That's because you're all about touch. That's why your clothes are so old, right? Because they're soft. New stuff doesn't feel right, and you have to wash them like ten times before you like them."

Josh twisted enough to shoot him a startled look. "How'd you know that?"

"Because I'm not as stupid as I look," he said. Then he adjusted on the couch, lifting a leg and slipping it between the back of the couch and Josh, effectively putting the man between his legs. "Now don't freak out by this. You need it, and if you don't get it, bad things will happen."

He felt the man stiffen. "What bad things?"

"You never fully ground into your body. You start to sicken and die. This is your first shift, so it's the most dangerous. We need to get you grounded back into your human form right away."

Josh swallowed. "How?"

"I told you. Touch. Human touch." He pulled Josh back against his chest, surrounded him with his arms, and pulled him into a big bear hug. He stroked the man's bare arms, up and down, and though he could tell Josh didn't trust him enough to accept this easily, he didn't fight it either.

"The woman on my team was like you. We called her Mother. It was short for 'I'm not your mother,' but that's a different story. She had to be touched after every shift. Not necessarily an orgasm, though that worked the best." He swallowed, trying to talk impersonally about something so very personal. "It's about taking care of a teammate, and it kept her healthy."

He put his head next to Josh's, smelling the scent of the man, sort of sweet and earthy—like cherry pie eaten in the jungle. It was a weird image, but Nero often categorized things by food. And he loved cherry pie.

"I'm going to touch you now. I'll stop if you want someone else or if you want to do it yourself, but you need to climax. It's the only way to keep you alive." He slipped his hands under Josh's T-shirt, stroking his right hand across the man's belly. His skin was soft, the hair was minimal, and Josh exhaled as if he had been waiting for a very long time for this sensation.

"I could try eating something else," Josh said quietly. "Go slow. Get a Gatorade or something."

"We could, and it might have worked thirty minutes ago, but not now." Nero stroked his hand up Josh's chest. The hair was amazingly soft, and the guy was too thin. His ribs were noticeable bumps along his path. Damn it, he should have seen that earlier. No one this thin was into food. "Really think, Josh. Do you want something in your stomach now?"

The man shuddered in revulsion. "No."

"Then trust that." He slid his other hand under the shirt, pulling it up and gently maneuvering it off. And now that Josh was naked from the waist up, Nero could see—and feel—the attractive details of the man's body. There was muscle definition here. Strong pecs, tight abs, maybe 6 percent body fat. He must work out some, or maybe he was naturally sculpted like a thin Michelangelo statue. Either way, he had the right body to send Nero's libido into overdrive. There wasn't any distance between Josh's glutes and Nero's dick. Nothing except Josh's old jeans and Nero's easily ripped khakis. Nero's cock began to thicken and pulse with hunger.

Just another mission.

Meanwhile, he continued rubbing Josh's chest. Up and down the silky, smooth skin while he felt the man breathe. Every inhale pushed into Nero's hands, and every exhale dropped Josh closer, tighter against him.

"I should have realized this before. That woody you had when I tackled you, that was because of this. It was your body telling you you need this."

"I didn't.... I wasn't attracted to you," Josh muttered. "It happens sometimes."

"Of course it does. Because this is what you need. It settles you." And before Josh could object further, Nero pinched his right nipple.

Josh gasped, his body arching in surprise, but Nero didn't let him escape. "This will ground you back in your body," he argued. Then he pinched the other nipple. Josh's reaction wasn't startled this time, but his response was surprising. Instead of pulling away, he sank deeper into Nero's embrace. He let Nero stroke him, pinch him, and arouse him. And Nero was all too willing to comply.

And didn't that set off alarms everywhere? Nero reluctantly pulled his hands off of Josh's body. He'd already proved to Josh that it was necessary. "I'll stop now so you can finish it. The process has started, but you need to orgasm. You can do it yourself or—"

"You can." The words came out husky and filled with need. Josh didn't want to want this, but he obviously did.

"You want me to jerk you off? You need to say it out loud." His lips quirked, though Josh couldn't see it. "We do have ethics, though I'm sure they're not obvious to you right now."

"I.... Yes. Please... jerk me off."

Yes.

Nero didn't examine the surge of lust that rushed through him at Josh's words. He simply returned to stroking the man. Josh's earthy scent was growing stronger—muskier—as his body flushed with heat and arousal. He let his head drop back onto Nero's shoulder, and Nero watched their reflection in the dark TV as Josh's eyes drifted shut.

"That's the way," Nero encouraged. "Just go with it."

Nero pressed his lips to Josh's neck, tasting the salt of sweat and feeling the throb of the man's pulse. And then he opened his mouth and ran his teeth along Josh's skin. Josh moaned, and Nero's own dick stiffened to painful. Anything he touched with his teeth and tongue was burned into his memory. Food and lovers, both held a cherished spot in his mind, never forgotten. Josh was there now, and Nero knew the taste of this man would haunt him. Even if this was the only time, whenever Nero smelled cherry pie, he would think of this moment.

So he did it again. And again. Letting his tongue and his teeth scrape across Josh's skin, rubbing and tasting as if Josh were a fine meal to be savored, a delicate dessert to be enjoyed, or a special lover to be pleasured in a slow, sensuous exploration of taste and texture.

He slid his hands down to Josh's jeans. He didn't fumble with the button or the zipper, but he stilled when Josh gripped his wrist.

"You swear this isn't some sick kind of game?"

If it was, then Nero was going to be the loser. He was going to live with this memory every night while he jerked himself off in a frenzy.

"Check yourself, Josh," he said. "If I stopped right here, right now—"

"No."

"See. Your body wants this, but you can do it yourself. I can leave you alone—"

"No. This is okay." Josh released Nero's wrist. He even shifted his hips enough to allow Nero to shove jeans and boxers down. And the very impressive erection that sprang free all but leaped into Nero's hand.

"Damn," Nero murmured appreciatively. "Are all the men your family this big?" Nero had a large hand, and it didn't come close to covering the full length of Josh's swollen cock.

"I never looked," Josh said, though his voice held a note of pride.

"Bullshit," Nero answered. "All boys look."

Josh exhaled in relief as Nero began to stroke him. Strong, solid pulls while Josh gripped Nero's thighs.

"Okay," Josh confessed, "I did look. And I'm special, at least between my cousins and me. And I'm definitely bigger than my brother."

Figured. And yes, the man's cock was just the right size. Thick, hard, and with a nicely shaped mushroom head. Nero watched that head, seeing the color shift darker, feeling the pulse in the stalk, and loving the rhythmic tightening of Josh's ass as he thrust. It was torture, that movement against Nero's cock. And it was all he could do to prevent himself from thrusting up in tandem, from pushing himself against the sweet peach of Josh's ass.

Just another mission.

It took a while for Josh to near the end. It was a measure of how close he'd come to not settling into his body, and it reassured Nero that what he was doing was absolutely necessary. Josh's life was at stake, and he was doing what was right and proper for the new werewolf.

He continued to stroke Josh's erection, roving his spare hand across Josh's chest and belly. He pinched the man's nipples, loving the sound of Josh's gasps. And when Josh's breath finally became erratic, when his hips were moving hard as he thrust into Nero's hand, that's when Nero lost his own control for a moment.

He shoved himself against Josh's tight ass. He flexed his hips and ground against Josh. And in his mind was a steady litany of *mine, mine, mine.*

Josh wasn't his. He was a temporary charge, a mission to get tech support and an answer for the plasma fire problem. This was business.

Except his body didn't feel that way. And the scent of Josh's musk, the feel of that huge dick, took a piece of Nero's sanity with every breath.

It's a mission.

Mine, mine, mine.

Josh gripped Nero's thighs. He threw his head back onto Nero's shoulder, and he thrust hard. Nero gripped him, squeezing with all his strength. And then one last hard pull, and it was done.

Josh cried out, exploding hot cum all over his chest and Nero's hand. His body shuddered with the release, pushing more and more out with every beat. And Josh was a man in his prime with a strong dick.

The force of the first release pushed his cum high enough to catch a drop on Nero's mouth. A hot wet drop that fell on the lower curve of Nero's lip. He licked it off instinctively, tasting the salt, knowing the texture of it on his tongue, and locking it permanently in his sense memory. Josh's seed. Josh's intimate release.

Josh. Josh. Josh.

Nero exploded in his khakis. Hot, hard, and with all the force of a man with his lover.

A mission.

Oh hell, he was well and truly fucked.

Chapter 8

HEAT SUFFUSED Josh's body, but there was no clear meaning attached. He knew he felt pleasure and a shitload of endorphins, but there was also embarrassment and shame. He'd been jerked off by his kidnapper, and he'd liked it. Hell, he'd asked for it. How fast did Stockholm syndrome kick in? Probably not within the first few hours, and yet here he sat, completely boneless in the man's arms, missing the feel of his captor's hand on his dick.

And what a hand it had been. Thick, hard, with the right grip. The calluses were sweet, and the feel of the big man surrounding him had taken him to an orgasmic peak he'd never experienced before. So did this mean he was well and truly gay? Or really twisted?

"How do you feel?" Nero's voice rumbled low and sweet through Josh's body. Both the man's hands were now stroking Josh's arms, up and down in a soothing, almost lazy rhythm.

"You did it too," Josh said, the confusing words spilling out without filter.

"What?"

"I felt it. You…." Exploded like a teenage boy. "You came too."

Silence. Josh wondered if the man was going to lie about it, but eventually Nero sighed. "Yeah, I did. That happens sometimes. Don't think about it. Think about your body. How does it feel?"

Like it had just had the best orgasm of his life. But Josh didn't say that. Instead, he focused on the heat on his skin, the gentle skim of caresses up and down his arms, and the steady heartbeat behind his back. Nero's solid *ka-thump*, *ka-thump* was like the beat of a big drum. It made him feel safe on a subliminal level. And no matter how many times he told himself that he couldn't get comfortable, that he didn't trust this man as far as he could throw him, he couldn't deny the way that *ka-thump* felt against his back.

"I'm good," he said.

"Then I'm going to get up and get something to clean up with. You okay with that?"

"Uh, yeah, sure. I can—"

"Stay right here. You feel good right now, but Mother used to faint if she stood up too fast. So do us both a favor and relax. Let me take care of things right now, okay?"

"Okay."

Nero shifted, drawing his leg out and twisting his large body around. "I'm also going to heat up some broth for you, so this will take me a moment. Please don't try to get up or run away. The windows and doors are locked, and you're likely to end up passed out on the floor. I swear I'm not trying to hurt you."

That harmonic resonance was back in the guy's voice, so he knew Nero was speaking the truth. He really was trying to look out for Josh, even if that meant jerking him off on the couch. God, he squirmed internally whenever he thought about that, so he gave up the fight. He didn't have the mental resources for it. And though he'd likely damn himself for it later, Josh nodded and closed his eyes as he relaxed back against the cushions.

Nero spent a moment helping him readjust some throw pillows so that his back was supported, and then Josh exhaled happily while someone else took care of him.

His mind went blank as he listened to Nero moving around the kitchen, putting something in the microwave. And then there were all those bathroom noises before his heavy steps returned to the couch. Josh opened his eyes to see the big man looking awkward as he hovered with a thick washcloth in his hand.

"I'm going to clean you up, okay?"

Josh could have done it himself, but when he'd given up, he'd done it all the way. He nodded, then closed his eyes in pleasure as the warm fabric brushed across his chest and belly. Then it slid lower, and he was already thickening in anticipation. But that was too far to go. A first ejaculation could be put down to being overwhelmed. A second would be intimate, and so he stopped Nero with a raised hand.

"I got it," he rasped. And he did. He took the cloth and cleaned up with a few quick swipes; then, while Nero took the cloth back, Josh tucked everything away. He even pulled his T-shirt on while Nero went back to the kitchen. By the time the big guy returned with a bowl of dark broth and saltine crackers, everything looked normal and yet felt totally weird.

"It's bone broth," Nero said as he sat down on the coffee table and held out the soup. "Take it slow, but eat it all."

Josh meant to reach for the soup. He really did. His hands went out and his mind said, *Take the soup, eat it all, get strong enough to get your head on straight*. But he watched with a kind of dumbfounded shock as his hands went to Nero's face instead. And while the big guy was leaning forward to pass him the soup, Josh pulled their faces together for a kiss.

Nero's body stiffened a moment, but only for a fraction of a second. And even so, his mouth was never hard. His lips were full and sweet as they moved across Josh's with gentle confidence. And when Nero's tongue pressed forward, Josh surrendered to him with openmouthed abandon. He let the guy touch him everywhere—tongue, teeth, and the roof of his mouth. And as excitement heated his blood, his own tongue came alive. It thrust forward, then ducked back. He dueled and fought for dominance while his heart pounded and his hands began to grip. He angled

Nero's head and he surged forward, thrusting into Nero's mouth like a man demanding his due.

And to his utter delight, Nero gave way. He opened up for the kind of foreplay Josh loved. Give and take, surrender and dominance, a back-and-forth that had him rising off the couch to pursue this further.

Nero was the one who broke free. His breath was coming hard as he jerked back. And then he cursed with a sharp bark of surprise. It took a moment for Josh to realize why. The guy had spilled hot soup on himself and rapidly set the bowl down before shaking off his wrist. The skin there was flushed red, and Josh had the strongest urge to lick it better.

Nero didn't give him the chance. He was already straightening up, away from the coffee table, and dropping the crackers. A second look told Josh that he'd spilled half the soup on his pants and more onto the floor.

"Damn it," Nero muttered as he stripped off his shirt and dropped it onto the carpet to soak up the spill. "Mother is going to bitch about that. I swear her human nose can smell spilled—" His words choked off, and for a moment the guy froze. He was crouched in front of Josh, his glorious torso flushed as he pressed his shirt into the carpet, but his whole body went rigid. And then Josh looked at his face and felt his heart lurch at the naked grief. Nero's mouth was open in shock and his eyes were wide. A sheen of tears reflected the light, but not a single sound or movement shook the frozen tableau. It was as if Nero held his whole body rigid in fear of what would come out if he relaxed any part of himself, even for a second.

It wasn't hard to put the pieces together. He'd seen grief like this before. Mother was gone—probably dead—and the event was so recent that Nero'd forgotten for a moment that she wasn't here.

Well, shit. Whatever else was going on, Josh instantly felt bad for someone in the depths of that much pain. So he reached down to finish sopping up the spill. He gently tugged on Nero's wrist and spoke in a gentle tone.

"I've got this. Go clean up."

Nero pulled himself together with visible effort. His body tightened and he shook his head. "You're the new wolf. It's my responsibility to care for you."

And responsibility was clearly a big deal to this guy.

"I'm fine, and your pants are a mess." He touched Nero's chin and caught his gaze. Damn, if ever a man looked lost, it was this guy. He was alone and yet still fighting with everything he had to hold it together, to do his duty, to be the alpha in charge. "I'm good," he repeated. "Get cleaned up." Then he sighed. "I don't think I'm going to run away anytime soon. There's so much to learn here." He let his lips curve into a rueful smile. "And I've never been able to resist that."

He saw doubt cross Nero's features. The man suspected a lie, but his exhaustion overrode any suspicion. Nero was simply too tired of fighting to question Josh's apparent surrender. He nodded.

"I'll… um… I'll just be a minute."

"Take whatever time you need."

Nero didn't respond. He'd already grabbed his shirt off the floor and headed into the kitchen. He returned a moment later with a roll of paper towels that he tossed at Josh before he headed off down a

hallway beyond the entertainment center. Bedroom
wing, maybe?

Meanwhile, Josh finished cleaning up the mess,
then carried his soup and crackers back to the kitchen.
He felt stupidly weak but was able to slurp down the
rest of the broth. That warmed his belly and steadied
his head, but it did nothing for his chaotic emotions.
He'd gone from trying to kill Nero a half hour ago to
feeling tender empathy for the guy's pain. And he had
no answer for the lust that happened in the middle.

And none of it even touched on the Big Bad in his
thoughts: the idea that he might be a werewolf, and
WTF did that mean?

It was too much to deal with. So he sat at the
breakfast bar in the kitchen and nibbled on saltines.
He focused on that one simple act, and before long,
he heard Nero come back down the hall. The guy had
changed into a navy blue polo and another pair of
khakis. His hair was wet, as if he'd ducked his head
under a faucet and then towel-dried it. His feet were
bare, though, and for some reason Josh found those
big dumb feet endearing. Like Fred Flintstone feet.
Big and strong enough to run a cartoon car down a
freeway on the way to the quarry.

Josh smiled at the image and was even more
amused when Nero's expression turned to confusion.
"What's so funny?" he asked.

"Just wondering how many pairs of khakis you have."

"Dunno. Five? Six? They're professional and casual. Allows me to dress up or down easy."

For some reason that honest answer tickled Josh's
funny bone even more. His grin widened as he pointed

to his empty bowl. "I finished the bone broth. I'm feeling better now."

As expected, the guy's expression relaxed and his shoulders eased. He clearly took Josh's well-being to heart and was pleased by the report.

"That's good. Give it another fifteen minutes and then try some real soup. Vegetables, definitely. Meat if you can handle it."

Josh nodded, though an assessment of his stomach told him that heavy foods were out for the moment. Instead, he nibbled on another saltine and waited for his opportunity to learn more about his very interesting captor. It came about three minutes later, after Nero had pulled out carpet spray to douse the area where the soup had spilled, and while they waited for the foaming cleaner to do its work.

"So was Mother your… um… actual mother?"

"What? No. She was a werewolf on my team."

"Was she anyone's mother?"

He shook his head. "She never had kids, but she was the only girl here. She used to point at garbage we'd leave lying around or stains that we never cleaned up, and she'd say, 'Do I look like your mother? Clean up your shit or else.'"

Intrigued, Josh leaned forward. "Or else what?"

"That's what we asked." He waited a moment, his focus distant and his mouth curved in delight as he no doubt wandered through his memories. "She said, 'Or else I'll leave my shit where you live.' And she did. Whenever we didn't clean up after ourselves, she'd shit on our stuff. Real turds, real stinky. We'd lock our rooms, put away our stuff, but if someone left a mess, so did she." He looked at the floor. "Her nose was really good, especially as a wolf. If you left a mess, it was pretty easy for her to tell who'd made it." He looked up. "We learned to pick up after ourselves, but we called her Mother as revenge."

"I suppose there are worse names."

"Lots. And she had her softer moments, for sure. But mostly she was this firecracker of a woman who gave as good as she got." He turned away, his movements heavy as he opened a closet and pulled out an upright vacuum cleaner. "I miss her. She... died last week."

"How'd she go?"

Josh didn't think he'd answer. Nero was silent as he plugged in the vacuum and sucked up the mostly dry cleaner. He was quick and efficient in his work, finishing up and putting everything away in silence. But when it was done, he crossed to a desktop computer on a nearby table. A few clicks later, he pulled up a picture of himself with four other grinning people at a summer barbecue.

"This was my team." He pointed to faces. "Mother and her partner Pauly. Cream and Coffee." He touched each face with a shaking finger, but his voice remained solid. "We got word of a demon eating ice fishers in northern Wisconsin. An easy run by our standards, since most demons are stupid, violent things. Like putting down a rabid dog. They're dangerous but not that smart. Everything started as usual, and we almost had the thing licked."

As he spoke, he clicked through other pictures of his team. The summer barbecue was over, and now Josh viewed Halloween costumes, then nap time on the couch while someone drew a fake mustache on

Coffee. Cream apparently loved waffles, and then Pauly mugged for the camera from a mountain summit. One by one, the images clicked through until the screen abruptly changed. Instead of grinning faces, he saw black, wolf-shaped smears in a blast zone.

"The demon had some sort of plasma fire. It killed them all in an instant. The only reason I escaped was because I was in the energy state between wolf and man, and even then, it was a rough ride. One second we were doing our jobs, the next—" His voice choked off. He couldn't even say the words, but then he didn't have to. Image after image on the screen told the story. They were all dead. He wasn't.

"And the demon?"

"Still in the water somewhere. It needs to recoup, recover, reform. We're not exactly sure. We're looking for it, but we haven't been able to find it." Then his gaze lifted to Josh. "I'm going to kill it. Soon as I'm done with you newbies, I'm going back there, and I'm going to blow that fucker into tiny orange chunks. And then I'm going to piss on every smoldering inch."

Josh watched Nero's face, seeing the fierce determination screaming through every cell in the man's body. If this were a movie, he'd be the first one to applaud. But life wasn't a movie, and the good guys didn't always win. All he had to do was look at the ash outlines on the screen to know that. It grieved him to think that Nero had nearly become one of those spots on the dead ground. And if Nero didn't have something more than fury in his arsenal, then he absolutely would be ash if he went up against the demon again.

That's what pushed him to poke a man who was so wrapped up in his grief that he focused on pissing over a demon's remains rather than the steps up to that glorious end.

"So, um, what are you going to do differently so that you can urinate in glory?"

He'd expected Nero to blink and come back to himself. Instead, the man's expression became laser focused on Josh, and his words were so clear and distinct that Josh felt the impact of the sounds like tiny pebbles against his sternum.

"That's where you come in. That's why we disrupted all five of your lives. It was a huge risk, but we had to take it—"

"Who you trying to convince?" Josh challenged, but Nero rolled right over him.

"We need a way to protect ourselves against magical plasma that burns. We need you to…." He took a deep breath. "*I* need you to get me close enough to take this bastard out. He was easy pickings until the boom. If you can get me through that plasma burst, I'll destroy the bastard." Then he slammed a fist down on his thigh, taking out his ferocity on his own body. "I think it was a one-time boom, or at least it'll take a while to recharge. If you can find a way to protect us from the fire, then we can finish it. We can end this nightmare forever and go back to how things should be."

His words were coming hard and fast, and Josh wasn't immune to the resonance of challenge in every word. Nero's voice rang like a clarion call asking him to save the day, solve the problem, protect the heroes, and be all that he could be in the service of good. Every video game he'd ever loved had a similar beginning.

But this wasn't a game. Josh couldn't ditch everything in his life to do what Nero wanted. Even though
Nero was as hot and inspiring as a call to action could
be, Josh was a slow one to leap. Savannah said he had
commitment issues, but either way, he couldn't jump
in. He looked at his hands, not sure what to say.

"I don't know anything about magical plasma.
Hell, I don't know anything about magic."

"We'll teach you what we know. Gelpack said
he'd help, and Wiz loves talking to anyone who will
listen about what he can do and how."

Silence hung heavy in the room. Eventually Josh
looked up. He couldn't keep staring at the floor, but
when he connected with Nero's gaze, he saw desperation. Like the man was consumed with the need for
Josh to say yes, to take the red pill and step through
the looking glass. One little yes and everything would
be Wonderland. It was the same passion Josh had seen
in Nero backstage before life had gone sideways. And
it was a thousand times more intense now that Josh
had seen those ash outlines.

Yet he still tried to wiggle out.

"I'm not Einstein. You don't throw people into a
lab and say, 'I need this. Invent it.'"

"Try."

No. It was on the tip of his tongue. The whole
thing was too much, too fast. *Hell no* would be a better
answer. He was a geek from the Midwest whose most
exciting moment in life before today was letting go of
the handrail on the Batman roller coaster at Six Flags.
Even his greatest moment of glory at MoreCon hadn't
happened. It had been upstaged by these guys.

They'd turned him into a wolf, then thrown him in a cage. He'd been poked with a cattle prod, met an alien, and been jerked off by the wolf version of G.I. Joe. This was crazy. And yet the moment he formed the word no, another word came through his lips.

"Yes. Okay, yes. I'll give it a shot."

Nero seemed to deflate before his eyes. He exhaled in relief and gratitude as he abruptly became normal-sized. There was no more verbal resonance urging Josh to enlist in the wolf army. Just a big guy with a hole in his heart whispering the words "Thank you. You won't regret it."

Sure he would. Because that was the way with Josh. He usually regretted every one of his passionate impulses. And this was the biggest one of all.

Chapter 9

THE BIOLOGIST died while Nero slept. Given the odds, having only one of his five recruits die was a huge win, but it didn't feel that way. To him it was one more body added to the weight on his heart. Worse was what Gelpack did in an effort to help.

"You did *what* to his *soul*?"

They were in the morgue, and Dr. Wesley Barren's wolf body had been pulled out of the refrigeration unit. He looked stiff and cold, his lush brown fur seeming flat against his body. According to the chart, his organs had stopped working one by one in rapid succession. It happened more often than Nero liked to think about. They guessed it occurred when the mind refused to accept the wolf body and chose death rather than to exist as an animal, but no one knew for sure.

"I tied his energy to his bones," Gelpack said. "Provided his sternum does not break, he will remain here in this dimension."

Nero stared at the alien as if he was... an alien. "But he's dead."

"But you have ways to make the body function. Pacemakers and artificial bones."

"Yes," he said as calmly as he could imagine. "But that's when the patient is alive."

"What is death but when the energy leaves the body? I have prevented that."

"But... not...." Hell. This was why they so desperately needed a doctor. It was so Nero could look to the medical officer and order him to answer. "We don't know how to animate a dead body."

"Wiz spoke to me about necromancy. Perhaps he knows how to perform the task."

"What! Since when?" Then he abruptly shook his head. "Don't answer. I'll talk to Wiz, but I'm pretty sure he was speaking hypothetically." He hoped. Unless it really was possible.... He stared at the corpse and tried to imagine what it would be like to have his soul trapped in a frozen, dead body. "Is his soul conscious? Does he know what is happening?"

"I cannot answer that. Indeed, I am most anxious to ask him about the experience when he reanimates."

Nero opened his mouth, but he hadn't the foggiest idea what he wanted to say. To buy time, he looked back down at the file and noticed a detail that Gelpack wouldn't care about, but for humans, it was pretty significant. "He's a devout Catholic," Nero said. "I'm pretty sure the Pope is against living as a zombie."

"Who is the Pope? I do not understand."

No kidding. And Nero didn't know where to begin.

"Do you wish to break his sternum? That will release his soul and he will die as usual. Though I am confused. You said of all the recruits, you most wished this one to survive."

He had. He did. They desperately needed medical expertise. "We don't want zombie doctors," he said. Except in the realm of the weird, was a zombie all that awful? Assuming he could still work and function as a normal person. "Will he be... the same?"

"He will be able to eat other foods, not just brains."

"That's not what I was asking!"

"You are angry. I have miscalculated." Gelpack twisted the wolf body such that the sternum was facing upward. "You must break his chest. I do not have the physical strength for such a blow. A quick strike with your hand or a mallet should be effective."

"No!" Nero recoiled, revolted by the idea of slamming his hand—or anything—down on the wolf's chest.

"I believe there is a vise in the garage—"

Nero held up his hands. "Stop! Just... give me a minute." So many things crowded into his brain. Ethical considerations, religious doctrine, even the financial commitment to keep a guy on ice with no idea if they could bring him back to the living. But if they could... wasn't it worth the risk? Better zombie than dead?

He had no idea what Dr. Wesley Barren would want and no way to make this kind of ethical choice in the moment. Which meant his best option was to kick the decision up the chain of command. "Don't break it yet. We'll keep him here and maybe the captain will know what to do." He'd never been more grateful to be a grunt.

With that, he pushed the body back into the unit and sealed it. He prayed the guy didn't get lost in the paperwork. Ten years from now, would someone open the unit and say, "Who the hell is this?"

Meanwhile, Nero rubbed his forehead and tried to focus on something more productive. "How are the others?"

"All awake, human, and eating under the supervision of their partners. I—" Gelpack cut off his words. If Nero had to guess, he'd say the alien was frowning, but it was difficult to say on a Jell-O face. Sometimes the guy's whole body rippled when he stood too close to an air-conditioning vent. "I believe you should see them yourself. I did not understand their reactions to becoming human again."

Great. Why couldn't anyone wake up human and be grateful they weren't dead? That had been Nero's reaction. But then his last memory had been of a wolf clamping down hard on his shoulder while his bones broke. Waking up alive had been a complete surprise. Waking up as a wolf had given him a badass feeling that had never fully disappeared.

"I'll go check on them now." He paused as he looked at the alien, pushing to express his thoughts in words that even an alien could understand. "I'm very, very grateful to you, Gelpack. I know that you're the reason most of them survived."

"I am the reason they all survived," Gelpack said with no apparent emphasis or ego.

He sounded like it was simple fact, which flat-out terrified Nero. He still didn't fully trust the alien, and yet four new members of Wulf, Inc. were completely indebted to him. Or five, if you counted the frozen doctor.

"Um, well, I'm grateful."

"You are welcome. Unless there is anything else, I will go make notes now."

"Yeah. Go ahead." And what he wouldn't give to get a close-up look at Gelpack's notes. "I'll go find the others."

JOSH WOKE achy from a deep sleep and did what he always did. He reached for his phone. There was email and news to read, a couple of games he liked to play to wake his mind, and all the myriad ways a smartphone could distract him from the things he didn't want to think about. He knew exactly what he was doing. Hell, he'd developed avoidance to an art form. He even had journal articles uploaded to his phone so that he could dive into science when his personal life got too stressful.

Except he didn't have his phone. Nero hadn't returned it, which left him staring at the utilitarian brown curtains over his window and listening to someone humming as they banged around the bedroom next door.

Werewolf. The word whispered through his mind, and he resolutely focused on something else. But the sound of ABBA being sung badly next door was just making the anger worse, so he got up and headed for the shower. His bedroom had an attached bathroom with toiletries. He could focus on that.

Which only worked until he was clean. But coming into the bedroom reminded him that he'd left his luggage back in the cage room. Cages and howling wolves intruded on his thoughts, not to mention the cattle prod–wielding alien. Anger boiled up, acidic in his throat, but he shoved it all back down. The emotions were too raw for him to face. Better to think about getting dressed.

He found sweats in the dresser. He pulled the pants on and prayed they stayed on his narrow hips. The T-shirt was loose, but comfortably so, and he distracted himself by studying the werewolf image on the front, complete with sparkly white canines and razor-sharp claws. Two days ago he would have sneered that the image was anthropomorphized to a silly degree. The wolf had human-like biceps, broad masculine shoulders, and a glint to his eyes. But now that he knew werewolves were fact, the image was unsettlingly real.

Werewolf.

Was that who he was now? A testosteroned-up werewolf who could rip people to shreds at will? The idea appealed as much as it revolted him. Who wouldn't want to be a big, bad wolf? How many times as a kid had he wished he could huff and puff and blow people into the next county? Or rip them to shreds like Wolverine did? And yet, as he'd grown older, he'd joined the ranks of people who made fun of bulked-up meatheads. He'd never been a Thor fan. He preferred

Iron Man, the smartass geek who built a supersuit so he could fly and blow up the baddies.

He could not be like this souped-up image on the shirt. And yet as he looked at the werewolf in the mirror, he wondered how it would feel to be one of these people. Maybe he'd actually fit inside these sweats instead of tying the waist knot super tight like a kid wearing his daddy's pants. Or maybe his big brother's pants. His older brother, Bruce, would probably brag that the sweats were tight on him. Asshole.

Sibling rivalry was a familiar anger, and Josh hung on to that. He aimed his emotions at the imagined picture of his brother preening about in all his muscled firefighter glory. What an ass! He'd definitely fit in these sweats, which made Josh yank them off and throw them back into the dresser. He'd wear his jeans from last night. The pair that had been at his knees while Nero had jerked him off.

He stilled in the act of zipping up his fly while more emotions buffeted him. The image of Bruce wasn't enough to hold his attention. Instead, his mind was caught by memories of Nero wrapping his big arms around Josh. He had thick, strong thighs that had cradled Josh's hips. And his hand had felt like heaven as it pumped his dick.

Josh started to sweat. He needed to burn off these thoughts with a video game or internet research. Hell, even the news would work. He needed his phone. Which meant he needed to get back to the cage room. His stuff was there. And he needed to find out how Stratos and the other wolves were doing.

Other werewolves.

He felt guilty for crashing last night and not going to find them, but Nero had made it clear that he wasn't allowed back downstairs yet. The last thing the other werewolves needed—according to Nero—was Josh hanging around confusing the issue.

So, wearing his regular jeans and the Wulf, Inc. tee, he tried his bedroom door and was reassured to find it unlocked. A quick walk down the hall brought him back to the game room and then into the kitchen, where a wiry brown-haired guy was dropping cheese onto an omelet while humming random musical theme songs. This was the guy who'd been singing off-key "Mamma Mia," and he looked up with a broad grin.

"Good morning!" he cried. Lord, even his voice belonged on a Disney soundtrack. It was happy, excited, and really ought to be making animated squirrels chirp along with him. "I'm making omelets. You want one?"

"Sure," he answered without thought. He never turned down food someone else cooked for him. But as he spoke, he wondered how his stomach was faring. There was no queasiness right now, but the idea of eating something heavy made his belly clench. "Um, better make that just scrambled eggs. Nothing fancy. I'll be back in a second." He saw the door to downstairs and headed for it.

"Sure thing. I'm Laddin Holt, by the way. That's short for Aladdin 'cause Mama said I was magical. Who knew she'd be right? And the door's locked. I already checked."

Laddin was right. Josh couldn't budge it. And the palm reader flashed red when he flattened his hand on it.

"You one of the regular wolves or a new guy?" Laddin asked. "I'm new," he continued without pause. "My trainer says there are five of us, but she still wants more recruits."

Josh turned away from the locked door and focused on Laddin. Information was key in every situation, and right here was some new info. Giving up on the door, he went deeper into the kitchen. "New one—"

"Wait. Let me try to remember," Laddin said, his face scrunching up. He also held up his hand to stop Josh from talking, and right there was yet another thing to focus on.

Laddin's hand was deformed. His thumb, forefinger, and a crooked pinkie looked mostly normal, but the middle two fingers were infant sized. But it didn't prevent Laddin from using the hand. He managed the omelet and pan without any problem, not to mention all the normal cooking utensils as he started thinking out loud.

"I was still half out of it, but I remember a lot of roaring and barking. There was a fight between a naked guy and a big guy. Gel guy had a... a stick?"

"Naked guy was me. Big guy was Nero. Gel guy had a cattle prod." Josh kept his voice neutral, but his side twitched in memory. The pain had burned through him like ants eating through his insides. His muscles had clenched, his body had jerked, and yet the fury of his attack hadn't lessened. If anything, the pain had tripled his anger.

And he'd attacked like an animal. Like a....

Werewolf.

Josh's side knotted up as he flinched away from the word. It was too alien for him to accept as being attached to him. His words were *boy*, *chemist*, *nerd*, *puny*, *gay*. Also *friend*, *man*, *son*, and *brother*. But not *animal*. And certainly not *werewolf*. And yet the word wouldn't go away.

Laddin did an exaggerated shudder. "I got an up-close-and-personal look at the weird guy's stomach." He blew out a breath. "Creepy."

Josh nodded as he forced himself to focus on Laddin. "Last I saw, you were being sedated. Which... um...."

"Cage was I in?" Laddin supplied. "Second from the last."

Was his transformation due to a Romani curse? Josh couldn't remember. There had been so much to absorb yesterday.

"Yeah," Laddin continued as he poured his omelet onto a plate before breaking a couple more eggs into a bowl and scrambling them with a fork. "I have no idea how long I snoozed. Next thing I know, a woman is calling me by name and telling me to get up and get dressed. We had things to do." He grinned as he looked up. "She sounded like my grandma. So I got up and got dressed as a man. It took me a moment to even realize I'd crawled out of a cage as a wolf. Weird, huh?"

"Definitely," Josh said, though he'd experienced something similar. He didn't even remember shifting, but he sure as hell remembered wanting to beat the shit out of Nero. And there was the anger again. The confusion and the betrayal, rising like acid in his throat. He pushed it down once more. He needed to focus, not emote. Fortunately, Laddin was a chatterbox.

"Captain M says it's different with every person, but there's always a trigger. She's the head honcho around here and the one assigned to me. She's in her office, over that way." He gestured down the hallway opposite from the bedroom wing. "Anyway, she just had to sound like my grandmother, and I obeyed."

"Yeah," Josh murmured. "Nero sounded like my father, and I wanted to humiliate him. I went human so I could correct his pronunciation." And beat the shit out of him.

He remembered the hatred burning like hot lava that he couldn't escape and couldn't control. He'd been all animal, teeth and claws. He'd needed to taste blood and feel entrails in his claws. Nothing like father issues to bring on the heat.

Laddin shot him a sympathetic look. "One of *those* dads, huh? That sucks. My mama ditched my asshole father when I was too little to remember. I used to want a dad, you know? But then I saw how many dirtbags are out there, and I thought, just having her and Grandmama wasn't so bad. We got along fine." He grinned. "And I can't wait to tell them that I'm not dead!"

It took a moment for Laddin's words to penetrate the memory of what he'd been, of what he'd felt.

Werewolf.

But eventually his mind cleared enough to replay Laddin's words. "You knew about all this?" he asked. "About being a...."

"Werewolf? Hell no. But Grandma's got second sight. She gives people readings at psychic fairs and stuff. It's mostly good intuition, but she's got a real gift too. She told me that I was born with this"—he held up his deformed hand—"because my whole life would change when I was twenty-eight."

Josh frowned, not knowing what to say to that. How did a congenital defect lead to werewolf-ism? Fortunately, Laddin wasn't one to let conversational silences hang there. He was filling up the space with his chatter as soon as he poured the eggs into the skillet.

"She said it was a life change. A transition thing. Like death, and maybe death, but she didn't know. Said it would happen in my twenty-eighth year." He pointed to his normal thumb and forefinger as he counted. "That's ten and twenty." Then he spread both hands, showing all eight normal fingers. "And that's eight. So twenty-eight."

"Your grandmother told you you'd die when you were twenty-eight?" God, what a horrible thing for anyone to say.

"Not die. Transition, or there'd be some big change during the year. I'd thought it would be re-alizing I was gay, but that happened when I was eighteen. Then maybe when I switched jobs or some-thing. I never, ever expected to become a werewolf." He nabbed a plate and scraped scrambled eggs onto it. "Honestly, I was beginning to doubt, but I should have known better. Grandmama is always right, at least with me. I turn twenty-nine in seven weeks." His expression fell. "I text them every night to tell them that I'm okay. Mama's probably planning my funeral, but Captain M wouldn't give me back my phone. Have you got yours yet?"

Josh shook his head. Worse, he knew that none of his family would even think to miss him until the holidays. His lab would notice he wasn't around come Monday, but…. "What day is it? I mean, it was Friday when—"

"Things went loco?"

"Yeah. How long were we…." He couldn't say the word, but it slipped out anyway. "Werewolves?"

"Don't know. For all I know, it could be Saturday. Or Sunday. Or next year."

"It's Monday," Nero said as he pushed opened the door from the lower floor. He stepped out, and Josh felt the zing of attraction tighten his insides. Then anger surged. He shouldn't be attracted to his captor. He shouldn't be looking at how the guy's strong hands dwarfed the doorknob or feeling that mesmerizing voice settle into his groin and thrum there. Josh got a low vibration of pleasure whenever Nero moved his mouth, and that was just *wrong*. But there was nothing Josh could do to stop it. Meanwhile, Nero kept talking while Josh felt every beautiful sound. "We found it's easiest to keep new recruits unconscious for a while. It lets their bodies rest before they shift back to human."

"Monday!" Laddin squeaked. "But Mama will be frantic—"

"Captain M already texted your mother and grandmother. They know you're alive and well and will contact them as soon as it's prudent."

Laddin shook his head. "That won't be enough. Not until she hears my voice and—"

"Pinches your cheek. Yeah, we know. We'll set up a time and place for your family reunion"—he glanced at Josh—"for everyone's reunions, but only when it's safe. New recruits are emotional creatures, and no one triggers a meltdown like family."

"But Mama—"

"Will have to learn patience. It's the way it is. I'm sorry, Laddin. No exceptions."

Laddin pressed his lips together in a show of annoyance. Josh had just met him, but he guessed that Laddin rarely went silent. But was he now pouting or plotting revenge?

Nero turned his attention to Josh. "How are you feeling? Can you handle food yet?"

Zing. Nothing like the focused interest of a hot guy. Josh hated that he warmed to the attention, but damn it, how could he not? Nero was looking at him like he cared. Worse, like he was *worried*, and even Josh's mother hadn't treated him like that in years. Casual disinterest was more her style, but she always remembered to pray for him before she went to sleep at night. Like that made up for how she turned her head whenever his father went on the attack. Compared to the other things going on right now, this issue felt almost comforting. He smiled as he shoved a forkful of eggs in his mouth and found it not-too-revolting. "Guess so."

Nero grunted. "Don't go too fast."

Yeah, he'd learned that lesson last night.

"And stay hydrated with electrolytes. There are lots of choices in the refrigerator."

Josh was about to say a sarcastic "Yes, Mother," but he cut off the words unspoken. That was too familiar and too creepy, given what they'd done last night and what Nero had revealed. He didn't know if Nero was his abductor, partner, or lover. The first, yes, the second, maybe, the third—definitely not, though there certainly were lusty feelings coming from his body. Which left Josh in an uncomfortable place. And uncomfortable places always made him angry. So he turned to the best distraction he knew and made sure irritation burned through his tone.

"Where's my phone?"

"Put away. And no, you can't have it."

"You can't keep us prisoners like this!"

Nero exhaled in a long slow release. Obviously the guy was trying to keep himself calm—and doing a better job of it than Josh—which pissed Josh off even more. "You'll stay like this—without your phones—until you prove you can handle shifting. It's for everybody's safety, including yours."

"What about your friends? I thought you wanted me to solve that fire blast thing?" It was horrible of him to throw that at Nero. The guy was still grieving, and Josh had implied that Nero had forgotten all about it.

Not surprisingly, Nero's eyes chilled, but he didn't lose his cool. "Any help you can give us on that will be richly rewarded. Things might even go back to how they were before all this ever happened."

Josh glared at the man for who-knows-what-reason. He was pissed off, and Nero was the best target. But he couldn't stand here, eating and throwing irritation at random targets. He needed to do something to distract himself from deeper emotions. From the fact that he was a werewolf now and that his family didn't give a shit that he'd been abducted. So he went for the second-best distraction.

"Fine," he growled, and it was a growl. Did he do that now? "Point me at the science."

Nero's expression didn't change, but Josh felt the ramp-up in intensity. Like Nero was holding himself back from leaping on the suggestion. "You sure?"

"You said you need me to figure out magical fire resistance, right?"

"Yes."

"So show me what you got. Point me at the diagrams, the biology, the facts and figures. Hell, I want to see your alchemy experiments. You needed a geek, let me go geek."

"Really?" The hope in his voice was palpable, but even so, Nero tried to give him a different option. "I assumed you'd want to get adjusted first. To understand what it meant to be a werewolf."

Like his identity could be figured out in an afternoon. Not if you were an egghead. "I'll bet you played football in kindergarten."

"Yeah, and it was called peewee ball. So what?"

"So you go at things from a body perspective. You approach everything from what you can hold, throw, or smash. That's how you get adjusted."

Nero straightened. "And you do what? Think at things first?"

Josh shrugged. "If I can conceptualize it, then I can deal with it. I can manipulate it, reverse it, and blow it up. So get me on your database and I'll take it from there." Plus, it had the added advantage of getting him out of proximity to Nero, whose simple presence was enough to muck up his thoughts.

"Works for me," Nero said with real enthusiasm. "This way."

Josh followed a couple of steps behind as they headed to the door downstairs. He tried not to notice the way Nero's body moved, tried not to watch the tight ass and broad shoulders. Didn't work. Same with trying to ignore the guy's scent or block the memory of orgasming in his massive hand. He tried not to think of a dozen different sexual things and only managed to get himself even more hot and bothered.

God damn it, nothing would stay settled. He couldn't be angry and attracted, but he was. He couldn't be science geek and werewolf—nothing like that ever happened outside of the comics. And he sure as hell couldn't be missing his family that he hated.

Right in the midst of all his conflicting, confusing emotional turmoil, another person came up through the basement door.

It was a measure of Josh's distraction that he hadn't recognized the guy last night. Even in wolf form, Josh should have known he who he was. He'd been in the last cage, and now that Josh saw the human behind the fur, everything slipped into place.

"Holy shit," he gasped, "are you Red Wolf? Like *the* Red Wolf?" He couldn't even remember the actor's name, but Red Wolf was as famous in manga circles as Wolverine was in comic book stores. The story had started as a series of manga comics but then spun off into a live action TV show with kickass martial arts. This guy played Red Wolf, the mysterious, moody loner of a werewolf who sometimes saved the day, sometimes destroyed it. The fans loved him.

And if this guy wasn't an actor but really was a werewolf, then…. "Are you saying that the manga is real?"

The actor/werewolf turned to him, his Asian eyes as flat as his mocking tone. "Yeah, dude, manga is totally for real. Obviously." He rolled his eyes. "*Not.*"

Josh felt the burn of embarrassment roll up his face. Jesus, he'd made a fool out of himself fanboying over a manga-turned-real-life actor. God, he was an idiot. And what a jerk this guy was to rub that in his face.

"Oh, right," he drawled, making sure the sarcasm dripped acid into the room. "Red Wolf is a sophisticated character. A complicated good guy beneath a scary exterior. That can't be you 'cause you're just an asshole."

He saw his words hit as the guy's skin flushed ruddy. He squared his shoulders and bulked out in the way that every Red Wolf fan had tried—and failed—to imitate. "Look, punk—" he growled, but Nero stepped in between them.

"And that's enough getting-to-know-you time until everyone's belly is full. Quick note to the new recruits: everyone is cranky on an empty stomach." He swung the actor toward the kitchen stool and shot Laddin a look. "Can you fix Bing some breakfast?"

"Sure thing," Laddin answered, chipper once again.

"And if you're done eating," Nero continued as he pulled Josh around, "let's get you to the lab."

That would normally give Josh a graceful exit, but Bing Wen Hao (as he now remembered the actor's name) was giving him the stare down. It was a Red Wolf trick that—on screen—came complete with glowing red eyes and an unnerving sound effect. And damn it, Josh couldn't break eye contact even if he wanted to, which he didn't. He was going to stare down this asshole until the bastard whimpered "uncle" in his puffed-up prettiness. Because, he had to admit, the actor had won the beautiful looks lottery. And that the hypno-lock was real.

Shit. He really couldn't break his eyes away.

Fucking hell. It was *real*!

Panic churned in his gut and he tasted bile. He might be a werewolf, but all of a sudden, even that status wasn't enough. Dammit!

Weak werewolf.

The impact of that thought nearly crushed him. All his insecurities rushed at him; all the emotions that he'd been so desperately trying to avoid came back to mock him. Even as a badass werewolf, he could barely stomach food, had been jerked off by his captor, and now an asshole actor had shown him how limited he was among the paranormal set.

He was going to fucking kill—

Nero stepped in front of him, breaking the hypno-lock and grabbing Josh's arm to haul him toward the stairs. "Time to geek out," he said loudly. In fact, it sounded very much like an order. He even gripped Josh's hand and slammed it down on the hand reader before half dragging him downstairs.

Josh followed, mostly because he didn't have a choice. Nero was bigger, stronger, and he had leverage. And then the idiot made the mistake of trying to be conciliatory.

"Look, I know that didn't go so well, but werewolves are really volatile, especially in the newbie stage. And we didn't even plan for Bing. We got him by accident. So don't go picking fights with people, okay? He's had his entire life turned upside down, and he's not handling it so well."

That was a really rational thing to say. Really great with the comrade-in-arms thing. Except as Josh felt fury physically rise in his gorge, he knew that rational wasn't going to cut it right then. Because his life had also been turned upside down. But all the change had shown him was that he was still the weak, puny creature he'd always been. And no amount of science was going to stem the tide of rage at that single thought.

Which is when Nero must have realized he'd said something wrong. His eyes widened and his hands went up in a placating gesture. "Um, maybe we should take a moment to reassess—"

Before he could say anything else, Josh attacked in the one way he always won.

Chapter 10

"ARE YOU fucking kidding me?"

Words started boiling out of Josh. Lots of words, most of them in a multisyllable, complex grammar fury. Nero could follow the words. Well, most of them. But after the first "Are you fucking kidding me?" Nero tuned them all out. He didn't need to hear the words, he needed to listen to Josh's body and understand the things that Josh's really big brain was ignoring.

First thing he checked—always—was whether a werewolf had eaten. Nero hadn't missed that Josh managed a couple bites of eggs at most. That meant his body wasn't fully grounded in the here and now.

"Are you even listening to me?" Josh demanded.

"Every word," Nero said.

Josh hadn't waited for an answer but kept screaming about his dissertation and mutant something or other. Nero focused instead on the color of Josh's skin. A guy in this much fury ought to have flushed ruddy, but Josh was getting paler by the second. And though he was gesturing and pointing, the movements had only average force behind them. About human normal for a guy his size, which on a werewolf was low. Any moment now Josh would get unsteady on his feet and Nero would have to catch him. No problem, but it was hard waiting for the guy to collapse before he could help. At the moment Josh was too wrapped up in his anger to allow any kind of support.

"…and you have the fucking gall to tell me that pretty boy…."

He had to watch the eyes. Josh's were growing darker. His pupils were dilating as he lost focus and connection to his own body. That was bad, but not dangerous. But if the eyes started to glow, the shit would really hit the fan. That would mean Josh was moving to an energy state before a shift, and it was way too soon to go there. Without being grounded back in his human body, Josh risked dissolving into energy and dissipating forever. He'd just sparkle away like fireworks. Nero had watched it happen once and the memory stuck as the most beautiful, horrible thing he'd ever seen. He'd be damned if he let that happen to Josh.

"…I need my phone…."

Josh's voice had lost its pitch, the words cracking or dropping.

"…fucking abduct…."

Grammar was going too as sentences became phrases, words became salad.

"…touch… couch… shit!"

There it was. The knees started to buckle, but Nero was there to catch him.

"No!"

"I've got you."

"No!"

"I'm keeping you from hurting yourself."

"No!"

Nero knew that each denial was shouted with fury, but Josh was losing breath. Instead of a loud exclamation, it came out as a puff of air. And even that was weakening.

"We need to take care of your body, Josh." He scooped up the man and carried him quickly into the gym. He didn't want to take Josh back into the cage room, and he for damn sure didn't want to go into the examination area. That was guaranteed to freak out everyone. Since he knew the gym area and where all the electrolytes were, he made a beeline there, kicking the door open with one foot while maneuvering Josh's lanky body through the opening.

"No."

He read the word off Josh's lips because there was no sound behind it. And damn if his heart didn't break at that sight. He'd known Josh all of three days, and in that time, he'd seen the guy go from a charming, fun showman readying for his big moment on stage, to this limp, ashen man too weak to even shiver. His body temperature was plummeting and…

Oh fuck. Fuckfuckfuckfuckfuck.

A light had just sparked behind Josh's eyes.

"Don't you fucking go there, Josh! You stay right here with me!"

He invested all his energy in those words, verbally willing Josh to listen. And it worked—for a moment. Josh's eyes widened and his mouth parted in shock. Best of all, the sparkle seemed to fade a bit, but it was hard to tell in the brightly lit gym.

As quickly as possible, he set Josh on the mat, and then he dropped down to his knees behind the guy.

"You've had your say," Nero barked. He wanted to moderate his tone, but his heart was beating too fast for any control. His next words would determine whether Josh lived or died, and he couldn't screw it up. "Now I'm going to tell you something you haven't thought of. Something that brain of yours needs to know."

The shimmer behind Josh's eyes faded a bit, and Nero realized he'd found the way in. Josh was a thinker, and so he'd latch on to new information like a lifeline of espresso shots. And so Nero pushed it, saying the one thing that he was pretty damn sure Josh had never once heard before.

"I screwed up your life," he said. "Me. No one else. I fucked you over, and I did it so royally that you're never going to be the same. It's my fault. Hate me, because I sure as hell deserve it."

Josh didn't respond, but he also didn't dissolve into pretty sparks of energy. Better yet, his eyes remained fixed on Nero's face, but that would change the moment Nero stopped talking. So he didn't. He let his confession roll out, with all its humiliating truth.

"I know you're a few months from graduation, about to get a doctorate. And I've just flushed eight years of education down the drain. Because you're not going back to that lab. You're not publishing any paper. We can't afford the exposure."

Josh's eyes widened, and Nero rushed to the next horrible truth.

"And your best friend Savannah? You can't talk to her. Not for a long while. I'm so fucking sorry for that, because I know you don't make friends easily."

A sheen of tears burned in Josh's eyes, and that ripped straight through Nero's heart.

"There's more," he rasped. Fuck, he was not going to allow himself the luxury of choking up. He'd done this to the man. The least he could do was own up to his own bastardy. "You know your big event at the con? I don't know if you remember. You were freaking out and a wolf, but everyone thought it was the most fantastic thing they'd ever seen. They were on their feet and cheering you as if you'd won the Super Bowl." Shit, not the Super Bowl. Not a sports reference. "Like… um… a Nobel Prize." Did they cheer at that? "Or… um… a cool *Star Wars* thing." Could he possibly suck more at geek references? "Anyway, they'd never seen anything like it, and you would have been the toast of the con. Years from now, they still would have talked about it."

He swallowed.

"But we had to wipe their memories."

Josh's mouth dropped open slightly, but then his jaw flexed. He was trying to clench his teeth. That was good. Anger was good. And it sure as hell grounded a man in the here and now.

"There's a magnetic pulse we can do to disrupt memories. It's not close to 100 percent, but it messes with short-term memory. Maybe some of them will remember what happened, but in a vague kind of way. Specifics will be lost, and the first thing to go will be your name. They might remember that something amazing happened, but they won't know you're the one who did it."

Josh's color was coming back. His eyes were narrowing, and his brows pushed together. If ever a geek could look like he was about to become a linebacker, Josh wore that expression now. He was pissed and growing more so by the second. Which was a good thing, because it meant he wasn't going to disappear.

"Your family ties aren't strong. They're not going to realize you've disappeared for a while. And worse, even if they do, your dad is just going to put it down to you fucking up again. Your father's a first-class bastard, and that was a positive in our book. The faster your family washes their hands of you, the easier it is for us to make you one of us." He dropped back on his heels. He wanted to touch Josh's hand. He wanted to soothe them both with a caress or a kiss. Something that shared empathy and support.

But what Josh needed right now was his fury, not a warm blanket of comfort. So Nero straightened away from Josh and told the damning truth.

"I am 100 percent responsible for the shitshow your life has become. I knew all these things, and that made you more attractive in my mind. You were the first guy on my list, even before all the others. And now you have the opportunity to make me pay. Get stronger. Get a handle on your abilities. The moment you're safe around other people, we can't keep you here. We have laws like everybody else, and that's one of them. We're not allowed to enslave you." He knew because he was usually the one reminding people of that law when certain über-powerful beings forgot that little detail.

"You're weak right now because you need electrolytes and blood sugar. Finding out how to balance a new physiology is hard for everyone at first, but you'll master it. And then we'll have no ability to keep you here. You can walk right out and go back to your life. Maybe you'll lose six months, tops, but you can finish school, reconnect with Savannah, and do your whole con show again another year. And you can do that knowing full damn well that you have fucked me over as much as I fucked you. Because we need scientists. We need doctors, chemists, and necromancers. Or antinecromancers. I don't fucking know because I'm a grunt. And without you, we get screwed over, me most of all. Because it was my job to recruit you, and my job to save the new werewolves when they eventually go out in the field, and my job to figure out how to defeat a fire blast. So if you really want to make me pay—like in blood, pay—then walk away. Force me to watch my people die. Again. And know that you will have destroyed my life just as effectively as I have dropped a bomb into yours."

His words ended, and God, he felt like he'd torn open his chest and exposed his own beating heart. He watched Josh's eyes, hoping to see some softening there. Nice that there wasn't any glow, but there sure wasn't any reassurance there either, let alone forgiveness. No, Josh just lay on the mat glaring at

Nero, and he had that right. So Nero forced himself
to continue.

"There are sports drinks in the refrigerator over
there. I'm going to get you one. You'll feel better if
you drink it. Choke down as much as you can and wait
fifteen minutes. You'll see what I mean. You'll feel
stronger. And once you do, we can talk some more. I
swear, I'll listen to everything you want to say. Cuss at
me, insult my parentage, whatever you want, because
I deserve it. Okay?"

Josh didn't answer, but he didn't object either.
So Nero got an energy drink and a straw, and then he
helped Josh sit up, propping him up against the weight
rack. He sat there quietly, watching as Josh took a single sip. The guy grimaced as it went down, but a minute later he took another. And later another.

It took twenty minutes, but eventually the bottle
was empty and Josh had color in his cheeks. His eyes
were the steady green color of new grass, and his body
temperature had risen to werewolf normal, which was
a little hotter than vanilla humans. He didn't object
when Nero brought him a protein bar, and he steadily
chewed that.

A half hour passed with Nero watching over a silent Josh as he doggedly gave his body what it needed
to survive. Salts and water. Protein and rest. After forty-five minutes, Josh was looking healthy again, but
just in case, Nero risked a question.

"Better?"

Josh nodded.

"Think you can stand up? I can take you to the
library now. Or you can go back to your room. Or we
can talk. Whatever you want."

Josh didn't speak, but he did roll onto all fours before pushing to his feet. Movement was good, so Nero got to his own feet as quickly as possible. He was ready to grab Josh if he teetered, but wasn't going to help unless asked. Every man had his pride, and he didn't want to trample on Josh's.

A moment later Josh was upright and looking steady. Excellent.

"So do you want—?"

Pain exploded through his jaw and face. His head snapped back from a vicious right cross. Fuck, he hadn't even seen it coming. He adjusted as quickly as he could, but he was reeling. Jesus, who had taught—?

Another blow, this time to his left side. He felt his body gather the energy. He could be a werewolf in a second, and then let the bastard try to take him down.

But he didn't go there. He didn't even raise his arms to defend himself. Josh had the right to beat the shit out him. And Nero deserved every blow.

Which is exactly what happened. Punch after wicked punch hit him until his eyes were swollen shut, his jaw was broken, and...

There it was. Shot to the temple.

Unconsciousness beckoned, and he dove straight into that cold, black void.

Chapter 11

JOSH PULLED himself back with a horrified jerk. His hands were bloody, his teeth ached from clenching his jaw, and the smell.... God, all he could smell was sweat and blood. He felt surrounded by it.

Nero was unconscious on the mat, his face a bloody mess. Nausea rolled in Josh's stomach, but he fought it down. He had to get help.

After stumbling out of the room, he dashed to the upstairs door, hauled it open, and bellowed, "Help! Someone—medic!"

The response came gratifyingly fast. He'd barely taken a step back toward Nero when a woman burst past him and sprinted for the gym. He followed while more people came thumping down the stairs. He was moving slowly, feeling disassociated with the throbbing in his hands and the twist in his gut. He watched in that numb state as the woman felt at Nero's neck for a pulse.

Oh fuck. Had he killed him? He didn't even remember hitting the guy, but the rage still churned inside him. He remembered the way Nero had detailed all the failings in Josh's life. No friends, no family, no fame. And the purpose and connection that Josh had cobbled together into a life had just been obliterated by Nero. That bastard had done it to him, and....

"Get it under control!" the woman snapped as she shot Josh a glare. "Why the fuck would you do this?"

Josh swallowed, only now realizing he'd been growling. That a raw animal fury was boiling inside him.

"Answer me!" the woman snapped. Was this Captain M? Probably, given the way she'd taken charge.

"He confessed." That didn't begin to cover what the bastard had done, but that's what came out. And before he could find his way to more words, she rolled her eyes.

"Of course he did. Jesus," she said, dropping a hand onto Nero's shoulder. "I knew this was a mistake. New werewolves are always angry, and Nero is desperate to be punished. God damn it!" She squeezed his shoulder. "Wake up, idiot. You need to shift and heal your face."

There was anger in her tone, but also fear. And as more and more people crowded into the gym space, Josh smelled so many things—eggs and bacon, formaldehyde, baby powder deodorant, and spices. Someone's body odor was acrid, another's had a fruity scent, and yet another's had a metallic tang. Added to that was the scent of his own sweat, as well as Nero's blood. God, he couldn't block that copper taste and the incessant beating of four words through his brain: *What have I done? What have I done?*

His stomach clenched, and he stumbled backward. There were voices everywhere, some soft, some anxious, and one in particular barking out orders.

"Get him the trash can!"

Someone shoved a wastepaper basket into his hands, and he lost the fight of trying to control his body. It felt like his stomach was twisting itself into rope, and everything was being squeezed out.

He vomited sports drink and protein bar. And then he continued to throw up absolutely nothing. Just pain, disgust, and he didn't know what. When his stomach finally ended the purge, he was on his knees, someone was pressing a hand to his forehead, and the scents had grown immeasurably worse.

"You done?" the woman asked.

He hadn't the strength to refuse to answer. He nodded weakly and whispered, "I think so."

"Laddin," she said, and the hand on his forehead disappeared.

"Yes, Captain?" he answered.

"Can you take care of that and then bring back my phone?"

Josh's head lifted at the idea that she had a phone. And she was letting Laddin carry it.

Meanwhile, the ball of energy being addressed responded with a crisp salute. "Right away, Captain!"

The woman shot Laddin a "seriously?" look before focusing on someone standing to Josh's right. "Wiz, you've got Mr. Angry Puker while Nero recovers."

The guy in question dropped a heavy hand on Josh's shoulder and squeezed hard. "Not a problem."

Then she looked down at Nero. "I don't think we should move him. Who knows what's broken in his face."

"It's probably the first real sleep he's gotten since…." Wiz let his voice trail away, but Josh had no trouble finishing the thought.

Since his entire team was burned to a crisp.

How could he be so angry at a guy and so wrapped up in sympathy for him at the same time? The riot of emotions was dizzying, and for a moment Josh really wished he was the unconscious one on the floor. Instead, he was held there to stare at the bloody mess he'd made of a guy who… who….

"You going to hurl again?" Wiz demanded as the grip on Josh's shoulder squeezed painfully tight.

"No." He gathered his strength and pushed to his feet. But once there, he didn't know where to look or what to do. He swallowed and looked at the woman. "Is he going to be okay?"

She shrugged. "He wasn't okay in the first place, but yeah, I don't think there's any permanent damage."

Hard to believe, given the ground-meat look of his face.

"Experienced shifters can heal most wounds when they come back to human, and Nero's as experienced as they come." Her eyes hardened. "And no matter what he said to you, your situation is not his fault. I ordered it, as did everyone else up the chain of command. I'm Captain M and the head of the Wulf combat packs. Your life sucks right now because I ordered it. And because you had a Romani ancestor with special woo-woo. Deal with it. And if you ever lay a hand on any of my people again, I will personally gut you. You got me, Mr. Collier?"

Josh swallowed. "Yeah. I got you." He resisted adding *ma'am*. He hadn't joined the military, and thanks to Nero's confession, he knew he didn't have to stick around. But he did need to get a handle on his emotions. If this was what happened when he got pissed off, then he really was a danger out in the world.

It was so hard to wrap his brain around it. He'd never been violent like that in his life. And now another question burned through his brain: *What did they do to me?*

He looked at the blood on his hands and fought down the need to purge again.

"I need to wash up," he said to no one in particular. And then he realized exactly what he needed to do. "And then I need to go to your library and start researching."

"What?" Wiz asked.

Josh trained his eyes on the captain. "I need to understand what has happened to me." He glanced at the other people in the room—Pretty Boy and Stratos. "What has happened to all of us." Then he swallowed as he looked down at Nero. "He said you want something to resist magical fire."

"Can you do it?" He heard hope in her voice, and he took perverse pleasure in squashing it.

"I can't even define magical fire yet, and it takes decades to develop good tech. You've just destroyed all our lives on a pipe dream."

"Your life was going to explode anyway," she argued. "It's in your DNA." Then she blew out a breath. "But whatever you can give us will help a lot of good people." She looked at Wiz. "Take him. Bury him in everything we've got and don't let him up until Nero's whole again."

Apparently she took perverse pleasure in squashing his dreams of escape. Little did she know that he enjoyed being buried in pages and pages of data. Or so he thought… for about four hours. By that time he was hungry and his eyes were burning.

Wiz didn't let him stop. He brought down a sandwich and a cup of coffee—for himself. What he said to Josh was "Nero's still unconscious," before he tossed Josh a Gatorade.

And with that reminder, Josh went back to the tablet he was reading that had access to a database of mismatched files labeled things like *Case File 2549* and *Fairy Declaration Magenta with Pink Sparkles*. It wasn't a database so much as an electronic pile of documents with no organization.

He kept reading.

By late afternoon Stratos joined him. She didn't greet him but just shot him a bitter look as she sat beside him with a tablet of her own. Three minutes later she'd discovered exactly what he had.

"No organization? Like at all?"

"None that I can see."

She sighed. "No wonder they need techies." And that was the last thing they said until evening. At least

Wiz brought them both food around six. Stratos got
another steak. Josh got thin broth that tasted like exactly what he needed. After the first few sips, he slurped
it all down before going back to his latest fascinating
read: Case File 1079. Inauspicious title, to be sure,
but it was about a team of werewolves tasked with
destroying a clay golem. They steadily chomped on
the creature's muddy legs until someone took a swipe
at its face and got a hold of the scroll in the thing's
mouth. Once they destroyed the scroll, the golem dis-
integrated. It was the standard way to disable a clay
golem, but clearly these werewolves had no idea. And
since the scroll was ripped to pieces and then burned,
no one could read the thing and find out exactly what
it said or how it had been created.

Idiots.

He made notes for his own reference guide and
then pulled up another file. It looked like he'd need
to read the entire database before he could start forming theories of his own. And that would take a really,
really long time. Especially since there seemed to be
a pile of arcane books hidden somewhere that no one
had bothered to digitize. And no way in hell was Wiz
letting him get access to that.

So he read. A lot. Thankfully he was a speed reader. And he tried to stay pissed off while he was working. It was the only way to avoid the crushing guilt
he had for going psycho on Nero's face. But the more
he read, the more he came to respect what Wulf, Inc.
was doing. The case files went back to the beginning,
when the wolves had first organized. Case number one
involved fighting a demon in Salem, Massachusetts,
and it made him wonder if there had been something

behind the witch trials other than human greed and religious zealotry. Either way, the wolves had taken out a really nasty demon and decided to organize.

Somewhere along the way, they'd run afoul of fairies and ghosts until an intrepid Englishman with mysterious powers decided to forge an accord in the late 1800s. That document was like the first Bill of Rights for magical creatures, or maybe the Constitution, because it set out three branches of weird and their governing bodies. All the case files were built on top of that as each branch policed its own and took out any magical creature that violated the Accord's principles.

And what was first and foremost under the Accord's rules? Don't freak out normal people. Don't eat them, don't hurt them, don't scare them into insanity. A little mumbo jumbo was forgivable, but anything that brought the population to real awareness of the woo-woo was punishable by death, dissolution, or reversion to "before the primordial goo."

Reading the case files was like reading scripts from *X-Files* or *Dresden*. He didn't get the full cinematic glory, but his imagination had no problem filling in all sorts of exciting details of heroic combat. And this was real life. Better yet, he was part of it now!

Or he could be. If he chose.

And God, he wanted to say yes. So what if his life had been turned upside down? How else was he going to keep a harpy having a really bad day from destroying a Swiss ski resort? Or barter for some luck from a real leprechaun? It was like stepping into the pages of his favorite books, and the little boy inside his heart was leaping with joy at every new case, every mysterious new adventure.

He managed to hold firm to his indecision until he started reading the most recent case files. All of a sudden the monsters were getting bigger and badder. Casualties started mounting because claws and fangs weren't enough to defeat bad guys with special abilities. And if they hadn't known ahead of time about the scroll inside a clay golem's mouth, then they sure as hell didn't count on vampiric pumpkins.

Worse were the files featuring Nero and his previous team. They'd been the stars of Wulf, Inc., dispatching demons and banshees with apparent ease. Until ten days ago. And that case file had been the hardest of all to read.

It was after midnight when he finally turned off the tablet. Stratos was still reading, her body posture as intense as when she competed in *CS: GO* for a $20,000 prize. Wiz was still here too, his posture relaxed as he turned the pages of something written on vellum that smelled like dead rats.

Josh's head was swimming, and that was nothing compared to the riot of emotions in his head. Tired of fighting it, he leaned back and closed his eyes, willing himself to sleep rather than face the guilt, panic, and desire that tumbled about his brain.

He let it all ping-pong through his mind, eventually quieting enough for three words to steadily grow to block letters in his brain.

CALL TO ADVENTURE

Normally he'd leap up and say yes, yes, yes to something like that. But that was in a video game or a novel. It was a thousand times different—and scarier—in real life. He could really die, in really excruciating ways.

His reading had revealed a secret network of werewolf packs who lived normal lives. In fact, this estate was perched right next to one. He didn't have to stay under the auspices of Wulf, Inc. to thrive as a werewolf. Hell, he could finish his PhD and teach at nearby Hope College if he wanted a nice, sane normal life. Or he could join the fight against dragons, demons, and the random bitter shapeshifter.

He let that question bounce around his brain for a while. He fell asleep before he had an answer, and his dreams took up the quest. Nightmare after nightmare had him dying by some monster's acid-throwing power or morphing into a putrefied goo that ate Savannah.

It sucked, and it terrified him. And by morning, it solidified exactly what he was going to do.

JOSH'S NOSE twitched. He smelled food, and his stomach grumbled in need. He was still in the library, and the smell came from a thick, fluffy omelet currently being consumed by Wiz with refined zeal. Josh watched the man's long fingers cut precise bites, and Wiz grinned as he read the hunger off of Josh's face.

"Want some?" he drawled.

"Yeah."

"Too bad. This is mine."

Dickhead.

"Good news is Nero woke up a couple hours ago. His face is fixed, and he said all is forgiven. So you're off my leash and can make your own food. Just try to puke into a toilet this time."

Josh flashed the guy his middle finger as he shoved himself upright. Half his muscles ached from the lousy position he'd been in. The other half were nonresponsive because of lack of blood flow. He growled low and deep in his throat as he moved, his annoyance put to sound. And then he froze as he realized what he'd done.

Shit. He sounded like Savannah's dog when facing off with the neighbor's Chihuahua. Wiz chuckled, clearly unimpressed, and Josh had to agree. The truth was, he sounded more like the Chihuahua than Savannah's bulldog. So rather than try a different insult, Josh headed upstairs for a bathroom and food.

He found both as well as just about everyone else. Stratos sat hunched over a mug of coffee. Happy, aka Laddin, was humming as he buttered toast. Pretty Boy chewed methodically on a carrot stick. The captain was enjoying her own omelet, and Wiz wandered up the stairs as Josh grabbed a bagel and threw the pieces in the toaster.

Except for Nero, everyone was here, which made this the best time to say his piece.

He cleared his throat. "I've spent the last day researching," he said. "I read fast, and there were things I wanted to know."

Everyone looked up at him—for a moment—then returned to their food.

"The thing is," he continued, "they can't keep us here. Not after we master our ability to shift. And there are lots of werewolf packs throughout the world."

"Bad idea," said the captain. "We're like the police. They're like cults. Nutjob, drink-the-Kool-Aid, David Koresh-like psychos."

"Not all of them," Wiz added. "Some of them just require absolute adherence to the alpha's demands. Whatever they may be."

Laddin frowned. "All of them?"

Stratos spoke up, though she never looked up from her coffee. "From what I read last night? Yes. It doesn't matter how they start. Eventually a nutjob alpha takes over and Wulf, Inc. has to take them down."

Josh agreed. It's what he'd read last night too. Which brought him to his next point. "They're not lying that they need help. Their numbers have never been huge, and their ranks have been thinning fast. They've only got two doctors, and both died thanks to a pestilence demon a month ago."

The captain straightened up as she glared at Wiz. "Just how much of our library did you let him read?"

"The case files," Josh answered. Then he looked at the new recruits, catching the eyes of each one in turn. "I was pissed about getting recruited or activated or whatever without my consent, but it doesn't change the facts. They need support, and what they've been doing is good stuff, as far as I can see." He took a deep breath and really committed out loud. "I'm a chemist, and I've decided to help. My guess is all of you have special skills too."

Stratos's lips curved, and this time she did look up from her mug. He saw the dark circles under her eyes, but also a flash of excitement. She'd been reading right along beside him, probably lots of the same files. "I'm a programmer," she said. "And yeah, I'm in too."

He glanced at Happy. The guy was grinning. "I'm organized," he said. Then he shrugged. "And I can blow up anything. I grew up doing demolitions."

Really? That was not at all what he'd expected. "Someone needs to organize their database. Their library—"

"I'm already on that," Stratos interrupted. When he looked at her, she shrugged. "I looked at your notes while you were asleep. Already started a basic sorting program."

Cool. That would be massively helpful. Meanwhile Happy gestured to the captain. "And I'm already helping her. If you think the library is a mess, you should see her office." His shudder looked like it came from the bottom of his feet and went all the way up his body.

That left Pretty Boy. But when Josh looked at him, the actor didn't answer. He just rolled the remains of his carrot forward and back between his fingers. Fine. He could keep his secrets, but Josh already knew about the guy's hypnotic stare.

"Okay, we're invested." At least three of them were. He looked at the captain. "And fair warning, I'm planning on changing your recruitment methods."

The captain shrugged. "If you can find a way without breaking the accord, then I'm all for it."

Great. He added "Read the Paranormal Accord" to his To-Do list. "What's the next step?"

She opened her mouth to answer, but Happy was there before her, practically leaping over the counter to tell them the news. "Today is one more rest day; then tomorrow we try to change into wolves. They've got exercises to bring out our doggie side. And then

we change back. That's it! As often as possible until we get comfortable with it. Comfortable and in
control. Those are her words." Then he spun around,
looking at everyone in turn. "Afterwards, she'll tell us
about our jobs, our pay, and benefits and the like." He
did a little hop. "They have full dental!"

"Yeah, but do they have a dentist?" Josh asked.

Wiz snorted. "We have a dentist, but he's dou-
bling as our medic right now. And believe me, you
don't want him in your mouth or in a wound."

"Really?" the captain snapped. "How are those
healing spells coming along, *Wizard*?"

"Pretty slow, considering I've been babysitting
new recruits. *And I'm not a cleric*." He paused and
Josh took a moment to realize he was referring to traditional D&D structure. Wizards had magic spells;
clerics had healing spells. Then Wiz flashed a truly
creepy smile. "But the necromancy text has been really enlightening."

At those words, everyone stared at Wiz. Necromancy? The idea gave him the chills. Meanwhile,
Happy was busy being cheerful.

"Anyway, in a few weeks to a month, we should
be all sorted out. Full werewolves with jobs and—"

"Dental," Josh finished for him. "We heard."

Then Pretty Boy chose to finally say something.
To his credit, his tone wasn't accusing but was more
like the flat, calculating tone of Red Wolf. "And what
happens to our lives while we are training? When
the police come looking or our families have our
funerals?"

The captain spun in her seat to look at Pretty Boy.
"I told you, Bing. We're doing everything we can to

minimize the damage. We didn't mean to activate you." Then her voice took on a more formal tone as she addressed everyone. "There's no police, no one has reported any of you missing, and we've dealt with those who would most likely be worried."

"How?" the actor pressed. "How did you *deal* with them?"

Happy stepped forward. "She texted your agent, Bing. He's handling things."

Pretty Boy's eyes widened in surprise. He glared at Happy for a long, uncomfortable moment, and then he abruptly got up from his stool and walked away. He headed down the hall and into what must be his bedroom. He didn't slam the door, but the heavy click was statement enough. Pretty Boy was pissed off.

Join the club. At least Bing had an agent who handled all the details. How sad was it that Josh didn't have any details to handle? Beyond Savannah, who'd had her memory erased, Josh didn't have anyone who would care if he disappeared for a month. His thesis advisor would be pissed, not to mention the faculty head of his lab, but that wasn't any different from usual.

And on that thoroughly depressing thought, Josh grabbed his bagel and headed out as well.

"What are you going to do?" Happy asked. In his defense, the guy just sounded curious, not like a paranoid mother.

"Research magical fire." He looked hard at the captain. "That's what you want, right?"

"Yes," she said. "It's what we want. And the sooner, the better."

"Roger that," he said, though he doubted she heard the sarcasm in his voice. He made sure he was out of earshot before he said the rest. "Right after Nero and I discuss a few things."

But he must have misjudged how good werewolf hearing was. He swore he muttered the words under his breath, but behind him, Wiz burst out laughing. And just before he made it to Nero's door, he heard the man's mocking words.

"Good luck with that!"

Chapter 12

NERO WAS sitting in his bedroom, thinking of all the times he'd been desperate to escape into the silence of his own room. Back when he was a kid, he and his sister had huddled together in the one bed while their mother screamed obscenities at her boyfriend, his grandparents, or worst of all, their landlord as he threw them out. Later, he'd longed for a moment's peace after he'd been infected with lycanthropy and was trying to sort through the new demands of a body gone insane. And then there were the more recent times, when his team had plagued him with their petty arguments, boredom, or simple need for attention.

How he'd longed to be right where he was now, settled in his suite in a mostly silent mansion. He could read, relax, surf the internet, or even stream a Miami Heat basketball game. They might even be playing right now.

But he didn't move from where he sat at his desk, staring out the window at a Michigan winter land-scape—snow on the lawn, snow in the trees, snow drifting down prettily from a cloudy white sky. This was the perfect time for a pack run through the forest. The snow might bite a bit between the toes, especial-ly when it was more ice than snow, but the rollicking good time more than made up for any discomfort.

Too bad he didn't have a pack to chase snow-flakes with.

Fucking A, he hated the silence.

As if in answer, he heard footsteps come down the hall. They were too heavy to be Captain M's and too light to belong to Wiz. That meant it was a newbie who didn't understand what it meant to come to his door. He already guessed it was Josh because no one else would dare, but whomever it was would learn the mistake. Nero readied a throwing knife.

No time like the present to make his point.

Knock, knock. "Nero? It's me, Josh. We need to talk."

Thunk.

Perfect throw, dead center. He knew that the point of his knife had shoved through the door to appear right next to where Josh had knocked. Take that, recruit.

Better yet, he heard the gasp.

"That's emphatic," Josh said through the door.

Take the hint. And just in case the guy didn't, he threw another. *Thunk.* This time the point protruded right where Josh had knocked.

"That can't be a werewolf skill. I'll bet you learned it young. Cool."

Nero frowned. Did he think this was a conversation? Apparently so, because he kept talking, proving he had a death wish.

"I'm coming in. We need to talk."

Thunk. Thunk.

Two more knives right by the handle.

"Yeah, yeah. You're big, bad, and surly. But I need my hands to do your research, so keep your pointy objects away. I'm coming in."

There was a lock on his door, but Nero never used it. His knives were usually enough to keep people away, and if there was an emergency, he wanted his team to be able to run in. Clearly that was a policy he'd have to reevaluate. Because Josh turned the knob and opened the door, and Nero hadn't the heart to stick him with either of the extra two knives he had at the ready. Of course, Josh had done the smart thing and stepped to the wall side of the door before opening it, so he wasn't an easy target either.

Well, he'd never thought Josh was stupid. But then the guy just walked in and shut the door behind him.

"I could gut you in so many ways," Nero growled.

Josh actually rolled his eyes. "Yeah, whatever."

"I could!"

"I know you could! But I'm here to talk, so put away your big, bad wolf act and let's talk, okay?"

"Go away. I'm watching a basketball game. And you need to figure out magic fire." He flipped open

his laptop as he turned his back on Josh. Why exactly
he was being so surly, he wasn't sure. Truthfully, he
was grateful for the guy distracting him from his mor-
bid thoughts, but he kept his jaw locked tight and his
back aimed to the intrusion, steadily typing in what he
needed to get to the streaming service.

Fuck. The Heat weren't on. Bulls versus Cava-
liers. Whatever. He folded his arms and pretended to
watch. Meanwhile, all his senses were tuned behind
him. Josh hadn't said anything. Was he that scared?
Good. Except the more the silence stretched on, the
more Nero wanted to know what Josh was doing. Why
wasn't he being annoying and trying to get Nero to
talk about his feelings or something? That's what Captain M and Gelpack had both tried to do… which was
why he'd taken out his throwing knives and had put
more holes in his door.

Except Josh wasn't talking. There was rustling
and poking into things. He was sure of that, but the
TV was loud enough that he couldn't tell for sure.

He finally couldn't take it anymore. Nero spun
around in his seat to glare at Josh. Except the guy
wasn't where he expected him to be. He certainly
wasn't cowering like he should be. Instead, he was
poking through the stack of books and magazines lit-
tering the floor all around the bed.

Nero's suite was just like all the other bedrooms
in this wing. He had one large room that allowed for
a bed, a desk, and a closet, plus a bathroom. In his
case, that meant a king-sized bed and a lot of floor
space, because he didn't really have anything else except for some clothes in his closet, a laptop on his
desk, and reading material everywhere. He ought to

get a bookcase. He kept intending to, but he wasn't one to keep stuff around. Once he read something, it was in his brain, so he threw out the magazines or gave the books to the library. What remained all over his floor was stuff he intended to get to but hadn't had the heart.

No need to read *Car and Driver* anymore because Pauly wasn't around to discuss engine details. He'd learned cooking from Mother, and weird recipes weren't fun without her to critique the disasters he created. Coffee's passion had been sports, sports, and more sports. The *Sports Illustrated* was actually his subscription. Which left Cream's true adventure addiction. They told each other tales of derring-do and tried to get the other to guess if it was true or false. At this moment, Cream was ahead, thirty-seven correct guesses to Nero's thirty-five.

He'd never get the chance to catch up unless Josh figured out how to defeat magical fire. But what was the guy doing? Squatting down to inspect a long-buried *Scientific American*. Josh tilted his head as he opened it to the cover article and started singing softly that song from *Sesame Street*: "One of These Things." Nero didn't wait for the rest of the song. "You don't know jack about what doesn't belong in my room," he snapped. "But I'll tell you, okay? *You*. You don't belong in here."

Josh pursed his lips as he appeared to think. "You know about Savannah. You know she's my best friend, but I don't think you know how we got that way." He plopped down on the floor next to the stack that had held the *Scientific American* and kept talking as if they were chatting over pizza and beer. "We'd been dating for a while, but it never quite clicked. I always held a piece of myself back from her. I knew I had to break it off, but I didn't know how. We were in college, and I'd gone home for spring break, and that'd been a disaster. I came back angry and irrational, holed myself up in my room, and blew things up in a video game. So there I am, hating everyone and everything, and she comes in and sits on my bed."

Nero sighed. He knew where this was going. The girl had been patient and eventually Josh spilled his guts and all was made better. "Some people actually prefer being alone," Nero said.

"Yeah, I know. That's me, most times. But she just sat there for like an hour. I ignored her because I was being childish, and then she got fed up."

"Turn off your game?"

"Nope. She broke up with me. Said I sucked as a boyfriend and the sex was awful." Josh winced at that, but he kept going. "Then she said it was time I understood exactly what she thought of me." He blew out a breath. "And then she gave it to me with both barrels, holding nothing back. It took about two sentences."

Nero couldn't help but feel a pang of sympathy. He'd had a few exes give him the royal fuck off too. "Sorry. That must have sucked."

"Nope. She was spot-on. She told me that I was running from my father's tyranny and that I needed to grow a pair or I'd be in his shadow the rest of my life." He shrugged. "There was more stuff, but that was the gist of it. It was exactly what I needed to hear at the time. We became best friends right then, way closer than we'd ever been when we were dating."

Nero shrugged back. "And what does this have to do with me?"

Josh dropped the magazine on the floor, then hopped onto the bed, extending his long legs in front of him. The bastard looked like he was settling in for a long comfy chat, and Nero wanted to choke him for his audacity. But he didn't have the chance as Josh started talking again.

"The thing is, she split me wide open like a can opener. Told me things I didn't want to see, much less deal with. Kind of like what you did to me yesterday."

Oh shit. "We're not going to be best friends," Nero muttered, except the words came out more like a growl.

"Probably not," he said, though his tone was a little too casual, especially with the shrug he threw in, as if he was disappointed at that but didn't want to show it. "The thing is, you said exactly what I needed to hear, exactly when I needed to hear it." Then he gestured at Nero. "Sorry about your face."

"It's fixed." He'd shifted early this morning and repaired the damage. Although he was still smarting from the chewing out Captain M had given him for forty-five minutes on how irresponsible it had been to risk his own health just so a recruit could get his fury on. She'd given him a choice then. He could talk to Gelpack about his feelings or he could go brood in his bedroom. Obviously he'd picked the latter.

"Thing is, I can't help but think about something the captain said. She said you were so damned desperate to be punished."

"That's bullshit. I don't—"

"I know. I think she's wrong too."

What?

"I mean, she has a point. Survivor's guilt can lead to a twisted need for punishment. Makes sense."

"Not for me."

"Yeah, that's what I think too." He stretched his arms out behind his head and leaned back. "You really don't seem like a masochist to me."

"Don't go psychoanalyzing me. I'm likely to put a knife through your thigh and laugh while you try to learn how to shift without bleeding out." He flashed an evil grin. "When you die, I'll call it a training accident."

Josh snorted. "Yeah, not scared. Now back to how the captain has you all wrong...." He dropped his hands down by his sides. "I've been reading your case files."

"What the fuck were you—?"

"Research, remember?"

"That's not what you're supposed to be looking at!"

Josh flashed him a happy grin. "Well, without you to stop me, I looked at whatever I wanted to." He sobered. "You were the alpha of the best Wulf, Inc. team. And like every good alpha, you spent all your time focused on the pack. Its needs, its lacks, its strengths." He gestured around at all the reading material in the room. "Is any of that for you? What part in here is you and what part is all about the pack?"

None of it. It was all the pack. Even his interest in physics had started because Wiz liked to call them intellectual Neanderthals. No one else cared, but Nero didn't like his team being deficient in anything. Plus, he had enjoyed learning about science in the purest form. Forget magic. That was just woo-woo shit that he left to the fairies. Even biology was messy in his mind. He was all about force, mass, gravity. Physics in its pure state. Astrophysics, when he could wrap his mind around it.

And chemistry too, though most of it was beyond what his high school class had taught him. Which brought him right back to the guy who was looking way too comfortable in his bed.

"Where is this going, Josh?"

"You're not trying to get punished. I think you're trying to be the captain who goes down with his ship."

"Then I'm a little late. It already sank." *Liar, liar.* The truth was that he still hoped to save his team. Hell, he planned on it.

"Yeah, that's the problem. You're a captain without a ship. Or an alpha without a pack. That's why she assigned you to find the new recruits. She's hoping you latch on to us and stop mourning them."

Josh's gaze landed on the stack of pictures Nero'd thrown in the far corner of the bedroom next to the bathroom. Framed images of his pack from barbecues to birthday parties. He hadn't kept a lot of photos. He wasn't snapping pictures with his phone every two minutes like Pauly, but he had a few. Except that everywhere he looked in his bedroom, in the mansion, even out in the woods, he remembered them.

So he'd thrown the pictures in the corner in an attempt to run from their accusing stares. He didn't need to see their faces to remember that time was running out. That if he didn't figure out an answer to magical fire, they really would die.

Seven weeks. That's all the time he had to find an answer, and ten days of that were already gone. But no matter how he tried, he couldn't see a solution. Which meant it was all on the new recruits who—at the moment—didn't know their noses from their tails.

And he didn't need all those damned pictures reminding him of what he already knew.

"I won't move on," he rasped. "Not yet." Because they weren't completely dead yet. Not until his seven weeks were up. "And you need to—"

"Defeat a magical fire burst. I know. But sometimes not thinking about a problem is more helpful than the full-out attack. And I'm not going to go back to it until I say my piece to you."

Nero surrendered to the inevitable. Josh wasn't going back to science until he got this—whatever *this* was—off his mind. "Fine. Talk."

"Captain M thinks you need to bond to us."

"Not happening." It couldn't. Because every time he looked at them, he remembered his team. He saw Laddin and thought about how Cream had been the last to join their team, but he'd latched on to Coffee and they'd been inseparable afterward. He talked to Stratos and remembered that Mother had a mouth on her that could make Pauly blush. And that was saying something. Everything reminded him of the ones who had been his life for the past five years. How did he stop thinking about that? And how could a bunch of puny geeks push out feelings so strong that they were both the steel that threaded through his spine and the force that was going to break him into a thousand pieces?

They couldn't. No one could. And it was unfair for Captain M to ask them to.

"I just got one question for you, and then I'll leave you alone. Promise."

"Then get on with it," Nero growled.

"When we were on the couch. You know, when I needed to be....."

"Grounded back in your body?"

"Yeah. That."

Nero arched a brow. "Yeah. What?"

"Did you need that as much as I did? Not like I did, obviously. You said you get grounded by eating."

"I do."

"But what we did. The touching. The caring. Did you need it too? Like dying of thirst need. Like you'd suffocate without it?"

"You're mixing metaphors."

"And you're ducking the question." He leaned forward, his body and his gaze suddenly intense. "Did you, Nero? Did you need it too?"

Nero felt his belly tighten as his entire body went still. He could lie. He knew he could and get away with it. He needed to keep the too-smart-for-his-own-good geek away from the inner workings of his mind. But he was so fucking tired of no one understanding what he was feeling. Josh was right. He didn't want to be punished—he wanted his team back. He wanted to run in the woods with them as they tumbled into the stream. He wanted the camaraderie and the—

"Touching, Nero. Did you need to be touched too?"

"Yes." A thousand fucking times, yes. But not in a pervy way. Not like he needed someone to jerk him off. He just wanted someone to be with him like his pack had been with him. "Sometimes," he rasped, "we would go running, and afterwards, we'd stay in our wolf forms. All of us inside, where it was warm, and piled on top of one another. It wasn't about sex." Though, honestly, sometimes that happened. "It was about us being together. Physically, all together."

And now it was gone. And fuck, now his face was wet. Why was he crying? They weren't dead yet. And still, Josh was relentless. When he spoke, the gentle tone was like that fucking can opener slitting Nero's chest wide open.

"So when you jerked me off, that was about giving me something I needed."

Nero nodded. "Yes."

"So can I do it for you? Same thing? Let me touch you, let me give you something. It's not going to replace them, but it'll be something intimate from someone who cares."

Nero jerked forward, but he stopped himself. He wanted it. God, he wanted it with this earnest brainiac of a busybody. But he couldn't do it so easily. He couldn't just replace them with him.

"That's not fair. To them or you."

"What about you?"

He shrugged. He'd long since given up thinking about what was fair to him.

Josh hopped up from the bed. His long-legged stride was loose, but there was tension in his hands and his shoulders. And his eyes were wide and kind. Only Cream had looked at Nero like that. So damned kind, it had hurt to see him so vulnerable, as if a single harsh word would crumple him. And Josh was wearing that same look. Tentative, nervous, but still determined.

He came and squatted down in front of Nero.

"Are you gay?"

Nero shrugged. "For the most part." He'd been with members of his pack, of both sexes. It was about the pack. But for him to get really turned-on required a male partner.

"I'm exploring," Josh said. "So how about we explore a little together? No pressure. No commitment. Just—"

"Touching."

"And anything else you want to do."

Anything else? Everything else? Suddenly it didn't matter to Nero. Trainee, instructor, recruit, abductor. All those words didn't compute. It was Josh touching his face gently, rubbing his thumb over Nero's lower lip while he bit his own. Damn, it was so fucking endearing—this nervous possibility and the gentle stroke of someone who cared.

"Ever done it with a guy before, Josh?"

"No. Was going to do it at the con."

"Are you sure you want—?"

Josh kissed him. His mouth slammed down on Nero's, landing awkwardly and too hard. Nero allowed it. He opened for it, felt Josh's tongue thrust inside, touch his teeth and the roof of his mouth. And he felt the grip of Josh's hand in his hair and the scent of desire thick in the air.

Then Nero took control.

Chapter 13

JOSH DOVE into the kiss with rushed desperation. He didn't want either of them to change their
minds. After a lifetime of overthinking or complete
avoidance, Josh had landed in an upside-down world
that left him no base from which to judge his actions.
So he stopped weighing his every move, stopped
thinking, and just went with his impulses. Which were
to kiss Nero and do a whole lot more.

He landed hard and pushed inside. Nero caught
him by the arms but did nothing to stop his thrusting
tongue. Then Josh touched and tasted in a way that
startled him. He'd been kissing girls since he was seventeen. Though he hadn't had many girlfriends, he'd

known how to do it. He understood his own movements and how to tease his partner. Except this time it seemed different, and not in a male/male way.

He tasted things more clearly, scented more sharply, and he learned things about Nero that he had never been able to discern with a girl. Like Nero's coffee had been bitter and he hadn't eaten anything else. Like there was an orange tang to the guy's mouth and he smelled like winter pine and a wood fire.

Josh slowed down to focus on what he was experiencing, to let his mind pick apart what was new, what was old, and what was Nero. He teased along Nero's teeth and dueled, tongue to tongue, for a time.

A very short time. Because just when he was dropping into thinking again—his ever-present analysis of experiences—Nero took over. Where before, Josh had been pressing down on a seated Nero, now Nero thrust upward. He stood, and though he was a couple of inches shorter than Josh, his body was broader, stronger, and the way he gripped Josh's hips to bow him backward gave him the height advantage when they were fused mouth to mouth. And that didn't even take into account how Josh's mind completely shorted out when Nero ground their dicks together. Twin bulges separated by denim and zippers. Their clothing didn't seem to make a difference as the heat built in Josh's balls.

"You're new at this, so we're going to do it my way," Nero said.

"That's the idea," Josh said as his head dropped back in pleasure. "This is for you."

Nero wasted no time and putting his teeth to Josh's neck, biting down gently as he scraped, then sucked, the skin. "Doesn't work for me unless it's good for you."

Josh chuckled as he grabbed hold of Nero's hair. "I'm okay with that." Then he jerked the man's head so that his mouth came away from Josh's neck. Josh angled his mouth and went back in for a heavy kiss. The dueling was more forceful this time. It was hard and hot, but Josh won in that game. Until he didn't.

He hadn't even noticed that Nero's hands had slid to his hips. And then abruptly, Josh felt his feet being kicked out from under him. He started to fall only to have Nero lift him up with enough force that he flew backward onto the bed.

Holy shit, he'd never done gymnastics with a girl. Turned out he liked it more athletic. So did Nero, who dropped down onto the bed, his thighs caging Josh's hips.

"Strip," Nero said. "Fast."

Not a problem, except that Nero remained poised above him, looking all shadowy and hungry. It was the way the window threw fitful light onto the opposite side of the room. But it was also because Nero's face was rough with dark beard and his mouth was pulled back enough to show his teeth.

"Is that a werewolf look?" Josh asked as he unbuttoned and unzipped.

Nero's lips pulled back into a grin. "Yeah, it is. Want to see yours?"

Josh froze after shoving his jeans down off his hips. "I have a werewolf look?"

"You do." Nero straightened up, pulling off Josh's jeans as he went. Then he ditched his own clothing while Josh jerked off his T-shirt.

They were both naked, dicks jutting forward, the heads weeping with precum. The only difference was that Nero's was surrounded by a thatch of dark black hair whereas Josh's was lighter and was still man-scaped. He'd done it in anticipation of this kind of exploration at the con. And now he was glad he'd bothered, as Nero's eyes seemed to brighten in delight.

Nero dropped his hand—large and callused—running it gently through the hair while Josh reveled in the electric shocks of pleasure. "Nice," Nero murmured. "Kind of gay, but I like it."

Josh raised his eyebrows. "You do remember what we just did, right?"

Nero smiled. "That was pack sex." He wrapped his big hand around Josh's stalk and squeezed while Josh nearly jumped off the bed in surprise. Except he wasn't going anywhere even as his hips started working on their own. Nero's grip was solid, and his hand was huge. It felt like the guy was wrapping him up all over again. As if he was on the couch surrounded by him, smelling him, and—

"I'm going to get things started," Nero said as he dropped his head down.

They were started. Hell, Josh worried that he was almost finished, especially when Nero neatly engulfed his dick with his mouth. He went fast, licking everywhere. Nero's tongue circled around as he sucked, and then he pulled back, only to push into the hole at the top. It was wet and sloppy and thoroughly overwhelming.

Josh's body took over, and he writhed on the bed as he thrust into Nero's mouth. He made sounds too. Whimpers, moans, growls. Hell, he didn't even know what came from him and what came from Nero, but it was all hot and wonderful.

But it was too fast, too much. He was going to blow too early, and so he grabbed for Nero's head and tried to pull him off. But Nero was ahead of him, moving away as he flashed him that wolfish grin.

God, what a sight. Nero with his hair shaggy and his mouth wet. His lips were wide, and there was a feral gleam in his eyes as his nostrils flared. "You smell like hickory."

"What?"

"I love hickory." Then he leaned forward, skimming his hands up Josh's sides. Josh thought he was coming in for a kiss, but instead, Nero used both hands to roam to Josh's chest. And then he abruptly pinched the nipples hard.

Josh jerked and let out a yip of surprise. A real, honest-to-goodness yip. And Nero's grin widened.

"You like that?" he said as he did it again.

"Yeah," Josh said, nearly coming from the delight of this new sensation. Girls never did that right. Meanwhile, their groins were almost touching. Their dicks certainly were, and Josh seized the opportunity to rub them together. Not the pressure he wanted, but the wetness was slick and the sensation wholly new. "You like that?" he asked.

Nero moved his own hips, increasing the friction and the pressure as he lowered their groins together. "Yeah," he said with a growly undertone.

They stayed like that for a bit, grinding together, thrusting harder and faster. Josh went to grip them both, but Nero batted his hand away.

"Not like that," he said. "We're going to do your first time right."

"How—?"

"Doggie style."

Of course. And he would have made a corny joke right then if he'd had the breath. Or the brain. But he had neither as Nero abruptly pulled away, grabbed hold of Josh's hips, and flipped him over. Josh landed with an *oomph*, but he didn't have time for anything more as Nero lifted him so that he was on all fours and crosswise on the bed.

"Look up," Nero ordered.

Josh did and got the full image himself on the bed in the mirror. But not just himself. Because while he was on all fours, Nero was leaping up to tower over him, his chest rippling and his dark hair pointing down to a dark purple erection. But it was his eyes that caught Josh. They were bright, the light making his brown eyes seem like luscious mink. And his teeth were bared in that same wolflike grin.

"Look at you," Nero said, admiration in his tone. "That's your werewolf face."

Josh struggled to focus away from Nero, but he had to see. There he was in the mirror, his hair shoved every which way, hazel eyes narrowed as he peered at himself. That was him right there, except different. It was the way he showed his teeth: white edges clear, jaw thrust forward as he arched his neck. It looked like he was about to howl, and as he thought it, the sound built deep and raw in his throat.

He didn't let it out, though. He was too much of a man and still too self-conscious for that. And yet it was there in his throat and in the arch of his back as his rear pushed high. He didn't have a tail, but damn if he didn't feel it thrust high and proud.

"That's it," Nero said. "Stay like that. God, you're gorgeous."

Then Josh felt something right at his ass. It was cold and wet, but it quickly heated. Nero's fingers, obviously, rubbing in the lube. It was weird to feel that caress. More like a massage.

A thick finger pushed inside. Slow at first, but nothing prepared Josh for that first invasion. Wet, alien, and yet not so bad. In fact, it was starting to feel really good.

"Relax. See if you can focus on other things."

Other things? Other than— "More," he groaned. "I want more."

Nero's free hand moved fast. He was bowed over Josh now, so when his free hand pinched Josh's left nipple, it was a quick movement—sharp, startling, and exactly what he needed. Josh yipped again, and his stomach tightened. But Nero didn't stop. He slid his hand straight down Josh's belly until he wrapped it right around his dick. And wow, did that feel good, but it didn't completely distract him from the invasion in his ass.

Then Nero pinched the tip of his dick. Same sharp pinch, like with his nipple, but there was so much more sensation, so much more feeling zapping like a bolt of fire up his spine. Josh arched his back up, but the movement continued from a belly contraction to a hard thrust. His dick slid through Nero's hand as he did it. Pleasure exploded through his stalk, burned at the base of his spine, and rolled up his back. That was good. That was more than good.

Then he realized that Nero's finger was embedded inside his ass. It wriggled there, stretching and loosening. Josh thought it was as deep as it would go, but as Nero continued to stroke him in front, his finger pushed farther inside the back

One finger. Then two.

"God, yes," he groaned.

And then....

"Holy mother fucking—" Josh strangled his cry. Nero had hit a tiny ball of feeling that was throbbing in pleasure. It was like nothing he'd ever experienced, and he tried to still himself so that Nero would stroke it again.

"Say hello to your prostate," Nero laughed.

Josh couldn't say anything. He was writhing, his entire body moving in ways he couldn't control. Thrust, arch, wriggle, push. Anything, everything, just so long as Nero kept caressing him *right there*.

Then suddenly Nero was gone. Ass, dick, everything gone. Even the heat at the back of his legs disappeared.

"What?"

"Getting a condom. Hold on."

What? Right. Oh hell, he hadn't even been thinking about that.

"I'm clean, okay?" Nero said. "But the pack takes care of one another, and so we suit up."

"Even as wolves?" Josh couldn't imagine that. Wolves stopping in the middle to put on condoms. The image made him crack up.

"We try not to do this as wolves. Too many magical babies by accident."

Josh frowned. He was on fire, his whole body feeling like it was poised on the brink. He couldn't process the words, and magical babies didn't compute on a whole lot of levels. Thankfully Nero didn't take long. He came back and stood behind Josh, tall and proud like a painting of Hercules he'd once seen. Every muscle stood out in glorious relief, and the fierce lust on Nero's face echoed the explosive power of the demigod.

While Josh watched, mesmerized, in the mirror, Nero positioned himself. Josh felt him at the opening: hot, blunt, and impossibly large.

"Look at us," Nero murmured, seemingly equally fascinated by the image. Nero bared his teeth, and Josh echoed the expression. Josh tilted his ass up just as Nero leaned down and gripped Josh's hips.

And then there was the slow screwing in. Bit by tiny bit, while Josh burned with sensation. Tiny short thrusts while Josh growled and arched higher.

"Good?" Nero asked, the word a tight burst of sound.

"More," Josh answered from deep in his throat.

"That's the way," Nero said as his face tightened. His jaw jutted forward as he thrust again. He pushed in deeper this time, slipping past some muscle barrier. Then it was easy, and Josh was so full. His ass was open, his spine was on fire, and his dick was weeping with need.

Nero pulsed forward and back, tiny movements that Josh felt throughout his whole body. It was like his spine was a conduit for every sensation and his brain was bursting apart from the feelings. Nero shifted, adjusted, did something, though Josh had no idea what. The man's expression was fierce in the mirror, his brow furrowed while sweat beaded on his forehead. But his eyes were hot as they connected with Josh's.

"Come on," he growled, and Josh had no idea what that meant. "Come on," Nero repeated as he adjusted again. Deeper thrust. Harder—

There!

Nero went all the way in and banged straight against that bundle of nerves. The explosion in Josh's body ripped through every cell like a flash of power. And Nero kept doing it. Over and over while Josh's vision went white. He felt Nero's hand wrap around his dick, but Nero needn't have bothered. Josh had already come. Then again, maybe not, because he pushed and pushed against Nero's hand while inside, he felt everything building, bursting, then exploding again.

He absorbed Nero's growl this time, and the weight of his body as the man thrust and thrust. Josh felt like the arrow pulled and shot from Nero's body over and over. Deeper, harder, wilder.

In the mirror, he saw Nero's face tighten. His eyes closed, his throat worked, and his teeth showed sharp and white. And then he came.

Josh felt him release inside. He also saw the moment in the mirror. Nero's chest expanded, his head arched back, and his eyes shot wide. Hercules triumphant. Pulse after pulse continued inside him, and Josh echoed it, his dick spending when there was nothing left inside, his body so hot, so wild… so happy.

Nero too. A dazed look, a soft smile, and a low sound that wasn't a growl—more like a purr—traveled from one body into the other and back. Pleasure. Joy.

Pack.

Chapter 14

"BEING A werewolf has some unexpected perks."

Nero flushed at Josh's lazy drawl. He was more relaxed than he'd been in weeks. Lazing in bed next to Josh's hot body was the closest thing to heaven Nero could imagine. But.... "That wasn't just about being a werewolf," he finally confessed.

Josh gasped. "You mean being part of a pack doesn't include night-and-day orgies?"

"Um, not usually."

Josh twisted so that they were face-to-face, his lips curved into a knowing grin. "You don't say."

Nero stiffened at the implication. "I didn't lie about it. Physical affection is part of every good were-wolf pack. Just not—"

"Mind-blowing banging?"

"Well," he hedged, "I suppose it could."

"I think it just did." Josh chuckled.

Nero released a breath, unsure how to proceed. He decided to go with the facts. "Casual sex among packmates happens more often than among vanilla humans."

"You got data on that? Like did you do a sex survey on werewolves?" His voice shifted to a stiffly professional tone. "Press 1 if you have sex with your packmates more than once a month. Press 2 if it's once a week. Press 3 if you're banging everybody whenever you get together. Press 4—"

"Okay, okay, so we don't have survey data." He arched a brow. "I think I've already said we're lacking in the science department."

"Just not in the sex department."

Nero groaned. "Will you be serious?"

"No, I don't think I can." Josh ran his hand through Nero's short tufts of hair. "I'm happy. It brings out the goofy in me."

God, it did, and Nero couldn't help but feel a matching lightness inside. Josh's silly grin and the boneless way he sprawled against Nero made his breath ease. "I don't want you to think you can grab random werewolves and—"

"Howl at the moon?"

Nero groaned. "You know you are *not* the first person to make that joke."

Josh frowned. "Hmmm. Well, it's new to me. I'll make sure to google 'better moon werewolf jokes.'" Then, when Nero gave him an incredulous look, he shrugged. "What, you think I'm this funny naturally? It's what we geeks do. We research, just in case." Then he flopped his arms and legs out wide, and since he was on top of the covers, Nero got a prime look at his thickening erection. "And just *in case* we do this again, I want to have a dozen more jokes ready for afterglow. And by again, I mean any time you want, even if it's right now."

Wow, Nero didn't think he could get horny again, but there it was. A slow heat built down low as he imagined losing himself in Josh's body again. But as tempting as it was, this had been Josh's first time. A responsible lover would let the guy recover a bit before going again. And Nero was nothing if not responsible, so he flopped onto his back with a sigh.

And since they weren't going to be banging again, he might as well continue with Josh's werewolf orientation. He ought to send the guy back into research—magical fiery plasma wasn't going to douse itself—but a selfish part of him wanted to stay with the man. So he took refuge in the protocols for new werewolves that he had established a couple of years back. He'd created a list of leading questions to allow new recruits to work through their feelings. It was all part of the process, and Josh would have to answer them eventually. Might as well be now.

"Tell me how you feel."

"Amazing. Relaxed. Goofy—"

"About becoming a werewolf."

Josh's face scrunched up. "It's too soon for me to feel anything. I don't know what it is yet."

"You don't have to know it before you have feelings about it. When I first changed, I felt like power incarnate. The wolves I was with encouraged me to feed that power with hunger and lust. Now that was an orgy." And a feast, but he didn't like thinking about that part. It wasn't his proudest moment, but then he'd been seventeen, angry, and had contracted the lycanthropy virus. That was a recipe for excess of the worst kinds.

"Sounds like a story. Tell me more."

Nero shook his head. "We're supposed to be talking about you."

"Well, I don't have feelings until I have things to compare them to. So tell me your conversion story, and I'll tell you if that matches mine." At Nero's doubtful look, Josh threw up his hands. "You can emphasize your *feelings*, and I'll say yay or nay if that matches mine."

It was a solid way to get to the point, but Nero didn't like talking about his wolf beginnings, mostly because he didn't like thinking about the kid he'd been. It was like looking at the before pictures of a renovation project. Here was the house in all its disgusting, broken-down glory. And here is the home now that's got a solid foundation, a good roof, and some truly exceptional plumbing. Why look at the before picture? Why not stay with the now and maybe consider the future? The past belonged in the past.

But part of the protocol that he'd written was to listen and follow the new recruit's lead. He could hardly discard his own plan of action just because it made him uncomfortable.

"Fine," he said with a disgruntled frown. "But I'm not doing it naked." If he had to follow professional protocol, then he for damn sure was going to do it dressed.

Josh sighed. "If you must." Then he stretched his hands over his head with a grin. "But don't expect me to hide all this glory from you. I mean to tempt you back to bed."

Of course he did. And of course it was a serious temptation. "So you know, werewolves have above average hearing, even in their human form. Everyone on this floor probably knows what we were doing."

Josh's eyes widened at that, and no wonder. The idea made Nero squirm too. He gave it even odds that Captain M was going to have a serious conversation with him about trainer/trainee professional distance. But then again, if she had been against it, she likely would have stopped him long before they got to afterglow. Josh had been the one to come on to him, and according to the protocol, the trainee was king (or queen) as they worked out their new identity.

Meanwhile, Josh pulled his hands back to his sides and then sat more upright on the bed. He didn't cover up, but he wasn't flaunting himself anymore either. Nero pulled on sweats, sat down on his desk chair, and stretched his bare feet out on the bed to come within inches of Josh. He ached to touch the man—even in so small a way—but he held himself back. He wanted to leave the possibility open and allow Josh the choice of whether they touched again or not.

"I grew up in Florida," he said. "First in Miami, but after my mom ODed, my sister and I were sent to my grandparents in Jacksonville."

"Whoa." Josh sat fully upright. "That's quite a beginning. How old were you?"

"Nine. My sister was six. It made for a rocky start, but my grandparents did the best they could. I knew a lot of people who had it worse."

"And there are starving kids in Africa. Doesn't make your experience any better or less painful." Josh stretched out a hand and squeezed Nero's ankle, and damn if that didn't make Nero's whole body warm. "I'm sorry."

Nero smiled, taking a moment to feel the heat of Josh's hand and the warmth of his gaze. Then he had to force himself to keep talking or get lost in the sweetness of the moment. "My teen years were awful. Gramps and I always fought, and Gram didn't know what to do with me. She had her hands full with my sister, who went through more phases than the moon." He arched a brow at Josh to show him that he could make moon jokes too. Josh quirked a brow at him but stayed focused on the story.

"What phases?"

"Goth one day, preppie the next. Punk, pink, retro, and I don't even know what. Gram said she was searching for her own identity, but I thought she was trying to drive us all crazy."

"This her?" Josh grabbed the one family picture he had in the room. All the others were of his team, but there, half-forgotten on a stack of books, was a framed photo of everyone at his last football game. Gramps and Gran looked as usual—like they belonged in the fifties—and his little sister, Rachel, had been in her studious phase, complete with fake glasses and a high bun. It hadn't lasted more than a couple of weeks, but the persona had gotten her through midterm exams, and so he supposed it had served its purpose. Anyway, he stood in the middle with a big grin as he looked at his cheerleader girlfriend, who was taking the picture. She'd dumped him right before Christmas break, but he'd had fun with her before then. So that made this one photo the frozen moment when everything had been good—or at least, it had seemed so—until everything went bad.

"That was a good day," he said. He'd lost his virginity that evening, so honestly, it had been a great day.

"What are they doing now? Do they know that you're... that you...."

"She's just started in Miami as a forensic analyst."

"Cool! Real-life CSI."

"And no, they don't know."

Josh nodded as if he expected that. "What do you tell them?"

He swallowed. "They think I'm in jail for murder."

To his credit, Josh didn't even flinch, but he did take a moment before he quipped, "Well, that's not what I expected you to say. Care to elaborate?"

Not really, but he did it anyway. "It was right after high school graduation. We all went down to Miami to have fun on the beach. The police told my family that I killed my best friend in a bar fight and am now in a special rehabilitation program oriented at teens." He shrugged, though the movement was forced. "That was ten years ago."

"So what really happened?"

It was gratifying that Josh didn't seem to have any doubts that the official version wasn't the truth. Nero wished he had the same faith. "We got into a bar fight with werewolves. He was killed, I was bitten, and then…." He shook his head.

"Orgy?"

He shook his head. "I remember burning up, like waves of heat inside and out. I think I went rampaging as a wolf with their pack, but I don't remember much of it." Thank God. "I woke up hungry somewhere in the Everglades. We ate, had sex, and ate some more. And then Daryl's team showed up."

Josh nodded as he became more animated. "I read that case file, but it didn't say much. The team stalked and killed most of a group of lycanthropes. It listed three new recruits, and you were one of them. That's it."

"That's because there was nothing else to say. We were given the choice: join up or die. I joined up, as did Raoul and Vanessa. Raoul tapped out as soon as he proved he had control. He married into one of the southern werewolf packs and is doing great. Vanessa didn't handle things as well."

"Couldn't give up the… taste? The report said that most of the pack had to be put down because they'd never live without blood. Those were the exact words: 'Never live without blood.'"

He knew. He'd read the file. "That's a known problem with the lycanthropy virus. There's nothing like the taste of blood. It's like life on our tongues, and…." He shook his head. "Sometimes we become addicted." He constantly watched himself for that need. The good news was that demon blood tasted nothing like human, so he and his team specialized in the nonhuman problems. Or they had.

"Was that Vanessa's problem?"

"No. She had the other problem." The same one that sometimes haunted him. "What she did—what we did—before we were stopped…." His gaze canted away until he was looking out at fluffy white snowflakes drifting lazily down. "I was lucky. I don't remember much beyond flashes." Blood. Screams. The taste of raw flesh. "She remembered it all, and she couldn't live with it."

"That bad?"

"Yeah." His gaze went back to Josh where he sat with a serious expression. "She killed herself a year later." Another body in the lousy human-to-werewolf transition statistic. "It's something to remember when you meet a virus werewolf. We all have an ugly history behind us. I was fortunate enough not to remember it."

"Probably not something you want to tell Grams and Gramps, huh?"

Nero's lips curved up. "Yeah, probably not."

"But don't you want to tell them something? They probably think you're a psycho felon or something."

"I am a psycho felon as far as the world is concerned. I pled guilty to a judge in on the woo-woo secret and was sent to the frozen tundra known as Maine. I can't tell them the truth, and I sure as hell can't explain away the body count from the bar fight."

"But you could tell them you're alive. That you're doing well."

"And then what? Meet them for coffee? Share Thanksgiving dinner with them?"

"Yes. Why not?"

"Ask me that again after your first home visit." His expression softened. "This secret is hard to keep. It's easier to let them think I'm behind bars somewhere."

Josh snorted. "Easier on you, maybe. Look, my dad's an ass, but I still can't let him think I'm dead. And I like my mother—most times—so don't think I'm going the prison route." He flashed a mischievous grin. "I'll tell them that I'm living with my hot ex-felon gay lover. That'll horrify them enough that they won't speak to me for a year."

He knew Josh was joking, but Nero had heard worse cover stories. And the longer Nero sat there soberly considering the possibility, the less cheeky Josh's expression became. Eventually the guy tilted his head and let his blond hair fall messily over his eyes.

"I'm joking. I'm not telling my parents that."

"Fair enough. But you'll have to think of something."

"Actually, no, I won't. Look, so far, I'm on a long weekend. It can be explained away by a really bad flu."

"We talked about this. You can't go back to your former life."

"Why not? I get that you need to solve the fire bomb problem. I'm here for that. But I can close up stuff on campus normally. The last experiments won't take too long. And then I'll write it up in my dissertation and be done. I can say I got a job—which will be true—and then I'm all yours."

"You're not safe in public yet."

"I'm a fast learner."

Nero arched a brow.

"Put a guard on me. Chain me up in my apartment. Whatever—"

"You act like your schooling is important to you, but you haven't done diddly on it for a year." Josh opened his mouth to argue, but Nero wasn't going to let him run from the truth. "You think I didn't look into this? I called the head of your lab and pretended I was going to hire you. I wanted a recommendation, and you know what he said?"

Josh's face was ruddy with embarrassment, and he didn't speak. Just shook his head.

"He said you were delaying, not getting anything done. That maybe a job would be the kick in the pants you need." He spread his hands wide. "Consider yourself kicked. Come work for us now."

"I've worked for seven years to get my PhD. I'm not dropping it like I couldn't hack it. Yeah, so maybe I've been screwing around, but I've got incentive now. Trust me, I can get it done." Josh straightened up. "It's a reasonable request. You can't expect me to drop everything when I don't have to."

"It sounds reasonable if you have no idea what it's like to be a werewolf. It took a year before I felt like a person and not a freak. And by that point I'd realized how impossible it is to talk to anyone outside of the mystical community. Trust me, you'll have zero interest in meeting up with someone from your former life."

"Not Savannah. And not my family," Josh countered flatly.

"You've changed at a level you can't even comprehend," Nero insisted. "They won't understand, and you can't explain it to them."

Josh snorted. "I can go all scary. Rawr!" He bared his teeth and put his hands up as fake claws. "So that's freaky weird, and I get that I'll have to learn how to control it, but it shouldn't tank my life."

Nero shook his head. "It hurts, Josh. It hurts to *not* be yourself around the people who should love you most. It hurts them, and it hurts you because you have to lie all the time." Nero tensed in his chair, seeing that he'd have to prove to Josh that he'd changed in a fundamental way.

"Maybe for you, but I never talked about myself or my work anyway. They think I'm a major screw-up. Let me take the time to finish my PhD, show them that I'm not a complete waste of space."

"It won't work."

"Why not?"

Nero didn't bother arguing. He pounced instead.

One second he was sitting in his chair. The next he had burst forward, catching Josh on the shoulder with one hand and on his throat with the other. His grip was tight but not bruising, and he flattened the newbie on the bed with his body weight.

For about two seconds.

Then Josh reacted. He had to give it to the guy. Josh had some basic martial arts skill behind his moves, but most of his response was pure instinct. Josh exploded with movement. He twisted and kicked, biting what he could get ahold of and scratching what he couldn't. It was like his first moments out of the cage two nights ago, only he had more thought behind his attack, which made it twice as vicious.

He held nothing back, and Nero had to use all his skill to keep them both from getting hurt. Eventually he let Josh pin him to the bed.

"Got you!" Josh crowed. He was grinning at his success, his body was slicked with sweat, and his erection was thick and hard where it pressed against Nero's. His head dipped and his mouth split wide. Nero didn't know if he was going in for a bite or a kiss. Didn't matter. He wasn't allowing either yet.

At the moment Josh was off-balance, Nero flipped him over. He couldn't have done it without his greater weight or Josh's inexperience, but he used that to his advantage, and suddenly, their positions were reversed. And while Josh was still gaping in shock, Nero engaged his brain.

"Feel powerful, Josh? Like any minute you're going to throw me to the floor and take out my throat?"

Josh grinned and spoke with a low growl. "Fuck yeah."

"Ever felt like this before? Violence simmering in your blood, hot with the instinct to attack? There's joy too, isn't there? You know you're big and bad. That most people are sheep to your wolf, and you can take them out whenever and wherever you want."

Josh didn't answer except with a hungry gleam in his eyes. Then he surged forward. Nero had been expecting it. He'd felt the quiver in Josh's muscles a split second before the attack, but even so, without training or a wolf's reaction time, he might have been overpowered. Josh was that good. Eventually Nero had to resort to a headbutt to keep the guy contained. And while Josh howled and Nero fought the stars in his own vision, Nero pressed his point.

"Ever feel like this before? Think back to who you were one month ago. What do you think of that guy?"

"Timid fucker too scared to live." The words came out in a snarl.

"What about now? Are you scared?"

"Not in the least." Then, for emphasis, the guy thrust his groin forward. He shoved his hot, thick dick straight up against Nero's. Yeah, the guy had a hard-on for this type of power. Physical dominance with a side of hunger and lust. Every wolf did. The virus lycanthropes had it the most, but every wolf felt this, and Nero couldn't resist rubbing his own throbbing erection against Josh.

He meant to continue speaking. Fuck, he intended to stay rational and really engage Josh's brain. But Josh's scent was everywhere, and Nero loved this kind of sex play most of all. Hot, hard, and fast. And once he started thrusting, he couldn't stop.

Neither could Josh.

They worked against each other, rubbing below and biting above. He had on sweatpants, but that was the only clothing either of them wore. Nero used one hand to shove his sweats down, and then they were head to head, chest to chest, and dick to dick. He fisted them both and squeezed.

Josh's howl cut off into a groan of pleasure. Nero groaned too as they began pumping together. Then Josh wrapped his hand around Nero's, squeezing tighter as they thrust faster. Heat built in his spine— his skin prickled with it and his hair stood on end.

Yes!

The excitement of it burst through the dam at the back of his spine. He erupted in spasms while pleasure entwined with pain grew into one glorious explosion of carnality. Josh came at the same time. He threw back his head and howled again. A crow of delight and power.

They stayed that way for who knew how long. They both kept pumping out semen like a tidal flood. And even when the well was dry, they both kept thrusting as the pulses continued. Wet, hot, and still hard.

Glorious.

It took a long time for Nero to gather his scattered wits. He'd had a point here, hadn't he? Oh, yeah. He waited until he was sure his words would be steady, and a little longer to see the contraction in Josh's pupils that meant he was back from heaven. And then Nero spoke, his words clear and not very gentle.

"Is this something you would have done a week ago? Howling sex? Would you even have allowed a man to do what I did a half hour ago? Split you open and jam himself inside you?"

He watched as Josh's gaze narrowed. He thought for a moment that Josh would deny the change, but the guy was too smart and too honest for that. "No," he finally rasped. "This is new. This is…."

"Powerful. Raw."

"Awesome."

"Yes."

Nero eased back enough to impress his next words onto Josh. "Now imagine you're at the dinner table and your asshole of a father starts calling you weak. You're a screw-up because you hide in a lab and don't do shit for real work." Josh's father owned a factory that made special heat-resistant fabric. It was one of the many reasons Josh had been on the top of the recruit list. But though the business pulled in a shit-ton of money, the family lived like laborers of the heaviest, hardest kind. Josh's sister was an Army medic, and his brother was a fireman. Everyone worked physically demanding stuff except Josh, who had gone into academia. His hands were soft and his shoulders narrow. He binge-watched the SyFy channel and put his leisure time into cosplay. "What are you going to say to him?"

Josh didn't answer, but his growl was enough. And Nero kept going.

"How many times have you imagined impressing the shit out of your father? Maybe throwing him against the wall or busting the table with your bare hands? Not science shit, but raw physical power like the kind he respects?"

"Every fucking minute of my childhood."

"You have that power now. You could throw down with your brother and sister at the same time and best them both. You could shut your idiot dad up with your wolf speed and your animal instincts. Most people can't control their gun hand enough to shoot you. They're too frightened. And yeah, your dad would be shit-his-pants terrified."

Josh's mouth pulled into a grin. "Yeah," he drawled. He was loving the image Nero painted.

"You've got confidence now like you've never had before. And with training, that's only going to build. You'll be able to take out monsters he's only imagined in his nightmares."

Josh's breath came quicker in excitement. He wanted that future, and it was possible for him. It was possible for all werewolves. Now it was time for Nero to drop the hammer.

"But you can't tell him that, Josh. You can't show him the man you are. You have to appear weak and useless in front of him. You have to hide in his fucked-up image of you and not break it. Because he can't know the real you. He can't be trusted with the knowledge. It would endanger you, me, and everything we know."

"Bullshit—"

"Not bullshit." He rolled away from Josh, grabbing tissues in one smooth move. And while they both started to clean up, Nero continued with the paranormal facts of life. "Do you know what the most powerful force in the universe is? It's not nuclear fusion, solar whatever, or even a neutron star."

Josh frowned. "Black hole?"

"Human belief." Nero held up his hand to stop Josh's immediate reaction. His science brain was not going to accept this easily. "I don't understand it, but I've seen it happen. Every single paranormal creature was created from human belief. Someone believed in fairies strong enough for them to appear. Werewolves and vamps became popular in literature, and suddenly, wham, here we are."

"It doesn't work that way," Josh argued. "You had to show up first and then humans started talking about it."

"You'd think that, but that's not what we've seen." He threw his mess into the waste can with a quick flick of his wrist. "Vamps were mean, vicious monsters until suddenly they show up in romance novels as sparkly and sensitive. We stopped taking out the usual bloodsucker ten years ago because now they've all got tragic pasts and hate themselves for what they are."

Josh shook his head. "That doesn't make sense."

"I've seen it happen. Stupid things like that fucking doll Chucky. No one was fighting psycho toys until after that movie appeared." He surged off the bed so he could pull up his sweats. Then he plopped back down and faced Josh. "It was more obvious before movies and the internet. A new monster would appear in a place that had just created a fairy tale about such a monster."

"Monster first, tales second. It's the only logical—"

"No. First, some really good storyteller thinks up a monster. He invests it with his passion and his belief and tells it to a community who come along for the ride. They talk about it, they think about it, they love it. And then pretty soon, the monster shows up for real because they created it."

"You can't think something into existence."

"You can if you think hard enough, if you believe hard enough, and if enough people come along for the ride. What do you think a demon summoning is? Black magic rituals?"

"By that logic, Jesus would be walking the earth and angels would be among us."

"Jesus was crucified on a cross and, if not exactly dead, he's hanging out in heaven with all the angels."

Josh was obviously struggling with this concept. He shook his head as he stared at the twisted bedsheets. And when he got uncomfortable doing that, he reached for his jeans and pulled them on with quick, jerky movements.

"Belief doesn't create reality," he said.

"You so sure about that?"

"Yes!" And then after a moment, he hedged, "Well, obviously, if you believe you're good at something, that helps your performance. And insecurity has the opposite effect. That kind of belief."

"But believing something into existence can't happen?" Nero argued. "That the 'think yourself thin' meditation only goes so far without diet and exercise?"

"Right!"

"Wrong. I don't have the diet industry answer. There's obviously a whole lot of conflicting beliefs about weight loss, so that probably plays a part. But Josh, listen to me. I've seen it happen. Belief created us. Belief created our enemies. Belief created magic."

Josh threw his hands up. "I didn't believe in werewolves, and yet here I am."

"But people believed in curses and werewolves. Your origin story is well documented. Hell, the owner of this entire estate is one of your relatives. That's how we knew what you were."

"A werewolf?"

"Yes."

"Not true."

"It is true." He held up his hand to stop Josh's knee-jerk argument. "Look, assume for the moment that it is true. That belief creates reality." He waited until Josh gave a reluctant nod. "Now imagine what happens if people start really believing that monsters are real. Werewolves, vampires, child-eating demons? We're already seeing a surge in monsters because of modern media. Because it's in the public consciousness."

"As fiction."

"Yes, as fiction. Now imagine if someone managed to prove they're real. Imagine what we'd be fighting if suddenly everyone started believing in more than evil leprechauns. What about a planet-destroying demon or—"

"Red Wolf."

Nero blinked. "What?"

"Red Wolf." Josh spoke the words as if he was realizing the truth as he said it. "Pretty Boy out there plays Red Wolf on TV. You said he was a surprise. That you don't know how or why he became a werewolf."

Nero nodded. He'd already figured that out, and if he hadn't rushed getting a geek squad together, he would have realized that Bing might get caught up in things by accident. People believed that Bing was Red Wolf because he played him on TV. So add in Wiz's magic spell, and bam, the guy's role becomes reality. Meanwhile, Josh kept explaining what Nero already knew.

"In the cages, he looked like the wolf he plays on TV. And he does that hypnotism thing just like his character."

A shot of adrenaline spiked through Nero. He hadn't heard that Bing could hypno-lock anyone, but then the actor was closemouthed about a lot of things. Mesmerizing someone with his eyes was a power they could definitely use. "Hypnotism thing?" Nero prodded.

"Yeah. You've got to watch the show. The CGI is awesome." He paused. "Except I thought the story came about because Pretty Boy is really a werewolf."

Nero shook his head. "Like you, this was a complete surprise to Bing. But he didn't say anything about his hypnotism power."

"Maybe he doesn't know."

Probably true. That was the first job of any new recruit: figure out exactly what his or her abilities are. "I'll mention it to his trainer."

Josh nodded slowly. "You said you know my origin story. Anything cool in there? Claws of steel? Poisonous fangs?"

"If that was true, I'd be dead by now." He gestured to his shoulder. The bite wasn't bad and the bleeding had already stopped, but Josh had definitely punctured the skin.

Josh flushed slightly. "Oh, yeah. Sorry."

"Don't be. I loved it." He shrugged. "Virus wolf, remember? We are born from a bite and we love the rough stuff."

"Right. And I'm a...."

"Romani magic. I'll get you all the details we have." Then he touched Josh's hand and Josh flipped his around so they were palm to palm, holding hands like lovers. He intertwined their fingers and squeezed. "Do you get it now? The only way we're keeping Earth from total chaos is by maintaining secrecy. If people realized how powerful their own beliefs are, we'd have—"

"Every monster known to mankind rampaging the planet. But we'd have gods and angels too."

"And what happens to our cities when Godzilla and the Terminator go head-to-head? Not to mention Titans and the Avengers—"

"And all their villains." And again, Josh shook his head. "That can't be how it works."

Nero remained silent. Everyone fought this concept at first, but eventually, if they kept their eyes open, they saw it for the truth.

"We have to keep ourselves secret."

"Okay," Josh said, obviously reluctant. "So it's a secret." He rubbed a hand over his face. "But I can tell one person, right? Like Savannah."

"Everybody's got one person. But the answer is no. And you do not want to test the Paranormal Department of Justice. Punishments are swift and brutal."

Josh winced. "Okay. Okay." It wasn't okay, but that's the way their world worked. "But my family—"

Nero sighed. They were back to that. "It's going to suck. Even if you could have lied to your family before, you can't now. Your aggressive nature won't allow it. You won't be able to sit there and pretend to be a screw-up when you aren't."

Josh's jaw firmed. "I can. I will." He lifted his chin. "I'm not going to let my family think I'm dead or sitting in prison somewhere."

It was a direct hit, especially since whenever Nero thought about Gramps and Gran, he was beset by more guilt. Thing was, over the years, it was just one more screw-up to add to the list, so he'd been able to bury it. At least he had, until Josh dredged it up again. And maybe that was why he dug in his heels now. He did not want Josh to go testing the theory.

"You cannot contact your family. Not for a very long time. Accept it."

Josh grinned. "We are not slaves. You told me that yourself. Once I master this wolf thing, I'm out of here."

"That's the problem, Josh. The wolf never gets mastered. At best, it just gets integrated. And once you're there, you won't want to see your family of sheep ever again. Because you might eat them."

Josh stared for a moment. Then he did the most arrogant thing Nero had ever seen. He flicked his fingers at Nero and made a "Pfft" sound. As if he were flicking away a fly. "Challenge accepted," he said.

Chapter 15

JOSH HAD never felt so electrified in his life. Every aspect of his life felt better, faster, and definitely more passionate. His body was more powerful and his senses snapped to alert at the most interesting times. Coffee smelled crisp, food had textures like never before, and the lust he felt whenever he looked at Nero was off the charts. Normally that would tank his concentration as he bounced between Food! Sex! Smells! But the moment he dove into the research, his hunger for knowledge skyrocketed. He wanted to learn everything about magic and monsters, but thanks to Nero's challenge, he had a crystalline focus to his studies.

He was going to figure out the base structure be-neath magic. Nero's equation of belief = manifestation was bullshit. The world didn't work like that, and so he set out to understand the basic laws that governed magic.

Normally the scope of that kind of project would overwhelm him in a few minutes and throw him into run-and-hide mode, but he felt sharp and determined. Everything he read was just one more data point in an ever-expanding pool of knowledge. And knowledge had always been his bulwark against an aggressive world. Sure, he couldn't stop a bully from taking his favorite baseball cap in grade school, but he could fig-ure out how to make a stink bomb and put it in the guy's backpack. He'd terrorized his siblings with food that turned their pee blue and money that looked like it was on fire. And though he never made it onto any of the cool sports teams, he found friends and safe-ty in being the innovative chemist among the science geeks.

And now he had an entire field of study that most people didn't know existed, and he planned to crack it wide open and swim in its secrets.

That worked for less than twenty-four hours. Something about a 5:00 a.m. wake-up call the next morning completely destroyed his zest for life. He'd only fallen asleep an hour before—still in the li-brary—and suddenly he was kicked awake by the big-gest bastard of a drill sergeant he'd ever met. The guy was huge, had an Army buzzcut and the thick brow of a Neanderthal. He barked orders like he had a mega-phone—which he didn't—and he managed to terrify Josh's sleeping brain enough that it had him stumbling outside into the Michigan winter before he'd fully cracked open his eyes.

They only good thing about Megamouth Yordan was that he appeared to be Pretty Boy's handler, and that pleased Josh's childish side. Let the guy who made his living smiling for a camera learn what real sweat was like. Especially since Bing looked truly miserable as he shivered in the cold.

Josh would have launched into a really bitter tirade—at least in his head—except that this predawn punishment was being handed out to the other trainers too. Nero was here, looking disgustingly awake, as were Captain M and Wiz. Those last two didn't seem thrilled, but they did appear to grimly accept their fate as they stood—not shivering—next to Laddin and Stratos.

"Against my better judgment," Megamouth blasted, "we're not doing this naked. Werewolves need to get used to running around with their asses bared to the moon, but we'll save that for another day." He lifted his chin as if to show off that he was standing there barefoot, bare-chested, and with only a really loose pair of basketball shorts to cover his junk. "But we are going to do it barefoot, so let me see those lily-white feet now! I want to check them out before they're covered in your own blood." He laughed in a truly sadistic way while Captain M and Wiz toed off their slip-ons. Nero hadn't bothered with shoes in the first place, but the rest of them just stood there gaping.

It was cold outside in the Michigan winter. And though most of the snow was gone right now, there were still patches of ice lurking in the shadows on the frozen ground.

"I suggest you take them off now," Megamouth growled, his voice low and threatening. "Or I will take them off for you."

"You're not serious—" Josh argued, but he never got the rest of the words out. He'd been watching the drill sergeant, preparing for the guy to be a dick and attack him. But no, Nero was the asshole who took him down. He swiped Josh's feet out from under him and let Josh drop face-first into the dirt. And then, before Josh could react, Nero had a knee in his back and was hauling off his shoes.

Fuck, the ground was cold.

Then Pretty Boy glared at Nero, his expression hard as he said, "Try that with me."

Nero tossed aside Josh's shoes, then hauled him upright by the back of his neck, as if he was trying to grab hold of the scruff of Josh's fur, except Josh was fully human right then. And while Josh unsuccessfully tried to dislodge the guy's hand, Nero looked at Bing.

"You're not my problem," he said as he apparently got tired of Josh's struggles. He calmly swept Josh's feet out from under him again. And while Bing watched with an amused curl to his lips, Megamouth took him down.

Or at least tried to.

Wow, Pretty Boy could fight. Josh knew very little about martial arts except what he'd learned in a college tae kwan do class. He knew there were different forms of martial arts, but that was about it. And as far as Josh could tell, Bing was a master of them all.

Bing had been looking at Josh, but the moment Megamouth moved on him, he spun and landed blow after blow. Hands and feet, he delivered both punches and kicks in a whirlwind of fury that had Josh sitting up to stare. He'd always thought martial arts was a kind of dance, but this wasn't anything so tame. It was fury in motion. Anger, hatred, and pure testosterone.

Josh had to give it to Megamouth. The guy took it all without so much as a sound beyond the occasional grunt. And Bing was making mincemeat out of Yordan, keeping him on the defensive while he attacked nonstop.

Until Megamouth decided he'd had enough. Bing's mistake was that he stopped short of killing Yordan. Instead, he raised his hand and froze, just like in a movie where the hero has to decide if killing the bad guy is worth the cost to his soul. It was a pristine movement worthy of an Academy Award. But this wasn't a movie, and while Bing remained poised, thinking about what he wanted to do, Yordan made the decision for him.

Yordan punched him in the knee and then the nuts. Bing went down with a scream, and it took a moment for Josh to realize that the cry was not from the blow to the groin. Bing was gripping his knee as if his life was over. And maybe it was, given that Pretty Boy used his martial arts skills on TV.

"Back off, you bastard!" Josh bellowed as he jumped to his bare feet and advanced on Megamouth. And he wasn't the only one. Stratos was beside him, looking like she was going to rip off the guy's nuts with her bare hands. The only reason Laddin wasn't with them was because he had advanced on Captain M.

"He needs a doctor now!" Laddin was saying. "That's his livelihood!" And if glares could kill, Captain M would be a smoking pile of ash.

But the woman held up her hand and pointed at Wiz "Fix him," she said.

Wiz responded with an angry snap. "I'm not a cleric."

Before the captain could respond, Yordan growled everyone to silence. Or he tried. "I've got this!" He squatted down in front of Bing. Not a sound came out of the actor's mouth, but tears fell as he gripped his knee. "You want to walk again? Go wolf. Dig down into your animal fury and let it fly. It'll heal and you can try to kick my ass that way." The grin in his swollen face was truly grotesque, but he didn't let up. "Come get me, Red Wolf."

Josh didn't know what to do. He didn't have a phone or any first-aid knowledge. All he could do was stand there as Bing went into a staring match with Megamouth. His gaze was dark and filled with hatred.

Then something happened to his eyes. A red glow simmered beneath the pupils. Josh had seen it on TV, and it looked even freakier in person. Then Bing whispered two words.

"Stay human."

Oh shit. Josh knew what that meant. Bing was using his Red Wolf power to Jedi mind-trick Yordan. And sure enough, Megamouth blinked twice and echoed the words. "I'll stay human."

Bing lunged. It went so fast, Josh was still seeing human red eyes when suddenly there was a huge wolf on top of Megamouth. The guy screamed and toppled beneath the attack, and Josh smelled blood. He surged forward to help, but what could he do? Fortunately he didn't need to.

Nero and Captain M were there before him, both wolves now, as they tackled Bing, dragging him off Yordan, who was bleeding arterial blood from the neck. Then Wiz shoved Josh aside as he went to press one hand hard against Yordan's neck.

"Shift," he said in a low, soothing voice. "Shift now."

It worked. Yordan shimmered gold and stabilized as a huge black wolf, lying on his back with his mouth open and his bright pink tongue lolling out. Wiz jumped back as Yordan squirmed, then came up on his feet. That was good for Megamouth, but two feet away, Bing was not going quietly into the night.

Red Wolf was squaring off with Nero and Captain M. He had his wolf head lowered and his eyes blazing red, his body preternaturally still as he obviously decided who to obliterate first.

Captain M was a white arctic wolf, pristine and gorgeous. Despite being the smallest wolf here, she was the one in charge. She was face-to-face with Bing, her teeth bared and her body tight with power. Yes, she still had on her sports bra and sweatpants, which ought to detract from the image, but it really didn't. It was all in the way she was bristling and growling "back off!" She was scary enough, but with Nero standing to her left, Josh was crap-his-pants scared. Nero was a big timber wolf, dark brown with shoulders the size of a Volvo, thanks to a scary ruff, and sharp white teeth. He wasn't making any sound, but he sure as hell wasn't going to let Bing attack.

"Holy shit," Laddin murmured as he grabbed Stratos and started tugging her backward. A second later Laddin had hold of Josh's arm, and all three of them took slow, steady steps back from the wolf fight to come. Wiz went with them, shedding clothes with careful movements. Everyone watched Bing. If anyone going to initiate disaster, it would be him. Or Mega-mouth, as the stupid black wolf leaped into the fray.

Yes, the idiot leaped over Captain M, spun around so that his exposed back was to Bing, and then growled the captain and Nero back. It was almost funny the way those two shied backward in surprise. Even more so as Yordan stretched up onto his hind legs and became human, still in those huge basketball shorts. Except that wasn't funny so much as really cool. And damned if Josh didn't have the urge to drop on his knees and say, "Teach me!" like Benedict Cumberbatch in the first Doctor Strange movie.

Meanwhile, Yordan was grinning like it was Christmas morning as he spun around and clapped his hands in delight. "You did it!" he chortled at the wolf Bing. "Now prove that you're under control and come back to human." He squatted down stupidly close to Bing's jaws. "Then you'll get the day off to do whatever the hell you want. I might even let you send out an email."

Josh held his breath. He gave it even odds that Bing would lunge for Yordan's throat, but the wolf stood there with his teeth bared. Josh could hear the animal's breath too. In and out in a tight pant.

Then—without even a glow or shimmer or anything—suddenly Josh was looking at the human Bing on all fours on the ground. The guy looked pretty-boy perfect. He didn't even shiver from the cold as he rose smoothly to his bare feet. And then—in a morning full of surprises—Bing looked at Yordan and bent at the waist.

Bing bowed to Yordan in a show of respect.

Holy shit. Had hell frozen over? Meanwhile Megamouth accepted the gesture with a regal dip of his chin, and then he abruptly hauled Bing into a big hug, wrapping his huge arms around the man and clapping him heavily on his back. Bing accepted it with a pained expression. Clearly the guy wasn't used to such exuberant shows of masculine bonding. But his lips were curved in a smile. And when Yordan finally let him go, he was able to nod at everyone else as well. Then, with an increasingly smug expression, he sauntered past them into the house.

His parting words were enough to make Josh hate him a little more.

"I think I'll eat breakfast now," he said. "And maybe read in bed before taking a nap."

"Go on, buddy!" Yordan bellowed. "You earned it." Then, after Bing was inside the house, he turned to the other trainers. "And you all owe me five hundred dollars each," he crowed. "My guy—first to shift, first to manifest a special power. Woohoo! I'm going shopping!"

He started doing a happy dance which, honestly, looked a little disturbing, given how well his hips moved. Meanwhile, Wiz gaped at him while Josh realized they'd had a five hundred-dollar bet on which trainee would learn to shift first.

Wiz snorted with disgust. "Just because we're not bastards about it—"

"Doesn't matter," Megamouth answered. "Results are what count."

Captain M—still in her wolf form—blew out a snort, then turned around with her tail stuck up high as she headed into the house. Wiz leaped to open the door for her as she retreated. It was a very classy retreat, but Josh suspected she'd still pay up.

Then, when Nero started to turn, Yordan stuck a meaty finger at him. "Don't you dare!" he growled. "You're assigned here." He glanced at Wiz. "You too."

Which, apparently, was true, because Nero remained, though he refused to shift back to human. He retreated to a corner where he watched everything with steady wolf eyes. It was sort of like being watched by a police dog. The thing was polite, but it didn't lessen the scare factor. Which left Wiz shirtless, barefoot, and in low-slung jeans. He shrugged and said, "Bring it on."

Megamouth did. Calisthenics to warm everyone up, sparring outside to "show our stuff," and when no one wanted to fight him, he sent everyone off on a horrendously freezing jog around the estate. And to deter anyone thinking of jumping the fence, Nero was there in his wolf form to make sure everyone stayed in formation.

And the most humiliating part of it all? Josh was the slowest. He didn't mind being less capable than the trainers. They were probably subjected to this idiocy often. Laddin was Mr. Nervous Energy, so running was just another way to burn off calories. But being less in shape than Stratos—a woman who was the picture of a pale gamer geek—stung his male pride. Apparently even techies who spent their days and nights attached to their gear got more physical exertion than PhD students. It wasn't his fault. He'd been in a cramped lab nearly 24/7 for five years now. Of course he was out of shape. He just hadn't expected to be *this* pathetic, especially since Nero took great delight in nipping at his heels whenever he got too slow.

By the time they made it back to the mansion, Josh's feet were numb, which was a very good thing, because he knew they were cut all to hell. He stumbled back into the main backyard only to hear everyone groan about something. Oh hell, he wasn't sure he wanted to know what. But as he collapsed on the frozen ground, he stared balefully at Laddin. "What now?" he groaned.

"No food," the guy answered, his misery palpable.

Josh jerked upward. Dreams of a six-egg omelet were the only things that had kept him going for the last mile. "What?"

Megamouth came to stand right over him. "You able to shift yet?"

"I'm exhausted and starving. Plus, I was up all night trying to figure out your magical fire problem. Of course I can't shift. No one has told me how."

"It's not a *tell* thing. It's a *do* thing."

That was it—that was all he said as he stared at Josh, expecting him to somehow poof into a wolf. Just like his father, who couldn't understand why his son couldn't catch a ball or punch a bully or handle tools in his machine shop. Just because they could do it without thinking, suddenly Josh was deficient because he wasn't good with his hands. Or his body. Or anything physical at all.

"Spoken like every natural athlete on the planet. Congratulations. You're good at something." He straightened up onto his numb feet and matched the asshole glare for glare. And he said exactly what he'd been dying to tell his father since he was three years old. "Too bad you're lousy at *teaching*, which is what you're supposed to be doing right now. So if you want us to go wolf, then *tell* us how to do it!"

And just like with his father, his words meant jack shit. Megamouth poked him in the chest. "You're pretty pissed off right now, aren't you?"

Josh slapped the guy's meaty arm away. "Yeah, I am."

"What you going to do about it?" Another poke.

Josh slapped it away harder this time. Or at least he tried to. His swats didn't seem to have a noticeable effect.

"Want to attack me? Want to rip my throat out like Bing tried? Huh? Huh?" Poke, poke, poke.

Yeah, he did, but he wasn't stupid. No way could he take on Megamouth physically, and he didn't have the ability to do a surprise shift. So he went where he always did when threatened: chemistry.

"I'm going to put methylene blue in your Gatorade and stain your teeth. I'm going to put sodium iodide and hydrogen peroxide in your toilet and wait for the next time you flush. And if you don't take the hint, then maybe I'll make sure that whatever the fuck solution I have to your plasma fire problem doesn't work for you. And maybe then we'll get a teacher who knows how to teach."

It took a moment for his words to sink in, but when they did, Megamouth lost his snide grin. It faded slowly until it was replaced with a cold, dark stare. "You're threatening the life of a packmate?"

"I don't see a pack here. And believe me, if I did, I wouldn't be part of yours."

"That's right," he replied. "Because I wouldn't have you in mine. And for damn sure I'm not going to trust any tech you give me."

"Exactly—"

"Which means you can't trust any order I give you, any mission I send you on, or even any training scenario you land in." He gripped Josh's chin and tilted it up, forcing Josh to stare him in the eye. "A pack survives on trust, and you've just proven yourself too much of a whiny child to be worthy of it."

Josh tried to rip his face out of the guy's meaty fist, but the bastard's grip was too strong. He had a dozen smartass things to say back, but he couldn't move his jaw enough to say them. And right when he thought he might manage a garbled "Fuck you, asswipe," Megamouth shoved him away.

"Maybe you'll grow up after another run. Go!"

Josh wasn't going anywhere. He was done with—

A sharp nip at his heels had him jumping sideways in surprise. It was Nero, standing between him and the mansion. And when Josh made to go into the house with everyone else, Nero snapped at him again. The bastard made it clear that Josh wasn't going anywhere but on his run. Josh tried to feint left or right, but it didn't work. Even a small dog was faster than him, and Nero was a huge wolf.

So Josh stood still. He'd be damned if—

"Ow!"

Nero bit his kneecap. And it wasn't a light bite either. He'd drawn blood!

"What the—*ow!*"

Another nip, this time on the other knee. And when Nero came at him again, Josh had no choice but to shy backward. Which meant Nero could advance. Another nip, which Josh tried to block. He got a bloody forearm for his trouble. And before he could recover, Nero bloodied his thigh, a half inch above the other cut.

It was the triumph of brawn over brains, the whole fucking story of his childhood. Josh had no choice but to stumble backward or lose more blood. And the longer Josh refused to run forward, the more he was jumping backward to avoid getting bitten. So he could do the whole run in backward hops or turn around and run straight.

He ran. And with every step on his numb feet, he cursed Megamouth, Nero, and even Captain M, who had abdicated her responsibility by leaving a psychopath in charge. He let the hatred boil through him—for at least fifteen minutes. But that could only last him so long, and it took too much energy to maintain his fury.

So he switched to plotting revenge. For him, that took no effort at all.

Chapter 16

NERO FELT like an ass even though he knew they were doing the right thing.

Training new werewolves was a very straight-forward process. Piss off the new recruit enough until they attacked. Most times they unconsciously shifted to the wolf and tried to bite out your throat, like Bing had (though the hypnotism was new). Calm the biter down, and then suddenly new guy realizes he knows how to shift. It took time and practice to learn how to go wolf without being in a blind fury, but eventually everyone mastered it. And since Yordan knew better than anyone how to piss people off, he was an ideal drill sergeant. Especially since he was big and bad enough to defend himself no matter what attacked.

The problem was that Josh was nothing like the typical werewolf. When he got furious, he fought back with his mind, not his body. Physical attacks were no big deal. Mental weapons like whatever the hell Josh had said were beyond what Yordan knew how to deal with. So he threw Josh back into the body in the form of endless freezing runs and then left Nero to enforce the order.

Nero nipped at Josh constantly, forcing him to run, run, run while fury poured out of the guy like sweat. Nero thought for a bit there that it would work and Josh would freak out and explode into his wolf form. That was what had happened with Wiz, way back when. But something changed on the second mile. Josh went quiet. His shoulders locked in place, and his breath came in steady sawing gasps. He'd found a rhythm for the steady pound of his feet, and that set the guy's massive brain to thinking, which was the last thing Nero wanted him to do.

Nero did everything he could think of to break Josh's concentration. Biting, tripping, tackling—everything. Josh simply got up, started moving, and never really focused on anything his body was doing. He was all in his head, probably plotting revenge. And damn it, that was dangerous for everyone.

In short, if Yordan's method was going to work, it would have already, back in the gym when Josh went ballistic on Nero's face. Which meant that Nero had until they made it back to the mansion to think of a new plan.

Just like with the fire blast, he completely failed. No brilliant ideas sparked, no clever ruses. Fortunately Yordan stepped into the breech. While Stratos helped Josh clean dirt out of his many cuts, Yordan filled him and everyone else in on the plan.

"Right after your boo-boos are taken care of, you've got forms to fill out and questions we want answered." He dropped a six-inch-high stack of paper on the counter. Nero knew that the paperwork was another way to piss off the new recruits, but Josh might be the only werewolf who preferred filling out forms over beating the shit out of someone. "You know, if you shifted, your feet would be lily white again and pedicure perfect," Yordan taunted.

Come on, Nero thought as loudly as he could in his wolf form. *Give him a smartass response.*

Nope. Josh smiled benignly and said, "Good to know." Which told him Yordan was in serious trouble, because Josh was thinking up something truly devious.

Meanwhile Josh looked at Stratos. "Thanks," he said softly. "He letting us have any food yet?"

She mutely shook her head, her eyes glittering with her own anger. And here was yet another person plotting revenge. Nero sure hoped Wiz was ready for it.

"Okay," Josh answered. "I'm going to take a shower."

Stratos held his gaze for a moment, the look significant in a shared-prisoners kind of way. It said loud and clear: *Whatever you're plotting, I'll help.*

Great, the recruits were plotting against their trainers. And worse, Josh got the message. He nodded with a short dip of his chin and then winced as he got back to his abused feet. And Yordan was completely clueless as to what shit was about to hit the fan.

Damn it, he had to think of a solution fast.

Nero padded along after Josh, keeping within biting distance in case he had to disrupt a sudden chemical attack. Nothing happened, of course. There hadn't been time. But Nero was on alert as he followed Josh to his bedroom and muscled his way in enough to stand fully in the doorway. There was a long wait as Josh stared at him and Nero looked back. Then Josh finally curled his lip and drawled, "By all means, join me."

Which roughly translated to: *You can't do jack shit to stop me from destroying you. But go ahead, you can watch while I plot.*

Which is exactly what Nero did. He sat down in the middle of the bedroom like a freaking pet dog. He watched Josh's every move as the guy walked awkwardly into the bathroom and turned on a hot shower. Nero even watched as Josh stripped and stepped into the hot spray. Nero wouldn't put it past Josh to MacGyver together soap bubbles, toilet paper, and herbal shampoo into an IED, but if he did it right then, Nero didn't see it.

And then he got an inspiration.

While Josh was standing with his head bowed beneath the steaming showerhead, Nero finally found a plan. It was a radical thought, something they'd never done with the new recruits before, but what the hell. So far nothing had worked the way they'd intended. It was time to step outside of the box.

Taking a deep breath, Nero switched back to human, then went to sit on the bed and wait. He felt the strain on his system, the heat and the pain that always came from shifting. That was the curse for lycanthropes. Too many movies had werewolves shifting in agony, so he suffered from that concept. The good news was that he wasn't tied to the moon like so many. In fact, the current full moon boosted his strength, but not enough to want to go through that pain again for a while. He was staying strictly human for now, which made this next step more dangerous.

Josh came out of the shower bristling with antagonism. It wasn't an obvious thing. In fact, his movements were beautifully casual as he finger-combed his hair while keeping a towel neatly wrapped around his hips. He had the lean build that Nero found so attractive. Lanky, often flexible, and with a long stride and a laid-back carriage that seemed relaxed until the guy exploded into motion. Right now he was moving with practiced ease, though the temperature in the room seemed to have dropped twenty degrees.

"If you're thinking of getting it on," Josh drawled, "I'm really not in the mood."

Sadly, that was true. There was no indication that Josh's dick was doing anything under his towel. "Actually, I'm here to level with you, but we have to keep our voices down. We can't have the other recruits hearing this by accident."

"Uh-huh," Josh intoned as he leaned back against his dresser. His taut abs were on display, and there was moisture pebbling in his light dusting of chest hair. He stretched his long legs out in front of him. If Nero had ever wanted an image to jerk off to, this was it. And the arch to Josh's brows said he knew exactly what he was doing to Nero's libido. "So the artful arrangement of you naked in my bed is just convenient?"

Nero shrugged. It was and it wasn't, no sense in denying it. "Listen for a moment." He dropped his voice to just above a whisper. "The goal of training at this stage is to get you to shift back to your wolf. We do that by pissing you off, like Yordan did with Bing."

Josh's eyes widened, which showed he was listening.

"But you're not like most recruits. The more angry you get, the more in your head you get." He lifted his chin. "How many different plans do you have for getting even with us?"

Josh's lips curled in a truly evil grin. "A dozen aimed at humiliation, seven will maim, and countless lethal ones, but only two are practical."

Well, that was scarily detailed. "Which means we have to find a different way."

Josh folded his arms across his chest. "How about explaining the process to me?"

"That won't work. It's different for everybody—"

"It's a place to start—"

"And all I can say is that I let myself go wolf. Or human. I want it and I'm there."

Josh threw up his hands. "You're all fucking naturals, which makes you lousy teachers."

Nero couldn't argue, but he could share his experiences from when he'd first shifted. "Remember when I told you that I was bitten in a bar fight?"

"You came to in the woods with your entire pack."

"Such as it was. Pack means a whole lot more to me now that it did back then." He leaned forward on the bed. He hadn't bothered with a sheet to cover his nakedness, and he was pleased to see Josh follow his movements with his eyes. Nero wasn't exactly ugly, so maybe there was interest there. He sure as hell was enjoying his view of Josh.

"I was kept alive by a girl with more sexual appetite than I'd ever experienced. Hell, more than I ever thought possible. Anyway, she smelled like lust, and at seventeen, that was all it took. If she was a wolf, then I went wolf and we did it that way. If she was human, then I shifted to two legs and took her that way. Or her friends. Or they me."

"Wow," Josh breathed. "Sounds like every teenage boy's fantasy." There was envy in his tone that Nero was quick to squash.

"Like I said, pack means a lot more to me now, and endless sex gets boring." He flashed a rueful smile. "My brain doesn't crave the constant stimulation like yours does, and even I got tired of it."

"My brain will shut up for some things."

Nero smiled. "Good. Because that's exactly my plan."

"Come again?"

"We need to get you into your body. For you, that means touch, caresses—"

"Sex." It wasn't a statement so much as a snort of derision.

"Hear me out. The girl who smelled like lust taught me a lot of things too, including how to trigger the wolf sex drive." He pointed at the desk and the thick stack of papers there. "So we can sit here and fill out all of Yordan's paperwork, or you can let me do everything she did to me. Every wolf trigger I know—"

"Sexually." There wasn't derision in his tone. It was more like heavily layered doubt.

"Yes."

"You want me to shift into a wolf during sex."

Nero nodded. "It's a dominance thing. I'm not going to let you get off as a human. You're going to have to go furry to get your release."

Josh's brows rose into his hairline. "You want to have sex with me as a—"

"Never." No room for doubt there. "I've never gotten into cross-species sex." At least he hoped he hadn't. Those early sex-fest days were murky. "The minute you sprout claws and a tail, you have to stop. A human can get ripped to shreds by an enthusiastic wolf, and I'm way too exhausted to shift again. So decide on a safeword. Something to make you lay off. We just want you going wolf, not... you know... tearing me a new one."

"How about 'stop'?"

Straightforward and practical. "That'll work." But would this?

Josh blew out a breath. "So that's why you're sitting here naked. You want to—"

"Trigger the wolf sex drive."

Nero waited in silence, feeling more naked than any shifter should. He was comfortable with his body and at ease with being naked, but sitting here, vulnerable, while Josh considered the possibilities made him want to huddle beneath a parka.

He didn't. He sat there and tried not to squirm. Fortunately, Josh finally nodded. "I suppose it's better than paperwork."

Not a ringing endorsement.

Josh straightened up. "So... do you want to do this here? Or is there some sex cave for wolves?"

"We're not deviants," Nero snapped. "We're animals. And we do it right here." Part of him liked the idea of Josh smelling this—smelling him—on his sheets every time he went to bed. That, too, was a dominance thing.

"Right here where everyone will hear us?"

Nero shrugged. As a general rule, werewolves were much more casual about sex than people. "Maybe we can show Yordan that there's a better way than endless humiliation."

Josh snorted. "I can get on board with that."

Of course he could. And Nero was glad to get Josh focused on teaching Yordan a constructive lesson rather than a destructive one. So he leaned back on the bed, exposing his entire body, including his rock-hard erection, to Josh's gaze. He'd worried at first that he wouldn't be able to get it up, considering the risk. But one look at Josh coming out of the shower had that problem solved.

Meanwhile, he got the pleasure of seeing Josh's eyes go dark as he took in Nero's pose. He was looking, all right. And his nostrils flared, but he didn't move toward the bed.

"We're trying to bring out the predator in me, right?" Josh asked.

The words were low and dark with menace, and excitement skittered up Nero's spine. "Yes."

Josh exploded forward. He leaped onto the bed and flattened Nero against the headboard. Or he tried. Nero wasn't any tame bunny to be caught, and he quickly twisted away. What he didn't expect was for Josh to continue his assault with lightning-fast reflexes. Wasn't the guy tired from all that running?

Apparently not, because he surged forward to pin him again. Clearly there was wrestling in his background. Or more accurately, an older brother who had needed someone to practice his wrestling on.

Didn't matter. Whatever Josh's training, Nero had more. Not to mention thirty pounds more muscle. He rolled with Josh's body, and if they hadn't gotten tangled in the sheets, it would have been hard to say who would have ended up on top. Fortunately for Nero, Josh's abused feet caught, and he gasped in surprised pain.

Good. A little bit of pain was part of werewolf sex, and Nero wasted no time in taking advantage. He shoved hard on Josh's shoulders and forced him flat, belly up, and then he began to lick. It was both sensuous and excruciating for them both. Nero smelled the musk, and his dick pulsed with need. He tasted the shower soap and the tangy spice of Josh—distinct tastes in his mind—and he went in search of a stronger zing.

He was merciless. No creature liked his belly exposed except in the most intimate of situations. He pushed that to Josh's limit. He wasn't careful as he bit down, and he certainly wasn't easing up as he moved lower. And though Josh twisted and fought, Nero was stronger.

He took his time, but eventually he found his way to Josh's dick which put them nearly at 69. The scent was strongest down there, the textures intriguing, and the combination nearly sent him spiraling out of control. The only reason he didn't was because he was still fighting Josh. Every time the man started to relax into the situation—to surrender to the experience—Nero found a way to push him too far. He needed Josh to try to take control, and that would only happen if Josh was uncomfortable.

Biting was the easiest way, but Nero had other tricks. He scratched everywhere with his nails, and he growled whenever Josh moved.

"Fight me, you bastard," he ordered. And the next time Josh started to relax, Nero straddled his face and shoved his dick straight down Josh's throat.

He was risking a lot here. Some men would simply bite down, and then Nero would be a eunuch until the next time he shifted. He pushed hard with his hips, half choking Josh, half just getting too involved in the amazing sensation of Josh sucking him off.

And then he leaned down and began to bite Josh's dick. Lick, suck, and then bites that he knew would frustrate the hell out of Josh. It worked, if Josh's groans meant anything. But no matter how much Nero tortured the man, they were both getting steadily closer and closer to orgasm. Nero's balls had drawn up and his spine burned with precum heat. And Josh's dick was throbbing. Any minute now, he was going to come.

So Nero lifted off Josh's dick, and he wasn't careful with it. His teeth scraped along the shaft and caught for a moment on the head. And when Josh threw his head back with an ecstatic scream, Nero grabbed Josh's dick and squeezed the head as hard as he could. Then he balanced on his elbows and did the same with Josh's ball sac.

Josh's scream was louder this time—harsh and full of need. So to increase the pressure, Nero began pumping his hips. Harder, deeper, straight into Josh's throat. God, he was so close. If Josh swallowed, he was a goner.

"You want off?" he said with a strangled cry. "Then go wolf! Do it, damn it!"

He felt the grip of Josh's hands, hard like talons on his hips. This was stupid, stupid, stupid to push him so hard while he had his jaws around Nero's dick. But he didn't know any other way. There was only one thing left to do, one dominance play left in his arsenal. He leaned down and bit into the soft side of Josh's thigh. He didn't draw blood, but he came close. And suddenly Josh was sucking him like he wanted to milk him.

The pull was fast, over and over, and Nero lost control. He erupted like a teenager with his first orgasm. And while he was still trembling from the force of his eruption, Josh's body changed underneath him. At first he thought the tingling heat was from his own orgasm, but this was magic and Josh was midshift. Nero was still in the grips, his cock pumping out semen in ecstatic pulses. He barely had the wherewithal to understand what was happening and no ability to adjust for it.

In a split second, he was lying dick-first in a wolf's mouth. And that wolf was throwing him off with all the power in a revved-up werewolf. Nero went flying sideways and landed on his butt against the headboard. He bounced because it was a mattress, then gasped because he had a hundred-plus pounds of black wolf suddenly going for his throat.

He wanted to say something, but he hadn't the breath. All he got out was a garbled "Josh—" And then there was no more talking as Josh came down hard with his jaw on Nero's neck. One bite and Nero was dead. No way could he shift fast enough to recover from having his throat ripped out. He didn't even have the strength to cry out, but he lay there waiting for death.

One breath. Two.

Burnt orange eyes in a long black wolf face glared at him. Then the animal suddenly lifted his head and howled.

Triumph reverberated in the sound. Joy, ecstasy, and yes, pure dominant power. It was all there, filling the room until Nero joined, arching his neck and releasing the full-throated sound. Sure, he was human, but it didn't matter. He knew the howl of a packmate, and nothing was going to keep him from joining in.

Josh had done it. He'd gone wolf again, and now was the time to celebrate.

It took several moments for them both to stop howling. Long enough for Wiz to bang on their door and yell, "We got it. You took second place. Now shut the fuck up!"

Josh just turned his head and howled even louder while Nero laughed. Eventually they both reined it in. Nero sobered up enough to cuff Josh gently on the nose.

"Listen up, cub. How about I show you how much fun snow is for a wolf?"

He shoved Josh off him and got to see the wolf scramble to get his footing. Two feet, four feet? New wolves never could remember. They were like overgrown puppies as they tried to figure it out.

Nero wanted more than anything to go running outside as a wolf, but he had a responsibility to watch out for Josh. All sorts of bad things could still happen with new werewolves, and he would be better able to help as a human. But that didn't mean he couldn't be part of the fun.

"Ten minutes," he said to Josh. Then he went to the bathroom and cleaned up. Five minutes after that, he was dressed as they both headed outdoors. The air was crisp, a new dusting of snow was falling, and Josh wasted no time running across the frozen ground to catch snowflakes with his jaws.

Nero played with him exactly as he'd done with his pack. He tackled the wolf, he rolled on the ground with him, and they played tug-of-war with sticks. Josh needed to get the full animal experience, and Nero needed to remember what fun it could be just to be alive.

It was the most glorious day of his life.

Until he remembered the worst.

Chapter 17

WHO KNEW it was such fun to be a wolf? Josh
had never felt so much unadulterated joy as when he
was running around with Nero, chomping snowflakes.
Suddenly his body wasn't an afterthought but a delight. And the simplest things were brand-new. Assuming he remembered he had four feet and not two,
he could dive and pivot like a pro athlete. He could
leap into the air and smell everything. There was such
information in the world if only he sniffed. Pine and
rabbit, human sweat, and the musky sent of sex. Yeah,
that was great! And even that was nothing compared
to playing tug-of-war with Nero. All he did was grab
something and pull while Nero held on to the other

end. It wasn't that complicated, but he enjoyed it to a level that was insane. He *loved* it.

But most of all—in a universe of mosts—he adored the sound of Nero's laugh. When the guy let it fly, his laughter was a deep belly explosion of happiness. That sound could fill a black hole to bursting, and the more Josh tumbled, leaped, or rolled, the more Nero filled the world with joy. He could have stayed outside forever.

"Time to go in, Josh."

No, no, no! He was too busy pushing his nose into a mound of debris. The scents were amazing and a little disgusting, but that didn't deter him. Nero did, though, as he whacked him on the butt with a stick. Ha! It would take a lot more than that to make him stop. There was a weird smell deeper into this pile of whatever. Some sort of animal—

"That's a skunk you're scenting. I don't think you want to pursue it."

It took a moment for the words to sink in, but when they did, he paused and drew back to stare at Nero, who was chuckling.

"Okay, okay, you got me. That wasn't a skunk. I have no freaking idea what you're smelling, but you need to come inside now and get something to eat. You're going to need it before you go human."

Food sounded interesting. And though his human side revolted at dropping his nose into a bowl of kibble, the rest of him was increasingly interested in anything edible. And given what a wolf would usually eat outside, perhaps whatever Nero was going to feed him would be for the best.

He huffed out a breath and dipped his chin.

"That's the way." Nero turned and headed up toward the mansion while Josh paced beside him. Now that Nero had brought his attention to it, Josh was feeling tired. His tail was drooping and….

His tail! He had a tail that he could wag. How cool was that?

He spun around, doing his best to look at his own tail. He tried to hold that pose while he wagged, but it was hard to manage. He ended up spinning around and wiggling while Nero held his sides laughing. Josh would have given it up quickly, but it felt good to hear such lightness from the guy. And not just for Nero's sake. Josh hadn't ever made anyone so happy. Not that kind of hold-your-sides, giddy laughter that filled Josh with light. It healed him deep inside, in a place he hadn't even realized needed attention.

So he kept spinning and wagging until he got dizzy from his own antics. Just when he was going to sit his ass down or fall, a huge body tackled him, and they went rolling. It was Nero, who was making fake growling sounds as they tumbled in the snow. Josh tussled back, and it wasn't long before they were both flat out on the ground and breathing hard.

"Sweet Jesus," Nero panted as he canted a glance at Josh. "That's what my grams used to say. Sweet, beautiful, ever-loving Jesus, you make me laugh!" Nero reached out a hand and burrowed it in Josh's fur. Then he stared at the sky and kept talking, his voice laced with that laughter that had put light in Josh's soul.

"Pauly used to chase his tail. Like you, he loved being in his wolf body." Josh twitched, and Nero correctly guessed his thoughts. "Of course I know that you love it. No one chases snowflakes for two hours unless they love it."

Had it been two hours? He didn't realize. He barely felt it, with all his fur, but Nero must be freezing. Except the man looked completely fine with the temperature. It brought a healthy pink to his cheeks.

"He'd been turned a month and spent most of it as a wolf. Then he started chasing his tail, trying to chew on it. Said it itched." He grabbed hold of a handful of Josh's fur and shook it. It was an affectionate gesture, and Josh was surprised by how much he enjoyed it. "You can guess what happened. He had fleas. By the time we figured it out, he had infested the house. We had to fumigate the whole place. God, was Carla ever pissed." He glanced back at Josh. "She and her twin, Wes, own the mansion. They're your distant relatives."

Really? Josh perked up and tried to remember the pair from his research, but couldn't hold the thought as Nero kept talking about Pauly.

"Of course, we started calling him Fleabag. He hated it, but no one changes their handle here. No one. It took him two years of secret negotiations and bets. Those are the rules. Everyone has to agree on a name change. For two years he won bets, did chores, and swore us all to secrecy until he had the votes. I was the last to fall. The guy beat me at shots. I have forty pounds on him, but he drank me under the table." Nero chuckled. "As soon as I sobered up, he called a vote, and one by one, we all had to agree for him to change his handle. We still haven't figured out his new one. I'm pushing for Fleabitten, but Mother's partial to...."

His words faded away and that gentle burrowing into Josh's fur stopped. Every part of Nero had frozen.

It took Josh a moment to figure out the reason, and then he felt stupid for not realizing it earlier. Fleabag Pauly was dead. As was Mother and the rest of Nero's team. He'd been talking like they were off on a mission or something, not dead and gone.

For a few minutes Nero had forgotten his pack was dead, and now that he remembered, he was frozen in shock. As a human, Josh wouldn't have known what to do. As a wolf, instinct drove him to crawl closer to Nero, to nuzzle the man's neck and gently lick his face. Nero allowed it for a moment, long enough for Josh to taste salt and to feel a grief so deep, it permeated the very air they breathed.

Josh whined. He had to give sound to the despair. He would have howled if he'd had the breath, but lying so close to Nero kept his throat closed.

It was his sound that jolted Nero back into the present. He abruptly jerked away from Josh while shoving hard with his arms. "Don't get all cozy with me. You're not a dog, and I sure as hell didn't pick your mangy ass up at the pound," he snapped. "Get inside. You need to eat, and I need a hot shower after freezing my ass off while you chase snowflakes like a moronic puppy. You need to figure out that fire bomb now. I can't believe I let you waste time outside."

The words were like a slap to the face. Hell, he couldn't have hurt Josh worse if he'd kicked him, even though Josh knew that Nero's reaction came from pain and grief. He was acting out like everybody did when they hurt. It didn't lessen the sting, and it sure as hell tainted the joy of the afternoon.

So Josh expressed that in the only way he could right then. He leaped to his feet and barked at Nero. And when the guy jumped back in surprise, he followed up with a few more barks in frustration. Fucking hell, he needed his words right then. But he couldn't wrap his head around what he'd say as a man, so he kept barking, as if that made everything clear.

And maybe it did, because Nero's expression softened. He rubbed a hand over his face. "You're right. I'm being an ass."

No, that wasn't at all what Josh wanted to say. Nero had been an ass, but it came from pain. Josh knew that. He'd wanted to help, but Nero wasn't about to let anyone comfort him. Hell, that had been obvious from the first moment he'd allowed Josh to go ballistic on his face. Still, the pain of that ached inside. Nero's laughter had brought light to a part of Josh that had been dark. And now Nero's pain made that place inside weep. Josh wanted to give Nero some comfort, but the man was not willing to let him in.

Nero turned away and trudged heavily back to the mansion. Josh tried to change that. He barked again, but Nero ignored him. Then he rushed forward and danced in front of the guy, inviting him to play. He even spun around and tried to catch his tail. It was all he could think to do, but none of it worked. Nero simply patted his head and opened the door into the mansion.

"I'll get you some food. You need to eat all of it and drink a bathtub's worth of water. I'll show you the wolf door so you can pee outside."

What? No way. He was going to use the bathroom like a man. Except when he tried, he couldn't get back to his human body. Oh shit. How did he—?

"I know you want to go back to human right now, but stay wolf for a bit. There's a lot you need to lock in about being lupine. You think it's obvious, but some pups have trouble. Learn it now. And eat as much as you can. You know how hard it is to eat once you come back to human, so get your calories in this way. The wolf door is right here."

Josh wanted to argue, but he didn't have a voice, and Nero was throwing information at him fast. He listened with as much focus as possible on how to open the wolf door. There was a keypad designed for wolf noses, since a palm reader obviously wouldn't work, but it was pretty hard to press with the tip of his nose. It made him cross-eyed and headachy.

"I'll heat up the food for you, and no, it's not dog chow. It's my own mixture of ground beef, vitamins, and some leafy greens. I made it so it'd be easy on your stomach, but my guess is that after a couple days, you'll be able to chow down on almost anything."

A couple days? Josh barked sharp and loud at that, but Nero waved him off.

"Yes, a couple days. You need it. You can get back to your research after you're fully vested as a wolf."

Josh snorted.

"It's not bullshit," Nero responded. "Yordan is pushing Bing for his own reasons. Mine tell me that you need to get time and calories as a wolf." Then he sighed. "But maybe, if you do everything I tell you to today, I can help you come back to human tomorrow. I really need a way to defuse that fire bomb, Josh. And I need it soon." His eyes took on a distant look. "Remember that lake where the blast happened? Lake… hell, I only remember it as Lake Wacka Wacka. Captain M says that it's poisonous now. Everything in it's dead. Cyanide is in the water somehow. We're going to blast it to see if we can kill the demon that way, but it's not 100 percent certain it'll work. We can't even find the thing." He focused back on Josh. "Figure out how we can survive that fire blast. Then everything can go back to the way it's supposed to be."

Josh released a low growl of frustration. What Nero was wanted was impossible.

"I need you to try. Try hard."

Josh chuffed his agreement.

"But not today. You need the time as a wolf, and I…." Nero shook his head. "I need the break too. I just… need a break."

That, more than anything else, made Josh give in. Nero's pain was real and raw. Right now he needed to grieve, not play dog-sitter to a new wolf. And sure, it cut that he didn't want Josh to help, but sometimes a guy had to lick his wounds in private.

So Josh didn't argue. He mastered the use of the doggie keypad. He ate all his ground beef and greens. He even went outside and figured out certain other mechanics behind a bush. But while he looked at the cloudy sky, he ached for the Nero who had helped him chase snowflakes, tugged on a stick with him, and rubbed his ass. Because right now, damn it, his tail itched.

Hell, he was never going to live it down if he got fleas.

Even worse, he couldn't even tell Nero the joke because the man had gone into his bedroom and shut the door tight.

Chapter 18

NERO SAT at his desk, staring at a picture of his team at the last barbecue. He was torturing himself— he knew that. The memories were painful and wonderful at the same time. He missed them. He missed who he was when he was around them. And he really wanted to introduce them to Josh. They'd like him. They'd tease him mercilessly, and he'd probably do something to the food to turn everyone orange, and just like that, he'd become part of the pack.

Except there was no pack right now, and he was lost without it.

A knock sounded on his door. "Not now," he growled out.

The door opened anyway, even though it was locked. Only one person could do that, and he was the last alien Nero wanted to see.

"Not now, Gelpack."

"This is the appointed time."

Nero frowned. "We don't have an appointment."

"It is the appointed time. And Captain M told me to remind you that this is the arrangement. I kept the new recruits alive—"

"Not all of them."

"—and you must talk to me about feelings."

"Fine. I'm *feeling* like you need to get out of here."

"You need not concern yourself with my safety. In fact, Captain M said that I should offer myself as your punching bag."

"Great idea." Nero launched himself out of his chair, leading with his fist. He went right through Gelpack to thud painfully against the door. Then he damned himself for being an idiot, because he'd known that would happen. The vaguest residue of something remained on his throbbing hand, and behind him, Gelpack simply reformed without the fist-sized hole. Well, he'd wondered if surprise made a difference against the creature. Now he knew it didn't.

"Fine," he said, all the fight going out of him. "What do you want to know?"

"I wish to discuss your feelings."

Oh, goody. "What about them?"

"Please describe them to me right now. Include as much physical description as you can."

"I'm feeling the clothes on my body. They itch right now." He was in his softest sweatpants, but they still bothered him. Everything bothered him right then.

"I'm feeling angry at you because I want to be left alone." Except he'd just been alone and realized that steeping himself in misery wasn't doing anyone any good.

"I'm feeling like my hand better stop throbbing soon or I'm going to have to shift, and I'm too tired to do that. And that's another thing," he said as he glared at his bed. "I'm feeling so fucking tired, even my hair needs to rest."

"How does hair feel tired? There are no nerves in hair to feel—"

He sighed. "It feels heavy, okay? Like each hair is pulling my scalp down and I'm too tired to stay upright."

"Why don't you lie down?"

"Because whenever I do, I get antsy." Fitting words to action, he stretched out on his back on the bed and stared at the ceiling. "Happy now?"

"I do not experience happiness as you do. That is why I am here: to learn how you experience it."

"If I knew that, then I'd be happy, wouldn't I?"

"Would you?"

"Of course I would. No one wants to feel crappy."

"But you knew your hand would hurt after you punched through me to the door, and yet you did it anyway. What actions usually bring you happiness?"

Playing with his packmates. Eating a ton of burgers at a barbecue. And Mother's potato salad. One bite of that and he was in heaven. "Killing that fucking demon."

"And how will you feel when you accomplish that? What will your happiness feel like?"

He imagined destroying that gun-toting, ne-on-blooded asshole. He pictured himself ripping out its throat, shooting its head into a zillion pieces, detonating an atomic bomb on its ass. But every time he destroyed it, it popped right back into his head. He saw every detail of the emotionless, killing thing, from its dead eyes to the steady hold it had on its gun. He'd hamstring it, disembowel it, and then decapitate it before pissing on its remains.

And still it would pop up in his brain, alive and whole as it burned his entire team to ash.

"Quiet," he said. "It will feel like quiet."

"Thank you for your answer," Gelpack said as his arm seemed to ooze around his body to open the door. It was a disturbing sight. "It is a common one, and so I believe I have found a pattern."

Nero lifted his head. "What?"

"Many of your colleagues have said that happiness comes from quiet. And yet you all live such noisy lives."

Wasn't that the truth? "So what do you conclude from that?"

"That happiness comes from quiet and noise both, in the right balance."

"It has to be the right noise," Nero said. "And the right quiet." It had been utterly silent after his team had died. He'd been in the in-between state when the blast happened. Then he'd reformed onto the scorched earth and heard absolutely nothing.

"How do you know which is the right one?"

Nero felt a cynical smile twist his lips. "By whether or not it makes me happy." Let the Jell-O guy figure that one out.

But instead of being confused, the alien nodded as if that made total sense. "Thank you for sharing your feelings with me." Then he opened the door and left. He should have shut it behind him, but some human protocols were lost on the alien. Or maybe it was because there was an enormous black wolf waiting who shouldered his way inside the moment the alien passed.

"Josh," Nero said. He was about to tell him to go away, but he couldn't quite form the words. Instead he stated the obvious. "You heard every word, didn't you?"

The wolf dipped his head.

"You're not going to leave me alone, are you?"

Head shake, no.

"Fine." He got up and headed for his computer. "Then you can sit right by me and watch while I see if that demon has started eating Wisconsinites again."

It took forty-eight minutes for Josh to change back to human. Nero felt the temperature drop in the air and knew immediately what was happening. He turned fast enough to see the golden shimmer right before Josh reformed as a man on all fours.

"For the love of God, watching you at a computer is like watching a toddler trying to do advanced math. Get out of the way." He grabbed on to the desk and hauled himself upright before pushing at Nero.

Normally Nero would refuse to vacate the chair out of stubbornness, but Josh was about to feel dizzy from shifting and needed to sit. So he jumped out of his seat and guided the man into it. And then before he could say anything, Josh put his hands to the keyboard and started typing. Nero tried to follow it, but windows kept popping up and then disappearing faster than he could follow. He gathered that Josh was coding something, but he didn't have the skills to understand it.

"I'll get you some soup."

"I don't need it," Josh grumbled.

"Watching you learn how to be a werewolf is like watching a toddler trying to cook dinner. You'll eat what I put in front of you or I'm taking away your screen time."

Josh turned to stare at him, his fingers momentarily stilled. Then he nodded. "I'll code, you get food. Deal?"

"Deal."

Then a female voice came loud and annoyed from the main living space. "You guys know that I can code and cook you both under the table, right?"

Nero looked back at Josh, who tightened his face into an "as-if" expression. Then, as one, they said, "Challenge accepted."

A moment later Josh went back to typing and Nero headed to kitchen. Stratos glared at him as he passed, her hand gripping a pen where it rested on Yordan's paperwork pile.

"I can't help you," he said softly. "Wiz has to—"

"Fuck you," she snapped. Then she abruptly closed her eyes and exhaled. "Sorry. I'm pissed, and I hate this. I hate everything about this."

Nero was about to say something, but Gelpack beat him to it. He hadn't even seen the alien in the room, but the guy straightened up from a chair and came to stand in front of Stratos.

"It is time for your appointment," he said. "Explain 'pissed' to me in as much detail as possible."

Stratos gaped at the gelatinous being, and for a moment Nero thought she would throw a punch. Instead, she stood up and got nose-to-nose with the alien. Then she bellowed, "Arg!" right in his face.

And Nero laughed—straight-out laughed—surprising everyone in the room, himself most of all. How the hell had he just found the right balance of quiet and noise?

Two weeks later, Josh blew up the lab.

Chapter 19

JOSH COULDN'T breathe, but that was only because he was coughing so much. He blew out weak puffs of air filled with the horrendous stink of chemicals fried into vapor or ash or whatever the crap it was that he was breathing.

A face came into view, which was startling really, because his eyes were watering so badly he couldn't see anything. But then Nero appeared in a blurry kind of way, as did the man's words through the high-pitched whine he'd been ignoring.

"Shift, you pyromaniac. Get human, right now!" Nero had that alpha note in his voice, so Josh struggled to comply. He'd really rather just lie here and keep trying to hack up a lung. But that was becoming too painful, so he might as well fix it.

He gathered his energy and moved back into his human body. It was a smooth transition now, thanks to lots of practice. And within a few eternities of effort, his body reformed and he could take a full, deep breath.

Then he started coughing again. Shit. Whatever was in the air stank enough that it made his human nose shudder in horror. What *was* that…?

Oh hell. He remembered. What stank was his new fire-resistant compound that had indeed kept his test dummy from being fried by Stratos and Laddin's favorite flamethrower. In fact, it had worked perfectly… up until the whole thing destabilized and went kaboom.

"Don't breathe," Josh rasped. "Toxic." He wasn't sure it was actually toxic, but there was no reason to take stupid risks. Or rather take *more* stupid risks.

"Yeah, we guessed," Nero answered. "That's why we hauled your mangy ass outside. And why the hell were you blowing shit up as a wolf?"

Because his senses were more acute as an animal. And part of testing was seeing how things affected the people using them. And the people who would use his fire protection were werewolves. Or they would have been using it… if it had worked.

"Stratos?"

"She's fine. You're the one everyone's worried about. You were closest to the boom. And what the hell are you doing making explosive compounds? You're supposed to be finding a way to survive a fire bomb, not create—"

"That *was* my fireproof compound," he growled. That shut up Nero long enough for Josh to roll onto his back and stare up at the grayish-blue plume of smoke that lifted into the blue Michigan sky. He saw a singed Stratos sitting a few feet away and Wiz looking murderously at him.

"You said it was safe," the magician snapped.

Yeah, he'd thought it was. But guilt made him snap back with a flippant response. "We're not dead."

"Because you were lucky!"

Yes, he was aware of that. Then his gaze caught on Stratos's as he studied her head to toe. She looked good in a charred, rumpled way. And when she realized he was looking, she gave him a gleeful thumbs-up. "I always wanted to be in an explosion," she said. "Now I can scratch that off my bucket list."

"Glad I could help," he returned. His voice was light, but he and Stratos had developed a shorthand in the days that they'd been researching together. He ducked his head in an apology, and she snorted and shrugged in an "it's all good" gesture.

Then she waved her hands at him. "What I won't recover from is seeing all your private bits out and dangling. Cover up, will you? A girl's got to eat, and no way can I erase that shriveled horror from my brain."

Oh shit. Yeah, he was lying here naked. Nero was ahead of Josh, though, already covering him with a blanket. Then, after a narrow-eyed look, he shrugged out of his sweatshirt to give to Josh.

"Can you sit up?"

"Yeah," Josh answered after one last weak cough. "I'm fine."

A few minutes later he was sitting up, sipping bone broth, and wearing Nero's sweatshirt, which no longer felt like putting on another blanket. Sometime in the past few weeks, he'd started filling out. And though Nero was always going to be broader and taller, Josh no longer felt like a ninety-pound weakling next to him.

He sipped his broth as others filtered by to check on him. Captain M and Happy gave him a stern and amused look, respectively, then went down to inspect the damage. Bing and Yordan walked past with barely a glance as they followed the captain. And Wiz shot him a final glare before taking Stratos inside to the stable wing of the mansion. That left him alone outside with Nero on what would have been a spectacular day, if he didn't look at the plume of smoke still wafting out from the blown-out windows of the lab.

"Josh…," Nero said, but Josh cut him off.

"Save it, okay? I know I fucked up. It happens. In fact, it happens a lot with me, so get used to it or send me packing. Obviously I'm not the guy to solve your problem. You picked the wrong geek to turn furry." God, never had words burned so badly in his mouth. He wanted to be the guy who fixed things, who had the answers, who came up with the tech that saved the day. Hell, he'd been getting off on the fantasy for weeks. It was what had kept him working deep into the night, and it was the bright image that filled his mind when the numbers didn't line up.

Except now he knew it was all a fantasy. He wasn't a brilliant chemist. He wasn't even a good one—just an unorthodox one who took stupid risks, pushed things beyond the safety limits, and had nearly vaporized himself and Stratos. God, he was such an idiot.

"You probably ought to send me home," he said glumly, knowing it was true but really, really hoping it wasn't about to happen.

"Yeah," echoed Nero as he adjusted himself behind Josh. It was the way they often sat after Josh shifted back to human. And though he didn't need a full-on orgasm to ground him back into his body, it was always nice to lean back into Nero's arms and let the big guy surround him. "I can see why you'd think that, but there's something you haven't factored in."

"Yeah? What's that?"

"No one thinks you're going to succeed. So when you blow up the lab, you're doing what they expect."

It took a moment to absorb that, but when he did, it felt like another punch to the gut. "Well, geez, thanks, Coach. Should I go slit my wrists now?"

Nero pinched his thigh hard in response.

"Ow!"

"Don't go getting all huffy. *Listen.*"

Josh rubbed the side of his thigh. "I can't hear you over the throbbing in my leg."

"Bullshit. You love that."

Well, maybe. Rough sex was one of the best parts about being a werewolf. Pain and pleasure mixed in a wild cascade of sensations, and if it ever got out of hand, they both healed fast. Plus, it never got *too* out of hand.

"Fine," he grumbled. "It's hard to hear over my *throbbing* lower parts." Which was true. His erection was already heavy against his thigh, and he wasn't wearing anything on his lower half except the heavy blanket. It would be so easy to start rubbing backward against—

"That's not what you need right now."

Undeterred, Josh pressed himself against Nero's hot cock. "Are you sure?"

"Would you stop? I'm about to tell you something you don't know."

"Ha. I know everything." It was a lie, obviously, but it felt good to settle into their usual banter where he was the smart one and Nero was the dumb jock. It wasn't remotely true. Nero was incredibly smart about people in a way Josh could only imagine, but it was nice to pretend. "Go ahead, Obi-Wan. Teach the young Padawan."

Nero didn't respond to the jibe. Instead, he continued as if Josh hadn't said a word. And that, too, was part of their pattern. "Did you know that the first werewolf in your line is still alive?"

"Bullshit," Josh said with a snort. "The first werewolf in my line was born in the early 1800s. I checked."

"Yes. And he and his mother are still alive." Nero leaned back against a bench, adjusting his position so that he had back support while still managing to tuck Josh close. "His mom is… different. She's the magical power in the line, and where she gets it from is well beyond my brain. But he—in his own words—was a screw-up from the very beginning."

Josh mentally ran through the early reports he'd read for a mention of his ancestors. There was a whole lot of hero worship for a guy named—

"Ever read anything about Wulfric and his mother, Lovina?"

"Of course. They were the ones who brokered the alliance between the fae and the shifters in the late 1800s."

Nero shook his head. "Yeah. They're still alive. She was born in the late 1700s. He was born in 1815, I think."

"No way."

"They mostly keep to themselves nowadays, only coming out when the shit really hits the fan. That means you may meet them sooner rather than later, the way things are going. Anyway, according to Wulfric, he screwed up everything he touched for a hundred years or more."

"That's modesty."

"No, it's fact. You know why we never do fairy deals?"

"Because fairies have their own agenda?"

"Because Wulfric screwed one over, and the fae have long memories."

"Ouch."

"The point is that—according to your own living, breathing ancestor—screw-ups are the only people who ever get anything done because they think differently. They don't see or don't count the risks, and everyone underestimates them."

"Which is a really fucked-up way to pick a teammate."

Nero chuckled, a tiny bounce in his chest that jostled Josh's head. "Yeah, well, he didn't pick you. I did. And I think the best way—the only way—you'll ever figure out the answer is if we all get out of your way. You included."

"You get that I just blew up the basement, right?"

Nero exhaled. "Yeah, I know. And it scares the shit out of me. But Josh, you've got to understand that we don't expect you to succeed, and that's why you will."

And wasn't that a clever turn of phrase? Too bad it did jack shit for his self-esteem. He didn't want to be a screw-up. He wanted to save the day for Nero. Because Nero needed a way to survive a demon fire blast, and Josh wanted to be the one to give it to him. But he couldn't. Not because he was a screw-up, but because he wasn't good enough.

"Josh—"

"Do you know why I love being a PhD student?"

"Because you like playing with things that go boom?"

"There's that, yes, but there's something else too." He took a deep breath and finally said the one thing he rarely admitted to himself, much less anyone else. "In a university lab, we fail 99.99 percent of the time. It's expected. We're trying new things and guess what's going to happen next. Most of the time we guess wrong. And even when we get it right, it's because we did something wacky, then looked backwards to figure out how it happened. Then we write the paper pretending that it was what we planned all along."

"And you call us screwed-up."

Josh snorted. "It's why I've never finished my dissertation. The minute I write my paper, I'll have to go out into the world where they expect me to succeed. Against ridiculous odds." He twisted to give Nero a dark glare. "And then you step into my perfect-ly wasted life and turn me into a werewolf where—bam—you want me to guess right against even more ridiculous odds. And you know what else? To make sure I really fuck it up, you put people's lives on the line. If I screw this up, good people die. Your pack died." Josh twisted to look at the thinning stream of smoke. "I'm not cut out for this."

Nero exhaled, his breath hot as it wended around Josh's ear and ruffled his hair. Then he said one word. "Okay."

That brought Josh around again so he could look Nero in the face. He even sat up to study the man's body in detail. Nero's expression was relaxed, his body hard, and his eyes taking on a slightly lascivious feel, probably because the motion had rubbed hard against his erection. But for the first time, Josh wasn't in the least bit interested in sex.

"That's it? 'Okay'?"

"Do you want me to try to talk you out of how you feel?"

"You can't. I suck."

Nero shrugged. "How about I suck you off instead?"

"What? Nero, didn't you hear me? Ever since that first night, you've been telling me that I was recruited to solve your demon blast problem. I've seen you hover outside the lab watching me. Hell, I've seen you praying—actual on-your-knees praying—that I find an answer yesterday. And now that I tell you I can't do it, you're all, 'let me suck you off'? How much of that smoke did you inhale?"

Nero rolled his eyes. "I wasn't praying. I was talking to…. There's this pompous fae prick I talk to sometimes. He likes it when I'm on my knees, begging for more time."

Josh waited a beat for Nero to explain, but nothing else came out. In the end, Josh had to push him both verbally and with a poke to his ribs. "You are going to explain that, right?"

"No, because there's nothing to tell. I saved the asshole's life in a bar fight once, and he owes me. Er, owed me. Past tense. Anyway, the fae honor their debts, but they do like it when you're on your knees asking them to pay up."

"There is way more to the story than that."

"Doesn't matter." Nero rubbed his hand over his face. "Josh, what do you think is going to happen when you figure out how to defeat the fire bomb?"

Josh frowned. It was pretty clear that Nero was hiding something, but Josh knew he wouldn't get more now. So he allowed the distraction and tried to look ahead to his future. So far his entire focus had been on figuring out magic and mixing it with chemistry. Even defeating the fire bomb was secondary to this beautiful new playground of alchemy, which he got to explore. Sure, he was working night and day to solve Nero's problem, but he was also learning such amazing things.

Nero squeezed Josh's arm and answered the question himself. "I take your solution and disappear. You…." He swallowed as his gaze cut back to the mansion. "*All of you* are going to have to decide on your future. Will you work with us or find a wolf pack somewhere else?" His jaw clenched as his eyes drooped and his hands fisted against Josh's hips. "This is an in-between time before everything gets reset. None of it is permanent. I want you to solve this problem, but even if you don't, it doesn't matter. It doesn't change…." He cut off his words, but Josh could all but read the rest off his lips.

"It doesn't change what you feel about me. You didn't expect to like me, did you? All of us were just another mission. A means to an end."

Nero nodded.

"But now you feel for us." He pressed the flat of his hand to Nero's chest. "You *feel*."

"I always felt, Josh."

"Grief. But what about love?"

Josh waited, but he could see it in Nero's face that he wasn't going to say the L word. The man's body was as hard as a stone as he locked his jaw shut. And Josh couldn't really blame him, because Josh wasn't exactly blurting out the word himself. Not in the real declaration kind of way. But that's what was throbbing in the air between them. Love and pain swirled together. Love because they cared for each other, because Josh wanted to solve Nero's problem and Nero wanted to make Josh feel better about utterly failing in his task. Pain because it was temporary. Pain because no matter what happened, they weren't going to have a happily-ever-after together.

"What if I stayed here," Josh said, "and didn't— you know—blow up the lab again. Then maybe we could keep seeing each other."

Nero blew out a breath, shaking his head with deliberate care. "I won't be here. Even if you are, I'll be… elsewhere."

"This is the twenty-first century. We could still talk on the phone, maybe meet up in sleazy gay bars and have hot sex in the bathroom."

"Never. And gross."

"Never because you're not a sleazy gay bar kind of guy?"

"Because *you* aren't."

"And gross because you can't see yourself with me after all this? Because I'm a screw-up, and not in a good way."

"It has nothing to do with that!" Nero snarled.

And for once Josh didn't rise to match Nero's hot tone. He didn't taunt him or fight him. Instead, he kept his voice level as he asked the next logical question. "Then what is it? Why can't we be together?"

"Because we can't." He blew out a frustrated breath. "I can't explain it to you." And when Josh opened his mouth, Nero cut him off. "I *can't* tell you. It's classified."

That shut Josh up. For a moment. And then he frowned. "My love life is classified?"

"My future is."

Oh. "Like special ops classified?"

"Sort of." Nero held up his hand. "Don't make me lie to you, Josh. Just believe me that I can't tell you the truth. I want to, but I can't."

Josh believed him. Nero looked too miserable to be lying. Which brought them back full circle. Josh was a screw-up who couldn't solve the problem, and Nero wasn't going to offer him a happily-ever-after. Hell, he wasn't even going to admit to the L word because the whole thing was a temporary fling.

What Nero was offering was a suck-fest, but for the first time in weeks, Josh wasn't interested. "I'm tired," he finally said. "Maybe I should get some sleep while Captain M figures out if she's going to fire me or not."

"She's not—"

"Nero, allow me the graceful exit, okay?" Josh pushed up to his feet, wrapping the blanket around his waist so he looked like he was wearing a skirt. Hell, could life get any more embarrassing?

Nero matched his movements, straightening up to his full height with the gracefulness that seemed to come naturally to the guy. "Josh, you're not hearing me."

Josh held up his hand. "If I keep listening, I'm likely to blow myself up on purpose. So please, do us both a favor and—"

"I'm not good with words. Not like you are. And I'm sure as hell not that good at talking about personal stuff—"

"Which is weird because up until today, you've always known what to say to me."

"Not true."

Okay, not exactly true. "*Eventually* you know what to say to me."

"So let me take another stab at this." He took a deep breath. "I need you to figure out the fire bomb thing."

"I tried!"

"But whether or not you succeed is…." He made a vague gesture with his hand. "It's completely irrelevant to how I feel. About you. About us." He took a step closer. "I want you to be happy. And if that means you have to blow up our basement, then okay. If that means you give up and go back to civilian life—"

"I don't want to leave!"

"Good. Because I don't want you to either." He squeezed Josh's arm. "Look, with everyone else, I'm always trying to read what they want, to be what they need so that I can lead them. It's not like that with you. This pack is temporary. It's until all of you figure out what you want to do. Which means I don't have to fill in for anyone's lacks. I don't have to adjust for their needs. I can be myself." His voice trailed away, and he looked at Josh, but damned if Josh understood what he was trying to say. "I'm myself with you, Josh. And you like me just as I am."

"Of course I do."

"There is no 'of course.' That's a big thing for me. That you like me—just me—even when I hover over you or pray to that asshole fairy. Hell, we watch movies together, and I'm even reading your stupid sci-fi books."

"Really? Which one?"

Nero waved it away. "I can relax around you because you don't want me to stop missing my old pack. You let me do as I want while you do what you want, and together…." He shrugged. "We fit."

"That's…." He almost said *love*, but a different word came out. "…friendship. That's packmates."

"I've had packmates before, Josh. This is different. This is…."

"Better?"

"Lots. And maybe it's new territory for me."

Josh nodded. "For me too."

"Okay. So yes, I want you to figure out that demon fire bomb thing, but more than that, I want to hang with you. To…."

"Suck my dick?"

Nero's cheeks grew ruddy. "You okay with that?"

"Yeah. You okay with me still trying to figure out the demon bomb thing?"

"Yeah. If you want to. It's an impossible task. No one expects you—"

"I heard. I'm a screw-up—"

"In the best possible way."

Josh nudged Nero with his shoulder. "That doesn't help, you know. All it does is make me want to meet my two-hundred-year-old ancestor."

"Join the crowd. We all want to hang out with him. He's got this… aura… thing going on."

Nero fell silent, and Josh did too. They had just stepped onto new ground together. Neither had said the L word, but they were both feeling the shift. Nero liked him whether or not he succeeded at defeating the fire bomb. That made Josh want to kick the thing in its ass all the more. And Josh liked Nero because the guy made him happy. They could relax together, be themselves, and have the greatest sex together.

Was that love? Maybe not yet, but they were getting there. At least until they were forced to separate because of whatever classified thing was going on. But suddenly that didn't seem like such a big a deal to Josh. Sure, it was a huge axe hanging over Nero's head. Obviously. But somehow Josh felt like he had the right screwed-up mind-set to figure that problem out too.

Call it an optimistic frame of mind. Finding their happily-ever-after would be his next task. Right after he defeated a demon's magical burning plasma. And speaking of which, Captain M and Happy were coming out of the lab.

"It's not as bad as it looks. Or smells!" Laddin said as he bounced onto the deck. He hefted the flame-thrower. "And she still works!" He fit words to action and blew out a long plume of flame.

"Stop that!" Captain M snapped. Then she looked at Josh. "Windows blew out, as you can see. But we'd been meaning to replace them anyway. There's chemical debris everywhere, and you're going to need a hazmat suit to clean it up, but it's only minor damage. The mansion has magical reinforcement, so the foundation and both wings are solid."

"I'm so sorry, Captain."

She accepted his apology with a quick dip of her chin. "Have you figured out what went wrong?"

Josh hedged. "I think so." He'd been mulling it over while still trying to cough up a lung. "I'll have to look at the readings to be sure. Did any of the computer equipment survive?"

Laddin grinned. "Sure did! I had your computer reinforced when you first starting testing with fire. It'll have to survive all sorts of stuff when you're taking it out into the field."

"He's not going into the field," the captain snapped. "He's dangerous enough right here," she added with a visible shudder.

"But his equipment might have to," Laddin argued. He'd been making noises about getting into field work, but the captain liked him right where he was, keeping her organized. "Or someone using his equipment. Someone like me—"

"No."

"We'll see." Laddin flashed him a wink. "So anyway, your computer was mostly protected from the blast behind the shielding."

"Which reminds me," Captain M interrupted. "Why, exactly, weren't you behind the safety perimeter?"

Because he'd been trying to see with his other senses—his animal senses. But clearly he needed to rely more heavily on the computerized ones. "My bad."

Her stare felt heavy. "Don't screw up like that again."

Laddin grinned. "Pick a different way next time. Eventually you'll run out of ways to be wrong and then you'll have the answer!"

Josh flashed the guy a quick smile. "I bet you subscribe to a dozen affirmation lists, don't you? Every day a dozen new ways to think positively."

Laddin responded in his usual manner: with a quick grin. "You should see my mug collection. Not a sour thought in sight!"

"He's not kidding, you know," Captain M said with a sigh. "He's already filled my office with positive attitude sticky notes." She rolled her eyes. "'Don't worry that Josh just blew up the basement. Be happy.' Gah." She stomped away.

"But it isn't a worry, is it?" Laddin said as he bounded after her.

"Of course it's a worry," the captain replied. "Every single one of you is a worry."

"But you shouldn't—" The back door shut on their banter.

Josh watched them go. "How long before she gets sick of him and tries to rip out his throat?"

"Not her," Nero answered. "Yordan'll crack long before she does."

"Nah. My money's on Bing." His gaze shot back to where Yordan and Bing were leaving the lab and heading out into the woods to practice. At first Josh had thought they were doing something illicit, but on the one day he'd followed them, all they'd done was practice. Martial arts moves, boxing moves, even some wrestling moves that thankfully his brother had never learned. And when they were done, Yordan went for a beer in the main kitchen and Bing wandered off to God only knew where. "Loners always crack first, and that guy is itching for a way to blow."

"Nah," Nero said, as he tugged Josh into the mansion. "Yordan's watching him. And besides, they'll be leaving soon for specialized training."

"What? Mr. Grumpy is leaving? Be still my heart."

Rather than smiling, Nero's expression faltered. "I told you. Pretty soon you'll all be leaving. Only a couple more weeks of training until you've each got a good handle on your wolf selves."

A couple more weeks. The words seemed to echo in Josh's head. A couple more weeks until this interlude with Nero was over. And it felt like they'd only just begun. The knowledge was like a ball of lead in his gut. It bothered him enough that he slowed his steps.

"I, um, I guess I better go clean up the lab. I need to look at the data and see exactly how the compound destabilized." He said the words as a way to escape back into his work. He already had a pretty good idea what had happened, but studying the numbers was better than facing the reality of his time with Nero ending forever.

"You could do that," Nero said, his voice gentle. "I'll even help you. But…."

Josh looked up. "But?"

"Well, you did take a pretty good conk on the head. Maybe you ought to rest a bit first. Or at least, you know, stay in your bedroom."

It didn't take long for Josh to understand his meaning. If his time with Nero was limited, shouldn't he try to make the most of it? "You want me to suck." He deliberately phrased the words with the double meaning.

"If you wouldn't mind." Nero grinned. "And maybe I can suck some too."

Josh snorted as he headed toward the house. "Oh, you're going to suck, all right. You're going to swallow me down like—mmph!" Suddenly he was in a choke hold with Nero wrapping him close to his chest and locking him in tight. Then the guy leaned close enough to speak straight into Josh's ear.

"I'll tell you what I'm going to do. And just how much you're going to love it."

His words were specific and had Josh hard as a rock beneath his blanket skirt. A few minutes later they were acting on every single word. Then, afterward, Nero wore a hazmat suit as he cleaned up the lab. Josh stayed close as he studied the data.

It took two more weeks, though, before he finally found a clue.

Chapter 20

NERO WAS living the best and the worst weeks of his life. Everything happened as he predicted. Josh attacked the fire bomb problem with renewed vigor. Nero made sure he ate and practiced being a wolf, and the shift-back-to-human sex was spectacular.

Bing and Yordan left for some specialized training. Laddin had been recruited for his bomb skills, but that same meticulous attention to detail really helped in organization. When he wasn't creating test fires in the lab, he was overhauling something he called Asset Management and Flow. All that was after he got over an existential depression, though. The day after Josh blew up the basement, Laddin ate a family of wild bunnies on a run. Apparently he'd had pet rabbits as a kid, and the knowledge that raw bunny tasted spectacular really threw the guy for a loop. Even Stratos found her place. She, Josh, and Wiz would spend hours together discussing magic theory and then doing experiments that usually resulted in fire, flood, or blood. Fortunately they kept the disasters contained. And besides, it gave them practice shifting to their wolves in order to heal.

And so the weeks passed. *Weeks* that Nero didn't have while his debt to the fairy bastard continued to grow. He owed more every day that Bitterroot kept the mulligan available, up to seven weeks.

To add to the bad news, the government blew up what used to be Lake Wacka Wacka (or whatever it was called), but the explosion hadn't stopped every living thing from dying within hours of touching the water, or what was now mud in a huge crater. That meant the demon was still alive, and it was sucking the life out of the area one inch at a time. The soil in a five-foot radius around the blast zone was thick with cyanide, and the toxicity wasn't decreasing.

That's what had everyone flummoxed. Whatever was killing the land was pouring out poison at an ever-increasing rate. Last week the dead zone around the lake and been four feet. This week the cyanide saturated five feet all the way around. Predictions said it would hit six feet by Thursday, and then seven a few days after that. It would get bigger and wider until the circle of death touched Lake Michigan. Cyanide would pour into the water and create an ecological disaster with global consequences.

Everyone was searching for a solution. The normals had experts of every kind examining and testing the area—government, military, CDC, NASA, everybody. The media was rife with theories that were no more or less plausible than what the paranormals thought, which was a big fat *we have no solution*. Prayers from the Religious Crew weren't helping. The fairies were noticeably silent, and the shifters couldn't do anything but growl.

And if someone didn't fix things soon, Wisconsin would be a wasteland by midsummer. And once the Great Lakes got touched, worldwide disaster was imminent.

As far as Nero was concerned, the only hope was his fairy mulligan, but that was dependent on finding a solution to that fire bomb. He was back, full circle, and all he could do was wait… and enjoy his ever-diminishing time with Josh. His seven-week deadline was nearly here, and whatever happened with the mulligan, Bitterroot would demand payment.

Time was running out. Which meant that all the warm and fuzzy things he was feeling were going to go through the shredder. For both of their sakes, he needed to dial back on the postshift sex-fests and start looking for a way to break with Josh so that neither of them invested more than was appropriate into their relationship.

That was the plan, at least. Except every time he got close enough to prepare his recruit for what was coming, he was also close enough to kiss that same recruit. And do so much more. Josh was always willing and often the initiator. It always felt too good to stop, and so the discussion got delayed and put off and forgotten. For a time.

Until the day Josh knocked on his bedroom door. The guy looked a mess. His hair flopped over his bloodshot eyes and his body sagged against the doorframe, but his grin nearly split his face wide open.

"Josh?"

"I've got the answer."

"Is it forty-two?" Josh had told him about his favorite sci-fi books from when he was a teen, and Nero had been enjoying geek humor in Hitchhiker's Guide to the Galaxy series.

Josh blinked twice and then immediately clapped. "You read a book! Good for you."

He had, but Josh liked to tease him about being a stupid jock, so he played the part to the hilt. "Nah. Streamed the videos," he said even though the paperback was clearly visible on his bedside table.

"Yeah, figures. But no, that's not the answer I meant." He dropped his head against the doorframe, and Nero realized that the guy really was exhausted.

"How late were you up last night?" They'd both headed for bed around two, but Nero knew Josh often kept working in his room. And since Josh was a full-grown adult, Nero didn't feel like he could assign a bedtime to the man, even though sometimes Josh really needed a keeper.

"Um, what time is it?"

"One. In the afternoon."

"Ah. There you go. I stayed up until one."

Nero pushed away from his desk. "You're going to burn out and get sick. Let's get you some lunch and then—"

Normally Josh flowed along when Nero grabbed his arm, but this time he refused to budge. "You're not listening," he interrupted. "I found the answer." And when Nero stared at him, Josh huffed out a breath. "I found the answer to magical plasma that burns."

Everything in Nero stilled. "As in what it is? Or—"

"I can defeat it."

"In a practical way? Like enough to keep a combat pack safe?"

Josh grinned with the most adorably goofy expression. "Yes. It's cooking now, so we'll need to wait eight hours—"

"Awroooo!" Joy exploded out of Nero in a howl. Finally he could kill that fucking demon. Finally he could use the damned mulligan and save his team. Finally he would close the chapter of his life that had been hanging open like a raw wound. Revenge, closure, and the end of an evil that was about to suck up Wisconsin—he'd have it all. And most of all, he'd have his team back, healthy and whole! He could be with them again. They'd have a barbecue, they'd run in the snow, and he'd tell them everything—

"There are some details that need to be worked out."

Of course there were. Didn't matter. Josh would figure it out.

"And we'll have to construct a framework for the compound."

No big surprise. "But… it'll work?"

"I think so."

"Then you're a genius." He surged forward and kissed Josh hard. He wrapped the man in his arms, and he ravished his mouth in the most primal way he knew how. And when they broke to catch their breath, he gasped for a few seconds before going in for more.

Forget food, he thought as he hauled Josh into his bedroom. He was going to thank the man in the best way he knew how. And after he had wrung as much pleasure as possible from their bodies, he was going to gather his lover into his arms and break his heart.

Their time together was done, perhaps as soon as tomorrow.

Because while Josh spent his time constructing his magical-plasma-fire-defeating weapon, Nero needed to work out a new attack plan. One that he could tell his team in the short minutes they had before the attack. He wanted nothing left to chance.

And nothing—not even more time with Josh— would stop him from saving the lives of his pack.

Chapter 21

JOSH CAME awake slowly. His body felt languid, and his heart sang with happiness. He smelled Nero on the sheets, on his body, and in every part of his soul. Nero was part of him now, and he opened his eyes to find the lover who so pleased him.

He wasn't disappointed. The man was sitting at his desk, and as Josh watched, the guy popped the last bite of a sandwich into his mouth and grinned.

"Any left for me?" Josh asked, his voice rusty.

"You want a ham sandwich?" He held out a plate obviously set aside for him. "Or I could make you a burger."

"Sandwich." He'd actually prefer a burger, but he knew Nero would go make it, and he didn't want his lover to leave. So he sat up and grabbed what was offered while Nero stretched his feet out onto the bed.

Josh took the cue and snuggled against the guy's huge foot. In the five and a half weeks they'd been together, he'd learned that Nero might pretend to be standoffish, but he liked connecting somewhere: a foot, a hand, or the "accidental brush" against his back. Since Josh loved touching the big man, he wasted no time in snuggling against whatever body part was nearest. Even when they were out in the main room, they managed to bridge the space between them somehow so they felt each other, even when it looked like they were just sitting near each other on the couch.

Nero waited while Josh started gulping down food. He even had a water bottle nearby, which he tossed to Josh with practiced ease. And though Nero's expression was calm, Josh knew he was impatient. He spun the empty plate on his lap around and around. And he watched Josh eat like he was counting the bites.

"You don't have to stare at me," Josh said. "Ask."

"The weapon," Nero said almost right on top of Josh's words. "Tell me about the weapon that's going to destroy that bastard demon."

Josh frowned. "I didn't design a weapon." He polished off the water bottle and tossed it into the recycle bin. "Is that what you thought I was doing all this time?"

"You made something to defeat the plasma fire."

"I didn't *make* it, I designed it. There's still a lot of testing involved, but it's a beginning."

"It's the whole enchilada, Josh. What did you make?"

Josh stretched out his arms, clearly proud of himself. "I created a compound that will concentrate the fire away from the attack team."

Nero's eyes brightened. "Tell me how to deploy it, where we need to be. Everything."

Now came the hard part: talking about the disaster that had killed his team. Over the past five and a half weeks, they'd discussed everything but that. The minute Josh brought the subject up, Nero found a way to distract him, usually with sex or a wolf romp in the woods. Eventually Josh had learned to avoid the subject, though he knew Nero daily tracked the expansion of what he'd dubbed the Wisconsin Cyanide Hole. He said he was looking for data on the creature. Plus, he occasionally slipped and made a reference to some deal with a fairy. He'd immediately deny having anything to do with those magical bastards, but Josh knew he was lying. His voice lost its resonance when he lied, but Josh hadn't pushed. He knew how delicate the subject was.

So instead of talking with Nero, Josh had studied the images, Stratos had dug up every weird fable or tale relating to demons who could blow fire, and Wiz had given him a crash course in magic.

"It works like this," Josh said. "Plasma fire eats living tissue the same way fire eats wood."

"We know that—"

"But we didn't realize that it concentrates on tissue, burning in one direction, until it eats up the fuel. Then it continues on in the same vector."

Nero stared at him. "What?"

Josh grimaced. There was only one way to explain this. He squeezed Nero's foot. "Do you think you can look at the pictures of the blast radius? After your team—"

Nero tapped twice on his computer and the images popped up. Which meant he had them cued up and available whenever he wanted them. At Josh's surprised look, Nero shrugged.

"Yeah, I look at them. Whenever…." He sighed and his gaze wandered over to that stack of team pictures still piled in the corner.

"Whenever you start to feel happy?" Josh asked. "Like you could move on without them?" He knew he was a temporary body for Nero, a way to feel good while still grieving. And maybe they'd grown to be friends. He certainly felt friendship—and a whole lot more—for the guy. So it hurt to realize that every time Nero started to move to a different place emotionally, he purposely dragged himself back into despair. They'd never grow to be more than friends if Nero kept himself stuck in his grief.

Nero's gaze snapped back to Josh. "I need to kill that demon."

"And will that make you feel better?"

"Yes."

"You know it doesn't work that way. Revenge—"

"It's not revenge, it's a second chance." Nero picked up his laptop and dropped it on the bed between them. "Now show me want you want me to see."

What he wanted was for the guy to feel better, but obviously that wasn't happening. So with a grimace, Josh tapped through the images until he found the one he wanted. It was the picture of a black ash smear in the vague shape of a wolf and the silhouette of greenish grass behind him.

"Coffee."

Josh nodded, knowing that the smear had been the werewolf codenamed Coffee. He pointed to the image and explained what he'd figured out. And it had only taken him weeks of staring at that stupid patch of grass when everything else had been scorched earth. "I couldn't figure out why this grass was still alive when everything else was dead. But then I realized that the fire concentrated here, where there was fuel." He pointed to where Coffee's nose would have been. "It continued down this way." He stroked his finger down the length of what would have been Coffee's body. "And then burned outward from his tail, leaving this part untouched."

He looked up at Nero's face, hoping to see understanding there. Instead, the man just shook his head. "I don't—"

"Try this." He started tapping on Nero's laptop, pulling up his own files from the server and then scrolling through them as he talked.

"This is how the fire burned from the instant of explosion." He tapped a key and showed a slow-moving progression of the blast, complete with arrows. "See how it concentrates over everyone's body, burns through them, then continues on in a narrow point from the back side?"

He looked to Nero. Shit, the guy was about to lose it. Watching in slo-mo as his entire team was decimated had to be brutal.

"Never mind—" he said, but Nero grabbed his hand.

"What does it mean?" he rasped.

"That the fire concentrates over tissue and leaves what's underneath it untouched. So the grass here is clean. And here. And here."

He pointed at every single gray-greenish patch. They were all hard to see because the heat of the fire had torched the grass, but it looked different in those vague smears. Like the echo of a shadow. And it had led to his realization.

"Okay, now look. If we put a dense tissue in front of Coffee, angled up and back, then the fire will burn—"

"Over him."

Josh added a heavy, thick arrow-shaped thing to the simulation and set it directly in front of Coffee like a shield. Sure enough, the fire burned through the arrow, then sheeted over Coffee, leaving the wolf scorched but alive.

"It's a one-shot deal, of course. Once the compound is consumed, there isn't any more protection."

Then he clicked back to the slo-mo simulation. This time Josh put a shield thing in front of each of the wolves. He hit a key and the blast began again, but this time the fire got really intense in front of the wolves, but then sheeted over them. Every single one of the team remained alive.

The simulation finished, and Josh looked up at Nero, hoping to see understanding. Nope. What he got was a slow, silent blink before Nero tapped the key.

The simulation started again, burned through, and once again, the team was left standing.

Again. And again. And again.

Over and over, he stared at what had never happened: a team who survived the attack.

"Stop torturing yourself," Josh whispered as he tried to bring the laptop around. Nero grabbed his wrist, stopping him from touching the computer. "Nero—"

"Thank you," Nero said, his voice cracking. Tears were shimmering in the guy's eyes, and the air felt thick with emotion.

"I know it's too late for them, but—"

Nero shook his head, cutting off Josh's words. Then he pointed at the screen. "Build," he ordered.

"It's already cooking. I've made it as dense as I possibly can, but we need to test it."

"There isn't time. Make as much as you can. We'll figure out the rest in the field."

"No, you won't." Josh was horrified by the thought. Computer simulations were one thing, but actual tests were a thousand times better. "Besides, that's not the only problem. The heat will be intense. The wolves will have to be covered head to toe in something heat-resistant."

"Volcax."

Josh's stomach clenched at the mention of his father's fabric. On some level, he'd always known that any type of fire protection would involve his father's fabric. But to be faced now with the reality gave him a punch to the gut, because anything having to do with his father gave him that reaction.

"Yes." No use denying the obvious. There wasn't anything better. He should know—he'd spent years in the university trying to invent something better. "But the military has his stuff locked up tight. He can't sell it to anyone else without risking prison."

Nero shook his head. "He'll give it to you. To his son."

Josh snorted. "No, he won't. He didn't give the stuff to my brother, Bruce, and Bruce is a firefighter."

Nero wasn't listening. He had tapped the keyboard again and was watching his entire team survive. Josh sighed, his heart twisting in his chest. This was too much for his trainer/lover/alpha. He should have brought it to Captain M first. But he'd been so happy to have finally figured it out that he'd naturally gone to the one who cared the most. The one *he* cared about the most.

"Never mind," he said as he pushed up from the bed. "I'll go talk to—"

"I'm thinking," Nero said as he grabbed Josh's arm. "How do we deploy this? Is it just a digital arrow-like thing, like here?"

"I've got the specs." He clicked on his design. "I put the compound on a lightweight structure. Think of it like a cone-shaped shield. Carry it to where you want it and plop it down."

"Like a small shelter."

"Yes." Josh clicked over to some graphs that Nero didn't bother reading. "You said you felt the buildup in energy right before the blast."

"Yes. I was already shifting then, but it definitely took a few moments for the blast to go off."

"This is a picture of what it looks like when Wiz shoots off a fireball. See the readings build here? My guess is that the right equipment can see the blast coming as much as twenty seconds before it goes."

"Twenty seconds? A werewolf can cover a lot of distance in that time. If I can warn them ahead of time, then they can get behind the shield."

"Exactly. Then the worst of the blast will shoot over everyone."

"And your father's fabric will keep us alive through the heat."

Right. Except that they'd never get their hands on the fabric, but rather than repeat what he'd said before, Josh focused on the other complications. "Then there's all the normal fire blast problems, plus a zillion other problems I haven't thought of. But this is the beginning—"

"How long? How long do you need to get these shields built?"

"I've got one that should be cooled enough now. Just one. *To test.*"

"Then what we need are blankets of your father's material."

"Not a blanket. Long jackets like a doggie sweater with a hoodie. It's too hard for a wolf to flatten out beneath a blanket in twenty seconds." He should know. He'd tried.

"But your father can make that, right?"

"Of course he can. But he won't—"

"He will. We'll pretend to be from the military."

Josh sighed. "Fine, you work on that." Let Nero find out the hard way that it was a useless endeavor. His father triple-checked everything and wasn't one to be duped by fake papers. "I'll go back to testing—"

"No. We'll go now. Best if we surprise your father with an urgent demand from a desperate son."

Ice slid hard and sharp through Josh's veins. "No," he said flatly. "I'm not going, and I'm not talking to *him* about *this*."

"Why not?"

Josh struggled to put his objection into words. Unfortunately, every response was clouded by emotion. As a kid, he'd admired his father's efficient business discipline. The man was precise and had an iron fist of control that didn't allow for mistakes. But that was also coupled with constant criticism about how Josh had never measured up. He wasn't fast enough, strong enough, *manly* enough—by his father's own definition of manliness. He didn't even want to imagine the guy's response to finding out Josh was gay. It would probably be something along the lines of how it made sense because Josh had always been a prissy, finicky, indoor boy.

What he'd actually been was a kid with a delicate stomach who didn't like getting beaten up by his older brother, Bruce, and his friends. "Take someone else if you have to. Believe me, he won't give me anything but grief."

"What happened between you and your father?"

"He's an asshole! He hates everything I am. I'm finally *happy*, and he's going to find a way to ruin it!" It was a childish reaction, but that didn't make it any less real. All he'd have to do was step through the front door and he'd be seven years old again, being scolded because he'd let another boy take his new Colts baseball cap. The kid had been two years older, twice his size, and apparently had a real hard-on for a football team that hadn't found Peyton Manning yet. "I do not want him in my life!"

Of course, Nero had no problem pointing out the ridiculousness of still letting his father destroy him emotionally. "You're a full-grown adult, Josh. More important, you're a werewolf now—"

"And a wolf doesn't let anyone push him around, right? A werewolf stands tall and doesn't take shit from anyone. And if he does, he makes the bastard pay, right?"

Nero frowned, obviously not understanding Josh's bitter tone. "Uh… yeah."

"That's exactly what my father used to say about being a man, and it's bullshit. A man ought to be able to *think* of a better way of living than beating up anything he doesn't like."

"So *think* of a better way to deal with your father."

"You said I could never reconnect with my family. That I should just cut them out of my life. Was that bullshit?"

Nero swallowed and his gaze canted away. "It's truth, but we need that fabric, Josh. And FYI, I've been trying to get it for weeks now. You're my last hope."

"Then you're screwed." Josh pressed his fists tight to his chest to keep himself from punching Nero in the face. "My father responds to one thing: force. And unless you're going to let me go wolf on him and scare the shit out of him, then I suggest you start looking for a different way to get the fabric you want."

Nero's gaze went cold. "Look at you, Josh. You've got more power than you've ever had before in your life. More strength, speed, and stamina. You're a living magical creature. And yet here you are, reduced to a child throwing a tantrum at the thought of asking your father for help."

"This from the man whose family still thinks he's in lockup!" Josh leaned in and got straight in Nero's face. "You told me to ditch my family. You told me that it wasn't worth the pain—"

"And you said you weren't going to cut them out of your life entirely. You said you would find a different way."

Josh shook his head, feeling betrayal cut deep inside. "This isn't about me at all," he said. "This is about you getting the fabric. About your revenge and being too impatient for a better—"

"We're out of time." Nero's voice dropped to a deep tone all the more frightening for how calm it seemed. "*I'm* out of time." He took a deep breath as he pushed to his feet. "You're more powerful than you've ever been before in your life, but that's dangerous unless you control yourself. Not just physically but emotionally. Face your demon father, Josh, so I can take out the demon that killed my team." He tossed Josh his pants. "We leave in an hour."

"And what if I don't control myself?" Josh asked. "What if I go wolf and rip out the guy's throat?" It was a real possibility. There'd been times in his life when, if he'd had the ability to kill his father, he absolutely would have.

"I'll be there to stop you. And then we'll have to convert the rest of your family to werewolves to keep the secret contained."

Josh snorted. "Sure you would," he drawled. "Because anybody can be a werewolf."

Nero's brows raised in a mocking gesture. "Think, Josh. Use that big brain of yours. How did we know that you were a werewolf?"

It took a moment for him to remember, and then his eyes widened in horror. "No."

"Yeah. You're a direct descendant of werewolves, most of whom don't even know what they are. So no, we can't convert *anybody*, but we've got a pretty good shot with your father, your brother, and your sister."

Hell, why hadn't he thought about that before? When he looked at his family tree, why hadn't he realized that every single one of them could be a werewolf like him? "But you've got a less than 30 percent survival rate. If you convert them, two will likely die." And with Josh's luck, the only one to keep breathing would be his stubborn ass of a father. "You can wipe their memories."

Nero shook his head. "It doesn't work well on werewolves, even the ones who have never manifested." He arched a brow. "Does that make you think twice about going wolf on your father?"

Of course it did.

"Then maybe you should think of a way to get his help without reverting into a sullen, stubborn child."

Chapter 22

WHEN HAD he become one of those do-as-I-say-not-as-I-do people? Nero stared out at the Indiana freeway and tried not to feel like a shit as Josh glared out at the same flat landscape. Nero didn't know if forcing Josh to face his father was the right thing to do. Every recruit had family issues, and generally, Nero thought it was best to leave them in the past. But over the last six weeks, he'd realized how very ugly Josh's childhood had been. For some unknown reason, he'd been the family whipping boy. His father had blamed him for everything, his brother had enjoyed tormenting him, and his mother and sister had turned a blind eye to it all.

Which meant Josh's family wound was a great deal bigger and darker than anyone had guessed, and maybe it needed to be confronted instead of swept under the table. Because stuff that big never stayed under the table. In short, Josh had to face down the demon of his father's bullying before he could step into everything he was meant to be and do.

But the real reason he was pushing Josh so hard was because Nero needed to save his team now. He had a few more days until the fairy mulligan disappeared forever. A couple more days and all of this would be over, one way or another.

Plus, he'd already tried to get the special fabric. He'd done the research weeks ago and realized that the only stuff that had a prayer of working was Volcax. Except every attempt to get his hands on some had been rebuffed. He had to admire the company's security measures. Even the burglary attempt was foiled. Which meant the only person who could get some under-the-table Volcax was Josh.

So Nero had used the nearest excuse he could find to force that to happen. Just because it might be good for Josh didn't change the real reason Nero was doing it.

If only he could tell Josh the truth. If only he could break the thrice-cursed fairy contract on this one issue alone. He needed to tell someone, because lying to Josh was killing him. He needed to tell Josh the truth about why he was pushing so hard. He needed to say that despite all intentions, he'd bonded to Josh. No one had said the L word, but it was there like a big, fat accusing finger pointed straight at Nero.

He loved Josh, and that was going to kill him when he reset the timeline. Because the minute he went back in time and saved his team, all of this—everything he had with Josh—would disappear. And then how the hell was he going to go on? Because somehow Josh had become as important to him as his team, and he couldn't have both.

He was fucking tired of losing everyone he held dear.

He shoved that thought away. He had a mission here, and the deep-down ache in his soul wasn't going to go away if he spent the miles brooding on it. Right now his mission was to get that fabric. Then he'd get Bitterroot to duplicate the shelter thing that was right now sitting in his trunk and activate the mulligan. Fairy magic couldn't create solutions, but it could duplicate an existing design. That's why the fae needed humans. They didn't have the imagination humans did, but once someone thought of a solution—someone brilliant like Josh—the fae could recreate it.

He'd always known that Josh would find an answer when no one else could. The guy obviously excelled at thinking outside of the box. The thought almost made him smile, but then he saw the first exit sign for Indianapolis and felt Josh stiffen so tight, he thought the guy's bones might break.

Five minutes later Josh turned to him, his expression stony. "You missed the turnoff to the factory."

"We're going to your home."

"The hell we are."

"It's Sunday, Josh. Your father is at home."

He watched Josh absorb that with the confusion suffered by all new recruits. Training occurred on a remote estate where every day melded into the next.

Everyone lost track of time. And given how Josh buried himself in his work, Nero wasn't at all surprised that the guy had no idea what day it was. He probably didn't remember what month it was, but Nero didn't bother pointing that out. Instead, he gently tried to bring Josh back into the real world.

"What does your family usually do on Sundays?"

"Church. Dinner. ESPN."

Nero glanced at the clock. "So we'll find them at dinner."

Josh didn't respond. His eyes grew vague as he once again stared out at the landscape, and Nero couldn't shake the feeling that a time bomb was ticking. Reuniting with family was the hardest thing any new recruit did, which is one of the reasons Nero had avoided the whole thing. But Josh needed to do it, and Nero needed the Volcax. So off they went to Sunday dinner while Nero prayed he could find a way to defuse the bomb building inside Josh.

"Do you want to talk about—?"

"No. I want to get in and out. No talk, no food, no nothing. Beg for the fabric, get refused, and then we can leave."

"We have to make this work, Josh. I've tried other ways, and they failed. You're my last hope."

There was silence as Josh processed that. And while Josh's jaw hardened to granite, Nero pushed it a little further. "You said you refused to give up your family, remember?"

"You said it was a bad idea, remember?"

Nero sighed. "I might have been wrong."

Josh glared at him. "Might?" Nero shrugged, and Josh eventually turned away. "You're a fucking asshole, you know that?"

Nero couldn't argue. And as they did the loop around the city and headed toward the suburbs, Josh repeated his intention in a muttered growl.

"We get in, then get out. That's it."

That wasn't going to work and they both knew it. In the history of mankind, no visit home ever went "get in, get out." There were always emotional notes, but there was nothing to be gained by pointing out the obvious, so Nero said nothing.

He took the turnoff, following the GPS directions to a middle-class neighborhood that was showing its age. The houses here were generally built in the seventies. Some looked spruced up with new paint jobs or nice landscaping, and others were less well-maintained. Many had melting snowmen in the front yard and a few still had their Christmas decorations up. The Colliers' family home was clearly the best one, with neat flower beds under the patchy snow and a US flag out front proudly waving over St. Patrick's Day decorations. He'd bet his next paycheck that Josh's mother had homemade treats for Halloween, Christmas gifts for the delivery people, and probably dyed eggs for the neighborhood Easter egg hunt.

They pulled into the driveway behind a big truck, and Josh groaned. "Goody. Bruce is here." The sarcasm was heavy, and Nero wondered just what Josh's older brother had done to earn such animosity. According to the file, Bruce was a stand-up guy: a firefighter with a commendation for bravery.

Nero pulled in beside the truck, and as he shifted the car into Park, he confessed one of his lesser sins. "You should know they've been told the usual thing about your disappearance."

Josh pinned him with a heavy stare. "And that is?"

"Vague. You've been at a retreat center." The exact words were *specialized treatment facility*, but he didn't want to say that. Depending on the family, the words could be interpreted as a hospital stay or yoga retreat.

"Awesome," Josh said, his tone heavy with sarcasm. Then he got out of the car and walked up to the front door as if he was facing a firing squad. Jeez, what had gone on behind the Collier family closed doors that had turned his exuberant, exasperating, *animated* lover into this sullen pile of anger? Once they made it to the front door, Josh couldn't seem to ring the doorbell. So Nero pushed the button, then stepped aside so that Josh would be the one slouching front and center when the door was finally pulled open.

First thing Nero noticed was the scent of pot roast and fresh bread wafting out of the house. The second was a fit twentysomething woman with stylish short hair and large brown eyes. According to the file, Josh's sister, Ivy, was an Army nurse on deployment, but she was obviously home now. More important, she was staring at Josh as if she was looking at a ghost.

"Josh," she mouthed without any sound. Then she abruptly launched herself into his arms with a delighted cry. He caught her, his expression dumbfounded. And when she pulled back, she spun around and said, "Everybody! It's Josh!"

"Ivy," Josh breathed. "What are you doing home? You're not due until…."

She turned back to him with a laugh and playfully punched him in the arm. "Until two weeks ago, meathead. You missed my party!"

"No, you're back early," Josh argued.

She snorted, but there was worry in her eyes. "Just what kind of drugs did they give you in that hospital? My party was Friday. You missed it."

Josh frowned, clearly confused, but he didn't have time to say more as his mother came bustling forward. Her hair was dark, but the gray roots were showing. She wore an apron over a dress, and her face was all smiles.

"Josh, you should have called! I would have made up your bed. How are you feeling, honey?" She wrapped him up in a hug that carried a cloud of White Shoulders perfume and pot roast that Nero could smell from three feet away. And when she pulled back from Josh, her light brown eyes scanned him from head to toe.

Meanwhile, the men had shown up. Bruce came first, his square frame and green eyes sharp as he lounged against the doorframe. "The prodigal son returns," he drawled. "Guess the funny farm did you some good. You're looking strong."

Nero winced. Obviously Josh's family thought *retreat* meant mental hospital.

Josh's mother whipped around, casually thudding Bruce in the chest. "Stop it. We're not teasing about his medical problem—no matter what it is. Do you understand me?"

Bruce dipped his head. "Yes, ma'am."

Then came the patriarch. Josh's father ambled forward, and the sunlight made his hazel eyes seem bright blue above his square jaw and thick neck. The werewolf genes were obvious to someone in the know: in his spiky hair, all a dark brown, and the toothy way he smiled.

"Don't stand there letting all the heat out," the man groused. "I pay good money for that. Josh, if you're coming in, then come in. Tell us where you've been and what you've been doing." He chuckled as he spoke the seemingly innocent words, but Nero heard an edge of meanness there. After all, the family thought Josh had been in a mental institution, so his words couldn't be anything but a jab.

They all hurried into the house, Nero included. There was lots of hustle as Josh and Nero shed their coats and hung them up in a tidy closet in a neat entryway of a very clean two-story house. And that was all the time it took for Josh to finally process everyone's words. He drew in a sharp breath, then turned to Nero with an accusing glare.

"You told them I was in a hospital?"

"Nope. We told them that you were in a specialized retreat center, that you were undergoing a very specific treatment regimen and could not have visitors or outside contact of any kind." It was the family who had gone straight to *mental hospital*.

Josh gaped at him, and Nero could hear the tick, tick, tick of the Josh time bomb speeding up. His eyes flashed fury, but he didn't talk to Nero. Instead, he turned to his family and spoke slowly and clearly. "I was not hospitalized."

"Technically, you were," Nero added.

Josh shot Nero a glare. "I was—"

"Resting and recovering from the stresses of your program of study."

"Bullshit!"

His mother tsked sharply. "Mind your language," she said, though the words sounded like a reflex rather than intention.

Josh didn't even look her direction. "I was not hospitalized," he repeated loudly. "I was—"

"Performing a classified task in a classified facility."

Wulf, Inc. had a protocol when a recruit was introduced back to the family. The idea was to confuse the nearest and dearest with as much bullshit as possible such that no one knew what was real and what was teasing. And this was a game that Nero usually played to perfection.

He smiled genially at everyone. "Hello. I'm Nero Bramson, and I'm Josh's friend. He's not ready to drive yet, so I thought I'd help him out and play chauffeur."

"Not ready to drive!" Josh sputtered, and Nero flashed him a megawatt smile. It was the absolute truth—not because Josh was incapable but because they weren't going to let him escape yet. Not before the demon that was eating Wisconsin was destroyed.

Josh knew this, and it clearly pissed him off. But it was also a moment for the man to choose. Did he give the truth to his family—in which case they'd all be converted to werewolves and they'd see who survived—or go with the cover story that they so obviously believed?

Tick, tick, tick.

Josh picked the cover story. "Yeah," he said, bitterness heavy in his tone. "Nero's my driver."

"I prefer chauffeur."

"I prefer asshole."

"Ain't that the truth," Nero teased as he waggled his eyebrows, which was a really dickish thing to say. But it was the kind of thing that guys said about one another all the time, and Josh had long since proved that he could sling the shit along with everyone else.

Except Josh didn't react as usual. His face burned red-hot, a telltale sign of truth if ever there was one. There was a moment of stunned silence all around, and then his father abruptly growled, "It figures."

Obviously Dad was a homo-hater. No big surprise there. What did startle Nero was Josh's mother, who turned white as a sheet. She gaped at Josh and had to steady herself on the wall.

Ivy groaned, "Oh, great," and then she grabbed her mother's elbow and steered the woman into the kitchen. "Let me help you with the green bean casserole."

Bruce was the only one who appeared unaffected. He stood there, his gaze heavy as it hopped back and forth between Josh and Nero. It was a shrewd look, and Nero became aware that Josh wasn't the only smart one in the family. And what was Josh's reaction to all this? Nothing except for the heat from his bright red face.

A beat. Then another. And then his father turned and thudded to his seat at the head of the dining room table, dropping into it with a grunt. Without looking up, he poured diet soda into his glass, crushed the can with his bare fist, then banged the can down on the table in one of the best displays of passive-aggressive fury Nero had ever seen. All the man had done was pour his soda and crush the can, but every action filled the air with hatred. Then he looked up at Josh with a hot stare and gestured to a seat at the end of the table.

"Pull up a chair. Tell us how the stress of not working a damn day in your life has turned you into someone who sucks dick."

"Dad!" Bruce huffed out in a fair imitation of his mother's admonition, but Mr. Collier turned his darkening eyes on his elder son and merely glowered. To Bruce's credit, he held his ground with a raised chin. "That's not how it works."

"Really?" his father drawled. "Then tell me how it works, Josh," he said, completely dismissing his eldest son. "Sit down at my table in my house, eat my food, and tell me how you ended up gay."

Ouch. And didn't that make Nero feel like shit? He'd just been stirring the pot, throwing all sorts of things at the family to keep them confused. That was protocol. But he hadn't realized how badly everyone would react.

Hell. He'd screwed up big time. He should have realized that here, in the heart of the Midwest, Josh's family might be more homophobic than Nero's own relatives in Florida. And he should have realized that just because werewolves were very open sexually, it wasn't the same among vanilla humans. That was part of the reason he avoided time among the vanilla. He forgot how narrow-minded they could be.

He had to fix this fast, and the only way he could think of to do that was to confess the absolute truth.

"We're a secret military organization, and we needed Josh's help. We abducted him, trained him, and now he needs your help to save the world." Not an exaggeration and definitely going to get his ass in deep shit if any of the higher ups found out what he'd said. "Everything else was bullshit. That's the truth."

Josh gaped at him, clearly understanding how many rules Nero had just broken. "You can't tell them that."

No shit. But he didn't say that. Instead, he shrugged and tried to communicate without words how very sorry he was.

Josh understood. At least his eyes got soft for a moment before he squared his shoulders and addressed his father. "We're not staying to eat. We're here because we need some Volcax." He jerked his head at Nero without looking at him. "He'll pay you well for it, but we need it now."

Nero didn't miss the "pay well" part, but he had no room to argue. And though there was a limit to what Wulf, Inc. would fork over, Nero wasn't going to quibble over a few thousand dollars. Or tens of thousands, as the case may be.

"What?" gasped Nero's mother as she came through the kitchen doorway carrying a casserole dish. "What do you mean you're not staying?"

Josh turned to his mother, and from this angle, Nero got to watch Josh's profile as he all but begged his mother to understand. "I can't, Mom. We came for Volcax. Rush order. Super secret. Have to get back to—"

"The lab. Yes, so you always say." She lifted her chin as she set down the dish on the table. "Well, whatever the reason, your father can't get it while he's eating. So you will sit right down there and join us. Your… friend too." Her voice broke on the *friend* part. Clearly she was uncomfortable with the idea that he and Josh could be lovers, but she was trying. And then, lest he think he'd distracted her from the main secret, she pressed ahead. "And you will explain to me where you have been all this time. Savannah came here last month worried sick. We all were."

Mr. Collier reached out and patted his wife's hand. "He's here now. He's fine. You can stop worrying."

She turned to stare at her husband and her jaw tightened with anger. No words were spoken, but Nero could hear them, even without the sounds. *He's not fine. He's gay.*

Ivy came out with two extra place settings and quickly made up seats for Josh and Nero. And when Josh stuck out his hand to stop his sister, she hissed to him under her breath.

"Sit. Eat. *Talk* to them instead of running away."

Josh's gaze landed heavy on his sister, but she didn't so much as flinch. And again, the subtext was easy to read off Josh's face. His expression said, *Why? It always ends the same way.*

Ivy wasn't buying it, and as she pulled out a chair for her baby brother, Josh gave in. Then Ivy gestured for Nero to sit as well. He took the seat next to Josh and smiled warmly at Mrs. Collier.

"Thank you so much for sharing your meal with me. And to answer your question, Josh has been in a classified facility—"

Bruce interrupted. "Doing classified work. You said that before, but we need specifics. Exactly who are you and—"

"Unfortunately we can't say, and it will do no good to press Josh. I'm here to make sure he doesn't spill the beans." He gestured to the spread of food. "This smells fabulous, Mrs. Collier."

"Well, um, thank you," Josh's mother said. Again, it was an automatic response when her mind was clearly on Josh. But at least it got her to sit down. And as Ivy took her seat as well, everyone linked hands for prayer.

Everyone, that is, except Josh, who glared at Bruce's upturned hand like it was a venomous snake. But when everyone stared at him, Nero included, he snatched his brother's hand in a white-knuckled grip. In contrast, he barely touched Nero, extending his last two fingers to interlink with his. No-go. Nero used his werewolf reflexes to snatch Josh's hand fully and hold it upright as if he was in a revival tent praising Jesus with all his might.

Mr. Collier went through the Sunday prayer, his words perfunctory, the message one of thanks done by rote instead of intention. But as he was saying "Amen," Josh's mother added to the prayer.

"Thank you for bringing Josh home to us. See to his health, dear Lord, and shine a light on his path so that he may walk it with clarity and joy. And maybe find him a nice young girl to help him with that task. Amen." Clearly she was the religious force in this family, and right now she wanted Jesus to show Josh that he wasn't gay.

Everyone but Josh echoed "Amen," including Nero. He could get behind the words, if not Mrs. Collier's meaning. He did want Josh to find his path with clarity and joy. He just hoped it was with Wulf, Inc. and not in this homophobic pocket of America.

Everyone unlinked their hands, and Bruce held up his, shaking it out as he tried to get blood flow back into his fingers. "Damn, little brother, you've gotten strong."

Josh jolted. "What?"

Ivy snorted as she explained things to Nero. "My brothers had this childish game of seeing who could crush the other's hand during prayer. Everyone's going, 'Thank you, Lord,' and they're sweating and grunting like they're at a WWE match."

"He held his own all through high school, but this time I thought he'd break my fingers," Bruce said as he looked at Josh. Then, when Josh continued to gape at him, Bruce's expression tightened. "Did you think I wouldn't admit it?" There was a long pause as Josh clearly debated how to answer. Fortunately Bruce saved him the trouble. "It's been a long time since I've needed to prove my manhood against my baby brother."

It was a friendly overture, and everyone waited to see how Josh would react. And though it took a moment, Josh finally nodded. "I... uh... yeah. I've gotten stronger."

"Back in that place you can't talk about? Doing things—"

"I can't talk about. Yes." His gaze went to his father. "Designing something that needs that Volcax. Please."

Mr. Collier grunted as he scooped up mashed potatoes before passing the bowl to his wife. Ivy was tucking into her beef like a werewolf—or someone who'd been eating Army food for way too long— but she managed to smile around her fork. "Do we call you Dr. Collier now? Did you get hooded and everything?"

"Um…." Josh grabbed the potatoes and started plopping them on his plate. "Not exactly," he mumbled. "Not yet."

There was nothing wrong with Mr. Collier's hearing as he scooped up his own mouthful of beef. "Seven years and no degree? What the hell have you been doing?"

Nero smiled. "He's been working for me."

"Really? And how much does working for you pay? How soon is he going to repay me for all that tuition money?"

Josh glared at the table. "I have to repay my student loans first, but then you'll get your money." He shot a resentful look at his brother. "Have you repaid him all the money he put out for your fire training?"

"Most." Then Bruce shrugged. "Well, some."

"Well," Ivy quipped, "thanks to the military, I'm free and clear of debt. I just don't have anything to show for it. Except this snazzy haircut." She pointed to her utilitarian short bob.

Mrs. Collier smiled at her daughter. "You've got experience and training. And being free of debt is impressive, especially for a girl your age."

Ivy smiled. "Thanks, Mom." Which would have been a lovely exchange if Mr. Collier hadn't spent the whole time staring at Josh. But when he spoke, his words were aimed at Nero.

"And who do you work for? What do you do?"

"I train people like Josh."

"Do-nothing students who never amount to jack?"

"Henry!" Mrs. Collier huffed. "If you treat him like that, is it any wonder he ended up in a hospital?"

Josh ground his teeth. Nero could hear it loud and clear. "I didn't go to a hospital. I—"

"Yeah," Nero interrupted, "you did. Just not for very long."

"That wasn't a hospital."

"It wasn't *not* a hospital. And don't be so narrow-minded. It's good and healthy to ask for help when you need it."

Josh narrowed his eyes, which was bad enough, but the expression of hurt lurking beneath the angry expression did him in. "Why are you being such a dick?"

"Joshua Collier!" his mother cried. "We do not speak like that to our guests."

Josh whipped back to his mother. "He's not a guest. He's my jailor."

"So now we have it!" Mr. Collier's meaty fist landed on the table hard enough to rattle the dishes and silence everyone. "You got in trouble, didn't you? Something happened at that dress-up party that you went to. The one where Savannah said you disappeared. You did something stupid like you always do, only this time, you got caught and were put in jail. You didn't call us because maybe you couldn't. And in jail, something happened to you. And now you're here, asking me for some Volcax, which you know I can't get you. I'm not doing anything illegal. Not for you, boy." His glare landed hard on Nero. "Or you, whoever the hell you are."

Wow. Never had anyone gotten things so right and so very wrong at the same time. Everyone at the table was stunned into silence. Even Nero didn't have the capacity to form words. But Josh had enough built-up fury to shove himself upright so hard, his chair toppled behind him. He planted his fists on the table and glared at his father.

"I'm not—" He cut off his words, his face turning nearly purple. And then he lifted his chin. "Yeah, Dad. I've been in jail, and they turned me into something horrible. And this guy here, he's the prime asshole. Big ol' wolf of a dick. And the only way I get out of jail is if you give me some stupid fabric to save this asshole's life. I need it cut and stitched into something insane because I've gone off my rocker. Because I got turned gay in jail."

"Joshua, please," his mother begged, the words filled with pain.

"Please what, Mom?" he pressed. "Please don't be gay? Well, I am. And I'm a whole lot worse than that. So how about I make you all a deal? You get Dad to save this ass—jerk's life, and I'll get the hell out of your life. It'll be like you never had a gay son and I never had homophobic parents. But don't you worry, Dad. How about you tack on a nice big profit to whatever you're going to charge and consider it repayment of my tuition? All those wasted years in school, and all I have to show for it is an ABD, which will only get me a job that pays one hundred thousand dollars a year."

No one at the table seemed to know what an ABD was, and a few seconds of confused stares had Josh throwing up his hands.

"It means *all but dissertation*!" And then he stomped out of the house.

Chapter 23

JOSH MADE it outside, but then he didn't have a single place he could go. Nero had the keys to the car, so that was out. He could walk somewhere. Hell, he could go wolf and roar through the streets of suburban Indianapolis, but that probably wasn't the smartest idea either. So he stood outside, breathed the crisp winter air, and tried to just exist without exploding.

It didn't work. Because a few minutes after his screaming exit, Nero wandered outside to stand next to him. And when Josh didn't say anything, Nero eventually spoke, his voice low and soothing.

"I know that sucked," he said. "But now you've broken from your family. Now you can go on with your wolf life however you want without your past interfering."

It took a moment for the words to slip past his fury and coalesce into meaning. But once it got in, it was like setting a match to dynamite. He rounded on his former friend and let fly with every filthy curse word that flowed from the cesspool of his thoughts. And when those slowed down, he found his real words. And those he spoke with precision.

"Don't you dare pretend that this was for my own good. You think I don't know what's going on? I get the same goddamned alerts on my computer that you do. I know that Wisconsin is dying inch by inch, foot by foot, more each day. I know you want to kill that fucker more than you want to breathe—"

"Yes, the demon is back and eating—"

"How many times did you try to break up with me last night? This morning? You don't think I heard the long pauses and the heavy sighs? You've been getting that hangdog look ever since the first possum drank some lake water and died. And now we have a growing dead zone with no answer."

"I need to kill it—"

"And for some twisted reason, you think that means we've got to split, you and me."

"We do have to—"

"But you don't talk to me about it. You stare at me while I sleep and then kiss me like it's never going to happen again."

"Josh—"

"And then you do that." He pointed at his family. "You poke and you push until I fucking explode all over my family, so I will hate you." This time he stabbed him in the chest. "Congratulations! I do! I despise you because you didn't have the balls to talk to me straight out."

He watched Nero's jaw work and his shoulders hunch. His brow narrowed in anger, but he held it back. And when he spoke, Nero invested it with that goddamned alpha power he had. Good thing Josh was too pissed off for it to work on him.

"Wolf protocol encourages a complete break with the past, and that's never pretty—"

"I don't care! You wanted to do this. Protocol or not, you wanted to be the asshole so that I would break up with you."

He held Nero's glare, matching it with enough hatred to make sure his point stuck. Apparently it did, because Nero's eyes dropped first. He looked down at a crack in the driveway and slowly nodded.

"Maybe I did. And maybe that was cowardly of me."

"You think?"

"And maybe I don't know how to feel about a lover who is a trainee with a genius-sized brain." He lifted his head. "You're going to move up fast in the company. All the higher-ups are already clamoring for your time and are willing to pay you well for that. Me? I'm a grunt who is waiting for my next assignment on the front lines. There was never any future for us. *Never*. And I…." He looked away.

"And you love me, dickwad."

Nero's head snapped up. "What?"

"Holy fuck, you think I didn't know? You think I'd let anybody do with me what we've done? It's not just the sex. There's nothing you don't know about me. You're the first person I turn to in the morning and the last one I kiss at night."

Nero was shaking his head hard. "That's not I—" He swallowed. "That's pack. That's how we feel in a pack."

"And that's *love*. You love your pack."

"Yes." The word cracked as it came out.

"And it sucks when that pack is torn apart, however it happens." Josh looked past Nero's shoulder to the house behind him. "But you didn't have to do this. You didn't have to do it this way." And with that, he turned away. He still had nowhere to go, but he was done talking. He needed some time alone—time to hate, to rage, to grieve in peace.

So he turned his back on Nero and walked to the rear bumper of the car. And when Nero didn't move, Josh spoke over his shoulder. "The specs are in your phone. Get my dad to start making the thing so we can get the hell out of here."

He waited another few moments, his shoulders tight and his breath all but sawing out of his chest. There were tears on his cheeks, but he didn't want to give himself away by wiping them off. Nero saw everything, and that was a detail he wouldn't miss.

So he leaned back against the bumper of Nero's car and let the tears burn cold on his cheeks. In time, Nero sighed and went back into the house. That should have been great. It really should have, except that once his vision cleared, Josh saw a car whipping down the street. A canary yellow Mustang with a dented bumper and a cute brunette gripping the steering wheel as she careened into a parking space.

Savannah.

She slammed to a stop outside his parents' place, then burst out of the car and ran straight at him. He tensed, and thank God for his werewolf strength, because she was not a small woman as she leaped into his arms. And then she held him, squeezing him tight enough to make his eyes tear up again. It wasn't pain but gratitude. Someone loved him enough to hug him as if her life had ended without him.

"Josh." She spoke his name as if it were a prayer. Eventually she took a deep breath and slid out of his arms. Then she slugged him hard on the shoulder.

"Ow!" Now even his best friend was hitting him? What the hell?

"Don't 'ow' me! Where have you been? I've been worried sick. Your parents didn't know anything, you missed Ivy's party, and no one at your lab has heard from you. What have you been doing? And why does it seem like you've been working out?" She squeezed his arm. "You haven't been this built since... ever." Then she peered hard at his face. "And why does it look like you've been crying?"

"That's a lot of questions," he murmured as he dug a palm into his eyes.

"Start with the most immediate. Why are you crying?"

He thought about lying, but she was his best friend since high school. If anyone could give him perspective, it would be her. "My boyfriend just broke up with me." He tensed, waiting for the "you're gay?" confusion. Instead, she glanced over his shoulder at the house.

"At your parents' house? That's lame."

"Yeah," he said with a weak chuckle. "It was bad enough that he dragged me here, but then he pulled this douche move." He shook his head, not wanting to go into details.

"Well, he is a guy, and they're all morons." Then she leaned back against the car.

"I am a guy too, you know."

"And you disappeared on me for six weeks, had a gay relationship, and just ended it. I'd say that's moronic. Not the relationship bit. We all screw those up. I mean the disappearing bit. So what happened? Where were you?"

He turned to study her face. "What do you remember from MoreCon?"

"I—" She grimaced. "It's weird. I remember getting there and meeting you in the café, but then it gets all hazy. Were we supposed to meet after the opening event? I think I got sick or something, because I remember waking up in my room the next morning and you were gone. As in not in the hotel, your car gone from the lot, just gone. And nobody knew anything until Bruce texted me that you were here."

He nodded, having expected something like that. "You can take your pick of answers. I had a meltdown because I'm gay and was hospitalized. I did something shady at the event, was arrested, and became gay in jail. I was abducted by a covert organization and turned gay."

"Don't you think covert organizations have something better to do than mess with your sex life?"

He chuckled. "Trust me, they have a lot weirder things to mess with."

She was silent for a long moment. She studied him head to toe; then she squeezed his arm as she dropped her head on his shoulder. "So covert organization, huh? How much can you tell me?"

He jolted. "You believe me?"

"You've bulked out. That wouldn't happen in a hospital or jail."

"I could have gotten buff in jail."

"Not likely. So that leaves covert military something or other, and they probably forced you to do calisthenics. And boy, do I wish I could have seen that."

He snorted. "I think I would have preferred to die."

"Ah, so I'm right."

"Yeah, you are. But that's about all I can tell you."

A breeze cut down the street, and she huddled deeper into her coat. "Why aren't you cold? You don't even have a coat on."

Werewolf metabolism? He wasn't sure, but he wrapped an arm around her and pulled her close. "We can go inside," he offered, though that was the last thing he wanted.

"Not until you tell me why you're here."

"We need Volcax. Nero insisted we find a way to get it now. There's a time problem he's not telling me about. But it has to be now."

"Nero the asshole?"

"Yeah."

"Do you love him?"

"Yeah."

"Enough to fight for him?"

He paused to think about it. There were so many factors to consider. He'd just become a werewolf and was still figuring out what that meant. He might continue at Wulf, Inc. He might go back and finish his PhD. His future was in flux, and Nero's was no different. The big ass would probably join a new combat pack and go anywhere in the world, fighting who knew what.

All those thoughts ran through his head, and Savannah, being Savannah, let him mull them over, though she was shivering by the time he finally spoke.

"Not right now," he finally admitted. "If everything was normal...." He almost snorted that word. Werewolves were not normal. "I wouldn't let him end things like this. But he's going somewhere. I might be going somewhere."

She straightened. "Where are you going?"

He was about to say he didn't know, but he made up his mind right then and there to share the important stuff. Details didn't matter. This did. "I really like the work I'm doing," he said, feeling his way through his decision. "I love it. It's exciting and different." Understatement of the year. "And they seem like they really need me."

"You're staying in covert land." A statement, not a question.

"Yeah." Then he shook his head. "But as soon as I can, I'm writing my dissertation and graduating."

"What?"

He turned her so they were looking eye to eye. "You may not remember it, but you harassed me at MoreCon for not getting on with my life."

"That's no surprise. I do that every time I see you."

True enough. "That's because you're right. I wasn't graduating because I didn't know what I wanted to do afterwards. Nothing interested me."

"And now you've found it?"

He thought about the pages and pages of case files he'd been reading through. Demons with plasma fire were just the tip of the iceberg. Vampires and shifters were only a fraction of the world out there. And when the fairies got involved, everything went whacko.

"I love it," he said.

"But you're leaving it?"

"Temporarily. I'm going to finish the PhD so the bastards pay me what I'm worth."

She grinned. "That's the spirit."

Then he glanced back at the house. "Nero was a jerk today, but he was right about one thing."

She arched her brows in question.

"I need to close out my past. And though today sucked rocks, at least I know I won't be leaving my family in limbo."

"But you're still disappearing into covert land."

He shrugged. "Not to them, I'm not. Nero outed me as gay." He held up his hand to stop her from making a snap judgment. "He thought they already knew, and I know he was shocked by their reaction."

"Still an asshole move."

Josh couldn't argue that. "So Mom's going with the mental breakdown, and Dad's chosen jailhouse conversion."

"Oh my God," she breathed. Then she looked at Bruce's huge truck. "What about your brother and sister?"

Josh exhaled. "I don't know. They both tried to help, but there's only so much they could do."

"Okay, so your siblings are up in the air, but *I'm* not. I don't care what you're doing, I expect an email address and regular communication. And you better get vacation time off for MoreCon every year." She poked him in the chest. "Every single year."

"Every year. I promise."

"Okay. Fine, then—" Savannah cut off her words as her gaze zeroed in on Bruce. He was just now coming out of the house, and his steps hitched slightly as he saw her. Then his jaw tightened as he crossed to Josh.

"Hi, Bruce," Savannah said.

"Hi, Savannah. Glad you made it before the shit hit the fan."

Josh gaped at his brother. "*Before* the shit hit?"

Bruce nodded. "Mother's called a prayer meeting. They're headed over now."

"Oh God," Savannah breathed.

"To pray away my gayness?"

"To pray for you."

Yeah. It was to pray away his gayness. "What about Dad?"

"He wasn't going to make your doggie hoodies…." He looked at Josh. "This is some lame practical joke or something, right?"

"Sorry, it's real. Unless the joke's on me."

"Well, that guy Nero made it clear that the money's real, but only if the coats get made today. He offered Dad a shit-ton of money. And you know Dad's greedy. And given that the other choice is a prayer vigil instead of EPSN—"

Josh straightened off the car. "Dad's actually going to give us the Volcax? Are we headed to the factory, then?"

"Nero and Dad are," Bruce said. "But maybe you and I could go somewhere else. Maybe have a beer."

Josh frowned. Years of being duped by his older brother reared up in his mind. "You've never wanted to hang out before."

Bruce shrugged. "We've never been adults before. And you've never disappeared, come back gay, and mouthed off to Dad before." He grinned. "And for the record, I knew what ABD means. You've had it after your name forever."

Was that a dig? If so, it was true. Hadn't he been saying that same thing to Savannah? He opened his mouth to agree. There was no reason he couldn't try to mend some fences with his brother before disappearing into Wulf, Inc. forever. But just as the words were forming, Nero burst out of the house, flashing his phone.

"Josh, we've got to get to the factory. The fairy says it's now or never!"

It took a moment for Josh to reorient himself from family to weirdness, but he got there. Some fairy had probably located the demon, and Nero was hell-bent on taking the asshole down. Meanwhile, Savannah and Bruce were having trouble following their conversation.

"Is that a slur?" Bruce asked, understandably confused.

"Or a codename?" Savannah asked.

Given Nero's attitude toward the fae, it was both, but he couldn't say that. Instead he shrugged. "Classified."

Meanwhile, Nero gestured to the car. "Get in. Your dad's going to cut the fabric and then I'll go—"

"Test it in a lab," Josh interrupted. "It needs to be *tested*."

"No time. Fit it on me and—"

"Make time," Josh said as he squared off with Nero. "I'm the geek here. I'll tell you when it's ready for use in the field."

"And I'm the boss. I'll tell you where—"

"You ready to commit suicide? Because that's what will happen—"

"—we test. *In the field.* It's the only test that counts."

"No way—"

"Damn it, Josh!"

His father's voice cut through their argument. "You want this fool thing or not?"

They both turned and spoke with one voice. "Yes!"

"Then get out of my way!"

It took a moment for them to figure out what he meant. Sometime during their yelling match, his father had opened the garage door and was waiting to back his truck out, but Nero's car was blocking him.

"Right away, sir," Nero called. Then he hauled open his car door.

Josh rushed to the passenger side of the car and made it inside just as Nero turned the ignition. "You can't do this without testing."

Nero backed out of the driveway while Savannah and Bruce watched from the lawn. But then he had to pause on the street for Josh's dad to back out and lead the way. And in that pause, Nero turned to Josh. His tone was level, his jaw firm, and his eyes hard.

"I'm going to do this with or without your shield and hoodie. So, do I wait for it? Or do I head straight for Wisconsin now?"

Josh cursed under his breath. And then he cursed even louder when he realized that Nero was waiting for his answer.

"Fine!" he huffed. "Wait for my dad to make two of them. We'll go together."

"Bullshit. You're not trained."

"And you're not thinking straight."

Nero acknowledged that with a grunt. Then he spoke, his voice low. "I've waited six weeks and five days." He looked at Josh. "I know this doesn't make sense to you. I can't explain further, but the longer we wait, the worse it gets. So I leave tomorrow morning, no matter what."

Josh winced. He could feel the determination in Nero's tone. There was definitely something the guy wasn't saying. Something important that had colored his every action since the very beginning. "It's reckless to go out there alone and unprepared. I've read your mission reports—this isn't you. You're all about safety with your pack."

Nero didn't answer, and as the miles sped by underneath the wheels, Josh put the pieces together.

"You don't think they're going to let you in on the kill, do you? You think they'll give the task to someone else."

Nero shook his head. "No one else is going to drag paste-covered shields into combat, Josh. Or wear a hoodie. No one but me."

"They will if they're ordered to."

Nero shrugged. "I don't know. There's a limit to what some of them will do."

"I don't care. That's not your call and you know it. So what is really going on? Why does it have to be you, right now, taking stupid risks?"

Nero didn't answer. And as they took the last turn before they hit his dad's factory, Josh realized the truth. Nero hadn't answered because he couldn't. And yet he was still stubbornly, stupidly determined to go into the fight. Which meant his trainer, his lover, and his best werewolf friend was really fucked-up in the head.

"You need to tell me the truth," Josh said slowly. He invested all his passion, his determination, and his *love* in his words. Nero had to know that he was serious. "You will tell me what's really going on right now or I will delete the specs and destroy the shield. I'll erase everything and you'll have nothing." He stared at Nero and saw the guy's clenched jaw. "You've blown up my life, destroyed my relationship with my family, and I still fucking love you. So you will tell me what's really going on or I'll do whatever I have to, to make sure you survive. And if that means destroying the specs—"

"Do you know what the number-one rule in the Wulf, Inc. handbook is?"

It took a moment for Josh to pull back from his tirade, and even longer for the words to make sense in his brain. "We have a handbook?"

Nero glared at him. "No, of course we don't have a handbook. We're werewolves!"

Right. "Sorry," he said. "You were saying. The number-one rule is…?"

"Never, ever, under any circumstances, make a fairy deal."

Oh crap. There was good reason for that rule. Fairy deals never, ever went the way they were supposed to. Anyone who had ever played D&D knew that.

"You have to understand," Nero continued. "My entire pack was dead, the demon had escaped, and I needed to do something. Anything."

Cold terror gripped Josh's spine. "What did you do?"

Nero sighed. "I made a fairy deal."

Chapter 24

NERO PULLED into a parking spot next to Mr. Collier's truck, but he knew Josh wasn't going to let him drop that bomb and just disappear, so he tried to minimize the damage. "It's not as bad as it sounds."

"It sounds like, in a moment of shock and grief, you did the one thing guaranteed to screw you over. And possibly everyone else too."

Yeah, he'd considered that. Long after the fact, of course, but that was one of the things that kept him up at night.

"Enough with the stoic shit," Josh huffed. "What—exactly—did you say? And I do mean *exactly*."

"I don't *exactly* remember."

"Mother of—"

"Stop being so dramatic," Nero snapped. "I'm not even supposed to be talking to you about this."

"Screw that. Talk."

Nero sighed. If only it was that easy. If he gave Josh the full details, then Bitterroot was going to make him pay. Period. But at the moment, Nero didn't care. He owed Josh the truth. More than that, he *wanted* to tell him the truth. It was too heavy a burden to shoulder alone. "Bitterroot owed me a favor, so I called him and got a mulligan."

"Bitter—you know—is the fairy?"

"Yes." And obviously Josh already knew the dangers of saying a fairy name out loud. That's why Nero hadn't said the guy's full name.

"And a mulligan is a what? You get to replace your team with someone else?"

"What? No!" He stared at Josh. "Where did you get that idea?"

"That's what a mulligan is in gaming circles. You get to replace your hand with new cards and do the turn over."

Nero's eyebrows rose. Apparently there were some things the über-geek didn't know. Score one for the sports reference. "A mulligan in *golf* is a do-over. A repeat. I'll get dropped back in time—"

"Oh! An Omega 13 device." And when Nero stared at him, Josh blew out a breath. "*Galaxy Quest.* We'll watch it…." There probably wouldn't be any more movies together, no matter what happened tomorrow. "Never mind. How does it work?"

"I'll start up right before the attack, and this time I'll save every single one of them and kill that fucking demon—"

"No! Don't go and attack. It's still suicide to go in with untested equipment."

Nero watched as Mr. Collier unlocked the factory door and disappeared inside. How he longed to be done with this conversation, but he already knew Josh wouldn't let him go so easily.

"A fairy mulligan has specific rules. We still have to attack. There's not a lot I can change." He looked at Josh. "But I can bring a weapon for each one of my team. Your design—"

"Is not a weapon!"

"Fine! Your plan and your tech will keep them alive. I just need them to survive the blast, then we can kill it. I know we can."

"No, you don't know that. All you know is what the demon *did*. Not what it *will do* after it shoots off that plasma blast."

Yes, Nero had thought about that, but there was only so much he could plan for. "I saw the… creature afterwards. It was a pink blob and completely defenseless."

"Except for the gun. Except for whatever demon powers—"

"Stop arguing with me, Josh. It's done, and I've run out of time. I go tomorrow morning at dawn, whether I have your tech or not."

Josh reared back. "Dawn! There's no way I can make five shields in that time—"

"I need the one. I've been texting with Bitter. He says if I've got one, then he can duplicate it."

There was a moment of silence as Josh processed that, but his mind obviously wasn't where Nero's was. "Fairies have cell phones?"

"Um, yeah. Of a sort." He did not want to get into the technological weirdness of the fair folk. "Anyway, if we get one shield and one hoodie, he can make four others."

"And what is he adding to them?"

"What? Nothing—"

"Bullshit." Josh blew out a breath. "That's incredibly stupid. Fairy deals—"

"It's not like that!" Nero huffed, praying it was true. "Bitterroot owed me one. I helped him out once."

"Time travel is not a small favor."

"And what I did wasn't a small favor either!"

Josh leaned back against his seat and stared blankly out the front windshield. "So it's not an Omega 13, it's a whole Star Trek reboot, dead planet Vulcan and all."

Nero turned to him. "I have no idea how to answer that."

Josh waved it away with a depressed sigh. "This Bitter guy owed you, right? He didn't ask anything in return?"

Not exactly. Nero didn't say the words out loud, but his face must have given the answer away, because Josh abruptly pointed at his chest.

"I knew it! What did you promise him?"

Nero's hands fidgeted on the steering wheel. There was no going back now. He might as well tell it all. "After the mulligan, no matter what happens, I go work for him."

"For how long?"

Nero didn't answer. He didn't like thinking about it, but if it meant his team survived, it was worth the sacrifice. It was worth a thousand times the sacrifice. He just hadn't expected to meet Josh before he left the mortal realm for Fairyland. And he hadn't expected to fall so hard for the guy.

But fairy deals had to be honored. The alternative was always worse, as in skin-burning-off-for-eternity worse. And that was one of the nicer possibilities. "How long?" Josh repeated.

"A year for every day that the mulligan stays available. Payable whether or not I use the portal."

"But it's been weeks."

Nero nodded. "Six weeks and six days. The fairies have a thing for the number seven, so at seven weeks the portal closes, whether I use it or not, and either way—"

"You're living the rest of your natural life in servitude to the fae."

"Actually, it's natural and unnatural. If I die before the contract is up, they'll resurrect me as something…." He shuddered. "Something unpleasant, and I'll keep going."

"Wonderful." The sarcasm was heavy in Josh's voice, and Nero rounded on him in fury.

"Stop with the judgment already. I don't need it, and frankly, you're wrong. I don't regret my choice for a second. Not a goddamned second. And I'd do it again if it was a hundred years for every day. They are my pack. I'd do anything for them. *Anything*."

"Even give up the rest of your life—"

"Yes."

"Give up a new pack—"

Nero winced. He hadn't counted on finding friends, much less a new pack in the trainees. "Yes."

"Me."

Nero looked down at his hands. He didn't have to say the word yes—they both heard it loud and clear in his silence.

"Well, I guess I understand why you broke up with me today."

"We were never supposed to be a permanent thing. Even without the fairy deal, we would have gone our separate ways."

Josh didn't answer in words, but one look at his face told Nero more than he ever wanted to know about what the guy was feeling. Hurt and betrayal burned hot in his cheeks. Pain shimmered in his too-bright eyes. But what was a thousand times worse were the words that Josh said next and the flat intonation in his voice when he said them.

"I loved you," he said. "I don't trust easy, and I certainly didn't want to fall for the meathead trainer who blew up my life. But I loved you, and I would have done a lot to make this work."

Nero's throat closed down, tears and pain choking off his words. But Josh deserved some sort of acknowledgment, something to show that Nero appreciated his bravery in saying the words out loud. That was the kind of courage Nero didn't possess. Because even though he felt it, he'd never let the word *love* slip out. Even in the past tense.

But he did love Josh. And if the lives of his packmates hadn't been on the line, he would have done a lot to see things work out too. He almost said that now. He nearly found the strength to admit his own feelings, but he hadn't missed Josh's verb. He'd said *loved*. As in past tense. Josh had loved him, but he didn't now.

So be it. But Josh still deserved something.

"Thank you," he finally said. The words burned in his throat because they were so much less than he felt, and so miniscule compared to what Josh deserved. "I— That means a lot—" He kept tripping over his own tongue, and the right words wouldn't come. "I'm sorry, so fucking sorry for how this worked out." Or didn't work out.

"Yeah," Josh said into the increasingly cold car. "Me too."

They both sat there a moment. Nero wanted to do something, to say something to bridge the space between them, but there wasn't anything he could do. And then, as if they were still in sync, they both opened their car doors at the same second and headed inside.

"Let me handle my father," Josh said as they made it to the shop door. "You just keep upping the money."

"Deal," Nero said.

"And stop making deals!"

Chapter 25

HIS FATHER was an asshole, and apparently a greedy one. Josh didn't know how much money Nero had promised the man, but it obviously did the trick. His father looked at the wolf hoodie specs, pulled out a roll of Volcax, and started cutting. He sewed the single garment himself, using specially designed thread, and he even had the sensors and other tech on hand, which went into the appropriate pockets. And in all that time, he never said a word.

And since Josh wasn't in the mood to talk either, he spent the time researching fairy deals. He did not want everything that had happened in the past six weeks to reset. The fairy mulligan might work for Nero—he'd get his team back—but then Josh wouldn't get recruited. He would remain a lost doctoral student with nothing in his life but a cosplay weekend once a year.

He'd grown, and he did not want to lose that, so he made a plan. Which was when his father cut the last thread and handed him the cloak. The man still didn't speak. Not until they were walking outside to Josh's Uber and his father's truck. The garment was carefully hidden in a large reusable grocery sack.

"Thank you for this—" Josh said, but his father cut him off.

"I know what you are," he said, his voice thick and scratchy. "It's the family curse, and you got it. It's not your fault; it was in the genes. But I can't have you opening your brother's or sister's eyes. They can't know or they'll be howling at the moon too."

The air froze in Josh's chest at that, and all his words choked off. But it didn't matter because his father kept talking.

"That's why I made this. That's why I'm risking jail and worse giving you a wolf covering." Then he finally lifted his eyes to stare right at his son. "Maybe it'll keep you alive, maybe it won't. Either way, you're dead to us. I won't lose another child to this curse."

"Dad—" Josh protested, the word half-strangled as it escaped his lips.

"Good luck, Josh. If a cursed soul can have luck." Then he turned and walked away.

Josh thought about calling him back. He had so many questions, so many feelings. But none of them resolved into words. And while he was still struggling, his father got in his truck and left. Josh echoed the movement, climbing into the Uber while his thoughts

spun. And damn it, he didn't even have Nero as a wit-
ness. Around midafternoon, Josh had convinced Nero
to check into the nearest hotel and get some rest. He
needed to be sharp tomorrow, no matter what happened. Josh even promised to pay for great delivery
pizza as soon as Nero texted him the hotel and room
number.

Which meant his job was done. All of it. Nero had
the prototype shield in his car, Josh had the Volcax
hoodie, and his father had closed the door on Josh forever. Done. He needed to get back to Nero.

He ought to let the guy sleep. He really shouldn't
say any of things bumping around in his head. And
yet the idea that he would never get another chance
burned like fire in his gut. He slipped inside the hotel room and looked around. The room was dark and
smelled of deep-dish pizza, but Josh's werewolf senses could easily make out Nero lying on his back on
one of the two queen-size beds. His arm was thrown
over his eyes and his breath was steady, but Josh had
been sleeping next to the man for almost six weeks.
He knew when Nero was asleep and when he was just
pretending. Right now the man wasn't even faking
sleep well.

"Have you gotten any rest?" Josh asked.

"A little."

"Do you want me to get another room?"

Nero dropped his arm from across his eyes to
look at Josh. "Do you want a different one?"

Josh shook his head as he went deeper into the
darkness. "We've got a single hoodie," he said.

"Bitter will duplicate it and the shield."

Like he trusted a fairy with Nero's life… *not*.

"Is there any way I can talk you out of going tomorrow?"

"No. I'm sorry."

He figured as much. "Then I hope it works out for you."

"It'll work out for you too. If my team doesn't die, then Wulf, Inc. won't go looking for tech support. We'll never force the shift on you and—"

"You *need* techies. And you said I'd probably change at some point anyway."

Nero blew out a breath. "You might. You might not. Your father has the gene, and he's never gone furry. Neither has Ivy or Bruce. Just your one uncle."

"Yeah, I read his file." The entire family thought his uncle had died in Vietnam. Nope. Meanwhile, Nero brought him back to the painful present with a surprising apology. "Look, Josh, I know I've been a real dick today. You were right that I was pushing you away." He shrugged. "Somehow that felt easier."

"Because it is easier. For you."

Nero had the grace to flush. "Yeah. It was, and I'm sorry. And now you get to go back to your real life as if none of this ever happened to you. As if *I* never happened to you."

Josh dropped down on the second bed, abruptly too exhausted to deal with Nero's bullshit while on his feet. "You sound like that's a good thing. Like I'd want to forget everything that's happened in the last six weeks."

"Don't you? You've been bitching this whole time about how we blew up your life. How we've taken you from your family, screwed up your PhD, taken you away from Savannah. Well, now none of that will happen."

Josh rubbed a hand over his face. "Yeah, you did." He blew out a breath. "But maybe my life wasn't so great to begin with. Maybe it needed to get blown up."

Nero's brows went up and he flicked on the bedside light. "Come again?"

"The way you guys go about recruitment sucks. It's fucking awful, and I'm going to make sure that gets fixed. But in my case...." He shrugged. "I was drifting. I wasn't going to leave school until they kicked me out. I didn't have anything I wanted to do and was afraid of going out and looking for it." He stared hard at Nero. "But now I do. Now I have Wulf, Inc. I like the work there, and you guys sure as hell need the help."

"We've been doing fine for centuries."

"Well, it's a new century, and things are changing." Josh leaned forward. "But I won't remember any of this, will I? Because you're going to wipe it away with one big fairy deal. Say you win tomorrow. Everything will go back how it started, and I'll never be recruited." Josh stood up. "For the record, I don't want to erase that. Yeah, you fucked up, but that doesn't mean I want to forget you. To never have what we did? What we—" His voice broke, and he felt like a wuss here, trying to express how much he felt for Nero. How much he still *loved* the guy. And come tomorrow morning—no matter what happened—it would all end. If Nero won, then Josh would never be recruited. This timeline would disappear. And if Nero failed, he would still be whisked off to Fairyland. Assuming he survived at all.

Which meant that even if Josh got recruited to Wulf, Inc., it wouldn't be like it had been. It wouldn't be Nero holding his body when he came out from a shift. It wouldn't be Nero poking him into calisthenics or forcing him to eat meatloaf and broccoli when he'd really rather have had nachos and a soda. He wouldn't have the big lug in his bed, in his heart, in his body.

"We balance each other, asshole. And you're going to wipe all that away."

Nero sat up, but his head seemed to hang heavy on his shoulders. "Don't ask me to choose between you and them. They came first, Josh. Do you know why I fought us so hard? Because I knew from the beginning that it wasn't real. I knew I'd go for my do-over, and either way, we wouldn't happen."

"It was fucking real!" Josh screamed.

Nero had been waiting for Josh to lose it. That was how they worked. Nero poked and pushed until Josh faced whatever he was feeling. Until it all came out in an agonizing rush of anger and pain. And no matter how violent the explosion, Nero was always there to catch his pieces. To hold him while Josh released everything he'd kept trapped inside. And together they weathered the storm.

This was no different. Josh screamed and lunged forward. Nero caught him when he was trying to both hit and kiss the man at the same time. He let Josh's momentum carry them backward onto the mattress, and then, when Josh's bellow became a choked-off sob, Nero held him even tighter.

"It is real," Josh kept saying. "It's real."

"Yeah," Nero murmured into his hair. "Yeah, it is."

Josh held on to Nero's broad shoulders as he clutched the man tight to his chest. Josh wrapped his legs around Nero's thighs, and he held on as if that could keep them from getting ripped apart. As if it would keep them from getting *erased*. But it couldn't, and they both knew it.

When Josh lifted his face for a kiss, Nero met him with his lips. And then they were devouring each other. Mouths, hands, legs, dicks. Everything entwined with everything else. They sucked, they rubbed, and they *needed*.

The sex was hard and fast. They spread, shoved, sucked, and rammed with a brutality only werewolves could withstand. And when they were face-to-face with Nero deep in Josh's ass, he held the man still and growled into his ear.

"You're mine," Nero said. Then he bit down into Josh's shoulder until blood dripped onto the sheets.

Josh howled, arching backward not to get away but to impale himself deeper. And then he flashed his own teeth before he bit down on the thick part of Nero's deltoid. No matter what happened, Nero would bear the mark of Josh's bite. He wouldn't forget even if Josh was erased.

"Mine," Josh echoed as his body began to pulse around Nero.

"Yours," Nero agreed, and together they rode the whirlwind to bliss. And even when it was done and they'd collapsed boneless on the bed, they still didn't stop. Nero reached for Josh, and Josh reached back. They caressed wherever they touched. They kissed what they could reach. And their groins ended up rubbing against each other while they both hissed in pleasure.

There were no words. Just the sounds of sex— harsh and raw. Then sex—gentle and slow. Then sex without sex—just holding one another in silence.

Eventually they cleaned up and settled in to sleep. But even then, when languor made his whole body heavy, Josh didn't sleep. He knew Nero was awake too, and he refused to miss a moment of their time together.

Eventually Nero spoke.

"I'll tell them. Before I go with the fairies. I'll tell them to recruit you."

"It won't be the same."

"No. But maybe it'll be okay."

It didn't feel like anything would ever be okay again, but Josh nodded because Nero seemed to need him to. And then, in the darkest part of the night, Nero kept talking about something that seemed completely irrelevant. But nothing about Nero was irrelevant, so Josh listened as if he was being told state secrets.

"I liked a couple of my mother's boyfriends, back when I was a kid. They were good guys who watched out for us. I still remember their names: Dan Ellis and then, a few months later, Junior Merrill."

"What happened to them?"

Nero shook his head. "One day they were there, the next they were gone. There was usually a fight, but there were so many fights in those days, they all melded together."

"You were a kid. How were you to know what was going on?"

"I did know, and it was really simple. Everybody leaves eventually. It could be quick, could be slow, but one day they're gone. It's the nature of life. People appear...." He caressed Josh's shoulder. "And then something happens, and they go." His hand flopped down to the mattress.

Josh blew out a breath. "It's not always like that. Some people stick around for the long haul." He would have.

"So I'm told." Nero pushed up on his elbow and looked down at Josh. "That's what I swore when I took over as leader of my combat pack. That I would stick with it for the long haul. That I would do whatever it took to stay with them, no matter what."

So this was where Nero was going. "You don't have to justify your choice. I get it. How many times have you talked about the importance of your pack? That loyalty goes to the pack. That love is held within the pack."

"I can't let them die. Not when I can stop it."

Josh looked away from Nero's fierce expression. He stared at the ceiling and spoke from his heart. "*I get it*," he said. And he did. "I even love you for it." Nero was someone who was faithful. He wouldn't abandon someone he loved if they screwed up, and he sure as hell would cover that someone's ass when the shit hit the fan. Josh understood that. He just hadn't realized that Nero wasn't making a new pack. He was going back to his old one.

"I didn't know I'd fall in love," Nero whispered, and Josh's gaze snapped back to him.

"What?"

"Yeah," Nero rasped as he dropped back onto the bed. "It's love. Fucking thing hurts enough. It's gotta be love."

"Yeah," Josh echoed, feeling the pain in his whole soul.

"But I can't—"

"I know," Josh interrupted. No point in belaboring it. Nero couldn't abandon his first pack, so he had to abandon Josh. "You need to get some rest. You need to be fresh in the morning." He started to get off the bed—Nero was a big guy and he liked to spread out in his sleep—but Nero grabbed his arm before he could go far.

"Stay," he said. "Stay with me now. Just until—"

"However long you need," Josh said. "I'm here for you. I promise."

"Thanks." They snuggled together, bodies entwined, breath intermingling as they pressed forehead to forehead. And then, right when Josh started to relax, Nero whispered again. "I'm so sorry I was such a dick. I didn't want this to hurt so much."

"How'd that work out for you?"

"Like I'm cutting out my own beating heart."

"Yeah," Josh whispered. "Me too."

They slept hard and deep for too little time. And when the alarm went off, neither of them spoke. They got their stuff together and headed out to the nearest park. Fairies liked greenery, and Bitterroot was no different. Once there, Josh laid out the harness, and Nero spoke in an undertone that nonetheless carried the throb of his alpha voice.

"Drake Bitterroot, I call thee. Drake Bitterroot, I call thee. Drake Bitterroot, I call—"

"Cutting it close there, aren't you?"

Josh jerked backward as a slender youth, about three feet tall, appeared in front of them. He wore dark green everywhere plus a couple of butterflies on his shirt, and his skin was the color of an oak tree beneath the bark. His eyes were sharp black points, and his expression was friendly despite his sour tone. And he missed absolutely nothing as he took in Nero, Josh, and the shield and hoodie that lay on the ground between them. He also wore no less than seven different types of watches.

"That it?" Bitterroot walked around the shield. He touched it, pushed his fingers into the sticky paste that Josh had created, and then prodded the hoodie with his toe. "Hmmm. Clever design. Your work, I assume?" he asked as he looked at Josh.

"Yes. I'm—"

"Don't tell him your name," Nero interrupted. He looked at Bitterroot. "He's with me. That's all you have to know."

Bitterroot pouted a moment, but then he shrugged. "All right, With Me, let's talk specifics here. Tell me what I need to know to duplicate these."

Josh frowned. "Um, I've got the specifications in my laptop."

The fairy rolled his eyes as if Josh were especially stupid. "Not specifications. Spare me from mortal *specifications*." He said the word as if even the sound of it nauseated him. "Tell me what you were thinking when you made it."

"My father made the hoodie—"

"When you got the idea. When you created—"

"He wants your feelings, Josh. Fairies deal in feelings."

Josh blinked. "What?"

Nero shrugged. "Hell if I understand it, but they do. Tell him how you felt when you got the idea. What emotions carried you through when you designed it for the first time? What were you feeling as you adjusted the specs?"

"I was…." Josh thought back. "I was excited. I was making something good." His gaze caught on Nero. "I was going to make you so happy." That had been the overriding feeling in every moment of the creation process: that he was going to make Nero so happy when it was done.

His gaze caught and held on Nero's for a long moment, and it was as though they were connected at a gut level. Josh was trying to say that every part of this harness had been a gift to Nero. And Nero was answering, *Thank you, I love you,* and *I'm so sorry it ended like this.*

"Done!" Bitterroot exclaimed. And when Josh looked down, sure enough, there were five full shields on the ground and a stack of matching hoodies. Even more confusing, Bitterroot carefully draped a large egg-shaped item onto each shield as they watched, binding it there in some magical fairy way with one of his watches.

"What is that?" Josh demanded.

"Something of faery that will absorb the heat. It wasn't the answer by itself, but it may help keep your people alive." Then, when the last egg was set, Bitterroot looked up with a grin. "Anything else? No? Okay, then, have fun catching the demon!"

And then Nero was gone. There was no clap, no snap, not even a blink. One second Nero was standing there with the shields at his feet, and the next the space was empty.

Gone.

Josh scrambled to keep up. His mind was reeling from how abrupt it had been, but he'd already planned for this. So before he lost his chance, he turned to Bitterroot.

"Before you go," he said, "I'd like to make a deal."

Chapter 26

NERO STUMBLED as he appeared in Wisconsin. He'd been thinking of his last goodbye to Josh, and suddenly he was here again, holding a *Crazy Cat Lady* T-shirt. Just like before, Cream and Coffee were already wolves, playing happily with each other while they kept an eye on whether Nero would wear the tee. Pauly stood defiantly in front of him, daring him to say no, and Mother....

Mother had leaped backward with her T-shirt half off. She'd been stripping before her shift but was now was reaching for her gun to shoot the shields that had abruptly appeared at her feet.

"What the hell?" she said.

"Don't shoot them!" Nero commanded as he dropped the tee. Then he took a breath, his gaze going again over every single one of them—even Pauly, with his smirk and his cell phone hidden behind his back so he could take a pictures of Nero in the T-shirt. Especially Pauly, who dropped the tease and was taking a defensive stance beside Nero.

"God, it's good to see you guys," Nero said, his voice choking up. He wanted to hug every one of them. He had so much he wanted to say to them, about how he'd missed them and that they were more important to him than he'd ever realized. All of those words crowded into his throat, but they didn't have the time.

"Are you okay?" Mother asked, her gaze still trained on the shields. Cream and Coffee had come closer as well, their noses working overtime as they sniffed the things.

Focus! Nero ordered himself. Reunions could happen later. "Look, I don't have time to explain. This is a fairy mulligan, and I'm trying to save all your lives."

All of their heads snapped up at that, but it was Paul who asked the question. "We die? From the demon?"

Mother had a different reaction. "We don't make fairy deals! You know that!"

"This is different. This is your lives." And before Mother could voice her next objection, he answered Pauly's question. "The demon has a fire blast that takes all of you out. You need to carry the shields and drop them in a defensive place. You'll have about twenty seconds to get behind them when the blast starts building."

"Sticky eggs?" Mother said as she pointed to Bitterroot's addition. "How is that going to help?"

"I have no idea. But you can carry the shield in your wolf form. It's got a harness I can strap onto you. Over the hoodies." He picked one up and shook it out. "Just before the blast, you flatten out behind the shields and under one of these."

Pauly shook his head. "We can't attack wearing one of those."

"Yes, you can." He hoped. "We've run simulations."

"Simulations!" Mother snapped. "You mean these haven't been tested?"

Nero ground his teeth. "No! Because *there wasn't time*! Now stop arguing. Coffee, you first. Pauly, you help Cream. Mother, get furry."

Everyone moved into place, working in a coordinated fashion even with the unfamiliar equipment. That's what happened in a good pack. When the time came for action, they all worked seamlessly even with the unpredictable. And hell, these shields were unpredictable. The hoodies were obvious enough. They worked like a wolf sweater vest with a long back to cover the tail. But the straps to attach and release the shield were confusing, and worse, Josh's compound smelled awful.

"What are these supposed to do?" Pauly asked as he was closing the buckles across Cream's chest.

"Channel the plasma fire that turns all of you to ash. It's a one-time deal, so if he looks like he's going explosive again, run away from the blast area as fast as possible." He jerked his chin to a tall oak tree. "That's the edge there. The van stayed whole."

There was a pause as everyone turned to stare at him, at the tree, then at the van, and back to him. They were processing, calculating distances, and probably dealing with a massive "holy shit" factor. But to their credit, no one said a word. They just returned to work.

Mother was full wolf now, so Nero started putting on her harness. Coffee and Cream started moving around in the things, testing how easily they could run, pivot, and strike. It wasn't easy, but they were professionals. They adjusted, and the shields wouldn't be carried into the battle itself.

Pauly was the last to strip before going wolf, but then he paused as he looked at the remaining two shields.

"How are you going to get yours on?"

He'd... hell, he hadn't thought about that. God, that was something they'd have figured out if they'd been able to test the things. "I don't need it," he said. "I survived the first time." He didn't explain that it had only been sheer luck that he'd managed to live. The timing had to be perfect, and since he didn't intend for Coffee to get shot, he wasn't sure he could be in a full energy state when the blast went off.

"Nero...," Pauly said, obviously guessing at the problem.

"If I don't make it, finish off the damned demon. And don't mourn me. Believe me, my dying today might be the more pleasant of outcomes."

All of them stilled at that. If they hadn't understood the gravity of the situation before, they did now. But Pauly was the only one still able to talk. "Nero...," he said, his voice choked.

"No time," Nero barked out. "Get furry."

Then suddenly a familiar voice sounded from right behind him. "Huh. No tinglies. Somehow I always thought transporting would be tingly." Nero spun around as Josh shrugged and dropped his backpack on the ground. "I kind of miss the sound effects too. But this was just, bam, I'm here." Then he grinned at Nero's shocked face. "What, did you think I'd let you face this alone?"

"Josh," Nero breathed, and then he bellowed. "What the fuck did you do?"

Josh's expression softened. "Not everyone leaves when you tell them to. Some of us choose to stick around." Then he looked around at the wolves, identifying them one by one. "Cream, Coffee, you're both a lot prettier than in Nero's pictures. Pauly, stop bristling. I'm here to help. And Mother, please don't pee on me. Trust me when I say I've already endured the Nero initiation. I don't need any more hazing, thank you very much."

Nero's gaze shifted to Mother. It did indeed look like she wanted to piss on the newcomer. They all did. "He's…." What? His lover, his best friend? "He's one of us. I trust him with my life. More important, I trust him with all of your lives." And that was the best endorsement he could give for anyone.

"All right, everyone," Josh called, "let me check your harnesses. When it's time, they're quick release. Tug here."

While Nero got Pauly into his shield harness, Josh did a thorough job adjusting straps and checking… he had no idea what. Then it was time for Nero go to wolf, but he couldn't change without saying something to Josh, though he had no idea exactly what.

And when Josh looked up to see him staring, his expression turned surprisingly stubborn, as if he was fighting as much emotion as Nero was and was also refusing to let it out. "I made my own choice," he said. "It wasn't a noble sacrifice or a lovesick act of desperation. I've found my passion, and I'm not willing to let it all be erased. No matter what happens now"—his eyes glittered sharp with unshed tears—"or between us, this is what I want."

Nero couldn't argue with that, especially since he was suddenly struck by the difference between the Josh he'd first met and the one who stood before him now. The Josh from before had been drifting and was a bit of a whiner. The most important thing in his life was putting on a show at a convention in the hopes that he'd get laid that evening. The man before him now vibrated with conviction. He had a strength that was impressive and a determination to walk his path as he saved not only the lives of Nero's team, but a whole section of Wisconsin too. He was focused and stronger than he'd ever been.

"I'm so proud to know you," Nero said. "And I'm so grateful for everything, Josh. If it ends today—"

"Shut up. It doesn't. Get furry so we can get on with it." Then he took a breath. "Wait! I need a gun first."

"What? Why?"

"Trust me on this, okay? Do you have a .45 anywhere?"

"Mother's Glock." Nero pulled it out of a lockbox and handed it over. Josh checked it over with quick efficiency, then shoved it in the back of his pants. "Thanks. Now get furry."

Damn, the guy was even issuing orders now. Good for him. So Nero complied. He shifted quickly and stood calmly while Josh strapped a bad-smelling shield onto his wolf body. And if there were extra caresses as Josh worked, moments when Josh burrowed his fingers deep into Nero's fur and squeezed, then it was only because they'd always communicated better with their bodies than they had with words. And that was why, when all was in place, Nero tilted his head up and licked Josh's face—a big wet swipe right over his lips.

"Ew!" Josh wiped the slobber off with his hand. "That's disgusting." But he was smiling as he said it. And then he reached into his backpack and pulled out his computer plus a headset. He slipped on the headset first. "Okay, everyone, bark if you can hear me."

Nero jerked sideways at the sudden sound next to his ear. Apparently Josh had put in a tiny speaker, but wolf ears didn't need anything so loud. He barked loud and sharp at Josh, as did everyone else on the team. And then, when Josh didn't seem to understand, Nero went right up beside his ear and barked as loud as he could.

"Hey!" Josh exclaimed, and then his eyes widened in surprise. "Oh. Too loud?"

Nero nodded.

Josh quickly tapped on his keyboard. "Better?"

Five wolves yipped in unison.

"I'll take that as a yes." Then he pointed to his laptop screen. "Okay, I put cameras in your hoodies too, and some sensors, so I can see what's happening on levels you can't." He glanced at Nero. "You can thank Stratos for the programming. I didn't have a clue." Then he turned back to his screen. "I'm going to stay here and watch everything. I don't want to interfere with your attack, but if I tell you to move, you've got to listen, okay? Bark if you understand."

Silence. No one answered because they were all looking to Nero for his decision. Fortunately Nero had no doubt. He yipped once, and then he barked louder for good measure.

That was good enough for his team. They all yipped their agreement, and then it was time for them to go. Nero looked one last time at Josh, who gave him a thumbs-up. Everything was set on his end, and so he turned and began to run for the bastard demon.

It was awkward carrying a shield on his back, and he was grateful for the distance to the lake. It gave him time to test out the added weight, to figure out how to leap and how to strike. It would have been better to have more than a few minutes to do this, especially since he also had to mentally prepare for this attack. But he'd replayed this moment in his head so many times that it was a relief to finally be here. That he had Josh in his ear too made it especially sweet, though the guy sure was chatty.

"So it turns out that back in the fifties, a guy wrote a dime novel based on a real-life serial killer that liked to murder ice fishermen. Must be a Wisconsin thing. Anyway, since he was a horror writer—like an early Stephen King—he made it into a paranormal thing, a demon with weirdly colored skin and orange blood who haunted lakes in order to eat random Wisconsin-ites. The writer never made it famous, but the locals loved it. They retold the story countless times, and now it's an urban legend here. I think it's the origin of your lakeside people-eater. It's a good thing that I'm a fast reader, because I had like ten seconds to read the ending before I got zapped here. It told me everything we need to know to kill the demon. Bitter—you know who—gave it to me. The writing's not bad, but—"

Nero did a hard, sharp bark. They were nearing the attack area and needed to focus.

"What? Am I talking too much?"

Another bark, this time lower and more growly.

"Got it. Okay. Go on and take 'em out. Take 'em down. Do your… do your stuff."

Nero snorted. He doubted anyone else got the reference to *Independence Day*, but Nero recognized it from their last movie night. And then there was no more time for memories because he was starting the first attack run.

Chapter 27

JOSH STARED at his split screen and tried to calm his racing heart. It helped to focus on the five tiny images of the wolves as they ran through the woods, but he still had equal parts excitement and terror zipping through his mind. He couldn't believe he was actually doing this. He was the tech geek helping to take out a Big Bad. Lives depended on him and his tech, which was terrifying given how many failed attempts there were in any science. And yet he couldn't deny the thrill. This was him, nerdy Josh Collier, as part of the team.

Or more accurately, part of the pack.

That's what Nero had said. *He's one of us.* And from Nero, that was like being handed the key to his heart. But Josh couldn't bask in the glow of that because he had to do his job. He grinned. This was his *job*, and he loved it.

He focused in on the action, piecing it together from what he'd learned reading the mission file and watching the recording of Nero's report to the review board. From what he could tell, right now everything was going exactly as before. They were running in formation, headed toward the demon.

"Get as close as you can," he said into the microphone. "And space the shields as evenly as possible. You want to be able to get to one within twenty seconds."

There was no response, but then he didn't expect one. They didn't want to tip off the demon that they were coming, but then again, how could the bastard miss five shields plunking down into the snow? Even as light as they were—which honestly wasn't that light—they would still make a thud when they hit dirt.

It didn't matter. The wolves needed the protection. He watched from five different vantage points as one by one, they dropped the shields into the dirt and then veered around them, going for the attack run. Nero's team didn't waste time.

Josh focused on Nero's camera view, cursing the black-and-white image. If he'd thought for two seconds, he would have realized that he could put color cameras in and damn the extra expense. He wanted to see what a "weirdly colored demon" looked like, but all he got was a gray image of a humanoid crouching behind a bush. Not exactly Technicolor, but it was getting freaky large in the image because Nero was in attack range.

He switched over to Coffee's camera because that had the better view. Nero zipped in fast and low, then abruptly jumped aside as the demon twisted and swiped. It was like Nero knew the strike was coming, which he probably did. Then, when the demon was off-balance, Nero did a swipe with his claws and tore a huge chunk out of the thing's leg.

Pale stuff squirted out—demon blood—and Josh released a cheer. Mother and Pauly went in next. Their cameras dipped and swerved, making Josh a little seasick, but they managed to get the bastard from either side. Mother used some kind of leaping maneuver to get her jaws on the thing's arm. Pauly did the same thing on the other side, missed, then got a swipe in with his paw that widened the gashes that Nero had made.

Gunshots rang out, the sound shocking in the crisp morning air. Josh already knew it was the demon. The thing was a really good shot, even while being torn apart.

"Watch the gun!" he called into the mic. "Cream, this is where you get shot!"

Cream's camera abruptly dipped and swerved. Evasive maneuvers, obviously. And suddenly Coffee was leaping up and down in the air. Jumping?

A moment later the reason became clear. The demon hesitated, seemingly flustered for a moment, and shot wildly, missing both Cream and Coffee. *Good going!* Josh clapped his hands in delight, but even though the demon had missed this time, he still had a gun and was taking aim. What it didn't realize, though, was that Nero wasn't going to let it have the chance.

The alpha wolf, followed closely by Mother and Pauly, was already running full tilt at the demon. The demon had three pissed-off werewolves coming straight for it and another two right behind. And it was penned in by the greenery and the lake, which meant it had one last trick up its sleeve.

Josh checked the levels on the simple sensors he'd had put into their hoodies. They likely wouldn't survive the blast, but that wasn't the point. Sure enough, the demon's internal temperature was rising fast.

"It's about to blow! Get to the shields. If you can't—" A quick look showed him that Mother was out of range. Damn it! "Shift *now!*"

He wasn't sure it would work. Just because Nero had survived the first time didn't mean any of them could do it again. Worse, Coffee was an old-school werewolf. Lots of bones crunching and excruciating pain and no in-between energy state. That meant they couldn't get out of this by shifting. They had to crouch behind the shields and hope that the Volcax kept them from being burned alive.

"Please, please, please," he whispered.

The demon blew.

Even though Josh knew he was out of range, the blast still terrified him. He felt more than heard the boom as the earth shook beneath his feet. Then the heat wave came at him with a roar. He knew from the pictures that the nearest trees were vaporized, but that did nothing to prepare him for the wave of hot air that flattened trees farther out and set them instantly on fire. The air was sucked out of his lungs, and every cell in his body felt the heat as a living thing. Thank God he'd set up on the far side of the van and the vehicle had shielded him. Not just the van, but the wheels as well, because otherwise his feet and ankles would be blistered raw. And it was also a good thing he'd pocketed Mother's gun. The metal was now hot where it was tucked in the back of his jeans, and he prayed the bullets didn't explode and blow his ass off.

Thank God, he was lucky. His ass stayed exactly as it was. The heat was intense but bearable, and though his computer was blank, it didn't appear dead.

But what about everyone else?

As soon as he could breathe without choking, he took off at a dead run for the others. All the electronics were fried, so he stripped off the headset on the way. Mother's Glock dug into his ass with every step and his shoes were going to melt soon from the heat, but he kept running. It took forever to get there while his gaze took in the blackened landscape. Sweet heaven, nothing could survive this. Nothing *had* survived.

"Nero!" he bellowed. "Nero! Anybody!"

He was still running when he heard it. Nero's human howl. He'd know the sound anywhere, and it carried in the still air like a divine bell. And thank God, there was no mournful note in it. If anything it sounded triumphant, especially when it was repeated by four other voices, all howling with him.

Nero had survived. Better yet, the entire pack had survived.

Josh stumbled to a walk and shot back his own howl. It wasn't a strong as theirs. He was still breathless and had to get to them immediately, but he needed to answer. That was what packmates did.

They'd survived!

He broke into a run again and saw them long before he made it to their sides. All five in their naked human forms. Pauly and Cream had obviously survived and then shifted to human as soon as they could. And now they surrounded a pink, blobby thing that was bleeding orange blood. Gross.

"Don't. Kill it!" he bellowed. And when everybody turned to look at him in shock, he repeated it. "Don't kill it."

Nero said something that even wolf ears couldn't catch, but Josh could guess what it was. Something along the lines of "Are you crazy?" He wasn't, though he could understand why they thought that way.

He picked up the pace again and finished the last of the distance. God, he had to get back on the calisthenics wagon, because huffing and puffing like this was embarrassing. Fortunately they waited for him. And when the blobby thing tried to make a run for it, one of the pack was there to shove it back.

"You could have shifted," Nero said when Josh got close enough. "You're a lot faster as a wolf."

"I know, but it would have been harder to carry this." He pulled Mother's Glock out of his back pocket. "I haven't yet mastered the art of carrying something in my wolf mouth without slobbering all over it."

"Give me that!" Mother cried as she reached for the weapon, but Josh held it out to Nero instead.

"Remember when I was trying to tell you about this thing?" He gestured at the demon. "About how it's a local legend that started from a dime novel?"

Nero nodded, but he had his get-to-the-point face on.

"In the book, the thing keeps coming back. They stab it, burn it, even chop off its head, but it keeps coming back."

Nero's eyes widened, and he looked back at the demon. "But—"

"Then the hero shoots it between its eyes with a magic bullet he got from a fairy prince."

Nero's eyes widened. "Seriously?"

"Fortunately we both know one." He pulled out what looked like a normal bullet except that it had the image of a twisted tree imprinted on the casing. He'd gotten it from Bitterroot, the same time the guy had given him the book. "Care to do the honors?" Josh asked. He figured that out of all of them, Nero deserved the right to end this particular legend himself.

Apparently Nero agreed. He grabbed the bullet and the gun and quickly loaded the chamber. The demon wasn't lying still for this. He tried to make a break for it, but given that he was mostly torn to pieces, it was easy for Coffee to restrain him. Cream helped by grabbing hold of the thing's head and holding it still in an impressive display of strength.

"Don't miss," Cream growled.

"Not planning on it," Nero said. Then he pulled the trigger.

A dead shot right between the eyes. Josh would have cheered, except he had his hands over his ears in pain. He really needed to get used to big bangs.

Then, best of all, the demon poofed into ash, just like in the book.

Hallelujah!

That was when another sound intruded. Someone was clapping. And since it took him a bit to hear the sound, the others had turned around by the time Josh managed to look behind him. There, grinning at them like a proud papa, was the diminutive Bitterroot.

"Well done, well done," he was saying. From the looks on everyone's faces, they all knew him and felt varying degrees of hatred toward him. However, no one looked as murderous as Mother.

"What do you want?" she snapped. That wasn't exactly what she said. Josh wasn't hearing well yet, but he could read the curse words off her lips and guessed at the rest. And then his ears cleared enough that he could hear Nero's grim response.

"He's here for me."

"Actually, he's not," Josh said. Then he grinned at everyone. "Well, it was fun while it lasted."

Nero's face took on a horrified expression. "What did you do?"

"I convinced him that one geek was way better than one meathead, so I swapped in for you." He gestured at Nero's pack. "You'd die without them. You were dying every day that you were apart."

"That's not true. Not after...."

"Not after we connected. I know. But like you said, they came first. And since I've pretty much cut ties with my family, I'm free to choose where I want to go and what I want to do." His expression hardened as he invested determination in his words. "I like who I am now. I will not have it all erased and go back to who I was. I won't allow it."

"We can recruit you again—" Nero argued, but Josh cut him off.

"It's done. Besides, he said their Fairyland is way better than Disney's version. It could be fun." Josh was proud of himself for sounding so calm. In truth, the idea of going to Fairyland scared the shit out of him, but if it would give Nero back his pack, then it was worth it. The guy deserved some happiness, and Josh wanted to be the one to give it to him.

Plus, his lovelorn side got off on the drama of it. He got to act out his very own noble sacrifice, just like at the end of his favorite movies. Of course, with the reality of it staring him in the face, he could admit that he was weak-at-the-knees terrified, but right now he was determined to put on a brave face. Nero, however, had his stubborn one on.

"No," Nero said. "No way are you taking my place—"

Bitterroot held up his hand. "Your debt is paid," the fairy said calmly. "But if you'd like to negotiate—"

"No!" All four of Nero's packmates said the word loud and clear, even though Nero had shaped his mouth into a yes.

Mother's tone was sharp. "We do not negotiate with fairies!"

Bitterroot grinned. "And yet here we are." Then, before anyone could call him more crude names, he slapped his hands together and addressed Nero. "Hurry up and choose. The authorities will be here soon, and I wish to be gone by then."

"Choose?" Nero frowned at the fae prince. "Choose who pays my debt? It's me—"

"No," Bitterroot said with a heavy sigh. "Choose which timeline you wish to exist in."

This time it was Pauly who asked the obvious question. "Come again?"

"Did you think time travel was easy? You have created two timelines that exist simultaneously. In one timeline, your pack dies, you recruit Josh and have many nights of sweet passion. In this timeline, you kill the demon and they survive. You may choose to be in this timeline with them." He gestured to the pack. "Or you can be in the one where Josh plays with your diddle all the ding-dong day." He didn't even look at Josh as his face hardened. "You cannot be in both. So choose."

"Wait!" Josh gasped. "You can't mean that both timelines exist. I thought I'd be erased. I thought…."

"Is it my fault that you never studied string theory? Yes, both timelines exist in parallel dimensions."

Well, hell. Josh grimaced as he played through scenarios in his head. He still would have done the exact same thing, but it would have been nice to know his options. Meanwhile, Bitterroot was still talking, his voice as pompous as it was condescending.

"What will you pick, Nero? Your pack, which you have worked so hard to save? Or your boyfriend?"

Josh shook his head. "We're not—"

"The hell we aren't," Nero growled.

"Goddammit!" Mother abruptly interrupted. "You went and fell in love in a timeline where we don't exist. We didn't get to see it!" She sounded like that was the most horrible part of it all. The others murmured their agreement. But there were also a few sly smiles, and Cream gave Josh a surreptitious thumbs-up.

Meanwhile, Nero was staring at his team with his heart in his eyes. The agony in him was palpable—or maybe Josh was feeling his own—so he cut in with the obvious answer. It would hurt too much to hear Nero say it aloud.

"He picks them," Josh said. Hadn't Nero said that this very morning? That they were first. That they *came first*. "I'm going to be off in Fairyland, so stay with them. There's no point in us both being miserable."

Bitterroot sniffed audibly. "Some people do enjoy being in my employ."

Mother snorted. "Only the masochists and the mentally ill."

"I take exception to that," Bitterroot countered.

"I'm sure you do," she agreed.

And that was a whole lot of banter that Josh knew indicated a *history* between these two. Unfortunately he had no time to delve into that, especially as Nero grabbed Mother's hand.

"You were always my favorite," he said, interrupting what was probably another witty comeback. And then he looked at the others in turn. "Just like you. And you. And you."

"Aw, fuck," Pauly said. "He really is in love."

"You're alive," Nero continued, "and that's all I ever wanted. Even if it's in a different parallel dimension from me."

"Shit," Coffee murmured.

"It's been an honor and a privilege. I—" His words choked off as he stared at his team. Then he squared his shoulders and turned to Bitterroot. "I pick Josh's timeline."

It took a moment for Josh to understand what was happening, and even longer for the reality to penetrate. There were two timelines, and Nero had picked the one with Josh in it. Not his pack, not the dead demon, but the one where his pack died and Josh came in to save the day. "What?" he gasped. "No!" He took an abrupt step forward. "Don't be stupid. I'll be in Fairyland, and your pack means everything to you. You said so."

Nero turned to him with a shrug. "Turns out you mean more."

"But I'll be in *Fairyland*."

"What if I'm with you?" He eyed Bitterroot. "What do you think? Two of us is better than one. We make a good team. We'll both serve the sentence at half the time."

"No!" Josh said. Well, that's what he tried to say, but his throat had closed down. Nero had chosen him over his pack, and the magnitude of that cut off every sound, every breath, and every thought except gratitude.

"Well, that is an interesting thought," Bitterroot said. "Especially since we have to address the subject of you reneging on our contract."

"What?" Nero jolted. "I did no such thing!"

"I believe our contract required secrecy. That means you couldn't tell anyone about our deal." He arched a brow at Josh. "And yet you told him."

"That's different. Josh had to know. He had to get the shields and the jackets—"

"It doesn't matter why you broke the deal." Bitterroot smirked. "Only that you did."

"And this is why we never make fairy deals," Mother huffed. "Because there's always a fucking catch."

Nero advanced on Bitterroot. His hands were clenched and his brow furrowed. He towered over the diminutive fairy in the most intimidating way. Unfortunately Bitterroot didn't seem the least bit cowed.

"You owed me a favor!" Nero barked.

"Which is why you aren't right now covered in fairy boils. But a contract is a contract—"

Mother cut in, her voice unusually subdued. "I'll take his time," she said, and suddenly she had 100 percent of Bitterroot's attention.

"What?" he asked, his voice airy light, but there was an intensity to the question that could not be denied.

Mother folded her arms across her chest. "How long is Josh's employment contract for?"

Josh spoke up, his voice thick but still able to say the number that had been bouncing around his brain since the moment he'd made the deal. "Forty-nine human years."

"I'll do it—" Mother said.

"No!" Both he and Nero were emphatic. And in stereo.

"—I'll serve their sentence for them, but I'm not doing forty-nine years. I'll do one, because a woman has got to be worth at least forty-nine of these losers."

"Forty," Bitterroot offered.

"One."

"Forty-two and I'll pay you in rubies."

"One. And I'll take human money in my bank account."

"Thirty-five, and you'll be my consort."

"One, and I'll be your employee. Separate living quarters and duties we both agree on."

"You will be obedient to me and me alone?"

She swallowed. "I'll perform duties we agree upon ahead of time. For one human year."

Bitterroot glanced to the side, and his smile widened. Josh didn't even know what he was looking at until he spoke. "You may be my dragon master," he said.

She snorted. "Since when do you have dragons?"

"Since now," he said, and he moved quickly over to one of the blackened shields. Bending down, he gently sifted through the partially melted framework and ash to where that egg had been. A moment later he was gingerly lifting up a tiny dragon no larger than the palm of his hand. Then he walked it back to Mother, using one hand to lift hers, palm-side up, before gently setting the ruby-red creature in her hand.

"Wow," Coffee whispered. "You totally *Game of Thrones*-ed it."

Josh had to agree. All of them crowded closer to see, but Mother was the most entranced of all, her eyes wide as she stared at the delicate creature.

"There's more," Bitterroot said as he went to the debris of shields littered on the ground. One in each pile of ash, all different jewel colors. He gathered each one, warning Cream away from a shield with a dark glare and a snapped order to "Stay back. They're delicate and take special handling." Then he reverently set each one in Mother's hands. And when they spilled past her palms, he used her wrists and put one on her shoulder.

"They're gorgeous," she breathed.

"So you agree? You'll be in my dragon master?"

"I don't know anything about dragons."

"I'll teach you. And at the end of a year, you may keep one for your own."

Her head shot up, tears in her eyes. "One year?" she whispered.

"And I will pay you with a dragon."

"Yes." The word came so fast, Josh wondered if she'd spoken before she could change her mind.

"Yes," Bitterroot echoed. And then right before their eyes, he changed. Where there once had stood a condescending youth, there now stood a tall, dark fairy prince with a shimmering butterfly tattoo. His hair was sleek black, his eyes even more so. And when he touched her cheek, Mother shivered. Her lips parted in shock or fear, or maybe just a riot of emotions that flashed through her eyes too fast to catch.

The new Bitterroot smiled. It was a dark looked filled with a danger that sucked the heat from the air.

Then they were gone.

And so was Wisconsin, because just as quickly, Nero and Josh were back in Indianapolis, standing in the park on a brilliant winter morning.

Chapter 28

NERO DIDN'T stumble so much as reel. Everything had changed so fast. And when he looked at Josh's wide, startled eyes, he realized that they had collapsed against each other, that Josh was in his arms and they were holding each other so tight, not even a fairy crowbar could come between them.

Josh's eyes were bright, the sunlight sparking in the hazel color making them first blue, then green, then back. Nero knew he could get lost in those eyes, in the changing colors and the emotions they revealed. But mostly, he knew he could get lost in Josh. The man who had made him whole when every part of him felt broken.

"So it's done?" Josh asked. "We're… free?"

"I think so." Nero wasn't the smart one here, so he had to talk it through just to make sure he understood it. "I went back in time and killed that fucker demon."

Josh nodded. "I went with you and made sure you killed it right."

"Yeah. And thanks."

Josh grinned. "You can thank me with sex."

Nero had no problem with that, but his mind was still stumbling past everything that had happened. "So I created a new timeline, one with my team alive."

Josh's voice softened. "They're alive, Nero. You saved them."

"We saved them," he said. "And they're going to kick ass over there."

Josh nodded. "But now we're back in the original timeline. The one where I was recruited to save your ass."

"And I thank you with sex." He dropped his forehead against Josh's. "Of course I picked you."

Josh whispered, "Thank you," so softly that Nero almost missed it. But they were pressed so close together that even if the words hadn't had sound, he would have felt it straight from Josh's heart to his own.

"Thank you for saving me," he whispered, and he meant it in more than the physical sense. He'd have lost himself in grief if it hadn't been for Josh. And now he knew how much more he could feel, how much richer life was with Josh in it.

Meanwhile, Josh was picking up the tale. "But someone had to pay Bitterroot. I was willing to do it."

"So was I."

"But Mother—"

Nero gulped. Mother had taken the hit for both of them. She'd agreed to serve Bitterroot for a year in their stead. "She wanted to. She has a thing for dragons. She's going to get to raise dragons."

"Wow," Josh murmured, and Nero echoed the sound. And though his heart ached that she had to pay for his choices, he remembered the look of awe on her face as she held those tiny dragons. Her year's employment wasn't going to be as awful as he feared. She might even love it.

"But what about—" Josh said. Nero didn't let him finish. He kissed him quick and hard. And when Josh melted into him, Nero let his body surround his lover and cradle him the way he hadn't been able to before now. He held Josh with his whole heart and soul.

Then he whispered into Josh's ear. "No buts. No questions. Not yet. There will be time enough later. I just want to hold you."

Josh returned the hug, squeezing him until he felt breathless. And then Josh whispered back. "Can we do a bit more than hold each other? I mean, if you want…."

"Yes." A thousand times yes. But instead of saying more, he kissed Josh again, pouring all of his need into it, which Josh took and gave back, like an endless loop of lust and love. Then Nero broke the kiss with a gasp. "Hotel. Now."

"Yes."

Nero's favorite word.

It was a measure of their distraction that they only then realized that Nero was naked. He'd never dressed after shifting back from a wolf, and it probably wasn't a good idea to walk through a city park in his birthday suit.

Fortunately Bitterroot had been kind. They found a neat pile of Nero's clothes at the base of a nearby tree. And right underneath the clothes sat Josh's backpack, already filled with his laptop, headset, and the dime novel on the Wisconsin demon.

Nero dressed quickly while Josh hoisted his backpack onto his shoulder. Then they held on to each other as they walked. Neither seemed very steady on their feet, and yet Nero had never felt more filled with life. He struggled to put a label to this feeling welling up inside him that was more than lust and even bigger than love. In the end, the word whispered out from his lips before he even realized how right it was.

"Home."

Josh turned to him. "What?"

"This. You and me. It feels like home."

"Better than home," he answered. "At least my home."

Nero snorted. "That's family. That's different, and it's got good and bad in it."

"Ain't that the truth."

They kept walking while Nero settled into this feeling with Josh. It felt as if no matter where he was going or what he was doing, he would always come back to Josh. Because Josh was home in a way that even his pack had never been. That thought grounded him, pleased him, and gave him the strength to say his next words.

"I love you, Josh. I want us to stay together. I'll figure out how to work it with Wulf, Inc. I can lead a geek pack with you in it or bring you into a combat pack. Or if you want civilian life, I can work on that too. I want to be with you."

Josh stretched up and kissed him hard and fast. And when Nero would have deepened it, he pulled back. "I've already committed to you. Hell, I was going to work for that asshole for forty-nine years just to make you happy. I love you. Whatever you want to do, we'll work it out. I swear."

"Me too. I swear, I promise, *I do*."

"Yeah." Josh grinned. "I do too."

Their next kiss was tender, sweet, but it held the shared promise of forever. And it might have gone on that long if it weren't for a sound—a steady clapping noise that came from over Josh's shoulder. Eventually they heard it. They stiffened and twisted around, both startled to see Bruce leaning against a tree trunk and watching them with dark green eyes.

"Congratulations, little brother. Looks like you've found love." The words sounded sincere, but there was a dark look in the man's eyes and an envious taint to his expression.

"Bruce, what are you doing here?"

"Following you. *Watching* you."

Oh shit.

Josh blew out a breath. "Look, I know it seems strange, but—"

"It seems like you're werewolves who make fairy deals."

Nero tensed. Even if the guy had been following them for the past twenty-four hours, he couldn't have figured all that out. Bruce hadn't been in the alternate timeline, and he sure as hell hadn't seen either of them go wolf. "What makes you say that?" he asked, working hard to sound casual.

"The freaking fairy told me."

"What?" Nero exploded.

"The short one who acts like we're all idiots."

Josh jolted forward. "You didn't make a deal with him, did you? You didn't—"

"All I did was listen and agree to hand you this." He held up a light green piece of parchment, which he passed over to Josh, who shared it with Nero.

When you're ready, call me. I will have five shields, hoodies, and a magic bullet available for your use. No charge except for the dragons.

Nero frowned. "What the hell does that mean? We already killed…."

Josh groaned. The sound was thick and deep, and he slapped his palm against his forehead for emphasis. "We're back in this timeline. In *my* timeline, where I was recruited to find a way around the fire blast."

Nero nodded. "Yeah, I know."

Josh held up the parchment. "Don't you see? In this timeline, the demon is still up there killing Wisconsin."

"What? No, we…." His voice trailed away as he realized that it was true. This was the timeline where his team died, the demon escaped, and Josh was recruited. The demon was still alive and they still had to kill it. His groan was deeper and louder than Josh's but no more heartfelt. And even worse was that he was only now seeing Bitterroot's whole plan. "We risk our lives, and he gets dragons." He crumpled the paper in his fist. "Did I tell you that he's the one who told us about the demon in the first place? He's the one who sent us on this hunt. Unbelievable."

Josh looked at his brother. "Did you read this?"

Bruce snorted. "Of course I read it. He *wanted* me to read it. Otherwise he would have put it in an envelope."

Nero looked at Josh's brother. He studied the tense posture of the man, saw the underlying anger but also a need deep inside. Bruce was his father's son, that was for sure, and something was riding him hard.

"What else?" Nero asked. And when Bruce didn't answer, he put command in his voice. "Fairies don't just give up information for free. What else did he offer you?"

Bruce held out his other hand. Nestled in his palm lay a dark red cherry, completely mundane-looking, except that it was a fairy gift, and that meant it was dangerous. Bruce lifted it up to the sunlight, and all three of them were temporarily mesmerized by the beauty of the simple fruit.

"He said if I want what you've got, I have to eat this." Bruce's gaze lifted until he looked at the two of them. "And I do. I want it." Then, before either of them could stop him, he popped the thing in his mouth.

"No!" Josh cried out, but it was too late. As they watched, Bruce chewed quickly and swallowed. They waited for a tense minute, everyone prepared for something dramatic to happen.

Nothing.

Bruce's face shifted into a grimace of disappointment, and Josh released his breath on a relieved sigh, but Nero knew the truth. Fairy fruit was a lot of things. It was powerful and unpredictable, with a whole universe of possibilities in every one. But the one thing that fairy fruit never, ever did was *nothing*.

So while Josh held out a hand to his brother, Nero dug the car keys out of his pocket and slapped them into Josh's open palm. "Go get my phone from the glove compartment and call in. Tell them that we've got another recruit."

"But why?" Josh asked. "Nothing's happened."

"Yet."

And right on cue, Bruce's eyes changed, his body tensed, and he opened his mouth for a scream.

"Crap," Nero groaned. "I hope he fits in my car."

It took the two of them together to drag Bruce's wolf body to his car. They were both sweating and huffing. It wasn't that Bruce didn't want to go with them—he clearly did—but the agony and confusion of a first shift were riding him hard. He couldn't co-ordinate his body parts even if he did have the focus. Which meant that Nero put Bruce's head in a choke hold while Josh sweated and cursed while trying to carry his brother's back half.

Fortunately no one saw them as they dragged a twisting, growling wolf out of the woods. They were ten feet from their car when the Wulf, Inc. van screeched to a halt in front of them. Nero was doing his best to hold on to Bruce despite the slobber that was making his arms slick when Yordan leaned out the van window to bark a question at him.

"What the hell are you doing?"

Nero shot him an incredulous glare. Wasn't it obvious? Apparently not, because he had to gasp out, "New recruit."

With a curse, Yordan gestured to the driver, who got out and quickly trotted around the car. It was Bing, looking movie-star perfect as he crouched down in front of the still-struggling Bruce.

"Be still," he said, his voice resonant with command.

Bruce froze. Every body part, every hair follicle stiffened to rigidity.

From the back side, Josh blew out a heavy breath. "Great. Now help me carry him to the car."

Bing shook his head. "We are needed in Wisconsin. Now." And then he opened his mouth to say something else, but Josh threw his hand up over his eyes.

"Don't you dare Jedi mind-trick me. I don't care what's going on in Wisconsin. This is my *brother*."

Yordan groaned as he finally got out of the van. "Like we need family drama now. Here."

With a mighty heave, Yordan lifted up the rigid wolf, and all together, they crammed him into the back of the van. But when Bing went to shut the door, Josh grabbed his arm.

"Don't leave him like that. Order him to go to sleep."

Bing clearly didn't like taking orders from Josh, but it was a reasonable request. Bruce was a new recruit, and it was their job to help him, not make it worse, even if the idiot had brought it on himself.

To his credit, Bing didn't argue but adjusted until he was looking straight into Bruce's frozen eyes. "Relax and sleep for...." He glanced at Yordan. "How long?"

"Three days."

"Three days," Bing continued.

Right on cue, Bruce's muscles relaxed. He flopped flat onto the van floor and started snoring. Josh shot Nero a wry look.

"What I wouldn't have given to do that to Bruce when we were kids."

"I am not a parlor trick," Bing snapped. "There is real danger, and you have delayed us with this foolishness."

Josh stiffened, his mouth opening for some smartass response, but Nero stepped quickly in front of him. First things first. "What's going on?"

Yordan sighed. "The usual. World-ending disaster in Wisconsin."

Naturally. Because in this timeline, the demon was alive and well. And still killing the planet.

Nero nodded and pushed Josh toward his car. "We'll follow you. Call me on my cell and tell me exactly what is going on. And then we'll tell you how to fix it."

To be continued...

DON'T MISS WHAT HAPPENS NEXT!

www.dreamspinnerpress.com

Were-Geeks Save the World: Book Two

Paramedic and firefighter Bruce Collier became a werewolf to protect his family—and hopefully make amends for the way he treated his younger brother. His bitterness nearly turned him into the monster he thought his brother was… until he met Mr. Happy.

Werewolf Laddin Holt—aka Mr. Happy—likes things organized as he makes them go boom. He's Wulf, Inc's explosive expert and the only one calming the turmoil inside Bruce.

At least until they're drawn into a conflict between two factions of fairies living around Lake Wacka Wacka. Bruce wants to take them out, Laddin has other ideas, and neither of them sees the real threat lurking behind the scenes—or how their love could be the answer to everybody's problems.

Chapter 1

"YOU WANT me to put wallpaper on the teahouse wall," Laddin Holt said. And though he didn't phrase it as a question, his tone all but screamed, *Are you serious?*

His boss and the lead actor for this independent film nodded. "Yes. China invented wallpaper. This room would have a textile-type wallpaper."

"But the wall is only seen when it gets blown up. It's on screen for ten seconds at most."

Bing Wen Hao merely looked at him, his face an impassive mask. But Laddin had been working shoulder to shoulder with the guy for two months now. He could read Bing's opinion in the smallest shift of his chin. And on this point, Bing was being irrationally stubborn.

"It will take me hours," Laddin said, still hoping to reach some bit of sanity in his boss's brain. "I have a dozen other things to do today."

No-go. Bing was in a knot of anxiety because some Chinese bigwig was coming this afternoon, and when the boss got anxious, everybody suffered.

"Details matter," Bing stressed.

Laddin knew that. He was the king of details, which was why he'd gotten the job of assistant director on this movie set. It was quite a step up from being the explosives guy on five failed action shows. He was in charge of everything that wasn't acting or camera placement. That meant the entire set design was his department, and he refused to fail now just because his boss was being irrational.

"Perhaps we could try different lighting—" he began, but Bing wasn't going to let that pass.

"If you cannot do it, perhaps someone else will have an easier time of it."

Laddin ground his teeth. Those words—or versions of it—had plagued him his entire life. His right hand was deformed, with his middle and fourth finger never growing beyond infant size. It had never limited his ability to do anything, and yet it was always a question in other people's minds.

"It'll be done by noon," he snapped. He just had to figure out how to do everything else on his list as well.

Bing gave him a slight nod—his version of *thank you*—and then moved off to do his own work. And though Laddin was annoyed by the man's obsessive attention to a detail that wouldn't be onscreen for more than ten seconds, he couldn't fault Bing's work ethic. The guy lived on the set night and day, working to make this movie as spectacular as possible on a very tiny budget.

Which meant Laddin had to find some specialty textile wallpaper ASAP.

He'd barely pulled out his cell phone to start googling when his morning Grandmama call came through. He answered it even though he didn't have time for her because he knew she would call back every five minutes until he did.

"Hello, Grandmama. I'm still alive."

"Oh, you poor baby. It still hasn't happened."

He chuckled because, really, what else was there to do? "Most grandmothers would be happy that their only grandchild is still alive."

"You're not going to die. How many times do I have to tell you that?" Her voice settled into her performance tone. Grandmama was a psychic by profession, and sometimes—most times—she needed to put on a show. "The day we realized your hand was different, I had a vision. The great Angel Charoum whispered to me that in your twenty-eighth year, you would transform into magic—"

"I'm really busy right now. We're supposed to start filming tomorrow, and everyone's on edge." Grandmama hated being interrupted, and usually he'd let her prattle on, but he didn't have the patience today.

"Don't despair, Laddin. It will happen for you. I know it will. There are still two months left before your birthday. You remember who Charoum is, yes?"

Of course he did. "He's the Angel of Silence." Which was rich, since Charoum's prediction had been the topic of discussion for nearly every day of his twenty-eight years.

"Exactly! And when the angel of silence speaks, it's very important to listen."

"Yes, Grandmama." And he had listened for twenty-eight years as everyone speculated on what the vision could mean. Most thought he would die, but Grandmama had insisted it was a transformation into magic, which was an entirely different thing. He'd had ten months of daily calls from his mother and grandmother to make sure he was still breathing. Laddin just wanted it over. Death, rebirth, or becoming a crazed leprechaun didn't matter to him so long as it happened. Because at this point, he was pretty sure he'd spent his entire life anticipating something that was simply Grandmama's imagination creating extra excitement around her only grandson's birth. And if it warped his entire life into endless speculation about his twenty-eighth year, then so much the better for her.

Him, not so much.

He was about to invent an excuse to get off the phone, when the phone vibrated in his hand. A quick look had him rolling his eyes, but he knew he had to answer it. "I'm sorry, Grandmama. Mom's calling. I have to tell her I'm still breathing."

"Of course, Laddin. Don't worry. It'll happen soon."

"I'm sure it will," he lied. Then he clicked over to his mother. "Hi, Mom. I'm still alive."

Seven long hours later, the wallpaper was finished, the Chinese bigwig was here and wasting everyone's time, and Laddin had disappeared into his work area to double-check the special effects for tomorrow's scenes.

Which was when a deep, movie-star voice said, "Aladdin Holt?"

"Don't touch anything," he grumbled. It was what he always said when someone walked into his work area. He didn't look up until he was done with the C4, and then when he finally did raise his head, he wish he hadn't.

Two guys stood in his work area. One wore stripper pants, the other some sort of Doctor Strange outfit. "You want the set next door. They're doing that *Game of Thrones* wannabe thing."

Doctor Strange grinned. "We know. That's where we got these outfits."

The stripper—whose torso was movie-worthy—shook his head. "No, we didn't. They had way better stuff than this crap, but it allowed us to fit in while we found you."

Well, that changed their category in Laddin's mind from "thieves" to "groupies." They were both beautiful enough to be actors, but neither of them had the charm. Which meant they were hangers-on looking for any odd job so they could participate in the movie magic. Laddin pulled a business card out of his pocket and handed it over.

"Here's my email address. Send me your résumés and I'll look them over." It wouldn't help them. Not a prayer he'd ever work with a guy who wore stripper pants. And Doctor Strange was already poking things on the electrical bench. "I asked you not to touch anything."

The guy raised his hands and wiggled them in the air. "Not touching. Just sniffing." Then he gestured at the Quit Slackin' and Make It Happen poster taped to the back of his door. "It's like a Successories warehouse exploded in here. Tell us, Mr. Holt, do you find movie-making a little lacking in magic these days? If so, have we got a deal for you!"

There was a dryness to his tone that set up Laddin's hackles. What did this asshole care if he found expecting to die hard to take? He liked being reminded that maybe his grandmother was crazy and today was just another day in a long and healthy life.

"You need to leave here now," he said, his minimal patience exhausted. He advanced, his good hand tightening into a fist. He was small compared to stripper-pants guy, but he was fast, and he had some frustration to work out. Fortunately Stripper Pants held up his hands in a placating gesture.

"Ignore Wiz. He's an ass. My name's Nero, and we're here to offer you a job. It's rewarding work saving the world. That's not an exaggeration, by the way. You'd be doing good for a lot of innocent people."

God, could they get any more annoying? Every asshole in Hollywood thought they had the movie idea that was going to change the world. "I've already got a job, and even if I didn't, this"—he flicked his fingers at the guy's clothes—"doesn't impress me."

Wiz grinned. "Didn't think it would. But how about we try this?" The guy whipped up a three-ring binder and started chanting something. It was cheesy fantasy crap, and Laddin had absolutely no time for this nonsense. So he grabbed stripper boy's arm and whipped him around into a choke hold.

Or he tried to. Normally people underestimated his strength, given that he was a small guy among the tall, dark, and handsome actors in Hollywood. They might not be surprised by his speed, but when he got a hold of a guy's arm, he held on with a death grip, and that usually took everyone by surprise.

Not this time. Sure, he managed a quick grab, but Nero must spend all his time in the gym, because Laddin's best wrestling moves did nothing. As in the guy didn't even bend. Which left Laddin standing there holding on to a big guy's wrist and thinking, *WTF?*

Meanwhile, Wiz finished whatever the hell he was saying with a grand flourish, and then both men froze as if waiting for something to happen.

Laddin waited too. It was force of habit. Grandmama often spoke with a flourish, and it was only polite to wait for the dramatic results. Except these two yahoos had nothing but bad clothing and an all-too-familiar way to waste Laddin's time.

"I'm calling Security," he said as he pulled the walkie-talkie off his hip.

Nero grabbed his hand and held him firm, but his question was for Wiz. "What the hell happened?"

Wiz frowned as he looked down in confusion at his binder. "I don't know. I said it right."

"Damn it!" Nero bit out. "Call Gelpack!"

"I am!" Wiz said as he started texting one-handed.

Meanwhile, Laddin had had enough. He broke the grip on his wrist and pulled up the walkie-talkie. He had one hand on the button, but then his words choked off and his eyes widened in shock.

Goo oozed around and under the door to his work area. It moved fast and with purpose, and though

Laddin had spent his entire career on a Hollywood set, this sight was real life and worthy of the *The Shining*. He gasped and shrank back, thunking into Nero, who used the moment to grab the walkie-talkie with one hand and restrain Laddin with the other.

"Don't worry. He's with us," Nero said as the goo formed into the vague shape of a human.

"What is it?" Laddin gasped, but no one answered. They were too busy talking to each other.

"Why didn't it work?" Nero demanded.

"I said it exactly right," Wiz said, his tone defensive.

"Unless it's him?" Nero said, looking back at Laddin.

"You think it's the wrong spell?" Wiz returned.

There was an edge of controlled panic to both their voices, as if they were worried but used to working things out on the fly. And all the while, Laddin just stared at the goo as it turned to look at him. It didn't even have eyes but the vague impression of orb indents, and yet Laddin would swear it was staring straight at him.

"What are your feelings at this moment?" the gel-like thing warbled.

Nero groaned. "Not now."

"I cannot understand his emotions. I will fix the spell if he explains."

"Later," Nero grumbled, but the gel thing paid no heed. It advanced on them with steps like a man's and yet also appeared more like water being poured forward into leg-shaped molds. If he'd seen it on a TV, he'd have called it cheesy. In real life, it made the hair on the back of his head stand up in terror.

And then the truth hit him full force.

Today was the day. He either died or transformed into…. "Magic," he breathed, seeing his grandmother's prophesy play out before him. Then he laughed, though the sound had a hysterical edge to it. "It's today!"

"Um, yeah, this is magic," Nero said, confusion in his tone. "Well, the spell was. He's—"

"Magic!"

"—Alien."

Laddin shrugged. Either one worked for him. "I'm not going to die," he said as he started taking deep, relieved breaths. His grandmother's prophesy was coming true and it didn't involve his death. The relief sent waves of giddiness through him.

"Not intentionally. It could still happen by accident," Wiz muttered. Then he peered at Laddin. "Are you okay? Maybe the spell did do something. Maybe—"

"The spell was ineffective," the transparent creature said. "You did not say it with clear intent."

"The hell I didn't!" Wiz huffed. "I intend this guy to become a werewolf. I intend to get it over with so we can move on to the next guy. I intend to get myself a really stiff drink after this is all—"

Laddin's head snapped up. "A werewolf? Really?" The idea was exciting in a terrifying kind of way.

Nero twisted him around. "You believe in weres?"

Behind him Wiz snorted. "This is Hollywood. They believe everything."

"We do not!" Laddin snapped, the reaction automatic. It was his grandmama who believed everything. And had taught it to him.

Meanwhile, the gel thing addressed him. "I do not understand your emotions. Most people are frightened."

His hand raised and extended toward Laddin, who immediately choked on his giddiness. Except it wasn't giddiness anymore. The sight of that clear ooze coming close to his face was terrifying, and he squeaked in alarm.

"That is better," the thing said. "The spell should work now. His pattern has settled into fear." The head spun toward Wiz. Not the body, not the shoulders, just the head, *Exorcist*-style. "I will make it stronger to be sure."

Meanwhile, Nero blew out a heavy breath. "We were trying to do this nicely. Without trauma!"

"That was never going to happen," Wiz grumbled.

"Shut up and do the spell. With intent!"

Wiz started speaking, his words a mesmerizing mix of nonsense and real words. Laddin focused on it rather than the horror before him. Nothing here was odd, he told himself. In fact, he'd been waiting his entire life for this very moment. He felt his shoulders relax and his breath steady.

"He is not frightened enough," the alien said. "His mind appears to be unusually accepting. Are you sure this is the right man?"

"Yes!" Nero snapped. "It's Hollywood, for God's sake. Who knows what they think is true? For all we know, you're not his first alien."

"That is most unusual," the thing said, and there was interest in his warbled voice. "I should like to probe this further."

Laddin had no idea if it was intentional or not, but the word *probe* exploded in his mind and tightened areas of his body into hard knots of terror.

"Much better," the alien said as he turned toward Wiz. "You may flourish now."

Wiz did. His voice rose with an impressive crescendo while his free hand danced in the air. And then there was a boom. Not a heard boom, but a felt one, the power impacting Laddin like the biggest car explosion he'd ever done.

His muscles quivered and his bones rumbled with the power of it. His throat closed off and his shoulders hunched. But inside, he was caught up in Grandmama's prediction. Finally, the batty old woman was proven right, and that made him happy. The woman might have plagued his childhood with one wacky idea after another, but in this, she was 100 percent right.

"Do not be so calm," the alien warbled. "Otherwise you will die."

The line was so stupid that it actually relaxed Laddin more. His cells were bathed in an electric current that was almost fun as it coursed through his body in erratic and uncertain patterns. But before he could fully relax, a sound filled the room. A guttural roar as from a beast. It was harsh and terrified, but the fury in the roar spiked Laddin's adrenaline. That was the sound of a creature about to attack. And from the depth of the noise, it wasn't a small animal.

Probably a very pissed-off wolf.

The others must have had the same thought. Wiz and Nero stared at each other in shock. The alien, however, seemed to settle more firmly into its form as he warbled.

"Much better. You will survive now." Then he looked at the other men. "The other one will die without help."

"What other one?" Nero demanded. Then he waved off an answer, pointing hard at Wiz. "You watch this one. Gelpack, you're with me. At least you can get a leg ripped off without dying."

The alien oozed toward the door. "It is hard to stabilize a werewolf while being dismembered, but I will try."

Laddin turned to help. After all, this was his set, his workplace. But his body moved strangely. His head was tilted too far forward, and his vision was different—more side to side, less in front. His balance was off because his hands were taking weight.

He looked down and saw fur and paws, and when he gasped, his tongue was too long and his nose… mama mia, the smells! He could smell everything! He started spinning, stumbling as he tried to maneuver. His backside was wiggling, and he kept trying to stand up to see better, but he was a wolf. He couldn't stand like a man.

He was a wolf! The joy of that flooded his body, and he yipped in excitement. There was so much to explore. Not just his body, but everything in his office was new. Dust bunnies and spilled soda, cracker crumbs and gunpowder. He couldn't decide what to explore first.

"Settle down!" Wiz exclaimed as he knelt down with his arms wide. "You're going to break something! And in here, who knows what you'll set off."

That sank in. His office was filled with explosive charges and delicate electronics for special effects. He'd spent hours organizing things in the most logical and safe manner. The last thing he wanted was to mess that up. So he stilled, though not quite frozen. His backside was still wiggling back and forth. It took him a moment to realize that was his tail whipping around behind him. And with that knowledge came the need to see, so he twisted so he could see. But then his ass turned as well, and he was spinning like a top while Wiz groaned.

"They always have to see their tail. Hold still! I'll grab it so you can see it. I've never seen a happier wolf in my life."

There was a sharp tug on his butt, hard enough to make him yip in surprise, and then he lunged forward to bite. It wasn't a conscious movement. Hell, nothing he did right now was conscious. It was all instinct and fumbling. The more he thought about moving anything, the less he was able to do it. But he lunged and nearly took a hunk out of Wiz's hand.

Fortunately the guy was fast. One second his hand was right there, the next second it was gripping Laddin's muzzle tight.

"There'll be none of that!" he snapped. "But now that I've got you…."

Something sharp stabbed hard into his neck. A hypodermic needle, he realized as Wiz abruptly stood up, holding the thing high. Laddin growled in annoyance, but Wiz just shook his head.

"You're a new pup. We need to get you into a safe environment. Then you can chase your tail all you want."

Lethargy was growing fast. It was harder and harder to stay standing, and damn it, his head was dropping too. He whined, high-pitched and mournful, but that was all the sound he got out before he flopped down onto the floor. He could see his paws spread before him, but he couldn't move them. And pretty soon his head lolled to the side. He tried to keep his eyes open. If nothing else, there was so much to see from this angle. And the smells….

It was too late. He was going under.

But the good news still echoed through his heart, and his last conscious thoughts were joyous.

Grandmama was right! He'd transformed into magic! And being a werewolf was fun, fun, fun!

KATHY LYONS is the wild, adventurous half of *USA Today* bestselling author Jade Lee. A lover of all things fantastical, Kathy spent much of her childhood in Narnia, Middle Earth, Amber, and Earthsea, just to name a few. "There is nothing I adore more than to turn around on an ordinary day and experience something magical. It happens all the time in real life and in my books." Her love of comedy came later as she began to see the ridiculousness in life.

Winner of several industry awards including the Prism—Best of the Best, the Romantic Times Reviewers' Choice Award, and Fresh Fiction's Steamiest Read, Kathy has published over sixty romance novels and is still going strong.

Her hobbies include racquetball, rollerblading, and TV/movie watching with her husband. She's a big fan of the *Big Bang Theory* (even though it's over), and her favorite movie is *The Avengers* because she loves everything created by Joss Whedon. And she'd love to share all things geek with you in person at any of her many appearances. She's usually found at the loudest table in the coffee shop or next to the dessert bar. To keep up with all things Lyons/Lee, sign up for her newsletter at www.KathyLyons.com. You'll get early peeks, fresh news, chances to meet her in person, plus prizes and geeky gifts.

Facebook: KathyLyonsBooks,
Twitter: @KathyLyonsAuth
Instagram: KathyLyonsAuthor

FOR **MORE** OF THE **BEST** **GAY** ROMANCE

DREAMSPINNER
PRESS
dreamspinnerpress.com